About

Simon Marshall is a writer, born and raised in London. He studied modern history at UCL and received an MA in Imperial and Commonwealth History from King's College London. His research has led to an ongoing fascination with the politics of empire and the causes of both world wars, which has informed his novels to date.

He is a Real Tennis Professional and has lived and worked in France for much of the past decade. He is thinking about becoming Anglo-Saxon again.

The Passing Tribute is his second novel. It is the sequel to *The Long Drawn Aisle*.

THE PASSING TRIBUTE

THE PASSING TRIBUTE

SIMON MARSHALL

To Nick, Josh and The RTC. Best wishes Simon

Unbound Digital

This edition first published in 2019

Unbound

6th Floor Mutual House, 70 Conduit Street, London W1S 2GF

www.unbound.com

All rights reserved

© Simon Marshall, 2019

The right of Simon Marshall to be identified as the author of this work has been asserted in accordance with Section 77 of the Copyright, Designs and Patents Act 1988. No part of this publication may be copied, reproduced, stored in a retrieval system, or transmitted, in any form or by any means without the prior permission of the publisher, nor be otherwise circulated in any form of binding or cover other than that in which it is published and without a similar condition being imposed on the subsequent purchaser.

This book is a work of fiction and, except in the case of historical fact, any resemblance to actual persons, living or dead, is purely coincidental.

ISBN (eBook): 978-1-78965-017-4

ISBN (Paperback): 978-1-78965-016-7

Cover design by Mecob

Printed in Great Britain by Clays Ltd, Elcograf S.p.A.

For Ged. Thank you.

Dear Reader,

The book you are holding came about in a rather different way to most others. It was funded directly by readers through a new website: Unbound.

Unbound is the creation of three writers. We started the company because we believed there had to be a better deal for both writers and readers. On the Unbound website, authors share the ideas for the books they want to write directly with readers. If enough of you support the book by pledging for it in advance, we produce a beautifully bound special subscribers' edition and distribute a regular edition and e-book wherever books are sold, in shops and online.

This new way of publishing is actually a very old idea (Samuel Johnson funded his dictionary this way). We're just using the internet to build each writer a network of patrons. Here, at the back of this book, you'll find the names of all the people who made it happen.

Publishing in this way means readers are no longer just passive consumers of the books they buy, and authors are free to write the books they really want. They get a much fairer return too – half the profits their books generate, rather than a tiny percentage of the cover price.

If you're not yet a subscriber, we hope that you'll want to join our publishing revolution and have your name listed in one of our books in the future. To get you started, here is a £5 discount on your first pledge. Just visit unbound.com, make your pledge and type MARSHALL19 in the promo code box when you check out.

Thank you for your support,

Dan, Justin and John
Founders, Unbound

Super Patrons

Frederika Adam
Sophia Anscomb
James Barlow
Ben Bomford
Thomas Bomford
Emma Bonar
James Bromiley-Davis
Nick Browne
Tom Carew Hunt
Lucy Caulfield
Sue Caulfield
Kambra Clifford
Bill Colegrave
Richard Dalzell
Paul Danby
Ged (Gerard) Eden
Josh Farrall
Tony Friend
Emmanuel Gueroult
Lisa M. Harney
Brendan Hegarty
Christopher Herbert
Bill Higson
Richard Hopkinson-Woolley
Charlie Horrell
Mary-Ange Hurstel
Andrew Jamieson
Anthony Jenks
Adrian Kemp
Stef King
Roman Krznaric
Patrick Lawrence
Philip Lidgate
Michael Llewelyn-Jones
Peter Luck-Hille
Neil Mackenzie
Alastair Mackeown

Simon Mansfield
Indiana Marshall
Patricia Marshall
Seb Marshall
Desmond Maybury
James McDermott
Kathryn McNicoll
Graham Meek
Mike Norgrove
Rob O'Donnell
Ann Pear
Andrew Petrie
Roger Pilgrim
Fred Pilkington
Edwin Richards
Harry Saint
Ivan Semenoff
Robert Shenkman
Miriam Shucksmith
Stuart Thompson
Philippe Travis
Richard Vallat
Mariano Vanlook
Teresa Whichello
James Wilson

With grateful thanks to Simon Brewer for helping to make this book happen.

Part I

Love waxes as hope wanes.

Boccaccio, *The Decameron*

Part 1

Love is a sort of frantic frenzy.

Boccaccio, *The Decameron*

Chapter 1

Ears, they say, are optional. They are not the doors through which a single liveried column of words marches before being bolted shut. To hear is not to bring reason; it is not to understand and have the cymbal of clarity crash in one's head. It is to be snagged by barbs and skewered on the forks of tongues. It is to be at war against an army of spears as they jostle and tinkle in the mind's dark sky. This sound which rings, and rings, and rings:

'The bells of hell go ting-a-ling-a-ling' – ring, ring – *'ting-a-ling-a-ling, ting-a-ling-a-ling'* – ring, ring. Private Dawson paused, dredged some phlegm from the back of his throat, smeared his nose with the butt of his mittened palm, then continued in his low, tuneless rumbelow, *'The bells of hell go ting-a-ling-a-ling, ting-a-ling-a-ling'* – ring, ring...

'Someone's ears'll be tinger-lingin' in a bleedin' minute.'

Dawson smirked at Collins' grizzled threat; a wry look was shared between Bagley and Yorston. Lieutenant Edward Wilson's eye was then caught; a flash of blue in the night. The tips of Dawson's teeth sparkled as, with a familiar look askance, he turned away and concluded in an emphatic undertone:

'For you but not for me.'

'Ting-a-ling-a-ling, ting-a-ling-a-ling,' rang the bell in Edward's head. *'Ting-a-ling-a-ling, ting-a-ling-a-ling'*.

The advance was held. The men, hunched and motionless, were perched in frozen anticipation along a ridge of limestone on the steep side of the mountain. Edward looked up at the sky. Through the mist the clouds' mottled greys had begun to emboss themselves on the dawning, star-speckled night, giving form to the terrestrial shapes. A muffled score of machine-gun fire pulsed up through the valleys: the sound – rising to a height – seemed to hover like a woodpecker drilling the treetops, before sinking and pinballing to silence between the rows of shell-splintered pines. Concealed above, beyond the densely wooded palisade, lay the fortified summit.

Edward's legs twitched with propulsive desire. He turned restlessly to Lieutenant Colonel Backhouse.

Backhouse had already risen from his crouching position. He stood, bolt upright, his thick moustache glistening with sweat as he counted out perfectly calibrated seconds into the broken dial of his shattered watch face.

'Two minutes,' he concluded. 'That'll do.'

The advance resuming, the men scrabbled across the rocks and littered canopy of pine needles, rusted cans, bottles, bullet casings and twisted metal – here and there snagging a sleeve on a branch or mangle of wire as they clawed at the earth and half-buried cloth to haul themselves up the precipitous bank.

At the shrill sound of a shell overhead Private Tate slipped. The sound continued non-stop and dissipated in the fathomless expanse of sky. Dawson grinned his same wry, toothy grin as he overtook the prone figure.

'I fuckin' slipped,' growled Tate in defence.

'Sure ya did.'

Bagley licked his forefinger and held it aloft.

'That's a – force seven – *wind*.'

'Force *eight*, more like,' said Yorston.

Bagley chuckled.

'Oh yeah. Eight fer Tate.'

Amid a peevish mass of khaki, mess tin and rifle, Tate drove his legs into the ground and lurched on all fours. Because – so what if he *had* flinched? So what if the wind *had* whistled between his ears? That was what happened to any man with a wife and kids combed out and old enough to have a life to go back to. The match was over: he was not out. When the captains couldn't agree a declaration and let the game drift endlessly on, it was up to the players themselves (players like *him*) to draw the stumps and go home.

Edward's ascent was quickly superseded by Backhouse. And as Backhouse effortlessly slalomed his way up the mountain, now and again launching his broad, muscular frame with the expert use of a tree trunk or branch, so his stride seemed almost to lengthen with every increase of gradient – powered forth by mighty thighs that had been toned by years flanking one of his great steeplechasing mounts – *that* was how a man ought to climb, Edward thought, as if the mountain were simply an extension of his manorial rights. He, Edward Wilson, could storm a trench. Yes, he could do that. He could charge in a blind fog of fury a pillbox, gun-emplacement or trench – but he could not swagger across the land as if the enemy's existence was an affront, not like Lieutenant Colonel Backhouse. Not even Captain Ingham could do that – could *have done* that. Ingham's stroll between the snowfall of shells had been that of a man indifferent to whether one fell on him or not. But for Backhouse it was as if the idea of a bullet being fired never entered his thoughts. And if ever it did, it would do so but once.

Another volley of gunfire rattled the earth. The advance was again halted by Backhouse. His left leg propped on a fortunate protrusion, his beagle nostrils sniffed the air for blood and cordite.

'The loss of order and control by the beaten only prolongs resistance,' he said, glancing at Second Lieutenant Vivier, whose fresh cheeks were aglow with Arnoldian pleasure. 'A circumstance frequently injurious – but not useful to the whole.' He dismissed a pendulous stream of rheum from his nose with the back of his hand and looked at his watch. He resumed his steady, measured count. 'Chop-chop, Wilson,' he broke in peremptorily.

Upon the command Edward pivoted and scrambled behind the line. Collins, Tate and Yorston fell out and followed him. Bent-kneed, bow-backed, the four scuttled along the ridge past the flank of men and disappeared into the thick of the trees. A series of crags and depressions were quickly clambered up and slithered down before they reached the edge of a perpendicular hump on the mountainous back. They paused, snatching at branches and scrub for support, their breaths heavy in the thin air. From their panoramic elevation the hump could be seen continuing its rise until it flattened out to the towering wall of vertical rock on which the fort stood. In front of them, in a hollow below, was a clump of full-sprigged Tannen firs. Sheltered by the wall of rock, they were the only verdant life in the wide sweep of ghostly, withered land. Beyond lay the gentler, exposed eastern approaches that had been taken by the previous, midnight assault, when Ingham's men had been cut down a hundred yards from the fort.

Backhouse had believed the reports of the Austrian retreat in spite of himself, and because of this had determined to lead the present attack. But this time the approach was to be made from the southwest. The terrain would be harder, the climb steeper, but with the fort's western wall assumed by a sheer thousand-foot drop, he had been convinced that whatever defenders remained would be so surprised by the flanking manoeuvre as to be swiftly knocked out. Edward's perfectly timed feint to the east was to provide the cover of distraction. Backhouse had been blackly confident that the Austrians would have since abandoned the fort anyway though. They'd had their luck and a last taste of blood, he had said, so they would know when to run once they'd cut. At worst, he'd assured Edward, there'd be a couple of half-dead fanatics loosing a few final potshots. He'd be dashed unlucky to be hit by one of those! The war, Edward had long since learnt, was all about luck.

Edward looked down into the hollow. He estimated the drop to be some twenty feet or more. At the earlier binocular distance, Backhouse's instruction to 'slip down into the trees' had seemed straightforward; that the reality now proved otherwise could obviously only be attributed to bad luck. His pulse quickened as he scoured the darkness.

'Thar, sir.' Yorston's carrot eyes gleamed as he pointed to a ledge on the rocks.

'Don't e'en go 'alfway, Yors,' hissed Tate. 'We'll break our bleedin' necks if we jump.'

In the instant of speech Edward half hoped that Tate might. But the solution to any doubt, he knew, was motion, perpetual motion. A glance at each man was to impart this resolution by a look. But as he did he was snagged by a barb: in Private Collins' eye was the same steely, piercing glint he had sometimes glimpsed since Captain Monroe's tortured death in the shell hole at Ypres. He turned quickly away. Dropping to his haunches he moved down the slippery bank in a series of punchy, staggered steps. He rolled onto his stomach, clawed at the scrub, and hoisted himself over the edge. For a moment his legs flailed in search of a foothold. Finding it, he wriggled onto the ledge, pressed himself tight to the icy rocks, and spanned his arms for balance. He carefully inched his way along to where the ledge widened. As he turned his cheek from left to right to check on his progress, a sharp protrusion slit the bridge of his nose. A wince of pain saw the stone slapped in anger – he might have lashed the Hellespont if a whip were to hand. On reaching the wider part of the ledge he shuffled round to face outwards and looked into the blackness below. He could barely make out the ground – he presumed it was earth and not rock; they might all break their necks! But luck did not think, and another glance at the men was a spur to banish reflection. He levered himself onto his backside, took a breath and, with no further thought, leapt.

The landing was neither soft nor silent, but an acrobatic roll cushioned the impact. He got up, quickly instructed the men's rifles be thrown down, and cautioned a like roll upon landing. The following leaps were effected with varying oaths, and the rolls were completed with others. As soon as Edward was sure the men had all safely landed he hastened on through the trees towards the slope.

The time! he remembered. He had to know the time.

At the last tree of the line he stopped and took out his watch. He stared blankly at the ticking hands. He had no idea of the time, he suddenly realised. He had noted only the fixed hands in Backhouse's broken watch dial before wheeling away; he had not matched Backhouse's perfectly calibrated seconds to the moving hands of his own watch!

'The time?' he snapped at Yorston.

'Um... it be... um...' Yorston stammered, his long face flushed with incomprehension as his eyes danced between the watch face and Edward.

'When did we leave the line?' Edward pressed. 'How long has it been?'

Yorston's willing was never gainsaid; he made his best dead reckoning.

'Um... it were... at thirty-three. Yeah, at thirty-three. Ah be sure.'

Light-headed perhaps, Edward was not delirious. It had taken them more than *two* minutes to get as far as they had.

'Though maybe it were thirty-one,' Yorston hastily corrected. 'Yeah, thirty-one. Give or take.'

Which was exactly the kind of imprecision Backhouse cashiered officers for.

'Twenty-nine, and... twenty-six, twenty-seven, twenty-eight...' said Collins, his own perfectly polished timepiece displayed to effect as he calmly counted the seconds.

Edward's thoughts were immediately sublimated to the metronome of Collins' ticking tongue. Scanning the exposed sweep of stone, mud and ice, he saw a gust of Alpine wind flick the tails of an overcoat bundled in the middle. He wondered what fool soldier would discard his coat on the mountain. Such a man would surely have to be punished – if he hadn't frozen already. A sudden strobe of pale luminescence then filled the coat with deadened flesh.

'Thirty-five, thirty-six, thirty-seven...'

The ticking tongue shook Edward from his reverie. He pointed to where the slope levelled to the plateau and made a downward motion with his hands. The four then scurried into the open. A few yards short of the top of the slope Edward flopped on his belly; the men followed suit. Prone, perfectly still, Edward listened intently for any sound in the night, before elbowing his way up and peering over the brow. The fort was some sixty yards ahead across a stretch of frosted, limber-churned earth. If there *were* any snipers, he thought, it would take more than a dash of luck to avoid being hit. He crawled back to the men and tapped his wrist at Collins for the time.

'Fifteen, sixteen, seventeen – two minutes,' Collins returned in his metronomic burr.

Edward indicated the distance to the fort with his fingers and took his pistol from its holster. He assumed a crouched, set position and gave the men a confirmatory nod. He then immediately surged forward. But as soon as he thrust he slipped. His boots slithering on the icy rock, he frantically pawed at the ground to gain traction. Finally catching a hold he was able to launch himself onto the plateau with a great pantherian leap.

The tiny, inconsequential specks scampering across the open land could scarcely be seen in the occlusions of night. Only the crunched frost and furious panted breaths disturbed the ringing Alpine silence. In the blinkered charge there was something almost serene in their motion.

A nebular shift revealed the moon and whitened the vast looming walls ahead: at their foot was a chasm of black. The clouds rolled over again; the silence was broken. In the impossible darkness, the cavernous firmament suddenly redounded with hell. Savage, snarling, slavering – the baying of hounds throbbed through the night.

At the head of the pack, Tate tripped. Stumbling, he barrelled head first into the chasm-like ditch. Edward, Collins and Yorston tumbled down after. Righting themselves, they set their backs to the wall and frantically scanned either side.

'Fuckin' dogs. They've loosed the fuckin' dogs,' Tate snarled between his teeth.

'Baint dogs – be wolves,' said Yorston. 'Do us like 'em gippos in the east. I tell 'ee.'

Edward too had heard the rumours: of the Romanians, hunted through the Carpathian peaks, picked off by the wolves as they froze in the drifts. But fear, he knew, was greater than truth.

He hushed Yorston and sought Collins for sense. It was provided by a negative shake of the head and a hand which collared his throat. The gesture that the animals were shackled confirmed Edward's thoughts but made no difference to his actions, for they had to keep moving. The hands were spinning on the dial, the dial of the relentless, ever-ticking clock. He led them along the ditch, pressed tight to the wall. He stopped at the corner. Reclining his head to the stone he rolled his eyes round the angle. Just beyond, the ditch shallowed to an earthen footbridge that connected the main entrance to a supply track winding down into the woods of the north. But there was no one about; there was only the relentless barking filling the black sky. He raised his pistol and sidled round the wall. With slow, deliberate steps he advanced towards the footbridge. A gust of wind, funnelled through the fort, swung the door back on its hinges. Edward froze. As the gaping door creaked, the battered wood was varnished by a dusky orange glow from within, and the flinty chippings of stone on the bridge twinkled like stars.

'The loss of order and control by the beaten only prolongs resistance', Edward incanted to stiffen his nerve. *Ting-a-ling-a-ling, ting-a-ling-a-ling* – then rang the bell in his head. *Ting-a-ling-a-ling, ting-a-ling-a-ling.* He inched forward, his stoop increasing to the height of the ditch; he slowly moved out and away from the wall. Inside the fort the flickering shadows seemed to reach up the wall like a monstrous hand. The pistol shook in his grasp.

Suddenly boots thundered in frantic deployment inside; metal crashed; rifles' bolts were unbolted; the hellish barking deafened to a pitch. Edward dropped to his knees: his bright eyes flashed back at the men. *Ting-a-ling-a-ling, ting-a-ling-a-ling.* A faint smile split his lips at the sound of the bell in his head, upon which he leapt onto the bridge and charged into the fort.

Three shots rang out.

A whimper and whine brought a last single shot. In the ting-a-ling silence the three mangy Alsatians became one unified heap.

'Forty-one,' said Backhouse, turning to Edward. 'Ten minutes precisely – to the second. Bravo, Lieutenant. I thought you'd gone haring off without checking your watch.' He glanced beyond Edward to the trio who entered behind him, his usually affable, ruddy complexion given a dark solemnity by the light of the dwindling fire. 'One knows an officer's worth by his men, eh, Wilson? Their loyalty's the proof of his character, don't you think?'

'Of course,' Edward confirmed with conviction.

Backhouse studied Edward for a moment as the men of the company swarmed around him. He gestured to the dead heap before him.

'That's the problem with animals like that, you know, Wilson – they've got to be shot.'

'Yes, I'm sure.'

Edward's affirmation came after a pause; its tone, contrasting with his former conviction, was thus taken by Backhouse as doubt to the fact.

'Ha ha! Of course it is!' He let out an imperious guffaw. 'It's the only thing to do. That's what you learn in the country. *That's* the law of life – not that bunkum you get from books and the church.' The swirling wind whipped through crumbling arches and bullied the flames in front of a series of high, vaulted alcoves. Edward shrank his bristled cheeks into the collared carapace of his greatcoat. 'Ha! Yes, Wilson, we're going to have to find you some proper country air when you get back to Blighty, I can see. Teach you some of the hard truths of nature while you're there. What do you say, Vivier?'

'What? What's that?' Vivier, overspinning a spherical stone in his hand, bounded over to join them.

'I said we need to get Wilson out of that filthy city of his. Get him away from those damned morals of his to see a bit of life, eh?'

'Yes, absolutely – definitely get you up to the house, Edward. No morals there.'

'I never realised life in the counties was so hard,' rejoined Edward with gentle mockery. 'We shouldn't have bothered with war, should we? Just all gone there instead.'

'There's a city boy for you, Vivier!' exclaimed Backhouse. 'Thinks the only civilisation's to be found on the Piccadilly line with a night at the flicks and weekends on the Serpentine. He'll be telling everyone how bloody awful it's all been as soon as he's back, that's for sure.'

Backhouse's metropolitan prejudices were not to say he didn't like Edward. He did: he liked any officer who didn't complain and just got on with the frig. He knew that in an industrial war where the guns had a timetable as rigid as the urbanised day it was essential to have a cadre of officers who swore by their duty and clocked in and out. There would, of course, always be those for whom the spirit of the cavalry dash was inbred, and so a thoroughbred would have to be given its head, but the standard officer of the line was simply the military equivalent of an estate manager: invaluable, undoubtedly; vital, unquestionably. For he had to arouse enough respect in the men to ensure placid obedience, but not so much as to inspire recklessness, or for his loss to incite emotion. He was a man who would be referred to with the utmost sincerity as a 'fine fellow', but for whom the adjective was purely decorative. And whilst it might be entirely proper to chat amiably to such a fellow should their paths cross on

Jermyn Street – perhaps even allow for a whisky and soda if a few minutes were spare before one dined at one's club – one would never actually invite such a fellow to the club. Backhouse's frequent exhortations that Edward visit the country were consequently offered more as recommendations rather than any sign of social intimacy. That, of course, was no slight on the man.

Bagley scampered across and stood before Backhouse.

'Nuffink, sir,' he declared. 'Not e'en a pack a fags nor a proper souv'nir neither.'

'There you go,' said Backhouse indifferently, unsure as to why he was told. He was even less sure why Bagley then remained where he was. 'Is there something else, Lance Corporal?'

A wide, rapscallion grin greeted the question. Short, stout, a hairline receding with the angle of his cap, a round face with a pair of pert apple cheeks, and a set of proud upper teeth – he looked quite like a hamster. Bagley's eyes bulged as he turned to Vivier.

'I brung it up for yer, sir.'

'What? What are you on about, Bagley?' barked Backhouse.

Vivier's expression suddenly brightened.

'Oh God – yes – I completely forgot! Good work, Baggers!'

Bagley promptly knelt, slung his haversack from his shoulder, removed the entrenching spade, and untied the cord which bound the precious metal shaft to it. He stood up and ceremoniously presented it to Vivier.

'Nor a scratch on it neither.'

'Good God, Vivier – the bloody driver!' Backhouse finally roared with delight. 'I thought you might try and sneak it up here.'

'It's got to be done, sir. Couldn't miss the opportunity, could I?' returned Vivier. He essayed a couple of easy swings with the club.

'No, of course not. You ought to have brought the wood with this damned wind though. Give it some more oomph, don't you think?'

'I know, I know. But a bit too long for poor Baggers to cope with.'

'Nonsense – some posture would do the fellow some good.' Taking charge of the club, Backhouse proceeded to shape for a cover drive. 'Presume you've got yourself some competition, Vivier? I'd have a thrash myself but I'd be useless. Never seen the point of a game where you have to play fetch with yourself. Leave that to the dog.'

'Yes, sir. Bagley here. He's a professional golfer.'

'A *professional* golfer!' Backhouse's contempt could not have been greater had he been bowled underarm. 'Stuff and nonsense. That's what ruins a game, you know – paying people to play it. Well, come along, let's see what this so-called *professional* of yours can do, eh, Vivier?' He abruptly about-turned and strode towards the arches of the exposed western wall. Beyond them, as if on the other side of some great stone curtain, a promontory unveiled the louring majesty of the immense Alpine peaks like a grand Olympic proscenium. Passing beneath the middle of the three arches Sergeant Caulfield was stopped on his way. 'Need to get those scouting parties out right away, Sergeant. We move on in thirty minutes. Don't want any surprises at this stage, do we now? Chop-chop.'

*

"Ere, Tommy – look what I's touched.' Private Addison held his hand open and displayed his booty of cigarettes. ''Elp yerself. Don't tell Baggers, mind.'

Collins' swarthy, leathern skin crumpled with scorn. 'Don't touch that Austrian muck,' he said, and continued to polish his rifle.

'Suit yerself,' Addison said with the peevishness of one to whom largesse did not come naturally, and so when refused caused offence. He jacked himself onto one of the alcoves overlooking the fire and fanned the cigarettes out beside him. 'Eeny meeny miny mo – oh shit!' Spotting Sergeant Caulfield's instruction from Backhouse he hastily re-gathered the cigarettes, shoved them back in his pocket, and leapt down. 'I'm goin' lookin' fer an armistice,' he said, and bolted away into the fort's warren depths.

'No point dodgin' columns,' grizzled Collins. 'Always another behind.'

'What be 'n armistice?' asked Yorston, intermitting furious rubs of his hands over the fire with the feeding of items of forage into it to stoke it to life.

'The end o' the fuckin' war. That's what,' said Tate. Assuming

Addison's vacated position he hunched his shoulders forward and shivered. 'About bloody time too 'n' all.'

Dawson shook his head with incredulity. 'Hark at him. He's not even done a year yet. Seven not enough fer Eight; he has to go and do duration.'

Yorston stuck his hand in the air. 'Erm – yes, yes – end o' the war? Duration please.'

'I can just see him with the recruiting sergeant: "Why did ya not volunteer, Mr Tate?" "Cos I wanted to fight 'til the end of the war, sir."' Dawson's eyebrows arched in humorous befuddlement. '"Oh, I see. Well done, Mr Tate."'

'I were workin' fer the war since bloody day one,' Tate returned tersely. With his slightly curved spine, pinched face, and short spindly arms he possessed the sort of beetle-like features that led no one to doubt he had spent his life on a factory floor. The wonder was he had ever discovered a mate. 'Not my bloody choice – and not my bloody war neither. So the sooner I get this khaki off the better. And stop bloody callin' me Eight.'

'Don't yer believe a word of it,' said Collins.

'Word o' what?'

'The war endin'.' He stood his rifle on end and began cleaning the bolt. 'Some don't want it ter end. Wouldn't have no bleedin' clue what ter do next.'

'Whatcha on about, Bairnsfather? Who?'

Collins gestured to the promontory with his caterpillar eyebrows. ''Im, fer one.'

'Your favourite, Yors, isn't he?' said Dawson.

'Certainly be,' Yorston agreed, though he was not sure to what; he was preoccupied by the forage and fire. He turned a tangle of wood and string over in his hands. 'What that a be?'

'A bleedin' snowshoe, innit.'

Yorston examined the curiosity for a moment before tossing it into the fire. An old over-boot and half a crate followed in short order.

'He bears the danger cheerfully enough, but the privation…'

'No – I can't. I can't stand the cold,' said Yorston. 'It baint human, is what it baint. Man needs ter be a-warming ter be a-fighting.'

'An attack'll get you warm, won't it?' said Dawson.

Yorston's beanpole frame sprang to life with a marionette flail of limbs.

'What's that, raiding party, Lieutenant Wilson? Yes, please.'

'Patrol?' suggested Dawson.

'Er... me please.'

'Working party?'

'Er... er... love ter, sir.'

Dawson's playful grin broadened to a gummy laugh. 'That's what you want, isn't it, Yors? A sneaky little no-man's-lander, just you and Lieutenant Wilson.'

'I... er... er... yes *please*.'

'Yors!'

'Mine!' Yorston spun round and began theatrically searching behind him. 'Oh, oh – there yer be, Lieutenant. I didn't hear 'ee there. Sorry.'

'So sorry.'

'*So* sorry.'

'And he'll be standing there, like, just breathing heavily,' said Dawson, 'beck'ning you with his finger – 'Come with me, Private Yorston'.'

'Did yer... did yer... did yer –' Yorston's excitement pitched to the manic as he shot looks at Tate and Collins '– see 'im earlier when he be asking me the time? He be there, a-looking at his watch by the trees and be asking me fer the time! I mean – what? – sorry sir...'

'So sorry.'

'*So* sorry. But... er... there be yer watch – that 'ee be a-*looking at* – but *I'll* tell 'ee the time. Of course. Of course. No problem at all.'

'He loves 'im.'

'Oh yes. I do – I do. I fuckin' *love* him!' As if he might make the genie of his adoration reappear there and then, Yorston turned to the fire and rubbed his hands furiously.

'It's alright, Yorston,' said Collins, glancing beyond Yorston's shoulder; 'sarnt's gonna take pity on yer instead. 'E'll get yer circulation goin'.'

'Enough of the 'ow's yer father. War ain't over yet,' said Sergeant Caulfield.

'We've just been sayin', Sarnt,' said Tate.

'Glad to hear it. Now…'

*

Edward and Vivier stood beside Backhouse on the edge of the promontory as the icy wind cavorted around them. A thousand feet below, the jagged church steeples rose from the lurid ruins of Asiago like shattered headstones in a churchyard; ahead the soaring peaks and sickle valleys were adumbrated by the phosphorescent glow from the burning ammunition dumps. Another crackle of gunfire ricocheted around the sepulchred earth. Edward felt a strange thrill at the sight; of sadness and wonder.

Somewhere in the crevices and coombs, he knew, 100,000 men were scattered in the darkness, though not a single one could be seen. It was as if they didn't exist. Yet beneath the hoary black mantle was a picture as clear to him as any in a playhouse. Clearer, even. For there was no need to see to feel life – not when the shadows lived in the silence, and would do so forever in the ever spinning stroboscope of human imagination. This, after all, was what the war should have been. This was the war that Conrad had envisioned, the Austrian eagle swooping down from the heights with Carthaginian élan to snatch the Italian snake and tear it to pieces. The world might go under, he thought, but surely *this* beauty would last.

How different it was from the western front. There the millions were never silent. They were always heard: rattling their tins, popping their lice, etching their pickets, slurping their tea, and shuffling like rats. Everything done in one trench, Edward knew, was exactly the same as that done in another. It was what he hated the most, what he found so repulsive. Because there was always someone there, everywhere: next to him, in front of him, behind him, blocking him. And all he had wanted was to get away from them – to get *them* out of the way, to *make* them disappear and turn them to shadows.

And now, after all that, here it was – all but at an end. But as he stared out across the immense vista towards the invisible cartographic lines of Austria he felt the excitement turn slowly to apathy. Any moment the armistice would be signed and those 100,000 would dissolve in the daylight. There would be no bows for those shadows in the dazzle of day. What, then, he thought, was the point in going on and on, deeper and deeper into the wilderness, baring one's fangs for a mouthful of feathers? Surely it was better to turn one's back on the scene and quit it with beauty and life. Far better to let the shadows play on in the darkness than to have them disappear in the glare. Far better that, and then go back, than to continue pointlessly forward – after all that.

'Just because a man gets paid for hitting a ball doesn't mean he's any good at it, do you hear, Lance Corporal?' said Backhouse.

'Course not, sir.'

'No – in fact it invariably means he's worse. Isn't that right, Vivier?'

'Well…'

'Now don't go putting on the woman, Vivier. My money's on you, do you hear?'

'Money?'

Backhouse clapped his hands with decision. He set his back to the precipice and stood akimbo. 'Hang it, Vivier – I'm not about to watch you tee off without putting a bloody wager on it. If you're not playing and you're not betting, there's no damned point *watching*. That's for the ladies. A guinea. There we are. Wilson's my marker. Don't go letting me down either. I've had enough of losing my cash to those damned Rackets boys. Thrash, thrash, smash, smash – you've as much chance picking a winner as whose racquet snaps first.' Reverting to Bagley he let out a short wheezy cough; a film of watery redness glistened in his eyes. 'Come on, man – chop-chop.'

Bagley delved into his trouser pocket and removed two shiny white balls. An apprenticed stonemason, he had discovered that the socket joints of horses (cattle and sheep were better, but harder to come across dead) made a more than acceptable golf ball when correctly ground down. He got on his haunches and harvested some chippings into a pile.

'Stop fannying about,' said Backhouse impatiently. 'I want to see this *professional* swing of yours, not watch you create a damned rock pool.'

Bagley carefully balanced one of the spheres on the apex of the pile and stood up. Receiving the club from Backhouse, he made room for a couple of smooth practice swings; they educed a near-idolatrous nod from Vivier, a nod not lost on Backhouse.

'Just hit the damned thing,' he said, appalled that a Wykehamist should fawn like a Wet. 'A swing's as good as a miss.' He raised his binoculars in anticipation – then thrust them at Edward. 'You take them, Wilson. I can't see a bloody thing.'

Bagley aligned club face to ball, and then leaned into an easy, full-bodied swing. With a resonant ping the ball sailed into the sky. For a moment there was a rapt, awestruck silence, as if a bird of prey had just been spotted in flight.

'Great shot, great shot,' Vivier said at last, his lusty approval due as much to the purity of the strike as to the distance attained. The latter was acknowledged by Edward with a respectful pucker of lips. Backhouse sniffed his contempt.

'A bit mechanical that swing, if you ask me. Now, come on, Vivier, show us what natural talent can do – talent that's not been ruined by any of this *professional* guff.'

'Right you are.' Vivier received the club from Bagley, who, falling promptly to his knees, positioned the second ball on the undisturbed apex with the same precision as the first. 'I reckon the best line's over there.' Vivier pointed. 'A little bit of drift with the breeze should carry it like a dream, don't you think?'

The question notionally put to Edward (who didn't know one end of the club from another – though he did know a forward defensive was out) was met by the barbed observation: 'There's a breeze, is there?'

'Yes – a stiff one.'

Vivier windmilled his arm to loosen his shoulder. Backhouse huffed mightily. Whereupon Vivier took up his stance; rotated his hips; a lovely backswing – looked pretty good! – and then collapsed in the stroke with a resonant clunk.

'Oh God, oh God – I've hooked it, haven't I?'

Edward was scrupulous in pursuit of the flight. 'Somewhat,' he said, finally. 'But you might get another go – I think it's coming back.'

'Oh God, that's awful. That's so pathetically useless. I can't believe it. I'm so sorry. I'm *so* sorry,' said Vivier, his mortification nonetheless counterbalanced by the jovial spirit of his Corinthian heart.

Lieutenant Colonel Backhouse was not Corinthian; and he was frankly ashamed. Vivier would certainly serve spaniel the next time on the shoot.

'Well, you have credit in your account, Lance Corporal,' he said with bluff magnanimity. 'Serves me right for fighting the tiger. But as our subaltern here's clearly a junior part, I'll consider the stake in abeyance. Is that clear?'

Bagley had no idea what an 'abeyance' was. ''Course, sir,' he said. He flashed a guileless hamster smile. 'A lesson or two'd make 'im a top ama'eur, for sure.'

Backhouse laughed. He liked some gumption in his men. 'Ha ha! I'll be taking that wager, Lance Corporal – even for a hundred of your rotten lessons!' Upon which he marched away round to the front of the fort.

'I'll have to atone at the next summit,' said Vivier, handing the club back to Bagley.

'Wiv pleasure, sir. Li'l shor'er on the backswing, if yer don't mind me sayin'.'

'Yes, yes – I know, I know. I can't stop it. I just love a flourish.'

'It's definitely a flourish, sir. No doubt 'bout it. Well done.'

'Well done what?'

Bagley chuckled. 'Dunno, sir,' he said. He then waddled off back through the arches on his squat haunches.

Vivier took a couple of steps away from the edge. He sat on a stone block blasted from the top of the fort, flipped open his cigarette case and offered its contents to Edward. Edward gladly accepted; Vivier's limitless supply of Black Cats had been a boon since he joined in the spring – especially as he mostly only smoked for effect. For his part Edward took out his matches, waited for the wind to drop a touch, cupped his hands and lit first Vivier's, then his own cigarette. Vivier spluttered on the inhale, and the exhale was snatched by the wind.

Edward put his hand to the side of his stiff, grease-waxed black hair and pressed it down. The fine lines of his face hinted at a fraternal half-smile. A mere four years might have separated him from Vivier's flushing teenage years, but his age had come before the war.

'God, you know, if my mother knew I smoked she'd kill me,' said Vivier.

Edward shook his head. At least Vivier's mother might actually *know* if he smoked!

'Yes, you told me before. It's the least of her worries, I'd have thought.'

'Oh no, but you don't understand – my mother *hates* smoking. Absolutely loathes it. She thinks it's the most vulgar habit, that only tradesmen smoke – cigarettes, that is, not cigars or pipes. I'm sure she'd rather have a cross and a medal than have her son pop out for a spit and drag.' He took a quick, mouthy puff and gazed at the mountains. His soft brown eyes sparkled boy-scoutishly. 'My uncle'll be green when I tell him I've been here, you know. He was all set to join one of the Society's expeditions with Mallory before it was kiboshed by the war. That's what they're here for, he used to say.'

Edward threw him a narrow look. 'What here for what?'

'The mountains. To climb them. I'd love to do something like that when this is over.' He stood up and inhaled a bracing lungful of air. 'You know, it's hard not to believe all that stuff about God when you're up here, don't you think? I used to hate it at school – getting up every morning to listen to the chaplain bang on about the gospels – but I would've paid attention if he'd read them up here. That would've made me believe.' He held the cigarette at an affected arm's length and was lost in thought. 'My cousin – the one in the Guards – once told me most of his men had become either intensely religious or had stopped believing in God altogether. Is that what you think's happened – people have stopped believing?' The question posed, he appealed to Edward.

'In God?' Edward asked, his eyes fixed to the distance.

'Yes, I suppose so. What else is there?'

'Well, you can still have faith. You can still believe. It doesn't have to be in God.'

'What's the difference?'

There was a short pause, before Edward said in firm, deliberate tones, 'God is the word. Faith is the act.'

'The act of God, you mean? Faith in *that* act?'

'Yes,' he said. On the horizon the clouds were prismed by flashes of copper and blue. A moment later Edward suddenly turned on Vivier, his eyes eddying with the conflicting currents of his mind as he countered with feeling, 'No, no – only in the act. The act is the only thing that matters. Not God. Not *God*!' Then, just as swiftly as the currents had collided, they parted: calm was restored to his waters.

Shortly, muffled laughter was heard coming from inside the fort. Unsettled by Edward's outburst and the awkward silence that followed, Vivier sought comfort and favour by sharing the poignant drift of his thoughts. 'Poor old Ingham, eh? You know, I was thinking about him on the way up. About what stinking rotten luck that was.'

Edward drew hard on his cigarette and took a couple of steps towards the edge. Yes, it was true, he knew, the war was all about luck; in the same way that living was all about luck; dying was all about luck; and love was all about luck. Except if it was willed otherwise. He removed a strand of tobacco from his lips and spat it away in distaste. But he also knew that Captain Ingham's legs being blown off in the previous assault had had nothing to do with luck. No. It was spite: sheer, malicious, jealous spite. That was the act of *that* God. And when he had seen Ingham doped up to his harrowed eyeballs in the aid post afterwards, he had understood that Ingham knew that that was what it was too. That Ingham might have been blown up by a shell at any point in the previous two years, or shot himself as the proof of his indifference to life, Edward had known. Now, however, for him to shoot himself would not be an act of indifference, but one simply of mercy. People would no longer wonder on the riddles of his mind as he pulled the trigger by his head; they would merely pity him for his end. Ingham had understood that as he had lain on the stretcher, and Edward had understood it too. They had both understood that now he *had to* live, that there could be no escaping life if everything were not to be swallowed by pity.

Now the gods could not be spurned by indifference; they could only be defeated by the brute will to live.

'If that's what you call it,' Edward said with finality.

Edward's curt tone blushed Vivier to silence: he instantly recognised the crassness of his words. The simplest thing would then have been for him to skulk away in shame, but he did not. He had formed that peculiar attachment to Edward which, despite being founded on nothing more than transient propinquity, possessed an intensity akin to the spark of two stones struck together in the surf. At length Vivier spoke, a faint crack in his voice revealing his self-conscious search for approval.

'To think, we'll be in enemy territory tomorrow. I'd heard about it – but I never knew it existed. Not apart from on maps.'

The search succeeded; Edward returned a thin smile.

'It exists. It just won't be *enemy* territory when we get there,' he said.

Vivier flicked his cigarette into the abyss with his former gaiety assured. He gestured in the same direction. 'Which pass is it we're taking again?'

'The Val d'Assa.' Edward moved and stood beside Vivier. He indicated the barely discernible arc to his right; then pointed more or less left. 'The Italians are somewhere over there.'

Vivier ruminated on the topography; so too did Edward.

'I thought it was due north of Asiago?' said Vivier, at length.

'It is,' Edward confirmed, before asking, 'That's due north – isn't it?'

'I'm not sure. I think that's north-west.'

Edward was not sure either. He dug into his pocket for his compass and map.

'Vivier's quite right – No need for your rusty old compass, Wilson.' The authoritative orientation was issued by Captain Gardiner. A liaison officer to the Italian staff, he was accompanied by an Alpini officer who had been attached to the regiment to ensure the advance met General Diaz's objectives. When Bagley had first seen an Alpini soldier, sporting his forest-green uniform topped by a pointed brimmed hat with a feather in it, he had whistled 'Yankee Doodle' and nearly had his hamster teeth knocked out. The present officer seemed of a similar disposition: a heavy jaw and swarthy features conveyed a demeanour of stoic humourlessness. Gardiner's wide pancake mouth, by contrast, smiled amiably – and then he started his sermon. 'The Val d'Assa's the valley of the gods, you know. That's what it means in the *Cimbro* dialect. But the valley's not the "val", as you might think; it comes from the word "tal" – though it means the same thing. And the "ass" – well, that's certainly not what you might think. It actually means God.' He allowed himself a knowing chortle at the antithesis before assuming an aspect of gravity. In a speckle of moonlight his eyes glowed with a wan, romantic lustre. 'It's where the ancient gods of Germanic lore lived. Or still do – depending on your beliefs. It's also the valley where Dante envisioned the mouth of his hell. Yes, he and the poet descended hand in hand from this very same spot.'

'Really?' said Vivier.

'Oh yes, indeed,' returned Gardiner with feeling. '*Lasciate ogni speranza voi ch'entrate* – "Abandon all hope ye who enter here". I've heard the words are even chiselled by the entrance to a cave somewhere within.' He paused, wide-eyed and hypnotic as he stared at Vivier's rapt visage. 'I've not seen it myself, of course, but who can deny the truth of another man's word? Who can…'

He was suddenly interrupted. As if proof that the ancient gods were presently engaged in the defence of their realm against the heathen hordes of man, a roar of wasted artillery and ammunition shook the earth. When the noise had been engulfed by the immenseness of nature, Gardiner resumed portentously, 'The gods are indeed full of…'

He was interrupted again. This time it was due to a loud commotion coming from the fort. Wilson and Vivier turned and hurried inside.

*

'Look what we's found,' said Addison, the whitened bristles of his stubbled chin flecked with the spittle of rage, having earlier been found himself by Sergeant Caulfield. He leaned menacingly over the mound of filthy overcoat heaped before him. 'Tucked up nice and bleedin' cosy in yer little fox-'ole, weren't yer? Almost dead, weren't yer, fella? *Should be*, shouldn't yer, fella? I should've shot yer, shouldn't I? *Shouldn't I?* 'Oping we's wouldn't spot yer, weren't yer? But we's did, didn't we, fella? We bleedin' did – yer sneaky little weasel. An' yer near and bleedin' shot me when I weren't lookin', didn't yer? Yer *sneaky – little – weasel*.'

'Should've put yer tin op'ner through 'im,' said Tate.

'Finish the bloody job.'

'Yeah, I would've, but the little weasel weren't fuckin' lookin', were 'e? 'E weren't fuckin' lookin'.'

'Mind yer language now.'

Sergeant Caulfield's admonishment alerted Addison to the officers' presence. Addison looked up, his thin sallow features twisted by a restless, champing jaw while his eyes shone with a bewildered, sardonic fury.

''E weren't fuckin' lookin', sir. Can yer believe that, sir? Turned 'is fuckin' back – so all's I can do is belt 'im…'

'Mind yer language!'

'And then he fuckin' laughs. He laughs! Can yer believe that? So I belt 'im some more.' Addison emitted a shrill, mocking laugh before his face became rigid. He turned back to the heaped mound of cloth, as if suddenly struck by the fear there might be nothing within it, that he might have beaten only a shadow.

'Enough, Private!'

Edward's angry command at last subdued him. And as soon as it did the mass of mud-grey overcoat stirred; it was the first sign of life. At the movement, Addison bared Edward a feline grimace of pride, as if the bird he had caught were the proud gift of his hunt. The body then spasmed; an electrical charge was applied. The cloth heaved and rolled; the hunched back slowly straightened; the writhing form rose to its knees; the pieces of overcoat flaked away from the tunic beneath like an epidermis being shed. From within the loose sagging lapels a man's dishevelled brown head extruded from the putrefied mass. In the emboldened firelight the hollows and shafts of his face were like they were hewn from the rocks. He turned to Edward.

'Friedrich!'

At Edward's sudden wild cry there was a stunned, deathly silence.

Only a split second was required for reality to decry to the illusion. Edward's ejaculation was nothing more than the rendered presentiment of a sight he had so long foreseen.

'*Oriana is right about one thing: people never come back.*'

Ever since Friedrich had said these parting words to him outside Herr Braunthal's house in Vienna five years before – ever since the dark cloud and the train that had carried him away from everything, and Oriana – that world had been immured in silence. Too soon – he had left Vienna too soon! Since then all he had wanted was to return to Vienna to know what had happened. This was what had driven Edward insatiably on: on and on as the ticking clock chimed in his ear, all the while conceiving a million fractured sequences of loving fulfilment. On, that was, until now. For, at last within reach of the invisible cartographic line, he thought – what was the point? To go back, after all that? Surely it was better to know nothing.

The man's death's-head features delineated in the black-and-orange light did not belong to Friedrich. They possessed nothing more than a general Germanic and physiognomic resemblance, such as might have deceived anyone had he been glimpsed at the back of a tram in the throng of the morning rush. But even had Friedrich been dragooned at the bayonet's point to sport the Habsburg colours he despised, Edward knew he could not have survived. His furious nature could not have allowed it.

'D'yer know 'im, sir?' Sergeant Caulfield finally asked.

'No. No... I... I... for a minute I thought—' Edward shook his head. He was then brusque in command. 'For God's sake get him some grappa or something. And put him by the damned fire.'

There was a sudden clatter of reanimation: Dawson went in search of the grappa; Yorston and Bagley half picked up, half dragged the man to the fire; Collins righted an ammunition box for him to be set down on; and Addison turned his back in high dudgeon, as if his gift had been spurned and so its fate were no longer of the slightest concern.

'Not too close,' said Collins; a barricading arm stopped Yorston and Bagley as the embers spat from the damp, blistering wood. ''E'll go up like a bloomin' guy.'

Dumped on the box, the man slumped like a rag doll. On the crown of his head a patch of raw skin was reddened in the firelight through the strands of his matted brown hair. Yorston, casting a proprietorial glance at the box, bent down and hissed in his ear, 'That fire be thanks ter me, that a be. Don't yer be a-forgetting that, chum.'

Dawson returned with a small flask of grappa and passed it to Collins. A measure was poured into a canteen and held out.

'There yer go,' said Collins.

The man looked at the canteen, then up at Collins. In his hollowed face his pale eyes seemed massive like a bullfrog's either side of a sharp, flinty nose, his pinched lips being framed by a pair of protruding, blackened ears. He reached out for the canteen with his trembling fingers and drew it slowly to his lips. His swollen eyes hopped about the assemblage with a sort of fearful, watchful calculation.

'Not poison ya know, mate.'

'Best if it were if yer ask me.'

He sipped the grappa, took another suspicious glance, and swiftly drained the remainder. He held the canteen greedily back out to Collins, an expression of demand in his face. It was what Collins hated most about the Germans – and to him they were *all* Germans, wherever they came from. No matter whether they were given a canteen of grappa or had a bayonet stuck in their gut, their haughty look was always the same. It made him want to twist and twist the bayonet until it bored right through them to the earth. He grabbed the canteen and returned a brow-beating stare as he poured a second measure.

'One more for yer, Jerry. Then that's yer bloody lot.'

The man stared at Collins like some dumb, defiant fiend. The canteen released to his charge, he emptied it, then spat the dribbled afters at Collins' feet.

'Bloody pigs.'

'Fuckin' waste is what that is.'

'Bet yer he snuffs it 'fore 'e gets even 'alfway down.'

'If he ain't napooed before the fuckin' 'alfway.'

Collins grabbed the canteen back, but said nothing.

The restorative effects of the grappa were not long to take hold.

But the man's blood, too quickly warmed by the heat of the fire, meant he soon felt his exposure: he began to shiver uncontrollably. His face taut, he clenched his teeth in a struggle to master his body. When he had finally done so a smile of triumph flashed on his lips. His eyes whitening, as if infected by some powerful toxin, they feverishly flitted between Edward and the shadows under the arches. He then launched into a furious tirade of incomprehensible speech.

'Jesus. Tin op'ner – I *told* yer.'

'Bitten by the bloody barn mouse.'

'Told yer that were too much peg fer 'im.'

'What's he saying?' Vivier asked Edward.

'I've no idea.'

'Oh, ok. Is it not German?'

'Yes... no.' Edward made a negative gesture. His German was fit for paper and pleasantries, not *that*. 'It's not the same,' he explained.

'It's dialect,' said Gardiner, stepping forward, out of the shadows. The Alpini officer advanced alongside him. 'He's from here – the mountains.'

The man's arms suddenly sprang out from his sides. He ripped the frayed twine that fastened the buttonholes of his coat and threw it wide open. Collins snatched at the air for his rifle. Edward grabbed at his pistol. The man rummaged in the pocket of his shabby officer's tunic, found what he sought, and flung it at Edward; the object landed by his boots. For a split second Edward thought the enamel glint might be one of the man's rotten teeth. He picked it up and displayed it in his open palm. Attached to a red-and-white ribbon was a dirty Maltese cross. As he tried to decipher the inscription, Vivier leaned over to help.

'*Fortitudini*,' said Vivier. Then, to prove he could not only read Latin, he translated, 'Bravery.'

'It's the Order of Maria Theresa,' explained Gardiner.

Edward threw him a peevish glance; he had no need of the explanation. He let Vivier take charge of the medal and then examined the man with near anatomical curiosity.

'Yes. It is mine,' the man confirmed in clear, enunciated English.

'The highest honour in the empire was awarded for the bravery of Captain Beremberg.'

The Alpini officer let out a savage, mirthless laugh from between his wiry black lips. It resonated deeply around the walls. The man fixed him with a bold, scornful look, as if some grotesque emanation had just appeared beyond a dark glass. A moment later he settled his impenetrable eyes on Edward and continued in a tone of refined, prosaic conviction, 'It was given to at Monte Maggiore. Yes, to me. I was leading the attack. I was leading my men through the thick snows – though it was not white and pure like the image of snow. No, there is fog and smoke, and everywhere is yellow with the gas. Only when we triumph can we see everything clearly. That is when we see all the Italian traitors. They are helpless, just like beetles when they are turned on their backs with their legs in the air. I did not want to kill so many pathetic creatures, you know. There was in me some kind of disgust at the thought; but I had to do it. So we are strafing their trenches with many thousands of bullets. After there were so many bodies. But then I knew that it was good. I knew it had cleansed me. It was like a sacrifice I had to make in order to realise how worthless those creatures were.' He gestured to the medal. 'It is correct that the highest honour is given to someone who is killing so many traitors, no? Animals, traitors – it is the same, no? So it is right they are shot.'

He fell silent, his eyes filled with a fierce, searching expectancy, as if the parade of firelit men surrounding him might with a breath be turned into dust. After a moment an uncertain stir rose; more eyes looked at Edward. Another mirthless laugh then rang out.

'*Non l'è elo,*' cried the Alpini. '*Non l'è elo.*'

Gardiner turned to Edward. 'It's not him, he says.'

'Not who?'

'*Qui?*'

'*Il capitano. Non l'è elo. Non l'è elo.*'

'He says he's not the captain. The chap here – Beremberg, or whatever his name is.'

'What does that mean?'

'*Non l'è elo. Non l'è elo.*'

Gardiner shrugged. 'He just says it's not him.'

'Well how the hell does he *know*?' Edward returned hotly. He switched his attention between the Alpini and the Austrian. A rare gleam in the latter's eye pinned him. The instant it did, the Alpini stepped in front of Gardiner and ripped the medal from Vivier's hand. Hurling it on the ground, he stamped on it with a wounded, brutish frenzy.

'*Non l'è elo!*' he cried again. '*Non l'è elo!*'

The shock of the medal being torn from his hand blew Vivier's short, petulant fuse. A first snatch at the Alpini being swatted away, the red mist descended. He furiously launched himself at the Alpini and the pair collapsed in a heap of flailing limbs.

'For God's sake, control your man!' Edward shouted at Gardiner.

But Patrick Gardiner was not rough and tumble. He reached out his arms, shuffled this way and that, and could only implore, 'Steady on! Steady on! *Basta! Basta!*'

'Get 'em apart!'

With the call, Collins, Yorston and Tate dived into the fray.

'What the bloody hell's going on?' cried Backhouse. Silhouetted beneath the central arch, he suddenly shouted: 'Wilson! Watch the damned Boche!'

Edward *was* watching. His eyes, once pinned by the gleam, had become transfixed by it. They had not left the purported captain for one fraction of a second. So he had seen – in every fractional detail of hummingbird motion – him calmly reach out as the Alpini snatched at the medal; had watched as he picked up a rusted blade that had fallen unnoticed from the ammunition box when righted by Collins; had followed rapt as, with the world consumed by the scuffle, the man slowly leaned forward, stealthily rose, and held the blade out before him with bloody intent; and then he had seen him lunge.

And all the while the man had gathered the blade, leaned forward, risen, and lunged, *he* had not taken his eyes off Edward for one fraction of a second either. He had stared, proud and implacable, remorseless as the hunter, captivated as Edward tracked his every movement with his pistol.

At Backhouse's cry and command, Edward instinctively fired.

Chapter 2

At last! Well, who would have thought he had had so much blood *in* him? One might have thought that the simmering cauldron of time had boiled it down to broth and bones. Still, the better the reason for the ink to flow and garland the paper with those great calligraphic serifs and twirls. Oh yes, he has a fine hand, I won't deny that!

Perhaps, now that the blood has tickled his fingers and toes, here we might say *thus the book closes*. But then it would be *thus the book opens*. For it closes and it opens. It opens and it closes. There are no middles in these books. The spine is either stiff and the quartos uncut, or there are rips, wrinkles, folds, scribbles and dribbles staining the pages from cover to cover. There is none of this 'halfway', 'middle', or 'chapter five of twenty'; no, none of this book-marking and switching the light out to discover the fate of the kingdom tomorrow, when the world has fallen to a whisper and hush. No, there is none of this. The world will not fall to a whisper and hush: it will only be silenced. The muzzle must be forced on the dog. So there are only beginnings and ends. There is nothing else. One either returns, or does not; does, or does not; loves, or not; knows – or does not. There is nothing half. Nothing unfinished. Nothing unread.

He is becalmed now, it's true. His heart has been stilled by the wind, and the blood has dripped to a stain. He is the cork that floats the fisherman's net and stops it from sinking. But not *now*, I say! Now is not the time to vacillate and linger! The line must be crossed, and crossed again! Because when a picture is taken, *this* is how it is framed – so that the conversation can flow seamlessly forth with that tyrannical word of narrative life – *'then'*. *Then* did he continue his ascent towards the ever-changed constellation. *Then* were the pillars demolished and he, smiling, left alone, transfigured on the heights!

This, *then*, is what I would say to him, were he to heed *me* and not others. Go, I would say – *Go on!* Do not just stand lifeless, hovering between the cracks and the invisible borders of the worlds. Do not let yourself be flicked. Motes are flicked! Take wing from the nail! Onward! Onward! Life! Life! *Eternal Life!*

*

'And the tannin is in the cupboard next to the drawer. Because the tannin is always, *always*, where it ought to be.' The cupboard being opened, Millie frowned. Her lips puckered in disapproval. 'Except when it isn't and it's... somewhere else. Bother, bother, bother – botheroo. Now – *now* – where the devileroo are you? Ok – remember, Millie: close your eyes and count to five, the thing you seek shall come alive.' She stood up, clasped her hands by her waist, closed her eyes and counted. Count concluded, her eyes opened and bounced around expectantly. 'Five more, Millie,' she said, and closed her eyes again. Upon their opening, her freckles darkened. She emitted a short whistle as a signal of steam being released. 'No, I don't want to count any more fives. No, fives there'll be no more a-counting. No fives for meeeee –' she twirled on her toes and opened the glass door of the cabinet over the counter '– cos all I want is to seeeee –' her eyes glimmering, she reached to the back of the cabinet '– is my honey beeeee.' The elusive jar found, she upbraided it with a shake of her head. 'Now that's not where you belong, is it, Mr Jar?'

Nurse Millicent Fawley, assumed to have nothing to do one afternoon by Sister Billings, had been asked to tidy the dispensary. Finding the dispensary not just untidy, but arranged in a most haphazard and illogical fashion, Millie had therewith taken it upon herself to reorganise it from top to bottom. The overhaul had been concluded by the affixing of labels to indicate where the various medicines, balms, emetics, infusions and dressings were henceforth to be found.

Sister Billings had entered the dispensary a little more than halfway through the unexpected convulsion. She had immediately uttered a decidedly un-Sister-like oath. She had then listened in a fog of teapot rage as Millie had told her that such and such a medicine had been moved to such and such a place, that others had been moved to such another drawer or cupboard for such and such a reason, and that this and that bottle had been disposed of because... but there Sister Billings had had quite enough. 'Nurse Fawley, you are quite the most mixed blessing the good Lord has yet inflicted on the world,' she had said. Whereupon she had turned on her heels and thundered away, fulminating that she had no need of labels to tell *her* where things would go; they would go where they had always gone!

'*There was ham, ham, mixed up with the jam,*

'*In the stores, in the stores…*' Millie sang as she whizzed open the lid of the jar.

'*Ham, ham, mixed up with the jam,*

'*In the dispensing stores.*'

She measured a spoonful of yellow powder from the jar and tapped it into the mug of brown liquid on the counter. A brisk stir being imparted, the alchemic concoction bubbled before settling to a colour of richly tanned leather.

'And now we'll put you back,' she said, re-screwing the lid, 'where your label says you'll be.'

Mission accomplished, she picked up the mug, opened the dispensary door and bustled down the corridor with a busy-bee '*bum – de – dum – dum – dum*' refrain on her lips. At the end of the corridor she turned down a broad marble staircase, and at the bottom took a left and then right.

'Nurse Fawley!'

Millie came to a sharp stop in front of the steps leading down to the garden.

'Yes, Sister.'

'I've been looking for you, Millicent,' said Sister Billings. Executing a ninety-degree turn, she marched up to Millie. Sister Billings was always looking for someone. Whenever she found them, she'd been looking for them – regardless of whether she had or not. And if she had *actually* been looking for them, they knew because she'd been looking *all over* for them. 'You're to go and – What's that?' She pointed at the mug.

'Bovril – for Colonel Backhouse, Sister. He says it's an absolute wonder for his…'

'I'm sure he does, Nurse Fawley. The *lieutenant* colonel has no doubt led a very sheltered life.' Her feline eyes arrowed in as Millie inclined her body (and thus the mug too) away from her. But if Sister

Billings could spot the raising of a skirt hem by even one quarter of an inch from the distance of a full ward's length – which she most certainly could – she could without question tell a doctored mug of Bovril when she saw one. She clicked her fingers. 'Give it to me,' she said. A flush of pique coloured Millie's cheeks as she handed the mug over. Sister Billings sniffed the concoction, instantly determined its components, and conferred on Millie her usual withering, superior look. 'This is not Bovril, Nurse Fawley,' she said plainly. 'How have you got hold of this? Well, no – I know exactly how you have, and whose help you had in doing so.'

'But Sister, Colonel Backhouse feels so much…'

'Nurse Fawley! The *lieutenant* colonel is not here to feel – he is here to heal. And I don't care if the war's over, I'll not have you speak back, is that clear?' Noting a glistening of suppressed petulance forming in Millie's eyes, she let out a puff of infinite exasperation, and no little despair. 'Never, in all my good days, Millicent, have I ever encountered a more wilful, obtuse, disobedient, unmanageable—'

'Sister Billings! Sister Billings! I need you in the ward – now!'

The interminable list of synonyms applicable to Millie's character being cut short by the doctor's summons, Sister Billings' sun-dappled complexion turned winter pale. She gazed distantly at Millie.

'They won't let him go,' she muttered sadly. Her focus quickly returning, her voice bore a hint of accusatory bitterness as she added, 'They just bally well won't.' She spun away, stopped, and passed the mug back to Millie. 'Throw it away, Millicent. I will speak to you and that wretched accomplice of yours later.' She took a few purposeful steps, stopped again, and returned to Millie. 'Now, Nurse Fawley!'

Mug in hand, Millie remained as still as a stick insect, watching as Sister Billings disappeared off to the ward. Then, when she had certainly gone, she skipped on down the steps.

'Bum – de – dum – dum – dum.'

*

As Lieutenant Colonel Backhouse reached out to receive the mug he coughed so violently that Millie was forced to keep hold of it. When he had finally stopped coughing, she released it to his charge.

'You, my little ginger snap, are a bloody marvel.' He took an eager sip, and then coughed again – this time a prolonged, rasping cough that sounded as if his weakened lungs were being given their last garrotte. Catching Millie's softened expression he threw her a reproachful look. A moment later the familiar brusque signal indicated there was no more coughing nonsense to come.

Millie explained peevishly, 'Sister nabbed me on the stairs as I came out. She knows what's in it now. It's so stupid that she and the doctor won't listen. I'm only doing what's good for you.'

'You are indeed. Everyone should be drinking it, if you ask me. I don't know how the devil you came up with this, but it's a bloody nectar.'

'My mother came up with it. When me and my sisters were poorly she always mixed the medicine with other bits and bobs, to save money. She used to experiment with all sorts of things, telling us she'd come up with something extra-special to help us get better extra-quick. We were her little guinea-pigs.'

'Then your mother's a bloody marvel too!'

'Yes,' she said with a gush of filial pride. 'Anyway, cos of what Sister now knows, it might be a bit tricky next time.'

Backhouse took another sip and winked at her. 'A bottle of gin says it won't be.'

Millie's eyes lit up and she clapped her hands joyfully. 'Yay!

'*Gin, gin, marvellous gin,*

'*You know where you'll find me – and that's at the inn.*'

Caught between sips by the couplet, Backhouse's amusement spluttered into another cough.

Millie let out a coarse, gravelly laugh. 'Oh God, don't kill yourself with the Bovril!'

'This girl has near as damned well saved my life, Wilson,' said Backhouse once he had recovered. He turned to Edward standing beside him in the sun. 'Forget all that quackery about steam inhalations, cupping, and cuts here, there and everywhere – *this* is what medicine's about.' He raised the mug to his health. 'The right prescription for the affliction. Of course that damned fool doctor won't hear a word of it. Not in his bloody manual. Had the nerve to give Millie here the most beastly ragging in front of the sister last week for helping herself in the dispensary – and then tried the same thing on me, can you believe? Said I ought to be ashamed of myself for encouraging her. Ashamed for wanting the only thing that's doing me any damned good – ridiculous man! Much good it did him though, eh, Millie?'

Backhouse's violent strength of feeling brought on another coughing fit. Edward stuck out a hand to stop the contents of his mug from slopping. Backhouse would have none of the gesture though: he loathed any hint at being invalid. Shielding the mug, he withdrew it from reach. But all the exertion was too much. His legs started to quiver so that he was forced to lean heavily against the garden wall just to remain upright.

The effects of Spanish flu had transformed Lieutenant Colonel Backhouse. They had reduced him to a thinly fleshed skeleton of a man. His ruddy face had become ashen and gaunt, and where once it had been complemented perfectly by his thick moustache, it was now overwhelmed by it, like a cat that had been shaved and left only its whiskers. The sturdy torso and tree-trunk legs that had flanked noble steeds and powered effortlessly up the mountainside had atrophied too, becoming so wasted of muscle that they seemed barely able to straddle a goat.

The advance through the Val d'Assa had been debilitating. The sun, unable (or unwilling) to penetrate its deep fissures and forests, had shone for a solitary hour over the high peaks before retreating to leave them to plough on in dark, numbing misery. It was then that the imperial shadows of war had emerged in the gorge: shells of men trudged past in scattered groups in solemn, sullen silence, while gas-mask eyes were trampled underfoot, flat haversacks clung to face-down backs, carts lurched along the corkscrew tracks, and horses staggered – before being thrashed; the litter of corpses, limbers and lorries swarmed upon by the million mouths of the million buzzing flies. When at last the invisible line was crossed, the sun had returned and they were bathed in white light. As one they had turned their heads to the sky like a field of greedy sunflowers. And then, as soon as they had, it was over. Whereupon they had about-turned and marched straight back through the gloom of the valley – just as Edward had known that they would. By this time, however, Backhouse's headaches and fever had already begun. Although his convalescence had been long he had refused to leave Italy, remaining close to the battalion south of Vicenza.

'Come on, you, back in your chair,' said Millie.

Backhouse cast a malevolent eye at the wheeled contraption beside him. It had been out of the question he should meet Edward sitting in it – he had already told Millie this, so he had no idea why he should have to repeat it. As such, turning to Millie, his expression carried the same malevolence as his eye.

'In a minute!' he snapped. But even with the support of the wall Backhouse's legs would not hold out. At any moment they would buckle and he would collapse in a heap on the ground. His powerlessness to prevent this was the cause of his rage. To take this out on Millie was the height of boorishness though. His disposition therefore quickly softened, albeit more in thought than in tone. 'Yes, yes. But I only do it for you, you know.'

'Of course you do.'

He slowly lowered himself into the bath chair and planted his hands with distemper on the rests.

'There – I'm going to have to converse with Lieutenant Wilson as if he were a bloody giraffe. Happy?'

'Now there's a giraffe in the hospital – quite. Well… I'll leave you two alone for a few minutes. Do try and stay in the chair, won't you?'

Backhouse made no reply. He merely watched on with a sort of wan, paternal devotion as Millie marched away across the lawn and joined Major Mallinson beneath the arbour, the latter's pipe hanging lazily on his lips as he plucked the purple blossoms of the many sprinkled periwinkles.

'That girl is of use,' Backhouse stated, at length. 'Most of them aren't, but she is.' He turned his head to the white winter sun in the cloudless sky and basked in its glow for a moment. His ruminations were concluded by an angry thump of the chair. 'She'll be damned well wasted in England, that's for sure. Just like the rest of us. By Jove, who the devil wants to go back anyway? The *country*? It's all gone. It'll never be what it was... For heaven's sake, Wilson, come and stand where I don't have to twist my damned neck to see you.' A peremptory jerk of his arm swished Edward in front of him. He gave him a cursory look before propping his gaze back on Millie; she was laughing with the major. 'But you don't care a fig for that. Never have, I'm sure. Nor should you. All that *Shropshire Lad* stuff's nothing to you city types. Anyway, the whistle's gone; the referee's picked up the ball; time to get off the pitch. It's been a damned bad game, but there you are. It's done now.' The lieutenant colonel's strain of melancholy bluster was more a product of his present physical condition than any permanent psychological change. If it had indeed been a *damned bad game* that was only because in the last minute of the match he had been kicked in the shins when clean through on goal. There was nonetheless relief detectable in his voice as he added, 'They're packing me off south to Taranto next week. At least that's Christmas sorted – thank God. What about you?'

'About me what, sir?'

'What are you going to do with yourself, that's what.'

The shift of focus being unexpected, Edward had no idea what to say. 'Well, I... erm...'

'Just as I thought. Haven't a clue. That's what I told the War Office too. They're going to start sending trains up to Vienna next month – some kind of relief mission. The usual thing: food, clothes and whatnot. I told them you'd be game for that. Get you another pip on your shoulder, no doubt. You speak a bit of Kraut, don't you?'

'Well, I...'

'I told them you did,' Backhouse continued regardless, a negligent turn of his fingers indicating the question had been of the parenthetical sort. 'You'll be under Major B's command. There's no point you loafing around here doing nothing all winter, is there?' This question was of the rhetorical sort. 'Of course not. Nothing worse than an idle officer. You'd just drink yourself stupid. And you'd be about the last man in the batt to get your papers, you know – you'll be here for a good while yet, if that's what you're thinking.'

That was not what Edward was thinking. He didn't know what he was thinking. 'I really was...'

Backhouse's muscular eyebrows twitched in aggravation. He was not one for quibblers, not when his mind was made up. The boy clearly needed some guidance. He was thus acerbically blunt. 'What's your trade then, eh? Wool sorter, rag conditioner, oil presser? I didn't think so. Back in England you'd be as useless as all the other officers come to the gentleman rank like yourself. Before you knew it you'd be just another orphan tramping round Piccadilly Circus and selling flowers on the steps of Eros. But you can do some good in Vienna. It's a rum lot up there, so I hear. And we can't have them starve, can we? Not now the war's over.' Beneath the heavy shades of his brow he looked squarely at Edward. 'They need the sort of man there who's not going to have a thought about whether to use his pistol when he draws it – whatever the circumstances. Someone who's not going to expect someone else to do the dirty work for him, do you understand?'

Edward had no chance to reply. The moment Backhouse finished he started coughing again. Millie's ears pricked to the sound. She presented her bouquet of periwinkles to the major and returned with her most purposeful gait. Her approach spotted by Backhouse, he tempered his manner to Edward.

'You've got some leave coming shortly, I know, so you'd have to forgo that. If not, I'll just have to get one of the other officers to do it instead. But seeing as I've already told the War Office and Major B you're the best man for the job, it'd be a bit of a fish in a pan if you didn't go now. You won't be alone – far from it. There'll be a company to guard the trains and help distribute the stuff once you're there, and a medical detachment too. See?' he said to Millie, like a schoolboy in search of a sweet. She was once more before him, the fine strands of her flaxen hair stippled in the sunlight beneath her white nurse's hat. She beamed broadly.

'Well done to Colonel Backhouse for sitting down.'

The lieutenant colonel returned her a lolly-sucking smile; he loved a dash of mockery in his women. He then addressed her in the straightforward terms of one who knew what was best for her too. 'Now, I've just been saying to Lieutenant Wilson here that there's no point in a fine chap like him wasting his talents back in England.

None at all. Farewell, sad isle, indeed. Nor you either, Nurse Fawley. The lieutenant's going to be heading off with a relief mission to Vienna shortly. A practical, knees-dirty job. There'll be a medical detachment going too. I've just told him that that's exactly your kind of caper. Isn't that right, Edward?'

'Well – I – yes, there was some…'

'Vienna?' said Millie.

'Exactly.'

'But how would I…'

Backhouse batted away any 'buts'.

'Don't worry about that,' he said. 'I'll see to the papers. So what do you say?'

There was a short silence. She looked at Edward, her eyes sparkling bright as the sun.

'Sure, why not?' she said.

Chapter 3

'Where is it we're going again?'

Edward let out a half-laugh at Millie's ingenuousness as they walked out the front of the country palazzo, a laugh swiftly suppressed by the thought he scarcely knew himself. A large sedan swept to a stop at the foot of the main steps. A young naval officer then sprang out of the passenger door and hurried inside, a cursory twitch of his long upper lip seeming to Edward to dismiss his existence.

'What's the navy doing here?' he muttered peevishly.

'What navy?' Millie was not paying attention; she only glimpsed the young man's back after he passed them. 'I've no idea. Oh, actually, I think I saw someone dressed like that talking to Major... I've forgotten his name, the other day.'

Edward's curiosity was only incidental to the slight. 'Oh,' he said negligently. Then he remembered. 'Vienna.'

'Vienna what?'

'That's where we're going. You asked me just now.'

'Oh yes, silly me.'

They stopped and looked at each other for a moment, an expectant, mirrored glint in their eyes, as if each hoped the other would be first to move to peroration. A simple 'cheerio' would hardly suffice, after all. Not now that Backhouse had just tossed them together like a couple of shipwrecked mariners on a desert isle. But if not 'cheerio', it was not clear what ought to be said. In the end Edward, to say something (*anything*), repeated what she patently already knew – Backhouse had said it barely two minutes before – that he had to see Major B in Padova the day after next. And then, before the subsequent thought had even flickered in the filament of his mind, he had said it: he invited her to come to Padova too.

To which her unthinking response was, 'Sure, why not.'

Whereat Edward immediately apologised. It was foolish to think she could discharge herself of her duties on a whim and get a pass at such notice.

To which she replied gamely, 'Oh no, it'll be fine. I'll think of something. I'd like to come.'

It was not until Edward had quit the hospital grounds that he came back to his senses. For the rendezvous was the unexpected denouement to Backhouse's battery of injunctions that had left him in a state of near palsy. So much so, indeed, that even the notion of 'Vienna' had been briefly stripped of all meaning. He knew only that a decision had been made; an order (he thought it was that) had been given; a whistle had blown – and it was over the top! Ah, the comforts of military routine! As soon as this inculcated consciousness gave way to insight, however, he felt the kindling of newer flames give light to the rocks around him. His whole body was released from the weight of its chains. Of course he would return to Vienna!

This return would not be to the old Vienna though. It would not be to the Vienna of his past. It would be to a city destroyed, a city ravaged by the fell monster of war, a city starving and wracked by despair.

When Edward had first arrived on the western front south of Arras at the end of 1916, Backhouse had been quick to chafe his Methodism. 'Let's see if grace and God get you out of the mud,' he had said. They had not. Duty alone had done that. He had been knee-deep in the thicker Flanders mud the following autumn when the news of the death of his father and uncle had reached him. Backhouse had offered him a few days' leave, but had minced no words in telling him not to take it. There was nothing he could do, he had said, and nothing he would feel but self-pity and guilt. He had been right. For how, Edward knew, could he have left the trenches, thinking that *they* were more important than the lives that were every day under his wing? How could he have abandoned his men to mourn *two* when there were hundreds dead and exposed within feet? No, those bullets had simply whizzed past his head and felled two figures in a far distant land. One had to keep going forward: there was no ground to be gained turning back.

Backhouse's new instruction was thus clear. It reminded Edward that it was his duty not to fritter his days away organising football matches and revues, and in conducting pointless inspection parades of men whose only care for their rifle, khaki and kit was that they should never again have to polish it, wear it or sew it: men whose only interest was in getting drunk and getting home, or getting home and getting drunk: these men whom he had succoured as closely as a goose did its goslings. Because how could any man with a pretence of morality turn away from the consequences of victory? From the consequences of defeat? He could not let a city and its people be trampled to dust. Faith, he knew (for he *had* learnt), was not to be found in private life and prayer meetings, but in works. The soul of the sluggard had nothing.

Chapter 4

Major B was sceptical about Backhouse's recommendation. At least, that was Edward's impression when he arrived at his office and was acidly informed that, seeing as he was now there, the major supposed he would have to take Backhouse's word as to his abilities. He would accept him as his little Austrian fag.

Senior officers ought to have fags, the major declared. Of course, where he went to school they didn't have fags, but as there were so many public school oiks swanning around whose only talent was living, some fagging would give them some use. A major ought to have a lieutenant or a captain as his fag, didn't Edward agree? Edward did not answer the charge, not because the major's sandpaper delivery made it impossible to know if he was being serious or not, but because the question was clearly plain stupid.

Major B was of a height and proportions in accordance with his aloof and withering manner. With a lean, irregular physique, he had a tendency to jerk like the hands of a grandfather clock. A pair of small, dark, deep-set eyes possessed a glazed shiftiness which every now and again hardened to a cold, contemptuous glare, and a prominent, angular nose was employed primarily for sniffing his irritation at any displeasing remark. His head, crowned by a shock of curly brown hair, was not conventionally plinthed, but was as if set on a spring which inclined to the left upon speaking, backwards when listening, and bobbed from side to side whenever provoked. His office was on the first floor of a building in the centre of town that had been commandeered by the army. The shutters were open but, the window giving onto the back wall of the clock tower opposite, any natural light was purely reflection, a fact which clearly irked him as much as the endless quarter-hour chimes. For despite the room having no door, an array of twitches and tics suggested it was being constantly knocked; but there was almost no one about.

After the fagging preliminary the major moved on to the relief mission. However, explaining it in offhand, perfunctory terms, it was as if the whole process of war had been less an ordeal of armaments than a test of his threshold for tedium. Indeed, it seemed the only military position that might have excited his ennui was that of Commander-in-Chief – a position he would have surely spurned for the bore of having to speak with the king; and had he been offered the crown, he would doubtless have scorned that for the chore of having to put up with his subjects.

The major was heading to Vienna in a couple of days to sort out where to store the supplies. They could hardly dump the stuff on the streets and let the Viennese help themselves, he said, though on reflection he rather liked the idea – a kind of Darwinian exercise to weed out the unfit; they ought to try the same thing in Knightsbridge. Anyway, in his absence Edward would be in complete charge of the mission's organisation. There was a huge amount of preparation and work to do. There'd be no more time for Edward to go rolling in the hay with all the lovely *signorinas*.

Edward was quick to interject stiffly that he did not roll in the hay. He then said that, as Lieutenant Colonel Backhouse had furnished him with little more than the broad ambition of the relief mission, he was keen to know some of the details: what, specifically, would be his responsibilities? While he spoke, Major B's head first tilted backwards, before bobbing this way and that. As soon as he finished it angled left.

The major responded by repeating how much preparation and work there was to be done. He emphasised how busy Edward would be, talked in vague terms of trains, wagons, food, supplies and men, and by the time he had finished had explained the specifics of precisely none of the above. Thus was Edward led to understand that the major was the sort of man who was only too happy to give him the rope to hang himself with, but who would still insist on tying the knot himself.

Edward next proceeded to some pertinent questions as to the rumours of the true conditions in Vienna, upon which Major B reclined in his chair as the quarter-hour chimed. He dismissed them as a sentimental exaggeration of the normal post-war state of affairs. It was a case, no doubt, of lots of middle-class people imagining their situation to be far worse than it was: people who had to put on an extra pullover and didn't get their morning *viennoiserie*. The major was sure that when they got there they'd find the city to be the prettiest corpse east of Paris. The only thing they'd have to do was stop the Poles, Czechs and Hungarians from taking turns twisting the knife in the wretched thing's back. One would have thought that they'd all been dragged into the war strapped to an Austrian gun carriage! Luckily the Austrians were just like the English: they had no stomach for revolution. A sardonic smile then sat on his lips as he said that of course, unlike the English, they had nothing *in* their stomachs!

When Edward left Major B's office he returned to the train station almost more in the dark than before as to what he was in charge of. Despite this, the guiding light he had earlier seen remained bright; his moral obligation was completely undimmed.

The sky was once again cloudless and the air chill and crisp. Millie had indeed thought of something, although what that was was a mystery to Edward. All he knew was that he had received a telegram the morning after they had parted ways at the hospital informing him that she would arrive on the eleven o'clock train. And as he idly paced from one end of the platform to the other waiting for her train there could be no denying the peculiar enthusiasm he felt at her impending arrival. Nor could he fully explain it. In the hospital garden she had made no impression on him other than by a mildly amusing domination of Backhouse, such that his invitation to Padova had been marked by a complete absence of design, let alone amorous pretention. But this was reason enough. For one did so tire of the company of one's fellow man, and so the prospect of passing a leisured afternoon with a female wherein every accidental brush of fingers was not of histrionic, palpitating proportions was a thing to cherish. His only mild concern was that he might not recognise her!

However, if there was even the remotest possibility that he might not recognise her, there was none that she might not recognise him: Millie's jars were always found where she put them. Upon the train's arrival she hopped down from the plate to the platform, strode straight up to him and beamed a sun-wide smile.

'Hullo there, trouble,' she said. 'What time is it? I'm starving.'

Edward could not stop a smile. 'I see you think on your stomach.'

'It's not the only thing I do on it. I'm sorry – I—' She bit her lip faux-demurely.

'I've heard worse,' he said, only slightly aghast, 'Though not from a nurse.'

'The worst *is* the nurse.'

'I'm sure they aren't.'

'No,' she rejoined gaily. 'It's probably just me.'

'Probably.'

'Anyway – golly, that was a trial,' she said, letting out a great exhalation as they crossed the platform to exit the station. 'I had to put up with an OD the whole way on the train.'

'An OD?'

'An "Oh Darling". That's what Tabby and I call men who go all spoons over girls. There was this Yank in the hospital a while back who went completely dippy over one of the nurses, and that's what he used to say all the time – "Oh Darling" this, "Oh Darling" that – in this silly, sickly voice. Tabby and I couldn't stand it. But the nurse loved it. I told Tabby we should write it all down and read it back to them so they knew how stupid it sounded. That's an OD.'

'Ah.'

'If a man ever said that sort of thing to me on a train I'd push him off it.'

Edward stifled a laugh. However, a glance at her steely, freckled, resolved face was enough to assure him of her homicidal sincerity.

'I'll have to remember that,' he said lightly.

'I'll remind you if you don't,' she returned, fixing a clenched-teeth grin.

He gave a wry shake of his head, for no soldier did *that*.

They made their way south along the main tram-tracked avenue into the centre of the city, before Edward directed Millie down the same colonnaded side street he had earlier taken to get to Major B's office. Shortly thereafter they came to an empty piazza.

'How about there?' said Edward, pointing at a couple of *trattoria* tables varnishing themselves in the sun.

'What for?'

'You said you were hungry.'

'Are you?'

Not especially. But he would be. And she was – the moment they entered the square he had caught her eye up the tables.

'Yes,' he said.

And so they sat down. Not long after, they were provided with two plates of ham and eggs, it being not entirely clear if that was what they had ordered, what the waiter had heard them order, or all that was had to be ordered. But Millie was happy enough. Two large, appellant eyes saw a couple of glasses of prosecco swiftly added to the account.

If it could not be said that there was anything particularly uncouth about the gusto with which Millie attacked her food, nor, Edward thought, was there anything refined about it either. It therefore perfectly complemented her features. For these laid no claim to distinction, and any prettiness attributable was due to a lusty candour as opposed to any delicacy or conventional beauty. Her hair was of the sandy, flyaway sort that one could brush for a year without making it straight; her pale skin was here and there reddened by the sun and dried by the marks of some old worried spots; her freckles were a signal of humour, not note; and her large grey eyes, though lively and keen, seemed to only rest through exhaustion. But then, suddenly, and as if to settle all dispute as to her character, after she had cleared her plate and washed the food down with a last swig of prosecco, she belched. Not a discreet, suppressed, back-of-the-throat belch, but one which, although its natural egress might have caught her unawares, she made no effort to contain.

'Excuse me,' she said. She bowed her head guiltily, whereupon her eyes rose in puppy-like exculpation. 'I can't help it.'

Caught between horror and humour, Edward's response was facetious. 'I'm sure you *could*.'

'Oh yes,' she confirmed, unbowing her head. 'But I'm not very ladylike. I'm the runt of the litter, you see. The last piggy out of the sty.'

'I'm surprised they put up with you in the hospital.'

'They have to. I'm the best nurse Sister's got.'

'I'm sure.'

'It's true. It'd all go to pot without me.'

Edward found it hard to believe her; still, a large part of him did. 'Well she won't have you much longer, will she?' he said.

'Why's that?'

'You're coming to Vienna, aren't you.'

'Oh, that – I don't know yet. Maybe.'

'Ah,' said Edward flatly. 'Don't you want to?'

'Yes, of course. But I haven't said anything – Colonel Backhouse said he'd arrange it. Anyway, I heard Doctor Armstrong say the other day that they're going to be closing the hospital soon, so it won't matter. I'll be able to do what I want.'

In spite of Edward's desire to gainsay this approach, Millie's bullish tone persuaded him otherwise. After a moment he resumed in an idle, exploratory fashion. 'So what would you have done then, if you weren't coming to Austria?'

'Oooh, I don't know.' She pursed her lips together thoughtfully. 'Sister Billings said I should go back to England and train to become a proper nurse.' She sighed. 'But I'm not sure I want to do this in a normal hospital. Tabby said they'd never let us do half the stuff we've been doing here. I'm sure I'd be bored stiff. So this thing in… in…'

'Vienna.'

'That's the one. It sounds like fun.'

Fun?

'I'm not sure that's what you'd call it,' he replied loftily.

'It's got to be. Otherwise what's the point doing it? We'd go mad.'

Edward knew exactly what the point was, and it was not actuated by frivolity and japes. But as he watched her pick some gristle from her teeth with her nail and then clamp them together as if for hygienic inspection, he was once more inclined to play along with the bright tone of day.

'*Madder*, you mean,' he said.

Millie let out a coarse, back-of-the-tavern-type laugh.

'Exactly! So, come on then, what were you going to do?'

'Me? I would have been stuck here.'

'Ok, Mr Clever Clogs, what *are* you going to do – after Vienna?'

'We've not even got there yet,' Edward laughed, his amusement caused as much by the fact that she hadn't a clue either. 'I've barely got used to thinking two days ahead, let alone two months.' He dug into his pocket and placed a handful of coins on the table to cover the bill. 'Now,' he said, standing up, 'I'm not one for walking round with my nose in a map like a tourist, so I thought we'd have a wander and see what we find. What do you think?'

'Ok.'

'Is there anything you particularly like, or want to see?'

'Oh, whatever, I don't mind.'

Thus, with a mutually agreed peripatetic intent, they departed.

They ambled across the cobbled square and passed beneath a long, vaulted archway. On the other side it opened out into another, far grander piazza. Millie turned up a stone staircase beside the archway wall.

'Let's see what's up here,' she said.

At the top they found themselves looking out from a magnificent *loggia*. They rested on the parapet and gazed out across the sun-blanched stones, stones that for seven centuries had bustled with the Venetian empire's citizens and denizens, and which were being presently swept of the early-morning market detritus of grapes, tomatoes, salad leaves and figs by the halting, desultory strokes of a single wire broom. The swarthy brushman paused, leaned on the handle, drew on the stubby end of his cigarette and cogitated as he took a listless look around. A comment being passed out of sight, his reply was a curt '*Cosí*.'

'That'll take him the day,' said Edward.

'I think he's got some kind of hip wound.'

'Hmm, maybe,' came the doubtful reply.

Retreating from the parapet they turned to the doors behind them. They were locked. Millie peered through the top of the glass panels; Edward did likewise. In a great beamed hall beyond, the walls were filled with paintings, a rich blur of colour – of fantasy and judgement – that in the pale light that filtered through the high mullioned windows seemed to swirl round and round as if viewed from a carousel horse. And before it stopped they had drifted silently on, back down the staircase, back under the arch, back across the piazza.

'I wanted to have a look at... *that*,' said Edward, pointing at the clock tower as it came back into sight. He had only had time to glance at it when he had arrived in the morning, and had forgotten about it on leaving the office in his haste to get back to meet Millie's train. They stopped beside a dried-up fountain and looked up at the intricate face.

'Ooh, that's strange,' said Millie.

Edward agreed that the Roman numerals indeed had peculiar fives. Someone must have muddled them up, he supposed.

'Just like me!' Millie laughed. She then pointed out how on the outer circumference of the clock face the several zodiac signs were not aligned to the cycle of months on the inner. Someone must have muddled them up too!

'Just like me!' joked Edward.

After staring at the clock in unmuddleable silence for a short time, at the half-hour chime they moved on. In and out of the colonnades they went; in and out of the strips of sunlight and darkness of the narrow, winding streets, with resonant footsteps, as their arms now and again bumped like boats at their moorings as a cobbled ripple ran under their feet, or as they slowed to an almost stop to gaze in neck-tipped wonder at some passing fascia, cornice or carving. And on they continued, over the river bisecting the city, as the shadows on the brickwork imperceptibly climbed ever higher towards the deepening mazarine sky.

Then, suddenly, they were bathed in light: they stood on the edge of a great elliptical park ringed by a wide boulevard. On the far side was a columned arch like that of the Emperor Constantine, as if charioteers might once have entered through it before careering round to an ear-splitting roar from the surrounding balconies. They crossed the boulevard and sat on the low exterior wall between the crenellations of weathered stone statues.

Millie asked if Edward smoked. Edward obliged her: he took his cigarette pack from his overcoat pocket and offered her one.

'Thank youuuu,' she trilled as he lit it. No sooner having sat, she stood up and wandered over to the nearest statue. 'Let's see who this lot are, shall we?' She inspected the Latin inscription on the plinth: 'Never heard of him.' She wandered to the next one: 'Nor him.' As she moved along, Edward followed – if for no other reason than to proudly explain who the eminently carved figure was. His pride took a blow. The names were of such general obscurity as to preclude him from declaring didactically that X was one of the greatest... or that Y was a famous... until, at last, the figure of Galileo he did recognise. But as Millie had already asked him whether he knew that Jupiter had four moons, each of them bigger than planets (he did not – though he was sure that in some way, actually, he did) he decided to defer any didactic declarations.

By the time they reached the far end of the park the sun had dipped its head from the day. A closing burst of blood-red orange infused the Renaissance and Byzantine palazzi around the perimeter with a sumptuous palette of iron and gold. Then it was gone; the sky was covered by a speckled blanket of silver-blue, and the breeze bit hard from the north.

They began their return diagonally – if Millie wouldn't mind, Edward asked, which she didn't; Edward had spotted a cathedral at the end of one of the avenues forking off from the boulevard. On reaching the cathedral they passed through a chapter door at the side leading into the cloisters. Following a speechless, foot-tolling circuit they entered the cathedral's cavernous nave, and their paths slowly diverged. Edward wandered over to one of the candlelit chancels. He peered through the locked railings. One of the paintings within depicted a scene from antiquity: a man lay prone on a stone floor in the middle of a courtyard, an arm extended high in supplication to the crowd around him; behind him stood an elderly man whose white-bearded features were strained by the rock he held aloft – the rock he was about to cast down on the supplicant man. Edward stared at the image for several minutes with rare fascination. But it was not the plight of the man about to be crushed by the rock (some saint, he presumed) that struck at his heart; rather it was the elderly figure about to cause his death. For in neither the elderly figure's eyes nor in his countenance was there betrayed the least trace of emotion: not hatred, vengeance, ignorance or apostasy. It was an expression of ineffable blankness, as if all human sentiment had been subjugated to the sheer brute physical effort of lifting the rock. Moving on, he rediscovered

Millie in the reliquary: she was staring at a glass case containing the jaw and teeth of San Antonio. Remarking his presence beside her she looked at him bug-eyed.

'Gobble, gobble, gobble,' she said, and promptly spun away.

*

They exited the cathedral into a chill, mist-thickened evening.

'Well...' said Edward, and by way of conclusion.

'A quick drink?' came the procataleptical appeal.

'Um... well...'

Edward's hesitation was not because he did not want a drink. Far from it; such a thing followed the natural course of a day. But it was one thing to have a glass of prosecco over lunch, quite another altogether to take a nurse out for drinks in the evening, more so in light of their new-found assignment. Furthermore, aside from propriety, there was a far greater risk of bumping into someone he knew who would take his companion for one in whom he had a vested interest. Any subsequent denial of this interest would most certainly lead to the charge being assumed to be true, and before he knew it, it would be common supposition that he had managed to wangle his bit of carbolic skirt away with him on a tryst to Vienna. Hang the relief mission, they'd say, Lieutenant Wilson was on the batter!

'I have to get back,' he resolved. 'We've got an early inspection tomorrow.'

'So have I. There's a train to Vicenza at eight. You can catch that. Come on – the buttons will be just as shiny if you're not in bed by nine.'

'Yes, I know – it's just I do have to...'

'Write a letter?'

'No, I have to...'

'Be boring?'

'*No.*'

'Come on, you know you want to. Just a quick one, to warm us up for the cold train. Brrr. That's all we need, isn't it?'

The wheels were heavy but the ox was strong: Millie's face beamed like the moon.

And so, a short time later they found themselves back in the same square where they had had lunch. An even shorter time later Millie had sniffed out a bar.

'Here's fine,' said Edward, as soon as they entered. He indicated a table in plain sight by the door. But Millie had no harness; she was already nosing back to the sounds in the grotto depths. Edward's fear at the prospect of being embarrassingly wassailed by an acquaintance was suddenly supplanted by another: that she was now his responsibility. For Millie was not a raucous subaltern whom he could abandon the moment the feeling took hold. Their evening was entwined until it was decided to end it – *whoever's* decision that was. Then, before he could dwell any longer on that, that which he had first feared happening happened.

'Is that you, Wilson? Blow me, it is. What the devil brings you here? Let me get you a drink.'

Edward had hardly time to match Patrick Gardiner's voice to his face when Millie brushed up beside him.

'Hullo. I'm Millie.'

'So it would seem,' said Gardiner, his manifest delight accompanied by a knowing wink at Edward. 'Well it's my great pleasure to meet you – I'm Patrick Gardiner. Excellent, well, seeing as the introductions are all in order, allow me to get you both a drink. I presume you *both* –' here the enquiry was put to Millie '– would like one?'

'Yes please,' she said pertly.

'Jolly good. Jolly good.'

'Miss Fawley is going to be part of the medical detachment,' Edward hastily explained, 'that's going up to Vienna in a few weeks' time with a relief mission. We've just been going through some of the details at the War Office.'

'Ah, quite so,' replied Gardiner smoothly; he was a dab hand at that sort of ruse. 'Yes, I've heard some pretty dreadful things about the conditions there. Now, Miss Fawley…'

'Oh, Millie's fine.'

'Jolly good. Well, Millie – *Edward* –' He redressed his attention. 'I'm just having a drink over there with a few Italian friends who have unearthed a couple of quite charming American nurses. My friends don't speak much English so I'm providing my services as their appointed guide and latimer, as it were. So, if I'm not intruding…'

'No, not at all,' said Edward, reassured that integration to a group would vouchsafe his and Millie's formal connection.

'Excellent. Well then you must come and join us.'

Gardiner's three Italian officer friends were impatient for his return: he was required to translate a passage from Petrarch that had just been recited. Gardiner duly obliged. The effect, however, was noticeably less enchanting on the nurses than the original Italian, a repetition of which was immediately called for.

It was not long before Millie was at the heart of proceedings. Briefly cowed by the maenadic trio of women, the Italian officers nonetheless rose dauntless to the challenge so that Edward and Gardiner were soon relegated to the role of spectators. Gardiner ordered a carafe of wine for the table and, establishing Edward's preference, a couple of grappas. After laughing at an intentionally ribald misunderstanding by one of the flirtatious Italians, Gardiner subtly detached himself from the party, reached across the table and placed his hand on Edward's forearm. Edward was convinced he was about to apologise for the puerility of the company and scene.

'You know,' said Gardiner, between laughs, 'I was hoping I'd see you again.'

'Oh?'

'Yes. I wanted to speak to you about what happened at the fort.'

'The fort?'

Gardiner's hazelnut eyes, burnished by the soft sheen of liquor, were suddenly extracted from the hubbub to settle on Edward. In the dim light of the bare electric bulbs his expression was transformed to one of fabulous solemnity.

'Yes, the fort,' he said with breathless assurance. 'Do you know, before the war I couldn't stand the Austrians. To me they were as contemptible as—'

He was interrupted by the arrival of the grappas and wine,

wherewith health was proposed and the glasses were chinked all around. Gardiner's return to intimacy and exclusion was swift: he resumed in the hushed tones of the confessional.

'Well, contemptible is enough to describe them. I still can't stand them, of course, but at least I now understand them. You see, when an injured wolf is nursed to health with saucers of milk, the taint of humanity is set on its teeth; it is no longer a wolf to be feared, but the prey of other wolves. That is what I thought of the Austrians: they were weak, tainted, the prey of bigger wolves. A man cannot pity what he does not know, after all, only pity what he sees. Then the war came, and I began to understand what it meant to be them, what it meant to be weak when once you were strong.' He took a draught of grappa and levered a splinter of wood from the table with his thumbnail, as if to attest to the organic decay of which he spoke. 'Do you know that while everyone in England still believed a spade was for digging flowerbeds and not trenches – while we men were still being measured, weighed, and fitted for boots and tunics to cross the Channel and fight – the Austrians had already lost the war?' He let out a short, ironic laugh. 'Yes, it was over by Christmas for *them*. An infantry regiment – of the Tyrolean *Kaiserjäger* – had charged with bayonets against a Russian division at Lemberg. Can you imagine that – a single regiment against an entire division? Three thousand blades against ten thousand guns! *Magnifique?* Perhaps it was, perhaps it was,' he said with a meditative rap of the wood. 'I was not there to see it. *Mais, ce n'etait pas la guerre*, as they say – that was for sure. Two thousand were slaughtered in minutes; the rest were for God and the tundra. At the beginning there was already the end. But, you see, this was because of the code of the military caste. The whole army had been whipped up in a cyclone of maddened bravura to efface the shame of Königgrätz and Custoza. And so with madness came death. That was what happened in the fort with the Austrian captain, or whatever he was, the one you shot. He knew the futility of his act – of course he did. He knew he would be shot and would die. It was not patriotism or despair that led him to grab the rusted blade and lunge at my Alpini friend – it was not the act of some hopeless suicide. No, he did it because the code had to be obeyed. In doing so he acted with that infinitesimal flicker of true life that believed he *might* be victorious, that he *might* plunge the knife into our Italian friend and at last be avenged – even though it was impossible. That I understood. It was an act of sublime eloquence, I thought.' He emptied his glass and summoned another. 'Drink up,' he said.

Edward had not touched his drink. But at the instruction he drained the glass, and was instantly brought back to the boisterous revelry going on round the table. The sight of Millie's fulcrum ebullience caused the natural declivity of his lips to straighten with an indefinable mixture of pleasure and unease. Two more grappas arriving saw a swift return to his dark sequestration.

'I tell you, as soon as I heard that captain of yours speak, I knew what he was going to do,' Gardiner resumed with animation, the oscillation of his voice marking the thrill in his thrall. 'I knew it. I knew he would never leave that mountain. The end of the war would be only a torment to a man such as he. Your soldier said he found him half-dead, didn't he? Well, I say he was found not because he was half-dead and unable to flee, but because he was half-alive. Yes, he was found because of his will to survive so he could die for the code – with his honour intact. And that's what you did for him. You shot him in order to preserve his...'

'What's he saying?'

Millie's interruption was directed at Gardiner: her pidgin Italian and patience had reached a simultaneous threshold. Gardiner, his countenance rigidly pleasant, was compelled to oblige her. He listened in to the Italians' rough badinage for a moment, before a snort of amusement was followed by a dismissive twirl of his fingers.

'It's just a dialect joke. It's not translatable, I'm afraid.'

Millie's freckles darkened. 'That's alright. What joke? I told them that I was going to Vienna, so it'll be about that. I'm sure I'll find it funny.'

'I'm sure you won't, Nurse Fawley.' Gardiner shook his head and said with laconic reproach, 'The red wine here has a potency that can sometimes bring out a rather crude, carnivalesque side – even for those accustomed to it.' A glance at Edward sought to share the warning, and he raised his glass to Millie with playful good humour. 'Stick with the grappa, I say!'

But if there was one thing more likely to pique Millie than being dismissed by twirling fingers, it was an intimation that her evening was subject to supervision. Her cheeks flushed crimson and her smile, though fixed, hardened.

'It's ok, I've barely touched a drop yet. So you can tell me what was so funny about Vienna, Captain Gardiner, can't you?'

'Nurse Fawley,' he said, emitting a heavy sigh at her persistent entreaty, 'they are merely suggesting – in their coarse soldierly way – that you watch out for Austrian men when you go to Vienna. It's nothing more than that, believe me.'

'I don't understand – why should I watch out for Austrian men in Vienna?' Millie said with intransigence. She glanced at the Italian officers, upon which, one of them, noting her reddened complexion, shared an evidently coarser remark with his companions, for they fell about laughing. She turned fiercely on Gardiner. 'What did he just say? Tell me!'

Gardiner's irritation was now manifest; his ideal of womanhood was Beatrice and Laura, not the Red Queen or the Wife of Bath. Shutting his ears off to the continuing vulgarities on the far side of the table, he therefore responded in a stripped, functional, masterly tone.

'There have been rumours, Nurse Fawley – although I'm sorry to say that time has proven them to have more truth than simple rumour allows – that the... let's call it the Habsburg Empire, shall we, rather than attributing its evils to any one people... had a habit of removing some of the less fortunate women from Vienna during the war. Removing them for *service* on the front line, if I may put it that way. Do you follow my meaning?' Millie did with a nod. 'Good. Not the sort of women one would normally think of as being drafted for such service either. I have a friend – an Italian colonel – who told me that after the advances on the Isonzo they recovered a good number of these women. Decent, middle-class girls, who through circumstances unknown – though most certainly unpleasant – found themselves torn from their homes to be the subject of some of the more bestial treatment of the war. It's sad to say that in wartime a woman's foes are not limited to the ones in enemy uniform. Forgive me,' he said, his contrition merely a force of the circumstance, 'you surely now understand why I didn't think such humour fit to translate.'

Millie understood *that*, just not the joke.

'But you laughed, Captain Gardiner,' she returned bluntly. 'You laughed.'

He gave her a short, snide rebuke. 'I did indeed, Nurse Fawley. I've laughed at dead men too. But I wouldn't tell their mothers that I laughed at their son's corpse.'

'Were *they* raped?'

'Excuse me?'

'Were the dead men raped too?'

Gardiner's shock at the word was profound. It was like the tip of a blade that could never be seen, only felt when it pierced. In the uncomfortable, aggravated silence that ensued he floundered briefly for words. Finally, bitterly, he scoffed.

'I doubt it – though perhaps you'll accept after what I've just said that there is reason to my friends' crude remarks. That is what the Italian experience of the Habsburgs has been. It is not Strauss and balls – it is *that*. I'm sorry, Miss Fawley, I think you—' He broke off and turned with vexation to Edward, his urge to censor seeking a likeminded hand. But nothing more followed forth from his lips. Instead of finding empathy or fraternity Gardiner was hooked by the icy blue glare which had transfixed Edward's eyes.

And no sooner had Gardiner broken off than Edward stood up and hurried out of the bar.

Chapter 5

Edward's sense of duty towards the Viennese was not shared by the men. As far as they were concerned the duty had already been done. The imposition of *another* was therefore simply a breach of contract and an abuse of an Englishman's liberty. What lay beyond the snow-white tips of the Julian Alps was of as much concern to them as what a cat got up to when it went out at night, and the warmth of the Italian sun only heightened the contrast to the darkness they were certain prospected behind.

'Told yer,' said Collins. 'Nothing ter bleedin' do.'

'Last in, first fucker out,' said Addison, watching as Private Tate flapped his demobilisation slip paper in front of Bagley at the far end of the station ticket hall.

'Like bloody Vivier,' said Dawson, wide-eyed in disbelief. 'How'd he get slipped either?'

'Baint the... er... erm... start of the huntin' season?' said Yorston. 'Must be Colonel Thorpe a-needin' some beaters, I reckon.'

'Yeah, Colonel Thorpe'd *love* a beater or two.'

'Oh, yah, have to go and beat for the colonel on the shoot. So sorry.'

'*So* sorry.'

Tate and Bagley crossed the hall and joined the men straggled round their wooden bench.

'Cheeky little slipper there, Eight, eh?' said Dawson. 'Didn't realise you were a miner. Thought that black in ya hair was boot polish.'

'Piss off. Bleedin' wife an' kids I 'ave, mate.'

Yorston thrust his hand in the air. 'So sorry, wife and kids. Must go. Bye!'

'*So* sorry.' Dawson gave Tate an exaggerated, theatrical wave. '*Bye!*'

'Yeah, well, I've done my bit,' Tate returned testily. 'I'm not gonna be dragged off ter fight the bloody Ruskies. Nor should you lot neither. And that's what'll 'appen – mark me fuckin' words. That's what I's just bin tellin' Baggers 'ere. Got the right ter go 'ome when yer bleedin' well like is what I think. Waitin' around fer some jobsworth ter say we can go 'ome – it's a fuckin' joke. Two fuckin' months 'n' all. Essential fer the bloody war – not so bloody essential to send 'ome though, are we?'

'Alright, alright, Eight. Anyone'd think you're waiting for ya slip paper or something.'

'They don't bleedin' want us – any of us – that's what I'm sayin'. It ain't right that I'm goin'…'

'Got *that* fuckin' right,' said Addison.

'Yeah… an' you lot ain't, was what I was sayin',' continued Tate, irked by the bantering barrage of remarks. 'They're shittin' 'emselves. I tell yer, they'll send yer anywheres so's yer don't be comin' back thinkin' ter change things from what they was before.'

'Lucky for us you're going back to tell them we don't want to change a thing then, eh?'

Addison gave Bagley a dig in the ribs and pointed at Tate. 'Cheer up, Baggers. 'E'll be gone soon so yer won't need ter listen ter no more of 'is Bolshie bollocks.'

Bagley's mind had drifted elsewhere: not far from the pub and Tate's little pamphlet. 'Yeah, well done,' he said flatly.

'Well done *what*?' said Addison.

Bagley glanced at the men, let out a humourless chuckle, and shrugged his shoulders. 'Dunno,' he said.

*

Edward, meanwhile, had time for neither portents nor grousing. Major B was right about him being busy; he had barely a moment to do anything that wasn't to do with timetables, railways, wagons, supplies, and the logistical trauma of assembling them in a single location by the turn of the year. It had not taken him long to discover that, whilst the railways might have been the string that bound the world, that string was no longer a single thread; it was multiple lengths that had been severed and frayed.

Major B was at least true to his word: during his absence in Vienna he let Edward get on with the job. He did, however, conform perfectly to Edward's expectations upon his return. Half of the plans that were already in place were unilaterally changed, and the half that were not were accepted with acerbic remarks that he was a good little fag. Still, Edward was satisfied when, just after the new year, the wagons were finally loaded with the first two hundred tons of aid – despite the fact Major B congratulated *himself* for his having accomplished this feat.

The company of men who were to act as guards and garrison were then entrained at Padova and the first of their engines connected. Thence they were tugged the short distance to Venice. At Venice the engines were changed for the ere transnational line to Trieste, and an old imperial puffer pulled them across the flat, arid Venetian hinterland. When they reached Trieste they stopped several hundred metres short of the station, where a local Italian transport officer met them to explain that if the train pulled into the station then the thousands of starving ex-prisoners of war who were swarming the quays in search of a ship would storm the wagons. It was as much as the transport officer could do to keep the train out of sight to try and keep order. Major B was unmoved by the plea: he was happy to shoot as many wops as was they had to – that would solve the problem of them searching for ships! The transport officer was pitched into a frenzy at the suggestion of shooting, before the confusion of humour was cleared and the Alpine engine that was to take them up through the mountains chugged out to meet them. At the same time the carriage transporting the officers and medical detachment was also changed: no Italian stock would be crossing the border!

'Jesus, we'd have been better off with the nags and navvies in the bloody wagons,' said Major B when they boarded the replacement. For once Edward agreed. The carriage had seen as much service in the war as any soldier, and bore the scars to prove it. The light bulbs had either been stripped out or smashed, the seats had been eviscerated, the doors were broken, and the windows had holes in and swung open at the slightest incline or jolt. The sole benefit to this last was that it provided relief from the stench of iodoform from its previous hospital life, though the doctors and nurses swore they smelt nothing. Although the holes were filled in and the windows wedged shut as best they could be, as the engine began the long, slow trawl into the mountains, the darkness that ought normally to have been an inducement to sleep became instead a thin blanket for an interminable passage of coughs, shivers and uncomfortable, fitful dozing.

Slumped on a bumpy hunk of upholstery, Edward pulled his cap down low over his brow, buried his freezing hands deep in his overcoat pockets and tried to sleep. As he did a faint smile formed on his lips at Millie's unladylike canine contortions opposite, her arms and legs being spread at wild angles, her mouth agape, and her head lolling to one side. It seemed to him only a matter of time before her tongue fell out and rolled on the floor. Eventually, turning his head to rest on the cold black window, he slipped into vivid, unsettled half-sleep.

Millie's sleep – in all its contortions – was just as unsettled.

*

When the medical detachment had arrived in Padova for the general entrainment it was the first time Millie had seen Edward since their parting of ways after their tour of the city. Edward had had just enough time to buy her a coffee and promise to buy her lunch in Vienna before he had been called away by Major B to take care of some problem with biscuits, or such like. In the intervening weeks their only communication had been a letter from Edward apologising for his behaviour, saying he had new billets in the city and asking her to tell him when she knew if she was coming to Vienna. When she got round to replying it was to say that she was busy, busy, busy with the closing of the hospital, but that she *was* coming to Vienna and she hoped his head was now alright after all of those grappas he'd had!

*

Millie, to be clear, had not wanted to leave the bar. When Edward had got up and walked out she had tried to cajole him back in. But the final forcefulness with which he had told her he was leaving and that she could do as she pleased had had an unpleasant, conflicting effect upon her. However much it annoyed her, she could not rid herself of the pangs of sentiment she attached to the day. And so she had returned with him to the station. Uncertain as to whether the cause of his ill humour was due to her or not (and so what if it were? *She* had done nothing wrong) her determination not to probe areas she herself had walled up meant she had asked nothing on the way. Therefore:

> *'Diddlety, diddlety, dumpty,*
> *The cat ran up the plum tree,*
> *Diddlety, diddlety, dumpty, dumpty, dumpty.'*

That this, followed by several skips and her most winning of smiles, had failed to elicit the least flicker of humour from Edward had left her feeling quite desolate though. And the only way she had been able to prevent emotion from making itself apparent on her face was through a brisk *'bum-de-dum-dum-dum'* – the which refrain she had continued in various scales until their final parting on the platform.

'I'm sorry,' Edward said in an undertone as he helped her onto her train. 'I didn't mean to spoil your evening.'

For a moment, when Edward looked up at her with his sad, whirling blue eyes, she half expected him to say something else too. But he did not, and simply averted his gaze to the distance.

'Oh, not at all! Plenty more evenings to come!' she replied breezily, as if nothing had happened.

On the train back to the hospital she gave herself a couple of sharp rebukes: 'Stop it, Millie,' she said to herself. 'Stop it!', and pressed her fingers into her glistening eyes as hard as she could.

*

Edward had been relieved that Gardiner had come out of the bar before Millie and joked that Edward could clearly not handle his grappa. That, after all, was more palatable than the reality. For the reality was nothing less than obscene. 'Obscene – obscene – obscene,' he had repeated to himself on his way to the station, with Millie humming beside him, as if by repetition of the word he might be scourged of the image that had transfixed his eyes and brought a watery sickness to the back of his mouth. It was a reality – an *obscenity* – that in an instant had stripped him of all his pretences. And in the absence of any irrevocable code to which *he* was bound which might have seen him return to his room, lock the door and discharge his pistol, the resolution he reached on his way back to the billets – and which was confirmed by the whiskies that despatched him to sleep – was straightforward. He would not go to Vienna. He *could* not. He would inform Major B of the fact at first light.

The whiskies imbibed meant that the first light he saw was not the first light of day. Oversleeping, in his haste to prepare for the battalion inspection the fulfilment of his resolution was necessarily deferred. When military matters were concluded for the day, logic and reason took hold. Aside from the fact that his posting was no longer a matter of choice, reason told him his duties could not be simply hanged in the noose of emotion. So of course he would go to Vienna. Reason could not suppress the image though. And in the ensuing days it leapt on his back and, no matter how many times he tried to beat it off with penitential repetitions of its obscenity, like the merciless *djinn* of Arabian lore it drove him on and on until exhaustion nearly ruined the meticulously prepared timetables and trains.

The image was crude: whilst Gardiner explained the lamentable fate of the Viennese women, Edward had transposed Oriana's face onto his conception of their abused bodies. It was an illusion no less fantastical than that of Friedrich on the mountain. But an image, Edward knew, was a unique possession: it was a secret garden of flowers and poisons; and no matter how delicate and fragrant the details ascribed it by its creator, it could never conform to anything other than the desires of he to whom it was given. However desperately one wished it were not so, and however shameful and repulsive the truth, the nether recesses of the mind could impose whatever they wanted on the image of an innocent or beloved. This was permissible only because incitements to outrage, disgust and fear were reliant upon these selfsame transgressions. Emotion was aroused by making the impersonal personal. Hereby faces acquired features, thoughts acquired forethought, winds acquired strength, and pens acquired a colour of ink to flow with serifs and twirls from their nibs. Thus, what might otherwise have provoked nothing more than a sigh of vacuous compassion at the sad tale of middle-class women was elevated from the slough of negation, and brought to fervour, barricades and revolution – by transgression. It was consequently not the image in isolation that had so sickened Edward, but what he had felt when he saw it.

The feeling of triumph was fleeting. It was a comet that flashed through the sky before disappearing into the blackness of space. That it had crossed Edward's mind at all was repellent enough. What was worse was that the tail had scarred the night sky, and the tail wagged: it wagged furiously.

He would return to Vienna – yes. He would return and would find Oriana where he had left her. And she would be freezing. She would be shivering in the ice. She would be weak and hollowed out of her former life. She would be a bundle of bones, begging for scraps and for food. She would have lost her love and been dragged back and forth through the rocks and the trenches. She would have scars on her skin and scratches in her eyes – those large, round, appealing eyes that would stare at him, pleading forgiveness and bread. And he would keep her warm and would feed her. He would find her blankets. He would wrap her in serge. He would stop her from shivering. And then he would bend down, pick up the abacus beads from where they had rolled – onto the floor, under the cupboard, under the table, down the stairs and into the gutter – and place them next to her bed, beside the broken frame of the abacus. He would do all this: he would fulfil his duty. And then, when his duty was done, he would leave. He would walk away proud and triumphant – because *he* had done this, and because she had not. For now that the sums had been counted, the weight was all on one side. That was what happened after the sails turned black when he had returned; when *she* had abandoned him.

So was that it? he had asked himself, and he asked himself, and he asked himself. Was that *his* love? Was that what he had *felt*? *That*? So fleeting, this love?

In the absence of Ingham he had several times considered unpacking his thoughts to Vivier, in spite of his youth. But on each occasion he had been beaten back by the realisation of the futility and inevitable apathy that would result if he did. For how could he go with a bag of words, toss them like seeds at the birds, and believe they would be carried away with the same beating wings as his own? How could they turn shoes into 'v's and torrents of rain into the gluttony of fat Germans? These things existed only as *his* images, as *his* sensations: they did not exist in his words. The words alone meant nothing. Only in their sequencing could there be found truth; only in their rhythm and flow; only in the total immersion of the imagination, diving into the thin spaces that split one word from another so that one swam from shore to shore between them, could one hope to pass over the dark holes of understanding. And so to tell all to Vivier required something which was in reality inconceivable, because reality demanded each sentence be delivered as a short, compact whole, garnished with a vulgar splodge of livery in order for the narrative to be driven on. On, on, always on. *Then*, he would have to say – *Then!* And how could any truth be expressed or understood like that? Even as he spoke he would feel the words falling from his lips like fading coals. He would know they were nothing but a shadow of the thought.

And when they had been stuttered out, haphazard and incoherent, scattered on the table before him, Vivier would glance at his empty glass. He would nod with feeling, utter some well-meaning phrases of ruth and compassion, and then, standing up to go to the lavatory, upend the table and tip them all on the floor. The table would be righted, more beer would be ordered, another cigarette would be lit, the talk would turn to the humdrum of football, cricket and the mess – and everything would be butchered by the drift to banality.

Two days before Christmas the option to unpack was removed: Vivier received his demobilisation papers in the morning. By the evening he had gone.

*

As the train began the long descent into Vienna, the creeping onset of dawn was only discernible through a wild wall of snow. When at last they outran the blizzard, shafts of watery sunlight stole in through the windows and roused the bleary-eyed passengers to stare in a stupor of wonderment at the glittering white snowscape. Slowly, the deep drifts thinned as the daylight hours rocked gently by, so that by the time the fields gave way to bricks, and quadrupeds turned into suburban bipeds, in the re-gathering afternoon gloom only scattered fragments of snow and ice were left to cover the ground.

Any notion that the thinning of snow might represent a concurrent elevation of temperature was immediately dispelled upon arrival in Vienna: a Siberian front had a beast-like grip on the city; and the line of lorries awaiting dispelled any thoughts of escape for some warmth. It was therefore not until several hours later that the enervating process of unloading the wagons and reloading the lorries was complete and Edward finally ordered their departure for the depot – Major B having left him in charge as he went with the medical detachment in search of their billets.

Chapter 6

The depot was the huge, cavernous former cattle market in the north of the city, where the smell of the long-departed ruminants still lingered. It took Edward and the company more than a week to unload the supplies, clean the building, construct the compartments, install the shelving, and for all the various items of clothing, blankets, boots, tinned foods, preserves, chocolates, medical dressings and sundry necessities to be categorised and accounted for so their efficient distribution to the wider network of local depots and welfare centres could be effected as smoothly as possible.

This activity was the only antidote to the cold: a dry, desiccating cold which needled the eyes and scoured the skin, a cold lardered between the grey stone and grey skies, a cold which numbed all thoughts to the primal wants of food and warmth. If a burning heart were the symptom of a malady, its cure could be found in this cold. Any moments of idleness Edward consequently passed with the men by the brazier. But even though he enjoyed the men's company and banter, he felt diminished by it: his comfort in comradeship always needed some sort of command. That said, anything was better than returning to the glacial solitude of his unheated hotel billet.

Edward had not heard from Major B for two days when he received a cable telling him to meet him at the British Military Mission at eight o'clock the next morning. The Military Mission was in the heart of the city by St Stephen's cathedral, and when Edward left his hotel, it was the first time he had walked through the city since the early autumn of 1913.

Ah, Vienna – lovely, tragic Vienna, hopelessly broken and destitute: the capital of all that was left. No longer the heart of a thousand-year empire directing the lives of 60 million with an ancient roll-call of tongues, but a simple conurbation of an insignificant province.

So, *this* was how an empire ended, Edward thought as he wandered along the bleak streets; this was what happened when the stallions were removed and mounted elsewhere. The great imperial edifices that Herr Braunthal had censured still stood, magnificent and proud – they had not crumbled in the sand as he had said they would. No. Their fate was far worse. They had become hollow façades that administered nothing and ruled over nothing: they were like the crab that had abandoned its shell to the tide. And so in that case, he thought, it would be surely better if they *were* all torn down. Yes, better that the grandeur lay in ruins – and be seen as all that was which now destruction is. That would at least be something for a future age to imagine with awe. Far better that than to be a façade and pretend to the glories long gone.

When Edward reached the Military Mission, Major B was already leaving. On the pavement outside, the major said he was being sent to Berlin, and as a mere hour before he had received orders to go first to Prague, he was in a querulous hurry to catch the next train. No one in the War Office clearly had a clue what they were doing, he declared. He had no idea how long he would be gone for, but was thankful he was going at all: he couldn't stand Vienna; he couldn't bear the weather; he couldn't stomach the people. On account of the indeterminate length of his posting the War Office had therefore promoted Edward to acting captain. Major B had made the recommendation himself, he said – he much preferred having a captain as his fag! – although he had no idea why the War Office had made the rank only 'acting': he wasn't doing five nights a week at the Leicester Square Empire. *Was he?*

'No,' said Edward.

Major B's opinion on the promotion was shared by Colonel Carrington, whom the major hastily introduced: the colonel was in charge of the Military Mission. Major B then cut the formalities short, wished them good luck and promptly departed.

Colonel Carrington was also leaving: he had an appointment with the chief of police to discuss the pressing crisis in Hungary. But in light of the major's departure he was keen to know a little of Edward. As such he proposed he accompany him a short way. They looped round the cathedral and headed west down Kärtnerstrasse in the rain-speckled cold.

With a well-gamed girth, a fluff of white hair poking out from his cap, and distinguishing side-whiskers which framed a round, amiable face, Carrington's appearance was more country parson than colonel. He spoke in the calm, sonorous tones of someone who, when presented with a problem of any complexity, would seek to solve it by an afternoon's weeding. That the Military Mission was primarily a diplomatic posting – which he was at pains to point out – clearly accorded with his urbane disposition.

Flushed with pride at his new elevation, Edward was eager to impress its merit on the colonel via his interest and (albeit limited) knowledge of events in Budapest: he had heard rumours of a communist takeover.

Colonel Carrington's response to this was unequivocally sanguine. Though Count Károlyi had indeed become a virtual prisoner in the Buda Palace since declaring the country a republic, it was hard to find sympathy with a man whose wife was a virtual Lady Macbeth. All the evidence the colonel had indicated that Mr Kun and his cohorts were rather practical communists, and a practical anything was better than a count with an ambitious wife!

The colonel said that Major B had told him Edward had been in Vienna before the war. Edward confirmed that he had.

'And how do you find it now?' the colonel enquired.

Edward's reply was light-hearted: he had had no time to see anything of the city since his return other than its depots and warehouses. That morning was the first time his feet had managed to get out of the lorries' footwells! After a laugh and pause, he then proceeded with a touch of discretion. He was struck by how quiet and empty the city seemed, although he suspected much might be due to the cold.

That, interposed the colonel with feeling, was exactly what he intended to maintain – *quiet*.

'Good, good,' the colonel said, satisfied, then continued by way of appraisal, 'When the major told me you'd been here before I was concerned you might be one of those chaps misted over by the idea of tragic little Vienna. Contrast is a pointless tint to put on a lens, dear boy, quite pointless. The world is no better nor worse than the shade that it is. Remember, dear boy, storms are best to read about; calm seas are best to sail on.'

The colonel had only been in the country two months and, despite being loath to be as severe as Major B concerning the character of the native population, he could hardly deny he found them to be both perplexing and vexing. 'They seem to find a perverse comfort in their own wretchedness,' he said, quite confounded. 'They are always complaining, always threatening – yet are willing to put up with nearly anything at all. Anything, that is, except that someone might try and help them!'

He presumed Edward knew something of the Viennese character? Edward did – though only a little. He had not been there long, he said; he had only been visiting his brother. As he spoke his thoughts turned organically to Friedrich. For *he* had certainly complained, he had certainly threatened, but he certainly would put up with nothing: his hatred of the Habsburgs, his commitment to the (Austrian) workers, his busting pride at his city would never allow it. Friedrich was a storm on his own. And even if that storm existed no more, the recollection of its passing was still enough to assure Edward that Colonel Carrington would not wish to hear of it. Edward therefore drily agreed that the colonel was right, but that now of course things had considerably changed.

'They have indeed, dear boy,' the colonel replied in a tone of deep satisfaction. 'Austria has had its revolution. That is quite change enough.' He came to a stop at the junction with the Ringstrasse and waited for a tram to totter past on its rusted rails, the rattling wood, windows and rivets so loud that the removal of a single bolt seemed likely to cause its flat-pack collapse. Once it had passed, however, Carrington showed no inclination to proceed any further: he would conclude what had to be said where he stood. He looked at Edward squarely as he resumed with pulpit solemnity. 'No one has noticed and practically no one has died. That is by far the best type of revolution, dear boy – by far. The country may now be a republic without republicans, but that's what always happens when the middle classes refuse to fight for their king. So they'll just have to lump it. Have you heard of the *Arbeiter Zeitung* – the workers' newspaper?'

Edward soberly replied that he had.

'Yes, yes, I thought you would have,' said the colonel. 'Well there was an article in it the other day which said that so many foreigners had flooded into the city since the end of the war that soon the workers wouldn't know if they were foreigners in their own country or not. Those so-called foreigners are all from the old imperial lands, of course – they're new foreigners, as it were. But that's the problem when you break an old vase into a thousand pieces, dear boy: one quickly finds that when one tries to put it together the pieces no longer go where they ought to. So at present the city's nothing but a knock-down emporium; it's a place where everyone knows you can get things on the cheap, from a pocket watch to a palace. Some people are making fortunes from it, that's for sure – *fortunes* – while everyone else survives on bread and potatoes, and maybe a cat if they're lucky to find one to skin. Some of the old are even setting light to themselves rather than freezing to death!'

The colonel paused. His earnest grey eyes gleamed with the hours of considered reflection. It was the black market, he then intoned, which had created the worst of these fortunes and misfortunes. It sowed the seeds of division between native and foreigner. And it was the *Schieber* – those detestable shady dealers – who were the outsiders that the people saw every day, and who were multiplied by rumour and hate into thousands. They were the ones against whom every sense of injustice would be sworn. It was, he stressed in conclusion, the black market that had to be stamped out to ensure peace and good order. That was the true purpose of the relief mission: to feed and clothe the city's inhabitants on equal terms, to negate the injustice, to destroy the black market.

'That's why you're here,' averred the colonel sententiously. 'I advise you and your men not to forget that. Calm seas, dear boy, calm seas.' A firm pat on the arm was accompanied by a benevolent smile. Whereupon he bade Edward farewell and continued his passage south down the Ringstrasse.

Edward remained perfectly still for a moment. A sharp gust of wind soon chivvied him back into life. His first thought thereafter was this: he was now Captain Wilson. And the first person he thought to tell the news to (indeed, who else was there now?) was Millie.

Chapter 7

By the time Edward reached the Meidling hospital in the south of the city he would have been frozen solid had his blood not been warmed by irritation: it had taken him almost an hour, and he had twice got lost. He found Millie on the fourth floor. She was in a ward room partitioned by a series of glass panels and poles, adjusting the weights on a large set of scales. On the scales stood a small, half-naked boy. To one side a nurse with a high, alabaster forehead bound in a like-coloured scarf sat at a desk with her pencil ready; to the other was a gaggle of children awaiting their turn on the machine. Edward was not interested in any of them though; he was after Millie. Not even the cold had diminished his enthusiasm at conveying his news.

'Oh hullo, trouble,' she said with a cursory glance.

'I see I'm still trouble then.'

'Trouble is as trouble does,' she said negligently.

Edward turned to the plump, jowly nurse of sanctified complexion. *She* was evidently no stranger to the black market, he thought; then conferred his regards. '*Guten Morgen*,' he said.

A beaky nose and a pair of owlish green eyes returned a novitiate glare. '*Guten Morgen*,' she returned in High German.

'What are you doing here?' asked Millie.

'I came to see how you were getting on.'

'Why?'

'Well, I... I...' He changed tack. 'I thought I'd take you to lunch. I said I would.'

'Did you?'

'Yes, I did.'

Millie's delivery was attacking and querulous, Edward's position defensive.

'Hmph. I'm not really hungry. And it's not like there's much to eat anywhere, is there?'

Bustling the boy off the scales, she summoned another. Edward's shoulders slumped forward. 'I don't know,' he said.

'I suppose we can pop out to a café if you like. But we'll have to be quick.'

'Ok.' And then, like a boy whose birthday balloon she had just burst, he turned back to the door and said heavily, 'I'll wait downstairs.'

The prospect of his departure roused Millie. For it was one thing for him to arrive unannounced, quite another for him to then *go*. She looked up and, with clear bright eyes, threw him a sportive smile.

'Don't be a silly-billy. I'm almost done. Come in. You can help.'

Edward was not to be bought off that easily. Having burst his balloon she now wanted to give him some cake? '*Help?* With what?' he said disagreeably.

'With me. That's what you're in Vienna for, isn't it?'

'Well, yes... but—' He let out a sigh. 'Well what do you expect me to do?'

'Help. Come on, chop-chop.'

'*Chop-chop?*'

Millie's smile turned into an impish grin. 'Please,' she said.

Edward's physical submission was quicker than the mental; he closed the door and stepped forward with a face on. The final confirmation of his entry provoking a flurry of tittered animation among the children, a sharp clap by the nurse restored order; a glower at Edward then firmly apportioned the blame for the disruption. As soon as Millie returned her attention to the new boy on the scales, Edward became suddenly aware not just of the boy's physical condition, but that of all the children. They were of a mixed, indeterminate age. Although some were mostly naked, and some only partially, there was uniformity to their anaemic complexions. Malnourishment was pronounced by the general protrusion of shoulder blades and bones, the distension of bellies, and by rippling, tapered ribcages. A few of the smaller children's heads seemed swollen, scarcely able to balance atop the deformed bodies beneath, whilst the faces were marked by shadows round the hollows of the eyes. There were signs of scoliosis, and each one of them was in some way rachitic, their puffy, twisted legs like wobbly strips of plasticine rolled out and stuck to their torsos.

'I've seen a few kids with rickets in London but... it doesn't look like we've been fighting the same war,' Edward said, after a moment's reflection.

'I know. It's ghastly, isn't it?' Millie agreed. 'Most of them are like this too. The healthy ones are the abnormal ones! They've hardly had any milk for five years – that's the biggest problem. The littlest ones – those born in the last couple of years – will be fine... and the big ones too; it's the ones who are five and six who are the worst. They'll never recover, not properly.' She leaned forward and announced the figures on the scales. '*Eins, sieben, und eins.*'

The nurse noted the weight, and Millie tapped the boy on the shoulder to signal the end of the examination.

'I see you speak German too now,' said Edward, his mood lightening with curious admiration.

'I speak German numbers. You'll be amazed how much communication you can have with someone just with numbers. It's like a whole new language!'

Millie beckoned a girl forth from the group; the little girl did not move.

'*Kommen,*' Millie encouraged her sweetly.

The little girl frowned, pursed her lips and crossed her arms. '*I mag net,*' she said, then repeated, '*I mag net, I mag net.*'

'Ha! I've learnt that, though – she doesn't want to.'

'I can tell,' said Edward, half smiling. 'She doesn't need to say it.'

'No.' Millie laughed. 'She's like you a minute ago.'

But whilst the little girl might have been an amusement to Millie and Edward, she was not to the nurse: her actions had proven Edward's presence to be an excuse for the children to act up. She therefore stood, with the intention of putting the girl on the scales herself. Her rise alone was enough to bring order. It not only silenced any objections Edward had to Millie's teasing, it induced the rest of the children to give the little girl a decisive prod forward. The girl's arms still intransigently crossed, Millie helped her onto the metal platform and carefully balanced the weights.

'This girl's ten – can you believe? You'd think she was half that age, wouldn't you?' Edward nodded in agreement. '*Zwei, fünf, und drei,*' Millie said, before making a couple of scribbled notes on sheet of paper next to the scales and then helping the girl (her arms still immovably crossed) down again. 'You can weigh the last two, can't you?' she asked Edward. 'I need to quickly check on the condensed milk rations. As soon as that's done then we can skip out for lunch.'

'Erm... I...'

'It's those two there.' Millie indicated a boy and a girl. 'Just tell the nurse what they weigh. Even a soldier can do that, right? Ok, I'll be back in a jiffy.' Wherewith she signalled to the nurse, pointed at Edward, and with no more ado bounced away in glass multiples out the back of the ward.

Suddenly alone, Edward looked down at the children; they were already looking up at him. He glanced at the nurse; she was already staring at him. He felt as exposed as if he were on top of a trench! His eyes flitted self-consciously about the room; then he collected himself. His brow lowered in responsible earnestness. He moved to the scales and called the boy forward first. Clad in a pair of large polka-dot underpants, the boy had short, cropped hair, a lazy, half-shut eye and a little pot belly. He waddled forward on his wide bow legs, buckled at the ankles. Edward reached out and provided the necessary elevation onto the scales. A dimpled smile cracked the boy's face, and a ripple of mirth came from the children. They were sharply shushed by the nurse. Edward then proceeded to scrupulously balance the weights. As soon as they had aligned he cleared his throat.

'*Dieses Kind wiegt siebenundzwanzig Komma vier,*' he said.

The nurse almost twirled with delight at the beautiful roll of his German. '*Danke,*' she cooed, with an owlish flutter of eyes.

'How old is he?' Edward continued in German.

'That boy is ten. What a nice little smile he has, don't you think?'

Edward didn't catch the question at the end, only the compliment before: she spoke a touch quickly to understand everything. He therefore gave no reply. Instead he examined the boy. He would have taken him for six at the most. He leaned over and lifted him back onto the floor, prompting the same dimpled smile and ripple of mirth. He next turned to the girl. The tallest of the group, her nascent maturity made her age more apparent. Her small, delicate face was fringed with blonde hair that was otherwise plaited in a traditional *Tracht* on the top of her head, a pair of straight brown eyebrows hovered inquisitively over two elliptical blue eyes, and her lips were tipped to just the hint of a smile. As she advanced towards him Edward remarked the inward curvature of her legs.

'*Siebenundreißig zwei,*' he said, on completing her weighing. He glanced at the paper on which Millie had scribbled. A full list of the children's names was annotated with their height and physical normality. He hesitated over whether to write something, then simply put a tick by the final two names. Turning back he saw the girl was still on the scales. 'Oh, *danke,*' he said hastily and, as instinctively as he had picked up the boy, he reached out to assist the girl down. Her eyes flashed at him as his fingers feathered her back. A light flush on her cheeks, there was a twinkle in the hint of her smile. Edward drew his hand away quickly.

'All the girls like an officer,' Millie chirruped, bouncing back into the ward.

'Millie, *please,*' Edward admonished her.

'Oh, come on – it's normal to touch people, you know.'

'Yes, but...'

'Right, all done?'

Edward had intended to mention the list of names on the paper, but forgot. 'Yes.'

Millie turned to the nurse and pointed at the clock. '*Zwei,*' she said. The nurse, understanding perfectly, clapped her hands and ordered the children to dress. 'See,' she said to Edward, '*that's* communication.'

'No, that's pointing.'

Unhooking her cape from the wall, Millie swung it over her shoulders and puffed out her cheeks. 'Come on then, Mr Grumpy, let's go.'

'I'm not grumpy.'

'Yes you are,' she laughed. 'You were grumpy the moment you walked in, doing that silly frowny thing you do with your eyebrows.'

'What? What frowny thing? I wasn't grumpy. *You* said...' He stopped and rolled his eyes to the ceiling: it really wasn't worth it. And, anyway, as soon as they left the ward and turned down the stairwell, Millie skipped breezily on.

'It's a good job you came today, you know, actually. It brought a bit of cheeriness to the poor little things. They always look so miserable. It's hardly surprising what they've gone through but... but... what was I going to say?'

'I've no idea.'

'Oh yes – Nurse thingamabobsy. She's not one to crack a smile, is she? No wonder the kids look so glum with her about.'

Well she had fluttered her eyes at *him*, Edward thought. But then, he was not sure that she had actually *smiled*. So he said, 'I didn't dare look at her long enough to see if she smiled.'

'Exactly! That's what I mean! Anyway, where is it you think you're going to buy me steak and chips for lunch, mister?'

'Not sure about the steak. I'm not sure about the chips either. You might have to put up with a glass of wine and some biscuits.'

'Even better! You can have the biscuits. I'll have the wine.'

'I'll have some too, if you don't mind. I'm celebrating.'

'Oh yeah, whatcha celebrating?'

'I'll tell you when we get there.'

Exiting the hospital they paused at the top of the steps. Edward hurriedly buttoned his overcoat and turned the collar up. Millie pulled her cape tight round her breast.

'Which is where, actually?' asked Edward. 'I don't know this area. I got lost trying to get here.'

'Really? Do you want me to teach you map-reading? Oops, no, I forgot, you don't do maps. You prefer to have a wander and get lost instead, don't you?' Edward's lips remained only partially clamped. 'Come on,' she said, 'there's a café round the corner. This way.'

As they descended the steps the pair's ongoing sartorial adjustments meant that Edward, although dimly aware of hurried footsteps passing him in the opposite direction, and then that those same footsteps came to a sudden stop behind him, paid them no more attention than that. And because this happened at the same time as Millie asked what he'd been up to for the past week, he did not hear his name being called out. Not the first time. The second time, however, he did. He turned round and looked up. For a moment he stood in dumb silence staring at the figure above him. Then the silence was broken.

'So, you have come back.'

Chapter 8

'Oh, God no, he's not anything like that.'

'No, nothing like that,' Edward chorused, unable to entirely mask his pique at the vehemence with which Millie denounced any romantic attachment to him. Surely she might at least have said it a *little* less forcibly – if only as a concession to the fact that she (or any woman) would be lucky to have the chance.

'Good,' said Kashia.

There, *again*, Edward thought, as Kashia gave way to Millie in front of the stove to add some ingredient to the simmering broth with a word of culinary explanation, was the same stripped, emotionless – almost brutal – tone with which she had assailed him on the hospital steps. That was not how Kashia had spoken to him when she had once said that Oriana was wrong, that they were glad he had come to Vienna, that they would not forget him. And that was not how she had looked at him when, with a cloth quivering between her fingertips, she had dabbed his cheeks with arnica, nursing him as she might have done a thousand other young innocent bodies on the fields of Königgrätz or Austerlitz. Yet it was the same person. She was thinner, yes, her face not so rounded, her Slavic cheekbones more pronounced, her skin unblemished and whiter, her black hair no longer curled round her ears but cut short at the fringe and bobbed at the back. There was, in short, nothing to suggest she had ever once flushed with a frail, girlish femininity. Everything about her aspect was harder, more practical, more pure.

Without proceeding to such pleasantries as to how he was, or what he was doing in Vienna, Kashia had said on the steps with blunt force, 'Now you can see what they've done.'

'It's frightful, isn't it?' Millie had instinctively said.

It was this interjection, Edward was certain, that had brought forth more from Kashia than would have otherwise come. Without it he was convinced Kashia would not have uttered a single word more –

merely turned her back and departed. As it was her gaze had been enlivened, and it had fallen with intrigue on Millie.

'You know each other?' Millie had asked Kashia first.

'Yes, we meet here in Vienna before the war, before everyone puts on uniforms and begins marching and shooting.' Millions might have done likewise, but Edward had not needed Kashia to address him directly to feel that he alone was being charged with complicity in the crime of soldiery. Then, as if Millie had been the animator of her past, she had said to Edward, 'There is something I must tell you. You must come to the apartment. Do you remember where it is?'

Yes, he remembered.

And his friend had to come too, Kashia had said with compulsion.

It had been a relief for Edward that, following a fixing of a time and a day for the encounter, he had been able to while away an hour afterwards with Millie, narrating events pertaining to his previous *séjour* in Vienna: of how he had been invited to stay at Herr Braunthal's (a friend of his father's and Mr Bellman) to begin his second education, of how he had been accosted by Friedrich in a shop because he had looked at a toy tram, of how Friedrich and Kashia had taken him to a workers' demonstration where they had been charged at by the Imperial guards, of how he had been knocked unconscious in the melee and nursed by Kashia after, and of how Herr Braunthal had been so enraged when he had found out where Edward had been – and that Edward had lied to him when he'd asked – that he had hastened his return back to England. Edward confessed his shame at his follies of youth – but had mentioned nothing of Oriana. He could not bear the thought that those words might be scattered on the café table, unsequenced and haphazard, and then fade and mean nothing.

It was a relief too when, three days later, he entered the courtyard of Kashia's tenement block with Millie beside him, her presence distracting him from the pulsing muscles round his heart. That is to say – when he entered the courtyard of *Kashia and Oriana's* tenement block. Remember the apartment? Of course he remembered it! He remembered every fractional detail. He had climbed its stairwells with Oriana, been led through its rooms, and left without once looking back a thousand times in his dreams.

If it was not relief that Edward then felt when Kashia opened the front door, told them her friend would be eating with them, and presented a dishevelled young man in an oversized Russian uniform and coat to be such a friend; it was instead something closer to nervous exhaustion. But that was not the end, he knew, for as yet Kashia had told him nothing.

Kashia's friend was not Russian; he was Hungarian: his name was János. His clothes were the only ones Kashia had been able to get for him at the welfare centre. There had been some old Austrian uniforms – but he could never wear those. Besides, it would be far too dangerous for him to be seen in the streets dressed in them.

Indeed, it seemed to Edward almost too dangerous for János to be seen in the apartment, let alone on the streets, because no sooner presented did he scuttle away. The floorboards creaking to the sound of his restless, scratching movements, he thereafter proceeded to reappear and disappear in the gloomy, steaming kitchen, sniffing around with a suspicious, brooding eye, like a traumatised dog.

The only daylight in the kitchen came from a small window above the stove which gave onto a narrow shaft. A paraffin lamp was set in the middle of the large, round table, and amid the clouds of steam and dripping condensation, a crepuscular shadow was thrown over the damp, peeling, yellow-black walls.

Kashia explained that János understood a few words of English, and spoke only as many as he understood. He would not say anything anyway though, she said, not to a man in uniform, not as it was *they* who had destroyed his life.

Edward did not respond. He did not need to. Kashia had already picked the lock of his thoughts.

'He has no choice to wear *that* uniform,' she said. 'It is that or he freezes. But it is not *his* uniform. He did not kill anyone on the orders of a king or an emperor because he was wearing that. Not like—'

'Yum, yum,' Millie interrupted, sipping the wooden spoon she had ladled into the broth.

'It's turnips and potatoes, Millie,' Edward pointed out, unconvinced.

'Ah, but there's the special ingredient. You'll see.'

'Yes, you'll see,' Kashia repeated with force.

Edward had seen the 'special ingredient' unwrapped earlier only from a distance; he had not enquired what it was. It was hardly his position to censure the black market when people had no choice if they were not to starve. Colonel Carrington's advice, he knew, was founded on idealism, not reality.

Kashia moved to the other side of the kitchen table and opened the cupboard door. She took out four bowls and set them down on the table. She then spoke to Millie. Their conversation being conducted at a volume not much louder than a whisper, Edward struggled to pick up a good deal of what they said: his hearing still suffered from the effects of the shell blast the previous year, so that some frequencies were muffled as if a wodge of wool were stuck in his ears. From what he did glean it revolved around the work they had done in the war.

János shortly returned again. His head was bowed, and his features were concealed beneath a mass of greasy black hair. He took an anxious pace forward, stepped back, put his hand to the doorframe, moved it next to a chair, rocked the chair on its legs, let go of it, shoved his hand in his trouser pocket, fumbled around, removed it, scratched the back of his neck, then the top of his head – before turning to leave. He was stopped by Kashia. She spoke in Hungarian; Edward only understood what was said by the outcome: János pulled out a chair and sat opposite him. As a gesture of friendship Edward passed him one of the bowls. The bowl was snatched and drawn possessively close. A single dark eye glared at Edward with a sort of tortured despair before, his head dropping, it was concealed again behind its greasy black veil.

Having been inclined to find out whether János spoke German, Edward was thus dissuaded from doing so. Instead, as if he were some dinner-party outcast, he diverted himself by laying his hand on the chair beside him, turning it palm up and gently opening and closing his fingers, opening and closing, like the petals of a flower, or as if a key were slipped into a lock and then held – held and released, held and released. He stopped. At the sudden memory of Oriana's key sitting next to him, his breath became shallow. The muscles round his breast pulsed fiercely again; his shoulder blade tightened; the tendons felt as if pricked by a million pins. He stretched out his arm, shook it and breathed deeply. That having no impact, he pressed his thumb hard into his armpit at the side of his breast to cut the blood from its source.

'You said you – Kashia –' he cut over Millie, shifting uncomfortably '– wanted to talk to me.'

'I do. But that can wait. It's not so important to you, I think.'

Kashia's offhand reply only increased his discomfort. Sitting down, waiting, excluded and impotent, he pressed his thumb even harder into his armpit. But nothing would still his fluttering heart. He gritted his teeth as his body tensed with impatience. *For heaven's sake – out with it!* She had said she had something to tell, so *tell*! After all, there could only be one thing to say.

But no, that wasn't true, he knew: there could be any number. He had turned over that in his mind a hundred times and more in the three days just gone. For perhaps she had just muddled her verbs: tell, say, ask – who knew the difference between them? Perhaps she had meant to tell him that she wanted to ask for his help; perhaps that's what she wanted to say. There were countless things a British officer could be needed for: food, medicine, travel permits, help with some papers, the finding of a lost someone, the release of an imprisoned someone, the disappearance of a found someone! This would explain Kashia's coldness of tone. It was not just for him, but simply indicative of one who, clinging fiercely to her pride, had become clinical in her means, one who operated of necessity, one who had moved on from the cosy bedside manner to the ruthlessness of surgery. In a city full of rumours, unrest and decay, it was her scalpel to slice to its heart – in order to survive.

Still, logical as all that might be, he couldn't just sit there and wait. He couldn't *do nothing*. Not when it was she who had wanted to tell *him* something.

'So what are you... what are you doing now, Kashia?' he asked.

'*Now?*'

'Yes. Not this afternoon, obviously, but... living?'

'Now we are not living. We are surviving.'

'There, bit of a silly question, Edward,' said Millie.

Edward's jaw stiffened. It was a perfectly straightforward question, *Millie*.

'But how? I mean, how are you earning money?'

Kashia swung round to face him, her expression contemptuous.

'That is the first thing you think about – to earn money. It's very English, you know, to think like that. I said we are surviving. To survive you do not earn money, you get it – however you can. And when you get, you have, and then you have not. It's very simple. Sometimes it does not seem like it is worth the labour – but in the end you live. There, it's like that. Is that enough?' Edward made a faint gesture of comprehension; Kashia's lip curled in response. 'Maybe,' she said scornfully, 'maybe you think you know… but you don't. You don't know anything about this life. When this is your life you are not thinking about the future; you are only thinking about today – or tomorrow: that is the future. It is never "with what" – it is only *how*. If we think of the money that is worth nothing – and that is worth more nothing every day – then we are having all the same wars, again and again. And again and again. And we –' she glanced in solidarity at Millie '– will be locked in the house once again. Yes, washing the bed sheets, emptying the chamber pots, giving babies, and smiling, always smiling as we tuck in the blankets and make the tea and the coffee.

'Do you know, Edward, the government here in Vienna does not want us to work any more?' Kashia continued with fervour. 'They forced us to work in the factories – to earn *their* money – so we can win *their* war. And now they lose it – yes, *they* lose it – they tell us to go home. "Go home," they say. "Go lie on your backs. Go queue for the food. Go make the food. Go carry the wood. Go scrub floors. Go and do all this… and say nothing!"'

'See, I told you,' Millie said to Edward. 'That's what it'll be like for me if I go back to England. I'm sure.'

'Of course. It is the same everywhere. But it's too late. Everything's changed. They can beat us as much as they like but it won't make any difference. Not now.'

'Does that happen a lot – the beating?' asked Millie, her sudden alarm prompting her to stop stirring the pot.

Kashia paused to adjust to Millie's misconstrual of her intent.

'Beatings? Oh yes. It's not so much seen now, but there is one young girl who I know is beaten by her father because he said the lentils she cooked him were too hard. Can you imagine – to beat your daughter because of lentils? She says her father behaves like that only because he was left for dead in the mountains and was found by a dog. She says that's where he gets his rage from: she says that's why he tries to kill himself. You see, there are always excuses. The same excuses, again and again. But the time for excuses is dead. Don't you think, Millie?'

Although her alarm had been heartfelt, Millie did not care to think more on such things at such times. 'Yes, it must be. Anyway, it's ready!'

Kashia, however, was not ready to hold her tongue at the sound of the gong and submit to the domesticity of the table. She took a series of fevered steps around the table. She stopped, gripped the back of a chair and fixed her eyes on Edward.

'Do you remember the demonstration?' she said.

'Of course. How could I forget?' Edward replied smartly. He looked at Millie and, in an attempt to restore some measure of past order, explained with compassion, 'That was when Kashia was my nurse.'

For a moment the adjunct had the desired effect: Kashia leaned back and rocked the chair on its legs. Her eyes darkening, they seemed to expand like drops of blotted ink atop the ridge of her bony white cheeks.

'I was,' she said, her voice involuntarily softening to the memory of when she had placed her fingers lightly on his skin – which seemed, as she looked at him now in the same dirty light, to be only more beaten by the weather than blemished by age or suffered further, deeper cuts – and dipped her eyes when she felt he was looking at her, and she wished that he hadn't. 'Little Kashia – always the nurse.' She turned to Millie and, retrieving her former hardness of her tone, added bitterly, 'We all thought a lot of sentimental rubbish back then. That's what happens when you're under a spell. Maybe we needed the war to break it. Maybe it's good the war happened.'

Millie's attention was concentrated on the food. She twirled round, picked up the nearest bowl from the table, ladled some broth into it and set it back down. She reached out to János for his bowl; it was released with a diffident glance.

'There you are, János,' she said, passing over the filled bowl. Edward reached out a helping hand for the relay.

'He won't take it from you,' Kashia snapped.

There was a short silence as Kashia and Edward boldly stared at each other. Edward then withdrew his hand, and János took the bowl from Millie. The first bowl was placed equidistant between Edward and Kashia; Edward pushed it to Kashia.

'It should be yours,' he said.

'Yes, you're right. It should,' she replied.

Millie filled the remaining two bowls and put them on the table. Serving complete, the two women pulled out their chairs and sat down together.

'Thank you, Millie,' said Kashia with marked courtesy.

'It's my pleasure.'

Edward and János mumbled their gratitude, and all took to their tin spoons.

'It's your uniform,' Kashia clarified, at length.

'I understood. You said earlier,' Edward said tersely as he made an exploratory probe of the fatty mystery floating next to the potato. 'You said they destroyed his life. I see that.'

'Yes.'

'Well, surely he understands I'm not an Imperial guard? Surely he understands that a uniform doesn't make every man?'

'It's what I started to say – about the demonstration. You remember?'

'Of course.'

'Good. You remember when the horses were charging and everybody was running away? János was there too. He was knocked over, like you. Then a soldier comes and – even though János is lying in the street and threatening no one – turns his great beast of a horse so that its hoof stamps on his face. He does it on purpose. He does it because a young man comes to listen to a speech; a young man who comes to the city to be an apprentice to a watchmaker. Not a revolutionary or anarchist – a watchmaker's apprentice! And so a young man loses an eye and his living because he cannot stand still, because he has pains in his head all the time. This happens only because the men in the uniform cannot stand that *we* – the workers – come to listen to a man who was not in uniform.'

'That's terrible,' said Millie. Her eyes fell tenderly on János as he shovelled the broth into the right side of his mouth. A patch covered the sunken socket of his missing left eye; below it his cheek was flat where the bone had been crushed by the hoof. The movement on the whole left side of his mouth was restricted by the nerves removed in its reconstruction.

'Yes, it is,' said Kashia. She continued to Edward, 'After you left Vienna we found out at the newspaper that there were lots of people injured at the demonstration – real injuries, not just some little cuts and bruises like you were having – and I went to the hospital to see them. I found János lying there: a boy with his face smashed in, unable to speak, who had no one to…' She brought her spoon down violently in presumption of the knowing glint in Edward's eye. 'Always the nurse, no? Yes, that was what I was. While everyone else is running making pictures and stupid dreams of – Yes, *I* am the nurse! Of course, when I told Friedrich about him and said he was Hungarian, he didn't care. *He* was not Austrian. *He* was not Viennese. "Let the watchmakers from Budapest take care of him" – that is what Friedrich said.'

'Equal…' the young man suddenly burst out in a fierce, food-spluttered drawl. His tongue pushed the masticated remnants to the back of his throat and, with a half-choked gurgle, he swallowed it whole. His eye fixed on Edward, then flicked back to Kashia. '…and different.' He slurped the frothing saliva in his mouth and repeated the hateful, tormenting words: '*Equal*… and… different. Ha!' Anger surging through him, he spluttered an invective stream of unintelligible Magyar. Kashia put her hand out to calm him.

'For the Austrians, people like him have always been different first and equal second,' she said. 'Second and last. It is the same for all of us – always second and last. I am from Czech. Maybe I live my whole life here – but for some people I will always be Czech. I will always be equal second. That is not equality. You see, everything has changed, and nothing has changed too. The Habsburgs have not gone. They are only hiding, waiting for the opportunity – the moment of weakness – so they can return to Vienna with their banners and horses and stamp on the faces of the workers again. And nothing will stop them, not unless we do it ourselves, not unless we are strong and follow the revolution they are having in Germany so we become one unified people against them. Then we will join together with the workers in Hungary, and then with Czech, and then with the other countries of the old empire. *Then* there will be equality…'

At the clarion word János – his suppurating fury unabated – shook off Kashia's shackling hands.

'Equality… Equality!' he cried. His arm wrestling free, he violently pounded the table. He was quickly restrained by Kashia and relapsed into his morose, vengeful silence. Kashia's gaze rested for a moment on the point where he had beaten the table. She then looked at Edward, a flickering smile of remembrance on her cracked, colourless lips.

'Now I can see it in your eyes too,' she said.

'What?' said Millie, after Edward said nothing.

Kashia challenged Edward with her defiant, imperishable eyes. For never again would his steady blue glaze shine through her. Never again would she be the one deceived first.

'He is not listening to me, Millie. He does not care what I am saying to him. He is thinking only about one thing. He wants to know what I have to tell him.'

'Know what?'

'Where he is,' said Kashia.

'*Who?*'

'Friedrich.'

Millie had been thoroughly confused in the café by Edward's garrulous narrative of his past in Vienna. It had been a jumble of names and a jumble of happenings. But she had made some appropriate sounds and ordered him wine when his glass had been empty. 'Who's Friedrich?' she therefore asked.

'Friedrich…' said Kashia, her smile dissolving as her pupils turned into pinheads, 'Friedrich was... Edward's friend – when he was here. And mine – when he was here. So now he wants to know where he is. He wants to know why Friedrich is not here. He wants to know what's become of Friedrich. *Don't you?*'

At her every repetition of the name Edward's body became more twisted and tense. He knew who he was – so why did she have to keep saying his name? What was the point in repeating the same thing, again and again, when they both knew who she was talking about? He swallowed his food and reached out for his glass, a glass that was not on the table.

'Well,' he said, affecting phlegmatic disinterest, 'it was the same in England. No one escaped, did they?'

'*Escaped?* Escaped what?'

'Conscription.'

Kashia let out an ecstatic, wild laugh. 'Conscription! You think Friedrich was *conscripted*?' She laughed again. 'You see, Millie, that's what happens when you meet someone only for a few days. You know nothing about them. But even if you do know them – even if you know them ninety-five per cent, or maybe even ninety-nine per cent, then the five or the one per cent you do not know is enough that you know nothing at all. No, Edward, Friedrich did not need to be conscripted – he ran to the war. Just like everyone else who so hated the Habsburgs – he ran to save them, with joy, with his arms open wide, because he was too afraid to live without them. He was too afraid that without them he would be nothing. Yes, believe me, a man can say one thing and do another so easily. He can look you in the eye and love, and yet he is betraying you at the same time, with even the same thought. What good are eyes when that is what they do? What good are people like that who have no honesty? Who have no belief? There are a million Friedrichs in the world, and every one is the same. They are the white heads of dandelions waiting to be blown by the wind.' She cast a sororal look at Millie, who continued to eat. 'How can people like that think they can be loved? How can they think that they are *worth* the love of another? And then, one day, they are blown apart by a shell, and everything's finished. There is no more. It is all dead.

'That's what happened to Friedrich, Edward. Just like those thousands of others who ran with such joy, he was killed at Lemberg for his empire. The rotting bits of his body were picked on by birds – fed for the Crown and the Altar.' She paused and, glancing down, turned her spoon in the bowl, as if stirring clear waters to wipe away an old vision. 'But maybe – maybe you can ask his father for a photograph... so you are not forgetting him. Then you are not forgetting us.'

Edward's darkened brow twitched at the disjunctive paternal intrusion. 'I don't need a... Why... What's it anything to do with his father?' he said.

'Like father, like son.'

'What does *that* mean?'

'It means you must know the character of the son when you live with the father.'

Edward half choked as a lump of fat slipped down the wrong pipe; he half choked too at understanding her meaning. He was given a couple of firm, flat-handed strokes on the back by Millie.

'Are you alright?' Millie said with rough humour. He spluttered his airways clear, upon which she enquired, 'Too many greens?'

Kashia shared Millie's humour. The sentiment did not accord with Edward. The flutters of his heart were overtaken by a tidal swell of anger.

'So that's what you had to tell me, is it?' he snapped. 'That a son follows his father? Is that it?'

'No,' said Kashia, at length, with icy concision. She turned her spoon in the broth again and slowly, deliberately, nourished herself. When she had finished, and when Edward's rage had clearly cooled in his face, she recommenced in dispassionate tones. 'That's got nothing to do with me now. I say it because maybe it's interesting that you know – if you are thinking to visit the old man again. Are you?'

If the thought of paying his regards to Herr Braunthal had even fleetingly entered Edward's thoughts – and fleetingly could be the only word for its transit – he certainly would not now. Not now that he knew *that*.

'Maybe,' he said stiffly.

Kashia hereupon shifted her tone and attention to Millie. 'You know, you must come to the soup kitchens with me. That is where the children in the worst condition come. You are finding only the children of the middle classes in the hospital...'

'I'm not sure about that,' Edward said sharply, his disagreement as much to do with truth as with his still-bubbling emotions, for if he had known this to be the purpose of the invitation, he would never have allowed Millie to come along with him.

'You've been to the soup kitchens, have you?' Kashia asked sardonically. 'You know all the city and the suburbs like Lichtental now, do you? After a week?'

'No, but I hardly think hospitals are discriminating against children because of their *class* – are they, Millie?' And then, with a swift, spiteful jab, he added, 'Friedrich was certainly right about that stupid word.'

Kashia did not flinch at the blow.

'That's what a man in uniform always says, Millie. They are always telling us: nothing is wrong and everything is working for the best for the people. But I know what it's like. I know the truth. I'm there every day.'

'Well, I'm sure there are kids who aren't going to the hospital, but that's got nothing to do with... anything else,' said Edward. Caught piggy between Kashia and Edward, Millie's eyes ballooned innocently. 'Anyway, Millie, I'm sure you've got more than enough work on at the hospital without going gallivanting round all the soup kitchens in Vienna.'

Millie's freckles suddenly darkened and a deep colour rose to her cheeks. 'Kashia's not asking me to go *gallivanting round* all the soup kitchens,' she retorted. 'She's asked me to go with her and see the children who don't come to the hospital – for whatever reason. And I'd like to, thank you, Kashia.'

'Good. You see, Edward, she doesn't need to be told what to do like the little soldier-boys in their uniforms. I will show her the real Vienna. I will show her the conditions of the real workers and how things must change for the future. We don't need you.' With a face of cold, regal triumph, Kashia returned to her bowl and slowly cleared away the remaining contents. When she had finished, she laid the spoon to rest. 'Now,' she said, confronting Edward once more, 'you want to know what it is I have to tell you, why I am asking you here. I do not ask you to come because of Friedrich, that is for sure. No, not for a dead man and his stupid father. I asked you to come so that I can tell you what happened after you left Vienna. Maybe you don't care now. It is even possible that you know already – but I'm sure that is not true. *They* would not tell you.' She paused, her eyes glinting in the reflection of the raised scalpel in her hands. 'So I will tell you. I will tell you what happened to your brother.'

Part II

*She should never have looked at me
If she meant I should not love her!*

Robert Browning, 'Cristina'

Chapter 9

Now, of course, one person having heard from another that a man they did not know had, they thought they saw – but could not be sure – been knocked down by a tram on the Vienna Ringstrasse might arguably be said to be of little more value than gossip or hearsay. But even allowing that all narratives require a splash of conjecture to brighten the drabness of life, there could be no disputing the facts. And these were plain enough. In a pitch of fury Richard Wilson had hastened across the Ringstrasse straight into the path of the aforementioned tram. The result was that he was to spend nearly seven months recovering in various Austrian sanatoria.

Facts established, cause can be explained – if, that is, an accident is insufficient explanation of a cause, and that a man's inattention in crossing a road must perforce be accountable to something greater than the seat of his temper.

The accidental epitasis had taken place in late July of 1914. Richard had just delivered his resignation as the assistant Vienna correspondent to the bureau of the *London Times* and was in the utmost haste to depart the country. But although the cogs of mobilisation had already begun to grind their teeth with admonitory vengeance (for an impudent child *had to be* slapped), this was not the cause of his haste. Oh no – it was motivated by more than mere continental discord. Mr Bellman had secured him a position on one of the popular American newspapers, where, at last unshackled, he would be free to conduct the great educational campaign that would arouse the righteousness of the American people to interpose in the coming conflict, to sweep aside the crumbling, corrupted stones of old imperial Europe. It was the very campaign that had been thwarted at his every turn in Vienna. So he had said farewell to Herr Braunthal; said farewell to the coffee houses, the waiters, the bishops and the rooks, and proceeded to the offices of the Canadian and Pacific Railway to collect his promised ticket of liberation from Mr

Mackenzie. For the following morning he would catch the train to Trieste, take passage to Canada, then head down to Boston!

Arriving at the Canadian and Pacific Railway offices, however, he was informed that neither Mr Mackenzie nor the ticket's whereabouts were known. The information imparted by some objectionable office girl, panic and rage had been swift to grip him; it was in this frenzied state that he had spun round and hastened back across (half of) the Ringstrasse.

He did not regain consciousness until five weeks after the collision, and it was some further time still before even the meagre facts outlined above returned to him. More than that it was simply a blur of causeless haste and fury. Whence he was coming, he did not know. Whither he was going, he was at a loss. For what reason, he couldn't divine. All he knew was that he had lost the use of his legs.

Not lost his legs, or their actual mechanical function, simply their use: a neurological trauma had led to the muscles being temporarily unable to receive their commands. He was, the doctor explained, effectively bedridden by volition. This being the case it was quite impossible to determine how long the condition might last. He might at any moment spring to his feet – to catch a vase as it fell from the mantelpiece, or a woman as she fell to the floor. It all depended on the unfathomable impulses of the brain. For some, priceless porcelain was the thing to be saved; for others, a woman. Still, as Richard's legs had only narrowly escaped being crushed beneath the tram's wheels, the doctor asserted he was fortunate to have them at all. Indeed, given the circumstances, he was fortunate to still have his life!

These blessings of good fortune were repeated with effusion by Ulrich Köstler. Not that Richard had any recollection of *him*, but being assured during his visits that he was a good friend, he was in no position to deny what Köstler's presence proclaimed. Indeed, on such occasions, Köstler later confided, friendship was most invaluable – memory being such a trifling concern when weighed against the graver afflictions of disfigurement or death.

As the truest test of his friendship Köstler had thereafter refrained from placing too great a strain on Richard's delicate condition by burdening him with the fuller details of his life. One such detail most certainly and most sadly included his nationality. For in a peculiar perversion of the customary English monoglottism the single tongue Richard spoke when he regained consciousness was German. Indeed, having no cause to speak any other language, for some time Richard had no idea that he *could*. How much this was attributable to the impact, how much to some repressed childhood trauma, and how much to having been read to daily in German by the young lady who attended his bedside during his state of unconsciousness, neither Köstler nor the doctor were prepared to attest. Richard had again been blessed by good fortune, Köstler told him, to be the recipient of such devotion from such a pretty young lady. It was a kindness (and, dare he add, *prettiness*) which had surely abetted his recovery – although the hint of a smile he concealed in saying so indicated the proximity of a certain truth to the tip of his lips.

The war and its progress could not be concealed from Richard forever though, and once its illuminating switch had at last been flicked on in Richard's head, it had soon sparked a thousand other lights of life: the connections that had hitherto fused were rewired and feeling had slowly returned to his legs.

The process had been nonetheless lengthy, and had taken place in a hospital on the outskirts of Vienna, whither he had been transferred upon his regaining consciousness. It was a relocation with two important consequences: firstly, it had put an end to the visits from Richard's mysterious reader – about whom he knew nothing other than what Köstler had told him; secondly, it had greatly complicated Herr Braunthal's search for him.

It had been many weeks after the telegrams, ultimata, and declarations of war had been despatched to the embassies of Europe before Herr Braunthal had received Mr Bellman's letter alerting him to Richard's disappearance. Herr Braunthal had been away at the time of the letter's arrival, but had replied promptly on his return that he would do all he could to find out what had happened. This had proved no easy task though. To unravel the fate of an Englishman amid the tumult of war – one who may or may not have still been in the realms of the Crown and the Altar, and who would have been an enemy if he were – had required all Herr Braunthal's perseverance and contacts.

Even with these it had still not been until the autumn that the puzzle had been solved. And then, as soon as it had been, the city hospitals were flooded with 100,000 more casualties arriving from the east and Richard was promptly moved further west, to Linz. Upon this new departure Ulrich Köstler had promised to help his good friend and facilitate his correspondence. However, naturally, Köstler had then said, the war meant that such correspondence would be subject to the almighty goddess of fortune. He hoped, he had joked, that Richard had not exhausted her benevolence – though even she was helpless in the face of the censor's ever-prying knife. It was a knife, Richard was to discover, that was to prove sharper than fortune. For despite several letters to Mr Bellman and Herr Braunthal he received not a single reply.

In late January 1915 Richard had been finally discharged. And as soon as he had been, he was interned at the nearby camp at Katzenau, where he had seen out the rest of the war. Or, better said, where he had endured it, imprisoned as he had been in the company of a motley assortment of English-language didacts barely able to pass muster in the language they purported to teach, and a ragtag of Italian irredentists scarcely able to comprehend a word of whatever dialect their compatriots spoke. His eventual liberation had come shortly after the armistice. Forced to resume his thwarted westward passage west via the Adriatic, he had first passed through Vienna to call on Herr Braunthal.

Despite the absence of communication Herr Braunthal was well, and he had welcomed Richard with a hearty, meat-rich meal, a fine Piedmont wine, and given him some clothes that he no longer had any purpose to keep. It was only after dinner that Herr Braunthal's humour had darkened; he passed Richard a letter from Mr Bellman that he had received at the end of the previous year.

Mr Bellman wrote that Herr Braunthal's letter telling of Richard's safety had only just reached him. But – oh, too late! Too late had come the blissful news! Oh – that the cup of joy should be poisoned by such woe! The long years of torment as to the unknown fate of his beloved elder son, combined with Edward's forsaking of his faith to join the king's colours, had been too great for his father's heart to bear: he had died but weeks before! The only salve to Mr Bellman's pain, he wrote, was to know that Richard would shortly return to carry on the great mission of his father's life, that which he was always destined to do.

The news in and of itself had been devastating to Richard, but it had been compounded by a feeling of guilt that he himself had been the cause of his father's fatal torment. It was an emotion that had only abated once he had reconciled himself to the unequivocal truth: that all the while he had been desperate to return home, his brother had decided to roam. Edward, it was clear, had abandoned their father. It was he who had strayed, who was the vagabond of the earth – just as he had always been. Why, Mr Bellman had said he had not even returned for the funeral! He had chosen to roll himself in the flag and frolic in the mud. That was what his brother had done.

After this revelation Richard and Herr Braunthal had sat on the verandah as the mist thickened in the twilight. Herr Braunthal apologised for not having forwarded the letter or written himself. He had been too wary of the censor's knife and had sought to protect Richard. His intention had always been to visit instead, but time – the thief – had outrun him. It had been the saddest thing for him, he said, to hear that Richard's father had died and to learn of the causes. It was terrible to be treated with such contempt by one's very own son.

Herr Braunthal scratched his white whiskers and sighed. There had been sadness everywhere, he said, and the war had exhausted him. Of course, he had not wanted to be involved in the war's prosecution – certainly not! He had not travelled the world building railways so one emperor could shake hands with another and pillage Europe together! But he had known that only an efficient railway could prevent the ravages of starvation. Hunger, after all, was the greatest fomenter of unrest. If the people had no food it always led to the sort of catastrophic social upheaval that would have destroyed all the advances in civilisation that had guided his life. Revolution, he said, was to be feared far more than defeat. One had to only look to the Russians to attest to that truth. For if only the tsar had constructed his railways sooner then the war would never have started: the Austrians would have known that a slap would be met with a fist!

So busy had he been, Herr Braunthal continued, wafting his hand dismissively at the new motor car on the drive, he had been forced into buying *that*. He stifled an ironic guffaw. It was exactly the same model as the one the archduke had been shot in! Of course he would have done without it – if he could; he would happily take back poor dobbin and the gig in a trice – if he could. He had then stood, spread his legs monarchically and, placing his hands on his abundant waist, surveyed his wintry domain and shaken his head with ruth. He should, he confessed, have left the country before the war. He should have travelled again. He should have gone at last to America. But such things were easier said than done when choice was the card on the table. It was only when choice was gone that regret was dealt in its place. He had stayed – and been compensated with trinkets. He would give them all up to go back five years – *if he could*. Oh, what man does not dream of impossible things when sadness fills his heart? he had said, as he rocked on the heels of his new leather boots.

Leaving Herr Braunthal and Vienna, Richard had proceeded south to Trieste. There he had joined the seething tide of refugees that had crawled back on their bellies, in rags, from the wastes of the east – desperately searching for a ship to somewhere; from nowhere. Three weeks he had then been stuck waiting. *Three weeks!* Three weeks, trapped at the bottom of the barrel of the world as the relentless *bora* blew its inexhaustible supply of cold, arid air across the quayside, scything down the men like sheaves of harvest wheat. Three weeks, convinced that at any moment he would be struck down by one of the many febrile afflictions which festered in such ports. No more – he had sworn to himself before the war – he would return to that city no more. And yet, there he was, *still*.

But it was as he had stood on the hills of San Giusto and watched the panorama of men swarming the quays like rats on the edge of the restless, turbid sea that Richard had had his great epiphany. His father had used to summon the Mission congregation to arms to battle the unvanquished beast that roared 'Protection'. Now, with his father's fallen sword gleaming in his eyes, the handle towards his hand, the form of the beast that had to be slain had been clearly revealed. Intimacy with the war had meant that, despite bearing the scars of the conflict, he himself was untouched; he was knowing, yet remained undefiled. And now that he understood, he had truly awoken.

He had awoken to see that it was not empires that had to be cast down; it was the people who had to be raised. For too long had they wandered the fields with the bridle round their necks. For too long had they drifted with the currents and been blown by the breeze. That was why the war had been met with such thralls of ecstasy: the reins had fallen slack; the waters had stilled; the winds had died. Everything had become listless, with neither breath nor motion. Little wonder the world had been trapped by such a deathly ship.

It was not the death of the archduke that had sounded this clarion though. It was not *his* heart that the bullets had blown holes in. Rather it was the heart of the printed word. The war had shown Richard that newspapers could do nothing to enlighten the masses – for it had proved the masses would rally to any cause if the banner print was big enough. No, it was no longer any use trying to turn the world with the word. It was no longer any use trying to teach with a fine hand, serifs and twirls. The kingdom of God, Richard's epiphany had told him, lay not with the pen. It lay in having one's hand on the hand that held the pen.

The age of the newspaper had gone: that of the typesetter had succeeded.

Chapter 10

By the time Richard stepped off the train at Victoria station in the new year of 1919 he was exhausted – perhaps even more so than Herr Braunthal.

As a series of whistle shrieks rang out over the cacophonous roar of engines, he was immediately engulfed by a billowing cloud of steam and smoke. He screwed his eyes shut and coughed; the salt of the sea was still in his lungs. Then, as if the whistles had been the locomotive signal of the morning reveille, his legs were suddenly swept from under him and he was borne along the platform by a frothing tide of khaki. At the end the wave crashed upon the concourse and the muddy waters sped across the concrete like a shadow over sand, before running away down the slopes and runnels, and out through the porous stone.

Tossed up like a piece of flotsam on a beach, Richard stood alone. He looked around expectantly. Ahead of him a warty sergeant with gadfly eyes brushed off the puckering lips by his wizened cheeks with a terse 'Stop fussin', girl. Stop fussin'.' To his right, a younger woman was a model of restraint, a glistening look being buffed away by a cheery 'Feedin' the dog aright, ah 'ope.' To his left, a pair of crinolined ladies harangued a guard about the delay to the 13:15 to Eastbourne, pointing out that it was 'All well and good to say *that*, young man, but what time *will* it leave?' There was all this, but there was no Mr Bellman.

Richard had managed to cable Mr Bellman from the docks at Southampton and receive the reply that he would meet him at the station. That Mr Bellman might be a few minutes late was therefore of little concern: his was not the fretfulness of the impatient lover. And so he bided patiently, or as patiently as could be expected of any man of an epiphanous disposition who had not slept for three days. But when the hands of the station clock eventually showed that he had been waiting for three quarters of the circular whole, he muttered, sighed, huffed, and determined it was impossible for him to wait any longer, even though he had no choice but to do so. It was at the very instant of this resolve to inaction that he was alerted by the call of his name. His interlocutor was not Mr Bellman, though: it was some grimy, plank-faced urchin.

Informed that there was a message for him at the Post Office desk, Richard followed the boy to the bureau, where he discovered there to be two items awaiting him: a telegram and a letter. Both were from Mr Bellman. He read the telegram first. Mr Bellman apologised: he had been called away on urgent business and would only return the day after next; he directed him to the letter and told him to open it. Richard did so. The contents of the hastily written script were as follows:

The Under Secretary at the Ministry of X was in need of an assistant secretary before the Peace Conference began. Mr Bellman had recommended Richard for the position – and had arranged luncheon for the following day at the Under Secretary's club in St James's. The Under Secretary was an old friend of Mr Bellman's, and so the interview – as the luncheon might be described – would be a formality, fully apprised as the Under Secretary was of Richard's history, character and capabilities. With a threat of strikes taking place at any moment, a room had been booked in a hotel off Piccadilly to save Richard from returning to the old family house in Hammersmith – a journey, Mr Bellman noted, that would be 'more perilous than crossing continents and oceans!' He had hired him a suit and had it delivered to the hotel: he hoped it would fit! He signed off with... but by then Richard had already folded the letter and put it back in the envelope. Immediately taking it out again to check the hotel's name and address, he then turned sharply on his heels and strode out of the station.

Outside he stopped dead. It had been nearly six years since Richard had last set foot on a London street, and the chaotic multiplicity of the metropolis took him aback. As far as the eye could see there was construction, destruction and rows upon rows of lights, billboards, and slogans affixed on buildings selling business, business, business, amid a dizzying whirr of steam buses, motor buses, taxis, trams, motor cars, bicycles, pony traps, carriages and carts – here and there swerving as lorries dumped coal, as navvies dug holes, or as steamrollers trundled backwards and forth, backwards and forth, while pedestrians scuttled between them, leaping and swinging like gibbons from pavement to platform. It was almost, it seemed to him, as if the Tyburn still flowed through the slums and the swamp had never been drained, as if the streets were not actually for living in, but for simply holding one's nose and traversing. The sight caused him to feel a momentary, wistful pang for the uncluttered Viennese boulevards and the gentle pace of the cafés, bishops and rooks. Whereat he turned his eyes away.

Determining that his own two legs (once neglected, now cherished) would transport him to Piccadilly far quicker than any public conveyance, he proceeded along Victoria Street a short distance before turning north towards Buckingham Palace. Once free of the rambunctious thoroughfare and on the quiet terraced streets a lucidity and enthusiasm that had for some time been absent returned to his thoughts.

His Triestine epiphany that he had to get his hand on the hand that held the pen had been undeniably momentous. It would, however, be a considerable exaggeration to say that at the time of its occurrence he had known how this was to be done. Moreover, the interminable wait in Trieste, followed by the equally interminable (not to say *rough*) voyage back to England had, rather than providing an opportunity to plot his ambition to its end, caused him to dwell on the pervasive disillusionment of his experiences of Charles Eliot, the *London Times*, Vienna and his internment. The result was that by the time he set foot on English soil he had sunk into a state best likened to the doldrums. Now, quit of the coast and reacquainted with the bounteous effects of the London air, Mr Bellman's letter blew a forceful, invigorating breeze back into his sails. His stride as he entered Green Park beneath the grey, blustery skies was consequently increasingly propelled by all the possibilities of working with an Under Secretary who would assuredly need him in Paris to help form the conditions of peace.

But fatigue and enthusiasm being currents of a natural ebb and flow, the sudden yapping of a territorial poodle as he crossed *his* path saw Richard's waters recede. A dark cloud of doubt shaped above him like a nimbus, a cloud more portentous to one approaching solitary middle age than to one still flushed with youth. He had returned to England in the full knowledge that the next steps he took would be the determinant ones of his life. As such, and as with all steps in the darkness, he could not help but be struck by a certain fear that when the light was switched on he would find this Under Secretary to be a man whose rudder and horsepower were not equal to his own ambition. Who was he indeed? Would this Under Secretary's hand really be the hand that he needed to hold? There were many hands, and many pens, but few that were ever worth clasping. It was a fear, it might be adduced, that was no more than a lingering consequence of the malign ocean, were it not for the fact there was something far more elementary – far more terrestrial – that had brought it to the fore.

Since departing England in early 1913 Richard had necessarily acquired an independence of thought as much as deed. To therefore return and find himself instantly gripped by Mr Bellman's hand – even if the apparent *fait accompli* of working with the Under Secretary could hardly be said to be unwelcome – was a cause of some minor recalcitrance. This feeling had arisen as the minutes ticked by on the station concourse (as if he were waiting for Mr Bellman like a schoolboy at the gates) and had festered as an undercurrent as he read the letter at the bureau.

On exiting Green Park onto Piccadilly, Richard rebuked himself. Such an emotion belonged to the churlishness of youth. After all, had Mr Bellman not been like a second father to him? Had he not always been a fount of wisdom and counsel? Had it not been he who had found him the post at the Ministry of X, who had booked his hotel, hired his suit – in short, everything? And had it not been he who had done all that, who would have instead?

His burst of self-reproach brought him to a stop: he had forgotten where he was going. His attention was suddenly drawn to a knife-grinder at the top of the Underground steps. Hunched over a spinning whetstone on his immobilised bike, the knife-grinder was an old man with craggy, dromedary features, and he sharpened the blade like a jeweller polishing a precious rare stone. Richard remembered occasionally seeing such men hawking on the quiet Hammersmith terraces when he was a boy. He remembered too that his father once had told him they would soon disappear. Free trade, he had said, would make steel so cheap that they would not have to scrape such a meagre existence. And yet, here the man still was on the streets. How many years, Richard wondered, had the man been turning his wheel, plying his trade, sharpening blades to cut the meat, to pare the bones, to trim the cloth, to carve the wood and shape the moulds of the shoes that walked right by him? The knife-grinder removed the blade from the spinning wheel; he inspected it with his deep, pinhead eyes. He was not content: a barely perceptible flaw was evident like a crack in the heart of a diamond. He set the blade back to the stone and resumed his timeless, rhythmic, perfecting motion, upon which Richard recollected his destination. He turned away and hastened on.

When Richard arrived at the hotel the concierge said he would have the suit sent up to his room directly. A surge of energy resolved Richard to try it on instantly and take a brisk, preparatory stroll around St James's. But neither energy nor resolve reached the top of the stairs: as soon as the bellboy left he collapsed on the bed. He was soon roused by the returning bellboy with the suit, whereat, receiving it like a wet towel, Richard tossed it over the chair and flopped back on the bed. Despite the stuffy, radiating warmth of the room he felt an ache in his limbs and he shivered. With his eyes tightly shut he tried to forget the discomfort and to sleep. After a short while he gave up the attempt. He stared lethargically, forlornly, at the enticing tub in the bathroom. Eventually he hauled himself from the bed, turned on the taps and undressed. As he awaited the slow filling of the bath he noticed a full-length mirror in the opposite corner of the room. Arched like a lancet window, and with a shiny gilt frame, its out-of-the-way position had been seemingly chosen to offer reflection only by intention. Suddenly the glass caught a glint: it beckoned Richard to fill the idle time with a gaze. He crossed the room and stood before it. The sight he beheld was deeply unpleasant. His cheeks, though drawn, were puffed under his eyes and suffused to a deep, Punchinello red, their fullness and colour a grotesque contrast to the thin, white, flaccid-skinned body which sagged beneath, marked here and there by a blotch of veiny blue and the odd clump of straggly, anaemic hair. He put his hands to his rising hairline and pressed back the widow's peak. A few strands of greasy blonde hair worked free from their flaky roots and hovered over his brown eyes and short, small nose. They were not the dark, linear features of his father: they were those of his mother. They were those of a man who was nearly thirty. And although it was indisputable that he had had his epiphany and would have luncheon the next day with the Under Secretary from the Ministry of X, that did not alter the stark truth that the mirror presented: that he had not yet sharpened a single thing of use in his life. He turned from the mirror in disgust and climbed into the bath.

The warm water had an instant effect on his senses. It transported him back to the previous languorous summer. He was sitting on the wooden steps of one of the camp huts playing chess with Signor Poyetti. Signor Poyetti's long ruminations antecedent to each move always gave the impression of deep strategic thinking, but were merely an excuse for him to continue his mapping of the mistakes of his past; however, they always allowed Richard to bask in the sun and to think of nothing, to drift away in a blissful, listless world. Hours might have passed in this state of suspension before Signor Poyetti had asked if his knight had been taken by the pawn. Whose knight? Richard had asked, and neither of them knew.

By the time the question was asked, Richard had fallen asleep in the water.

Chapter 11

'Ah, excellent, excellent –' the Under Secretary sprang from his armchair and shook Richard's hand warmly; his beaming countenance displayed an almost preternatural joy '– it's so wonderfully kind of you to come trekking across London in this weather to meet me. Really it is. I find I can endure any temperature so long as it isn't bullied by that wild spirit – the wind, don't you agree?'

Richard did; the enervations of the *bora* were embossed on his mind. A flush of fellow feeling rose from his breast and, commingling with the cigar smoke and heat from the fire, brought a stippled colour to his cheeks.

'Quite true,' he said, smiling, 'although I'm afraid I must disappoint you: I've only come from a hotel on Grafton Street. It's not much of a trek.'

'Oh really? No, no, indeed not – not for a Boer, at any rate. Quite a peregrination for an ant, I'd say though.' The two shared a moment of mirth, before the Under Secretary continued, 'I do apologise. I was quite certain Mr Bellman told me you would be coming from... from... um...' Being a man of inestimable refinement, the Under Secretary abhorred the misapplication of names; his hesitation as the word 'Hammersmith' yahooed round his head was thus excusable for the avoidance of a slur. '...um, Row, Roe...'

'Ravenscourt Park.'

'That's the one – Ravenscourt Park,' he confirmed with relief. 'Yes – I knew it had an "r" in there somewhere. Yes, that's right, it's very nearly the countryside, isn't it? So wonderfully lush and green. It makes one very envious, being choked up here in the heart of the city. But you've not come from there this morning, did you say?'

'No. I'm staying in a hotel on...'

'Grafton Street. Yes, yes, of course you are – do forgive me. Well that's splendid.'

'I thought it would be less of a risk, with the strikes.'

'The strikes? Oh, my dear fellow, I wouldn't worry about those.

Besides, one does not need strikes to excuse a touch of convenience now and again, does one? And after all you've been through a little convenience is the least you deserve. Why, you've only been back in the country a handful of days—'

'Just one.'

'One what? One *day*, you don't mean?'

'Yes. I arrived at Victoria yesterday.'

The Under Secretary's face, heretofore the very essence of joviality and ease, was transformed by an expression of utter mortification.

'Oh my – do sit down, please, please,' he entreated, as if Richard's continuing to stand was like a quiver of arrows loosed at his uncharitable Christian heart. 'My dear fellow, you must think me worse than the Pharaohs – dragging you to luncheon the day after your return! Please, please, do sit – *sit*.' A series of impassioned gesticulations provided a florid accompaniment and induced Richard to take up the armchair opposite. The barman was summoned with a magisterial wave. 'Let me get you something to drink. What would you like?'

Richard looked up and addressed the barman directly. 'A glass of water, please.'

'Of course, sir.'

'Are you sure you wouldn't care for anything else?' asked the Under Secretary, as if the ascetic request were yet another arrow loosed at his breast. 'A coffee at least, or something more...'

'No, thank you.'

'Well – but you must let me know the instant you do. Whatever you wish. I am as Publius to your Paul.'

'Certainly.'

'I had understood,' the Under Secretary resumed in an emollient, exculpatory tone, sitting back in his chair, 'that you were to have returned several days ago – not a single day. I would never have dreamed of inconveniencing you in such fashion had I known the truth.'

'No, no – there's no inconvenience. None whatsoever, I assure you.'

At this avowal the Under Secretary bound his hands together as a votive. A smile of worldly humility spread upon his lips and he bore the serenity of one transported to the Elysian fields of content.

Richard was equally content. He had dreaded the thought of the Under Secretary being some fusty old political hand, one whose hair – whatever little he still possessed of it – would be of the colour of wool, who would stand as if tilting to port, whose complexion would be of one dipped in it, and who would speak like one whose habit was to dine on it. It was an expectation confirmed by his officious admittance into the club, by the grand, busted corridor along which he was conducted to the wainscot and plumes of the smoking room, and by the full panoply of morning-suited elegance which greeted him there. Instead, he found the Under Secretary of a tall, full stature, with features that sparkled with all the vivacity and ideals of youth. He was elegantly dressed in a light grey morning suit and his features, though of unarguable definition, were softened at the edges to attain to an almost hermaphroditic equilibrium between virility and compassion. A high, noble forehead was crowned by silken hair sweeping left to right with strands which seemed to catch each shaft of light as if it were a single golden sunbeam, and his celestial blue eyes, tinted with light and candour like the pellucid waters of a mountain lake, were set with perfect symmetry beneath the sweeping arcs of his brows. It was a bearing unquestionably superior, possessed of a complexion of such delicacy and grace as to bless him with an ageless, waxen look: a physiognomy and visage to requite the desires of any sculptor's hands that desired a model for the great Patrician age of antiquity. A figure, in short, of such sublimity that any of a spiteful bent might have been tempted to ask what it was *he* had done during the war – were it not so ignoble a question to pose.

'You're too kind. Really, too kind. But the pleasure is entirely mine. You coming here, quite literally straight off the boat – why, it's beyond the call. It really is.' As if overcome by the mere iteration of this pleasure the Under Secretary fell silent. A moment later he added distractedly, 'We'll go through to the dining room shortly.' Another short, reflective silence followed. 'Well, I must say – and I do hope you'll excuse me for doing so – but the moment I saw you I was struck by how exhausted you looked. You were like a man who'd been battling the moon for a fortnight and more! But that explains it. Why, in your place, I wouldn't have left my bed for a week!'

Of Richard's exhaustion there was no doubt. Fourteen hours' sleep had failed to alleviate his fatigue, and the morning's liberal imbibition of coffee had only resulted in restlessness. Normally, therefore, the Under Secretary's piquant observation would have drawn Richard to the full hedgehog of prickles and denial. But the translucent honesty of the Under Secretary's eyes was like a serum which told that any concealment of deceit was impossible.

'I am exhausted,' he confessed, before remarking profoundly, 'But imprisonment is the wolf that howls at the window of sleep.'

The Under Secretary returned a nod of perspicacious empathy. He too had suffered many sleepless nights.

'Yes, yes, indeed. You were in one of those wretched camps for the whole war, weren't you?'

'That's right.'

'You poor fellow. And no doubt with a host of insufferable companions with whom you could barely exchange two civilised words?'

'I accepted my lot.'

'Quite so. One must, after all. The mind boggles – it really does. And you were in Vienna for two years before the war started, making it four… five years – heavens, my arithmetic has quite gone to pot—'

'Six.'

'Six years. Good Lord. Nineteen-thirteen – that's right, isn't it?' His supposition confirmed, he emitted an incredulous sigh. 'One can scarcely believe that year ever existed now. It's like a mirage in the sun. I imagine the whole of England must be somewhat like a mirage to you too. Or perhaps a vast circus hall of mirrors – with everything dreadfully warped and distorted – is a better analogy?'

Richard just about smiled. 'I've not had a chance to think about it,' he said.

'No, no – I'm sure you haven't.' The waiter returned with Richard's glass and set it down on the table. 'Splendid, George. That's most kind of you.' The Under Secretary blessed him with a paternalistic smile, before resuming to Richard, 'That's just as well. One must never look too closely in mirrors. It's best to keep them well out of sight – else before one knows it one finds oneself squeezing the pips, sucking the lemons, and left with nothing but the bitter taste of regret. Why, everything changes in six years, regardless of locomotives or war. That said, I couldn't imagine what the devil I'd feel like if I'd been plucked out of London and plopped back in the city six years later. Six days in the country is about my lot before I start to feel giddy. And now, here you are –' he clapped his hands in delight '– plunging straight back into the heart of the political jamboree. Well, it's splendid. Simply splendid.'

The Under Secretary broke off. A distracted look in Richard's eyes persuaded him to turn and track its course. The object was a portrait of Joseph Chamberlain above the fireplace at the far end of the room.

'Ah yes, Mr Chamberlain: a figure of much contention. Indeed, a portrait of as much contention as the man.' He suppressed a lordly chuckle. 'There are any number of members here who would far rather it were located significantly lower than its present position, I assure you.'

'Then why isn't it?' asked Richard sternly.

A faint elevation of the eyebrows was the sole ripple discernible in the Under Secretary's impeccably smooth waters.

'Our *engouement* for eccentricity, perhaps,' he returned light-heartedly. The remark did nothing to leaven Richard's countenance. But the Under Secretary was sensible to such emotions: Mr Chamberlain was a well-worn cause of antithetical feeling. 'Ah yes, do forgive me – your father's campaign against Mr Chamberlain's tariff reform. I've heard much about it from Mr Bellman. A great and noble campaign, without doubt. Alas, it was my misfortune never to have had the pleasure of hearing your father speak. I understand it was something quite electrifying – his words delivered with passion and of an adjectival vehemence like a cannonade.' The encomium achieved its objective; it educed a near vernal efflorescence in Richard's features. The Under Secretary proceeded swiftly to pollination. 'But a portrait is no more than a *souvenir*, is it not? It is there to make one think as much of the things of which we are proud as of those we are not. It is not purely to remind the rich how rich they are, or the handsome of their good looks. It is to encourage one to reflect upon a man's character and life, to praise his nobility and to find the reason in his faults. Here, I'm afraid, I confess I'm supporter of the portrait. But look – look at the fireplace.' He pointed at a large irregular segment missing from the marbled black mantelpiece. 'That too is a portrait – albeit of a very different ilk. A portrait of perhaps even greater significance than Mr Chamberlain though. Some high-minded fellow – muddle-minded, you might say – part of a cabal that was trying to force the government's hand over the unpleasant matter of Chinese labour on the Rand all those years back, managed to sneak a bomb into this very room and detonate it. Well, he did more mischief to himself than the fireplace, I'm sorry to say – but now we have our little *souvenir* to remind us how much money can threaten the moral content of our labours. There you have it. Two equally different but complementary portraits, one above the other. Now,' he said, rising from the armchair, 'it's time for luncheon, don't you think? We need to make sure you're well fed and in tip-top form for the coming months, don't we?'

And with that, so concluded the interview stage of employment.

*

'For oft' the sound of hammers, blow on blow,
The noise of strife
Confuse me till I quite forget He knows
And oversees
And that in all details with His good plan
My life agrees.'

Richard returned a beatific smile at the Under Secretary's homily, upon which the latter continued, 'Well yes, you are of course perfectly correct in what you say – but only so far as the principle. The body proposed by the American president – his League of Nations, as he calls it – cannot be the solution. It is a most laudable *principle*, certainly – a most laudable *ambition* – as an instrument to facilitate the spread of the rule of law and democratic government.' Finishing his consommé he dabbed the corners of his mouth with his napkin. 'But it cannot possibly be an instrument of *policy*. It cannot be an instrument of *action*. One can hardly invite countries to partake in a forum for global governance whose own institutions – in so far as they are even constitutionally formed, which is seldom the case, I add – are riddled with imperfections. For such countries to sit in judgement on those who have spent centuries expunging these imperfections would be ludicrous. Quite ludicrous. The whole thing would end up a farce – and a highly dangerous one at that. No, the responsibilities of the Allied nations cannot be shared around the world like so many pieces of chocolate. They cannot be abrogated by the handing over of however many millions Mr Clemenceau and the prime minister manage to wring from the benighted German nation. I told the prime minister that myself.'

'No, of course not. I wasn't suggesting that,' said Richard, his negation one less of conviction as to what he had actually been suggesting than of a desire not to oppose the Under Secretary. 'We must assume all of our responsibilities. That goes without saying. The blow of the hammer shapes the iron in the forge.'

The Under Secretary dropped his napkin on the table and clapped his hands. 'Splendidly expressed, my dear fellow! Splendid! I can envisage the words of the father as the son speaks before me! Indeed, now is the time for the metal to be forged in our mould. Peace, as you so rightly said, can only be the product of unity. But one cannot create unity by simply applying a rubber to a map. No. Unity comes only via the outward expansion of a communality of ideas from a core. One might, for example, imagine this core to be akin to a great canopy at the roadside. Beneath it travellers might freely seek shelter from the rain, and therein find a fraternity of discourse to while away the hours. However, the mere existence of the canopy cannot compel a man to seek refuge from the rain; a traveller is just as likely to bow his head and plough on like a mule, or, if he is possessed of an umbrella himself, to open that and continue on his solitary way. And if there should be two travellers side by side they might each open their own umbrella! Certainly, they do not *need* some vast canopy to shelter beneath. They do not *need* such a thing to continue conversing. And so, in order for the canopy to supplant the umbrella and the doggedly bowed head – in order for it to become a *necessity* – one must convince the traveller that it is more efficacious to pause than to tramp on soaked to the skin, that a great canopy offers far better protection than having one's single umbrella buffeted and broken by the wind. Thus, in the same way that a small child and a large man will profit equally from the canopy, so a small community and large nation will profit equally from being part of a federation. In this way too a national characteristic – a single umbrella, if you will – which might otherwise be a pointy or objectionable presence in the midst of a throng, will become a bright, colourful parasol twirled high overhead. It will become a source of celebration and joy – like a shiny bauble on a Christmas tree.'

Richard was entranced. The irresistible persuasion of the Under Secretary's intercourse was like a gentle lyre in his mind. It was as if he were listening to a concert whereby the musician's beauty had interwoven with the chords to create a sublime, melodic rhapsody, one which left him deaf to any dissonant shift that might otherwise have jarred the unwaxed ear.

At either end of the rectangular dining room the two fireplaces were in full flame, the orange glow tinging the pastel-patterned wallpaper with a dusky, confidential hue. Outside the daylight dimmed and darkened across the white stucco ceiling. Richard glanced up at the sober wing-collared portraits surrounding him. Their aspects, he was sure, seemed no longer to convey a distant hauteur, but rather jealousy – that they should be trapped in canvas and oil, and could not touch the hand before him: the hand that then caressed the wine glass stem before raising it to pink pure lips. That, after all, was a hand that any man should wish to clasp.

'An excellent claret this,' said the Under Secretary. 'Are you quite certain you won't have anything other than water? I feel as if I'm denuding you of half a lunch.'

'Not at all,' Richard returned earnestly. And to prove his contentment he drank his water. But he was not entirely content. On sitting down in the dining room he had thought to ask for some lemonade. He had changed his mind as soon as the Under Secretary had ordered wine: lemonade was for children. So he had asked for more water. It was an insipid, puritanical contrast to the alluring complexion of the Under Secretary's wine.

The Under Secretary held his glass suspended at a distance and studied Richard for a moment. He had been in search of someone not scarred by the morbidity of war, a trait he found had afflicted many once fine men. An assistant secretary was for him a man not just who carried out his instructions, but in whom he could have faith, and who would return that faith in him. Without faith a man was no better than a retainer whose colours changed from day to pay. What the Under Secretary's vision required most to fulfil it was not introspection and doubt (these he was well acquainted with in himself), but loyalty and conviction.

'Splendid, splendid. *In aqua claritas* indeed! Well, now, there is one matter we must tackle – before we advance to the main course, as it were. Mr Bellman told me in our discussions of your objection to the Habsburgs, that objection being directed quite as much to the empire as to the dynasty.'

There was a short pause.

'It was, yes.'

'Was – yes, *was* indeed! You're quite right. One has difficulty applying the past tense to things that seem still to be quite present! Yes, but I am correct in saying that – so far as the past is concerned, am I not?'

'Yes. The two were the same,' he noted plainly.

'Inseparable and indivisible. Quite so. Quite so. The two heads of one eagle.' The Under Secretary, once more sensible to a simmering of Richard's emotions, was malleable in his approach. 'Do forgive me. That's a perfectly abominable way to broach such a matter – and to one whose understanding of the convolutions of Austrian history is naturally far superior to my own. What I sought to propose – albeit in a very ham-fisted manner – was that whenever one reaches an end, there was once a beginning. That is to say that the division that has been the architect of such a terrible conflict was nonetheless once the cause of creation. For once the Habsburgs brought order; once they brought unity. And from that order and unity sprang peace and society. Without Austria – as Mr Talleyrand so rightly stated – there would have been chaos. It was only when concessions were made to the different peoples of the empire that rottenness crept into its once sturdy frame. The people began to forget unity to compete with each other for favours. The Habsburg crown became no more than a symbol. And, like all symbols, it was empty and worthless. All of this I don't need to tell you, I'm sure – indeed you'd no doubt express it with far greater clarity and erudition than I!'

Richard made a bashful, swooning gesture with his head. The Under Secretary, after a luxuriant sip of his wine, acknowledged the act with deep satisfaction.

'The question I was therefore attempting to address earlier was how to restore this ancient order to the *new* Europe: how to bring back unity,' the Under Secretary resumed forcefully. 'The answer, simply, is that we must construct a new society. A society in which a man may be proud of the soil to which he is born, but in which he does not seek conflict with another who is equally proud of the soil to which *he* is born. We must create a Europe wherein the colourful parasol twirled is as important to the whole as the canopy, but subject to the necessities which govern the livelihoods, happiness and survival of all. To achieve this there must be a confederation of the Danube states once ruled by the Habsburgs. Then will the umbrellas of petty nationalism be folded and set aside. Then will unity – and thus security – be created: by federation.' The Under Secretary suddenly leaned forward; his translucent eyes fixed on Richard like two otherworldly lights; his hand reached out to touch him. At the coming anointment Richard's heart beat hard; his blood soared to an ecstatic, giddy height. 'And the English must do the same. Yes, we too must fold our umbrella. We too must step beneath the canopy of federation. We too must accept that for the world to advance according to our beneficent principles – *our beliefs* – we can no longer exist alone as an isle on the edge of the world, an isle whose empire is propped on the crutches of alien alliances – injurious not just to our own morals and interests, but to those with whom we should most naturally seek to federate, those whom we are most alike in sentiment. That is what we must strive for in the coming months – together, Richard, you and I: to bring our states to federation, and the Japanese alliance to desuetude. These federations will be the true authority to preserve the peace of the world. Because for them not to act would be contrary – as I said – to every necessity which governs the livelihood, happiness and survival of all. Do you see, Richard?'

Chapter 12

See? Of course Richard saw! Federations: that was the answer!

As Richard strode back to the hotel he tipped his head to the sky, his face washed by the cold spitting rain. Why, if ever proof were needed of the organic brilliance of the Under Secretary's conception it was there up above: the disparate clouds of late morning had bunched to form a single impermeable shield. Until that moment, he suddenly realised, his thoughts had been nothing but brutish.

'We shall meet again. Come to me tomorrow.'

These were the soft words with which the Under Secretary had bade him farewell. Transfixed by the Under Secretary's gaze, Richard had agreed to the summons instinctively, upon which the Under Secretary had apologised: he was being a Pharaoh again; he had forgotten Richard had only just returned. Richard had felt compelled to accede to this truth; but he would need a couple of days – no more! – to put his affairs in order. He had lost five years already – he could not lose any more!

'A couple of days – of course, of course!' the Under Secretary had exclaimed with delight. A top-to-toe glance at Richard's ill-fitting suit had then prompted him to whisk a card from his pocket: it belonged to his tailor. A suitable wardrobe should be billed to his account, he had said, a noble waft of his arm sweeping aside Richard's incipient protest.

'Why, an assistant secretary is every bit as important as the ink in the pen!'

On returning to his hotel Richard's first act was to extend his reservation until the end of the month. A journey to and from Hammersmith was certainly far too perilous to undertake daily; the feckless functionaries would only ever throw off their stupor of municipal indifference in order to strike! He next sent a cable to Mr Bellman, then, wasting no further time, headed straight to the tailor.

The following morning he was fallen upon by Mr Bellman in the hotel lobby as if he were the returning prodigal and not the elder.

'My, how you've changed, Richard!' Mr Bellman cried. He clasped Richard's shoulder and rocked him with the familiarity of yore. He laughed, the same rasping, wheezy laugh as always. That, however, was the extent of the similitude to the past. For if Richard could be said to have changed over the course of nearly six years – and there was no doubt that he had – it was as nothing to the change that had overcome Mr Bellman. While the whole world had become encrusted with lichen and moss like a tree in the wold, Mr Bellman had become apparently younger. His crooked carriage had straightened, his sallow complexion had coloured, his sagging jowl had been nipped, his sandy-white hair had become thick, and he moved with a surprisingly leporine spring. It was remarkable. It was as if he had disappeared into the dark woods of war and re-emerged having discovered an elixir within.

'No less than you,' Richard returned with good-natured astonishment.

In the same familiar vein Mr Bellman then said that for a moment he thought he had seen a ghost: Richard was so pale, thin and drawn. There were flecks of grey on his moustache, did he know? And how his hair had receded and thinned. It was the same wispy hair as his mother's, that was why. But that was the lot of every man when he passed the age of thirty!

He would be thirty *next* year, noted Richard.

Mr Bellman let out another rasping, wheezy laugh and shook Richard heartily. 'Ha! Yes, of course! *Next* year!'

Mr Bellman already had a dinner engagement that evening with a couple of friends in Covent Garden, he said, but Richard would join them and they would celebrate his joyous return all together.

The restaurant chosen was accessed via a back alley through a nondescript door that Richard thought might equally have served it for trade. A steep staircase led down to the basement dining area, where through a thick haze of tobacco smoke a collection of tables were dimly lit by a pattern of candles and crackling bulbs.

Mr Bellman's friends were of the conventional city-underwriter type: polite, hearty, generous to a fault – and bone from the neck up. Mr Bellman himself was in ebullient good form though.

He hailed Richard's return, he saluted his father, he cheered his companions, he wished all future good fortune, and he ordered endless champagne with which he toasted the peace of the world. It was, all told, an evening Richard considered to be undeniably vulgar in tone (the contrast in milieu, and between the Under Secretary's red wine and elevated discourse and the froth of champagne and dull talk of the markets could not have been greater), but which he indulged for the sake of times past. Now that he dwelt on the upper floors he could submit to dine in the basement! After the main course he even allowed himself to be persuaded to a glass of champagne to toast the Ministry of X. However, not being a drinker, it went straight to his head, and after the initial gaiety and light-headedness, a mild but persistent headache set in over dessert. Mr Bellman and his companions carried the air of men for whom dinner was simply an *hors d'oeuvre* to the night, and Richard consequently soon after made his excuses: he wished to make an early start for the family house, Mr Bellman having earlier passed him the keys.

Accompanying Richard back to the street, Mr Bellman declared he would visit as soon as he could. It was only in saying this that he was informed that Richard would not be staying at the house. Mr Bellman's ascent of the stairs somewhat tardied by the evening's excesses, he took a moment to reply.

'Ah, yes, very prudent in the circumstances,' he said.

'And I'll be making arrangements to sell it,' added Richard.

The decision having only been made that morning, its first public iteration tolled in Richard's solemn tone. And, such being its weight, he did not instantly remark Mr Bellman's pause on the stairs behind him.

'And your brother?' asked Mr Bellman, at length.

Richard spun round, his cheeks colouring darkly.

'What of him?' he snapped.

'Well you'll need his consent.'

'What for? It's nothing to do with him. I can do as I wish. That's still the law, isn't it?'

'Yes, indeed – but only when there isn't a will.'

'A will? Who wrote a *will?*'

In accordance with the legal matter suddenly brought to the fore, Mr Bellman's voice assumed a plain, antipodal dispassion. 'We did, Richard. That is, myself and your father. You must understand, we hadn't any news of you, and so when your brother enlisted, we... well... we naturally presumed he'd be killed. Without a will, if both you and your brother were dead, the estate would've passed to your mother's relations. And could you imagine that happening? *Could you?* No – impossible! So, not knowing if you were alive or not, your father *had to* write a will.' There was a brief glottal pause, before he concluded, 'He settled the estate between you: between you equally.'

'Equally? *Equally?* When my brother did *nothing?* When he abandoned my father? When I am the—' Richard thudded an angry fist to the wall in place of the word; the hitherto mild pulsing of his temples turned into a throb. That after all he'd endured he should be subject to his brother's consent was almost unbearable. He stared down at Mr Bellman with wild eyes, as if the tormenting revelation had just been made by the devil himself. But Mr Bellman's position, equidistant between the light bulbs along one side of the wall, meant that with his face turned from the light, there was something intangible about him, as if even the shadows could not wrestle definition to his form. Richard felt a sudden, peculiar chill shoot through him; for a split second he was utterly convinced that Mr Bellman would vanish there and then and leave not a trace of existence behind. In subdued, truculent tones, he then asked, 'And if he refuses? If he does not consent?'

In the slight forward movement of Mr Bellman's head there was detectable the faintest upward turn of his lips at the question. '*Refuse?* Why on earth would he refuse, Richard?' he said. 'You think he wants to live in that house? You think he'd return to do that? No, no, your brother made his choice long ago: he went by his gate. His consent – when we find him – will be a formality.' Upon which elucidation Mr Bellman tripped boldly back into light, and with his leporine spring, bounded the stairs. 'Come, come,' he said soothingly. 'I was going to tell you as soon as I got back but... well... I didn't think it'd have to be this soon! It's hardly the first subject to go celebrating your return after six years over dinner with, is it now?'

'No, I suppose not,' Richard agreed lowly.

'Exactly – though maybe I should have known the first thing an Englishman thinks of when he gets a new job is to buy a new house!' He let out a sharp, discordant laugh and, leading Richard with his hand flat on his back, swung open the door to the street.

They were met by a vast wall of fog. Only the faint luminescence from the distant street lamps gave shape to the contours of night.

'Aha – the city's greatest habit! How about that for a welcome home, eh, Richard?' Mr Bellman rasped. His arm rising to Richard's shoulder, he steered him firmly left. 'Come on, let's get you a taxi. We don't want you getting lost when we've only just found you!'

However, Richard's incandescent humour had only been dimmed by Mr Bellman's emollient phrases; it had not been extinguished. And having navigated his way across Central Europe without so much as a Baedeker or Bradshaw's the idea of his being considered incapable of finding a taxi on his own, or even traversing the short distance back to Piccadilly on foot, made him bridle. He eased himself free of the hand on his shoulder and stepped away.

'I'll find one myself,' he said.

'Nonsense. I know where they stand. Come on.'

In blithe disregard of Richard's vexation, Mr Bellman reached out to direct him back to the appropriate path. But as he did he slipped on the kerb; stumbling into the street, in a trice he was swallowed whole by the fog. For a moment there was a profound, eerie silence, as if his body had been committed to the deep to be turned into corruption. He then re-emerged, lurching ghoulishly forward. As he swayed on the greasy cobblestones his face was twisted like a chamois, his teeth and gums bared and his blotted eyes huge and speckled with strange neon tints.

Richard was horrified at the grotesque emanation, unmasking as it did Mr Bellman's true state of inebriety. In the festive context of the evening such a state might of course be excused, but this could not counter the revelatory truth that Richard thus suddenly saw him not with any affection of old but in the bright light of disgust. And whereas two days prior he had suppressed such discordant emotion, now he did not. Now he let it infiltrate every pore of his being so that his only thought was that Mr Bellman might *actually* disappear into the fog and leave not a trace of existence behind.

As if detecting this horrored look, Mr Bellman assumed a reptilian stillness. His large reddened eyes began to glisten. Then, with a sad shake of his head he stepped stealthily forward, stretched out his arm, and wove it tightly through Richard's loose, pliant limb; a restive twitch at the coiling embrace provoked a gentle constriction.

He was afraid to go back to the house, Mr Bellman suddenly confessed in low tones, the stench of tobacco and turbot on his breath making Richard inwardly retch: that was why he could not go with Richard to the house in the morning. He had not set foot inside it since Richard's father had died. Oh, it was such a shameful thing to have to admit to a son. It was a torture to even admit to himself! For… oh – if only he hadn't returned to America for those months in '17! If only he'd stayed in England! If only, if only, he'd been there, then his father wouldn't have died all alone in despair! If only… if only, he said – the catch of emotion sticking in his pathetic, halting lament – he could have entered the study and found his poor father himself. If only – *at least* – he could have been there to do that… and not Joseph Childs.

'Joseph Childs?'

Richard jerked himself loose at the jar of the name. As soon as he did Mr Bellman untangled his arm and took a slithering step back. His body stood in relief against the fog, like a half-dissolved spectre.

'Yes, *him*, Richard. Can you imagine? Of all the people in the world, it was *he* who discovered your father. Oh, for your father to be mocked in such a cruel way! The very same man who took his place when your mother died was there in *his* place when he died. Oh, what God would find pleasure in such torture? What spirit would torment such a soul? The Lord knows what that odious man was doing there – if not to collect his bond. No doubt your father's kindness brought him to the door, but that was ever his weakness – he was too good to say no to such men.' Mr Bellman's whole body gave a sudden, violent shudder, as if his skin had been pounded within. He turned his head and threw a deep rasping cough into the impenetrable mass of fog. As he twisted back, a half-laugh was suppressed beneath a bitter, sardonic tone.

'The only good,' he said, 'is that at least now he has suffered his due. Joseph Childs has had his comeuppance.'

Chapter 13

Joseph Childs' comeuppance? Richard couldn't care tuppence. Why, until Mr Bellman had said his name Richard had forgotten he even existed! It was of course true that in a previous age he would have relished such a prospect, but not any more. Now Joseph Childs was of as much consequence as a twig in a wood.

What *was* of consequence was his waking the following morning with a throat like sandpaper and a nose in need of a plunger. To be incapacitated at such a moment (just when he was about to clasp the hand of the hand that held the pen) was unthinkable!

The diagnosis was simple: a concoction of champagne, cigar smoke, over-rich food and the chill, miasmic air had resulted in an enervating night's sleep that had made him ripe for infection. As a result he possessed no inclination whatsoever to drag himself to the far west of London to visit a house he could not even sell. His sole concern was the rapid restoration of his health.

That he did then set off for the house was entirely due to the Under Secretary. Even *in absentia* Richard knew he had to prove to him that he would bend to no ailment. If he did it would be the surest sign of his own moral and physical pusillanimity, a flaw that would be instantly exposed in the glare of the Under Secretary's pure, veracious eyes.

The combination of obligation and affliction was therefore enough on its own to account for his thoroughly disagreeable humour – without, that was, the importunate codicils to the previous evening. For during his slow walk back to the hotel through the Stygian fog, guided by the sulphurous glow from the street-corner acetylene flares, Mr Bellman's foul revelation had awakened him not just to the fact that returning to the small, provincial cottage-lined streets of Ravenscourt Park would be unprofitable, but that he had a debt to repay too.

The hardships of exile, internment and orphanhood may warrant to the greatest degree a man's self-sufficiency and grant him compassion, but they could not forget a debt. It was a debt as irrefutable as it was ineluctable. This was because it was not purely a financial one, but one with a far more straitening clause.

His matriculation to Oxford before the war had been largely funded by the Methodist Church and local congregation. There was naturally no stipulation that this subvention entail a commitment to at some future point follow – or indeed advance – in his father's ministerial footsteps, but there was no doubting the expectation that he would: the moral clause, as it were. And whilst the cataclysm of war might have written off this debt for some, Richard was suddenly only too aware that for others the account would have grown, more so since he had returned. The Ravenscourt Park Mission being a stone's throw from the house, there was therefore the very lively possibility of bumping into one of the congregation and being interrogated upon his intentions and duties, a circumstance that would inevitably shackle his new-found liberty, if as much in the spirit as in the flesh. Perhaps this was the real reason the daemon of disgust sprang so readily to mind in the image of Mr Bellman. *He* would never forget that debt, that much was certain: with him it would be like a Promethean shackle hammered into the rocks.

Like all grievances that manifest themselves in disagreeable humours, Richard's greatest was not against that which had happened, but against that which had not. And so like any reasonable man he took it out on the front door.

The key jammed in the lock; he gave it another violent twist and leaned his shoulder forcefully into the door. The door finally opening, it returned him a slap of dry, fusty air. Then, like a vacuum released, on entering the hallway it sucked every life-giving annoyance from within him: he was left with nothing but a feeling of barren disjunction. In this disinterested state did he begin a perfunctory wander through the house.

He went first into the kitchen. Through the dankness and gloom he remarked damp on the ceiling and the rotting window frames; he turned and left. He paused by the stairs. He noted an escalating crack in the wall and the threadbare patches of carpet. He was struck by how impractically low and narrow the staircase seemed. A man of, say, the Under Secretary's stature would look ridiculous attempting to climb such a thing. He went up. As he stepped onto the landing the floorboards deeply groaned, as if a giant had stood on their guts. He observed the four closed doors: two bedrooms, one bathroom and cupboard; the frames were battered and chipped and the wallpaper was peeling. He looked across at the diminutive steps leading to the attic bedroom, but he did not approach. There was no point: he was sure to be too big and get stuck. It was almost inconceivable, he thought, that a whole family could dwell in such a small space – that *he* could have dwelt in such a small space. He let out a sigh, and descended.

Poking his head into the living room at the back of the house he then entered his father's study at the front. There, there used to be papers, pamphlets, articles, cuttings, books, and who knew what else piled high over the furniture and floor, giving it a sort of magical, cavernous depth. As a boy he remembered undertaking vast expeditions just to reach his father, like some intrepid character in an adventure novel. But now everything had been emptied there was something sterile about the room. Whether this administrative ablution had happened at his father's behest, Richard did not dwell on: he was still too confounded by the size. Two strides took him from one side to the other and made him feel practically Gulliverian. He turned to the bookcase, removed a volume and cracked open the leather spine. His eyes first opened wide, then squinted at the thin double columns and minuscule print. He shook his head incredulously: there had to be a million words and more on the pages, impenetrable as a forest. How could anyone, he thought, be expected to read such a thing? And what would be the point of such labour? After all, now he knew that the words together meant nothing: it was only the hand on the hand which held the pen that meant something. That was the only thing that brought change. Not words.

He replaced the volume and moved over to his father's writing desk, positioned square to the window. Turning to the empty grating of the fireplace beside it he ran a cursory eye over the trinkets on the mantelpiece. Propped against a small, smiling porcelain tiger was a dog-eared card. He picked it up. An army field postcard, it stated via pre-printed lines that the sender was *quite well*, and had received no letter *lately*. He flipped it over; the address was in Edward's hand. He put it back. He leaned against the mantelpiece and stared blankly at the dirty net curtain. A few moments later his eyelids flickered to ward off some disturbed specks of dust. His focus regained, it fell on his father's high-backed armchair. Set slightly back from the desk, and at an angle facing the fireplace, it was almost as if his father – feeling a chill in the midst of his lucubrations – might have just pushed the chair out and risen to stir the embers to life. On the armchair's headrest a patch of the olive-green cloth had faded from the many years where his father's head had inclined to the right when he'd dozed. Slowly, imperceptibly, Richard's look hardened as he stared at the patch. And the longer he stared the more unpleasant the sight became to him, the more indignant he felt at its presence, the more violent and irrepressible was his urge to fall on his knees and scrub the abhorrent spot until the taint on the cloth was all gone. For this very armchair in which his father had spent so many years composing speeches and sermons by the fire, breathing life into the Anti-Protection League and belief to the kingdom of God, was remembering him with nothing but a bald patch of cloth!

Mr Bellman's words suddenly rang loud in his ears. '*All alone in despair*' – that was what he had said: that was how his father had died.

With one swing of the brush that sweeps the dust of death from the door, Richard had never once thought of his father dying alone. Alone, perhaps, in that his wife was dead, that neither of his sons were present, and that Mr Bellman was abroad – but not actually, in the physical sense, *alone*. There had surely been *someone*? Some friendly, caring presence to reach out with a soft, tender hand, to be a balm *in articulo mortis*? There had surely not been *no one*? Because if that were the case then would it not mean his father might have lain slumped dead in the armchair, undiscovered for days, his body rotting and his head decomposing into the worn patch of cloth? Would it not mean, in some way, that if this had happened he had been *forgotten*?

Then, quite unexpectedly, into the burgeoning horror of Richard's vision the image of Joseph Childs interpolated itself. This man who had discovered his father. This same man who had carried his mother up the staircase to the bedroom when she had collapsed in the kitchen for the very last time. He would know the truth. Yes, Richard thought – he would, this man who had had his comeuppance.

Chapter 14

Well now, *there* was someone Sarah Childs didn't expect to see on her doorstep when she opened the front door. That said, Sarah Childs had barely got used to opening the front door expecting to see anyone. A thoroughly disagreeable experience it was too: the opening of a front door was what husbands and maids were for. How else was one supposed to avoid callers if one didn't have someone to open the front door and say that one was not in, or that one was indisposed, or to declare that one was not inclined to receive such and such a person? Really, her husband had no idea how much torment his company's bankruptcy had caused her. And did he show any sympathy for her plight? Not a jot. He just talked of economies here and pennies there, piling stress upon strain. It was a miracle her nerve had held to be able to carry on with her needlework!

The very first economy of the Childs' troubled times had been the maid, an economy Sarah Childs had found to be quite unfathomable, if not a little irrational. As far as she was concerned when a man got into financial difficulty (an eventuality in which the woman assumed no blame) the marital contract (and, if one must, love) decreed that a husband's primary obligation was to preserve the dignity and station of his wife. If he was unable to do so then he was beholden to absent himself for as long as it took to recover the means that he should. That, in her book, was the first economy. But Joseph had not done that. Oh no. Instead he had caused her more suffering. And it had left her to deal with predicaments that were most invidious. Because, of course, what else could she possibly do but invite the young man in for tea? The Lord alone knew what she'd say to him!

Richard, for his part, would never have accepted the invitation had it been extended *after* she'd told him her husband was out. That information wasn't relayed until the door was closed behind him. For the Lord alone knew what he'd say to her!

'Do sit down, Richard,' she said, pointing to the settee as they entered the front room. Her round compact face beamed at the sight of the plump upholstery with its bright colours and intricate floral patterns. She threw up a scowl when he sat and paid it not the slightest regard. His indifference was symptomatic of the times: once, to remark upon the exquisiteness of one's soft furnishings would have been the watermark of civility; now men sat without even so much as a word. Considerably stouter of frame due to the physical burden lately placed upon her, Sarah Childs' waddle over to the teapot on the sideboard was notably Jemiman. 'I've just made some tea, so you're in luck.'

'Ah, yes.'

'Yes – I was just settling into my needlework,' she said, intimating that his arrival had come at a critical stitch.

'Ah, yes.'

She took an additional teacup from the cupboard and placed it beside her own. Both were filled with a couple of awkward, peremptory slops.

'Yes, the knock on the door quite startled me.'

'Oh.'

'I wasn't expecting any visitors, you know.'

'Hmm.'

Heavens above! Had the boy become an imbecile? He was grunting like a halfwit.

'Anyway, I simply cannot do needlework without tea. I find it's quite impossible.'

'No, I can imagine.'

Could he indeed? She set her teeth for the purpose of tutting betwixt. To think, all that church money spent on his education, and she got more sense from the birds! She turned round and handed him the cup. He half rose to receive it.

'Mind, it's hot,' she said.

'Yes. Thank you.' Richard set the cup down on the coffee table. He gave it a malevolent glance, and a grimace then passed for a smile; it was too hot to even start drinking.

Suppressing a sigh, Sarah Childs took up a pert position on the divan opposite and clasped her hands together. She purveyed a look of friendly condescension, as if, discovering a hedgehog snuffling round the back garden, she had just given it a saucer of milk. As such she would have been perfectly happy to watch in curious silence until it decided to peregrinate off again. But hedgehogs were quite different to men, she knew. So she would have to at least find out what garden he had come from, and then, perhaps – if time allowed – which one he intended to go to next.

'Well, it's very good to see you again. You've just got back from France, isn't that right? That's what the Hornchurches told me at church the other day.'

'From Austria.'

'Ah really, Austria – not France?'

'That's right.'

'Oh, I see,' she returned in a lilt of enlightenment.

Not, of course, that Sarah Childs was in the least enlightened. She had paid little attention to what the Hornchurches had actually said concerning Richard's return. It had been distinctly subservient to the scandalous news from the pews that old Mrs Lambert had turned High Church on her deathbed and left her money for a chantry. Anyway, wasn't it France where they'd gone? But now, then, what was this Austria he'd just mentioned? She had obviously heard of the *Austro-Hungarian* empire – that was where it all started – but she had never heard of anything called *Austria*. She had never seen any casualty lists of men from there before. But in order not to get bogged down in the self-evident insignificance of the place she moved swiftly on.

'Well that's very good. And you're well?'

'Yes.' His legs were given a reassuringly fleshy pat. 'Everything's still there.'

This, however, Sarah Childs *did* understand. She had not spent four years fundraising with the church mission for wounded soldiers for nothing. Her little brown eyes were burnished by a sudden pathos, and beneath her smooth forehead her flinty nose twitched with tragic emotion.

'Oh, thank goodness. Such a ghastly business the war's been. Why, some of the poor devils I've seen – well, one almost wouldn't wish that sort of thing on the Germans, you know.' She shook her head with commensurate woe – and glanced down by her side to her needlework. Of course, when Sarah Childs spoke of what she 'had seen', that seeing had been done from a distance. For even so much as to glimpse one of those unfortunates as she walked down the street was a cause of such distress to her sensibilities that she would be forced to cross to the other side. But she was an excellent fundraiser. 'And it's not just the ones who've come back either. The Davies family – you remember them, don't you, the children a little younger than you? The father a beastly liar and cheat, but the two boys such dear sweet things. Perfect cherubs, they were. Well, they died at Gallipoli – both of them, of dysentery – *both of them*! Can you imagine? All those guns and those little boys die like that. Horrid, perfectly horrid.'

Richard was suddenly restless. In his haste to get from house to house he had not thought of the consequences. Now, despite Sarah Childs' vapid discourse being both haphazard and tuneless, by hammering at the keys there was the risk she might eventually strike the right note – or the wrong one: she might refer to his debt. Joseph was certainly of a temperament too stolid to mention such a thing, but his wife? Stupidity was a kind of deception, after all, and one could never be sure whether the right note masked the playing of a wrong one, or a wrong note masked the perfect timing of a right. There was a short silence before, letting out an indeterminate grunt, he reached for his tea.

Sarah Childs sprang to her feet: she had forgotten her cup! Because that was what silence was for – drinking tea. Otherwise they'd be sat there all morning. Sip, remark, sip, remark – that was how it worked. And before one knew it the cup was empty; someone said, 'Oh is that the time?'; another said, 'Lovely to see you' and 'Do come again'; the front door was shut; and it was all over and a sigh of relief could be breathed. She collected the cup from the sideboard, sat down and took a sip. Placing the cup back on the saucer she opened her mouth to speak – then noted he was minded to take another sip, and followed suit herself. At length, like a pair of watchful duellists, in a slow, mirrored movement they set their cups on the table.

Sarah Childs glanced at the mantelpiece clock and then looked closely at Richard. Really, she thought in conclusion, it was such a pity when a mother's looks were spoiled by a son. Adeline was a pretty creature (too pretty for a charlatan like Jack Wilson, certainly), but where an appearance of femininity could be adorable in adolescence, by middle age it gave a man a distinctly prim and bumptious air. A man had far more distinction when he looked like a woman with the face of a horse.

'And so what are your plans now?' she resumed conversationally. 'Are you going to carry on with the... the... well – what you were doing before?'

'The *London Times*? No, that's finished with. I've just been engaged as a... private secretary, in the Ministry of X.'

'Oh my, that sounds very exciting,' she said with the flatness of one who found it to be anything but.

'Yes, there's a great deal to—' He broke off in the face of Sarah Childs' expression of frowning perplexity, then concluded simply, 'I'm certain it will be.'

Sarah Childs was indeed perplexed. A *secretary*? Was that not a little peculiar? Surely that was what women were, not men?

'Well, that's excellent,' she decided; she recollected the poster said that there were always those '*others*'. 'It's good to have something to come back to. Lots of the young men haven't got anything at all, have they?'

'No. It'll be difficult, I'm sure.'

'No doubt, no doubt. Still, one has to do something, doesn't one?'

Richard's reply was an economical nod. A silence again descending, Sarah Childs cast another covetous look at her needlework – and back at the clock.

'The devil finds work for idle hands, doesn't he?' she mused negligently.

'Yes, exactly.'

She turned to the window. 'But then one can't imagine being outside looking for work in weather like this, can one? Frightful this cold, isn't it?'

'Yes – although it was a good deal colder in Austria.'

'Where?'

'Austria.'

'Oh – and what's that?'

'It's—'

'Oh yes, of course, of course,' she cut across briskly – none the wiser. She rifled through her parlour questions. Then, with sudden pertinence, one sprang to mind and she asked, 'Do you speak French?'

Richard's brow furrowed in consternation. 'They speak German,' he said.

'No, no, not German. Do you speak *French*?' Sarah Childs' thoughts had motored ahead. A keen glance at the clock this time had purpose.

With an almost identical sense of purpose, Richard glanced at the clock too. And he would have swallowed the remainder of his tea in a single gulp had he not been pre-empted by the sound of the door latch and the sight of Sarah Childs bolting from the room.

Her sharp, hectoring tones were soon audible in the hallway. In attendance of Joseph's imminent entrance Richard finished his tea. His relief merely hastened his determination not to stay beyond a brief exchange of pleasantries. Whatever wind had blown him the short distance to the Childs' house had been deadened by Sarah Childs' prattling company. He would, perhaps, find another opportunity to speak to Joseph. Thus, putting cup back to saucer, he stood up – at the very moment that Sarah Childs came bustling back into the room.

'I've just noticed the time. I really must be—'

'You said you speak French, didn't you?'

The force of Sarah Childs' demand nearly threw Richard down again. His tilt was redressed by a forward thrust of his chin. 'No… um… well… a little.'

'Good. Can you tell Helen here that the blanket Joseph gave her yesterday he should not have done? I need to take it back.' Her face had turned rigid and pale, as if set in a cast. 'I'll tell Joseph when he returns to find her another she can have. Tell her that, please.'

Richard returned the *mitrailleuse* command with a flustered, dictionary look. Hovering in the hallway half-light behind Sarah Childs' stout frame he then discerned not the expected form of her husband, but that of a female. A female who forthwith advanced to the doorway with bristling intent.

'You want that I give the cover back?' came the pettish enquiry.

'Not the cover – the *blanket*.' A flush of intolerable sufferance rose to Sarah Childs' cheeks as she explained to Richard, 'It belonged to my mother. Joseph had no right to be giving it to anyone. I've told him a thousand times. So can you make sure she understands that I'm taking the *blanket* back.'

'*Oui, oui* – I understand.'

A warning wiggle of Sarah Childs' hips rattled both ends of her body. '*Oui, oui* – that's what she always says – *oui, oui, oui*. She says she understands, but she didn't the last time when Joseph gave her the wrong sheets. I'm sure she doesn't understand half of what she says she does. But I don't want her coming down bothering me for the blanket later. Tell her Joseph will bring her another when he gets back. She must understand that Joseph will do it, not me.'

Whereupon, in order that the physical evidence be brought forth as a sort of *ecce objectum*, Sarah Childs spun round, brushed the girl aside and hastened away up the stairs. The front room shortly resonating to the thumping sounds above, Richard took a moment to shuffle his vocabulary into order.

'*Elle... dit que...*'

'Yes, I understand,' the young lady cut in crossly. In accented English, she then proved as much. 'She is taking the blanket and 'er 'usband is giving me one more later.'

'Yes. I'm sorry... I...'

'*Non – merci.*'

Her countenance was leavened by the flash of a pursed-lip smile. Even with the benefit of the additional light of the doorway, however, the twisted mass of chestnut-brown hair that tousled down one side of her face concealed much in darkness that might otherwise have been lit. But it gave a striking boldness to her form. On top of a slender figure wrapped in a long, half-buttoned-up navy overcoat were features of dusky complexion and defiant angularity. Her face was like a slither of charcoal hewn out with an axe; it was all rough protrusions and geometry. A straight nose with a solid bridge stood out between the jagged foothills of her cheeks and jaw, and at its upturned tip arced down to a mouth as wide as a vale. Her eyebrows were fine and strong, and the shell of one ear that extruded her locks was embossed like a fossilised rock. Her eyes, well-spaced as they were, were set like a pair of half-sunk spheres, with which she stared at Richard with a sort of noble, equine pride.

'It's only sometimes she is speaking so quickly that I am 'aving some difficulties to be understanding 'er,' she said. 'That is the only thing.'

'Yes, of course,' said Richard. A palpitation caused his eyes to flit. 'Where – where are you from in France?'

'Not France. *Je suis belge*. And my name is "Hélène", *pas* "Helen".'

'Hélène is much nicer,' he smiled.

'It's true, yes? "Helen" – *mais c'est moche comme prénom, non?* – I'm sorry, you are speaking French?'

'No... but... *oui, un peu. Mais... "moche"* is...?'

'*Pas joli. Ce n'est pas beau.* You understand me? It is ugly. *Tu trouves pas?*'

'Maybe – *oui*. I'm sorry... *mon français est un peu...* How do you say "rusty"?'

'Rusty?' Her eyes hooded.

'Um... rusty – *comme le fer...*'

Her face wrinkled.

'*Oui, c'est quand tu... mélanges le fer avec l'air – avec l'oxygène.*'

Her nose sniffed. '*Rouillé?*' she posited doubtfully.

'Yes – *rouillé*, that's it.'

Her lip curled. '*Ça veut dire quoi exactement?*'

He hadn't the faintest idea. He went in search of saliva, then said with an oscillation, 'Sorry, I haven't spoken much French lately. But that's what I was... trying to say. *Mon français est rouillé*. It's rusty.'

'Ah, *tu es un peu rouillé!*' A thin smile countered the hint of condescension in her voice as she deciphered his meaning. '*Non, mais c'est bien.*'

'My German is much better,' he returned instinctively, mitigating his Gallic shortcomings by impressing his cultural breadth. It did not impress. Her expression instantly soured as her once leavened countenance darkened to pitch.

'Why do you learn *German?*' she said, the final word spat with such venom that he flinched at the force.

'Well... I –' he began, her torchlit gaze burning a hole in his throat as he desperately sought the right words '– I learnt German at university... and then worked in Austria – in Vienna – before the war.'

'Austrians, Germans – *ils sont pareils. Tous.* They are animals that...'

Her invective was cut short by Sarah Childs' thundering descent. Re-entering the front room she displayed the problematical blanket as exhibit one. 'There we are. I've taken this.'

'Ok. There is no problem.'

'Let's hope not.' Sarah Childs threw the girl a haughty look over her shoulder, clenched her teeth to a marmoset smile, and returned her attention to Richard. 'Helen here is our –' she removed the unpalatable word 'lodger' from her highly respectable mouth '– plucky little Belgian. She and her family had to flee when those beastly Germans plundered the country at the start of the war. Had their house burned to the ground and lost everything. Then little Helen came here as a refugee, didn't you?' 'Little Helen' returned 'big Sarah' a look of molten contempt, a look fully endorsed by Richard, and blithely ignored by the speaker. 'Yes, just like your mother's family as I recall, Richard. Huguenots, weren't they?'

'Yes, but I don't think you can...'

'Anyway, she's here now, aren't you dear?' She turned back to Hélène – but did her best not to look. 'She can count her blessings too – coming to a nice house in England. It's a much better place than that dirty, muddy old Belgium. And she's got herself a nice little job in an orphanage in Crouch End – haven't you, dear? You ought to visit, Richard. I've not had time to go myself yet; heavens, it's quite the other side of London – one needs to set aside a whole day for that sort of thing, you know – but it'd be a nice day out for you, I'm sure. Yes, the church is doing some wonderful work up there to help the little tykes. Really, you must go.'

'*Oui, viens,*' said Hélène. Her penetrating eyes settled on Richard to impart the wish that her tone did not so plainly convey. It was a look which, when allied to the words, thrust like two lances through his breast. His heart exposed, it beat fiercely and freely. 'Excuse me,' she then said, 'I'm sorry. But I am very tired now. I must get some rest. *A bientôt, peut-être.*'

'*Oui*,' said Richard.

'Yes, you do that, dear – get some rest,' Sarah Childs enjoined.

And with that Hélène turned away and disappeared up the stairs. Richard listened intently to the soft, beckoning diminuendo of her footfall. A moment later his ears were drummed by a cry of untold exasperation as Sarah Childs collapsed on the divan.

'Good heavens – that girl is a trial!' Her face cold and bloodless, she gasped for air as if she had just been fished from a pond. 'Rest, she says! She's always needs rest. You'd think she was down the pit fourteen hours a day, not looking after a few waifs and strays. Honestly, these continental women. It's the incense, you know. It's like one of those funny things the Orientals smoke; it clogs the body with indolence. How Joseph had the misfortune to come across her I've no idea. He could have found a nice young salesman who we'd never see from one week to the next. But no, he found some chit of a girl who sits in her room like a canary. She's always here, you know – like a wretched shadow. Every time I turn round she's beside me. I can scarcely breathe at the thought sometimes.' She flapped her hand in front of her face, though an inclination to hyperventilate was checked by a need to further lament, 'She doesn't go out. Hasn't any friends either, let alone anything like a—' She stopped dead.

Now, the idea that came to Sarah Childs did so quite unexpectedly. Indeed, when she had previously suggested he visit the orphanage she had done so in the offhand manner of one recommending a zoo to a vet as a place to shoot tigers. That said, even had she been privy to Richard's private heart-beatings or espied any amorous looks, she would have been impervious to the sound and indifferent to the sight: Sarah Childs was no Emma Woodhouse. She had not the slightest interest in assisting ill-starred lovers to find fortune. Whatever interest she did have was tackled with the same earthy pragmatism as that which presented love as the cure for anxiety, and then marriage as the cure for that love.

Her first remedial calculations were therefore primitive. If Richard could come to strike up a friendship with the girl, the girl would be less often in the house. If their friendship flourished, less often still, and so much the better. And as soon as this idea had come to her, her only regret was that it had not come sooner – before the girl had come back. Because then she would have been able to fix a date for the visit so he didn't end up wriggling out of the commitment after he'd gone. There was consequently only one way to ensure that no wriggling occurred: he had to be hooked.

'You know you really *must* go and visit her at the orphanage, Richard,' she resumed in a strain of sudden, heart-wrenched compassion. 'Now you've said you would, the poor creature would be devastated if you didn't. She's had such a terrible time. Lost all her family – and not a friend in the world, you know. Not one. Joseph and I do our best but... well, she needs someone to take her out properly, doesn't she? Someone her own age.' She paused and looked at him winsomely. Being of a mind that a lily could not be considered beautiful unless it was gilded, she continued breathlessly, 'And she's such a fragile thing too. When she's shut up in her room I can hear the little lamb crying her heart out. Oh it's awful, truly it is. So it'd be simply marvellous for her if you were to visit. Perhaps take her out for the evening afterwards: a show, the flicks, or something like that. Yes, yes, you *will* do that, won't you, Richard? For *her* sake.'

If Sarah Childs knew quite how superfluous her entreaties were (the whole time she spoke Richard thought of nothing but the logistics of reaching north London) she would have considered them a waste of valuable needlework time. As she did not, the solemn affirmation that Richard gave that he would do all she asked gladdened her immeasurably. So much so that she almost considered his having come to the house that morning a blessing. Indeed, it was lucky she had been home; her husband would never have thought of the benefits he might bring to her. Oh no – not *him*!

And so, with the morning brought to a satisfactory conclusion, it was with a touch of something approaching warmth that she concluded, 'Now, you said you were off, didn't you? It's a pity you couldn't stay longer, but it's been lovely to see you. I'll be sure and let Joseph know that you passed. He'll be delighted. Anyway, we'll see each other again very soon, I hope.' And then, as she ushered him out the front door, so as to make absolutely sure, she repeated, 'Don't forget the orphanage, will you? Crouch End. Number two, Nelson Road. You *must* go. She's there every day.'

Well, almost every day. But exceptions provided excuses.

Chapter 15

The Under Secretary was a blizzard of action. With the Paris conference about to begin there were any number of recommendations and representations that had to be put to the prime minister, the Treasury, the foreign secretary, the colonial secretary, and a whole host of attachés, delegates and underlings for approval. Then, once put, that had to be rephrased and put again: myopia was as common an affliction as deafness! This was supplementary to all the regular correspondence with this or that Member, one place or the other, some official or clerk (with recommendations, representations etc. etc.) – all of which had to be conducted with a delicate balance of diplomacy, persuasion, tenacity and concession to ensure that, when the moment came, the Under Secretary's vision would be triumphantly acclaimed by the requisite numbers.

Paris, the Under Secretary declared one evening over dinner (Richard partook of a glass of Margaux, the Under Secretary having poured scorn on the thought of champagne: he couldn't abide the stuff – it was dry as dust and gave him a headache for a week), was simply the start of the journey; Mr Wilson's points were nothing but towns to go through, or else to go round. No one had yet marked on the map where the end destination was to be. Yes, yes, he affirmed, there would be handshakes en route, and no doubt treaties galore; but what terms were then signed, what countries were formed, where the borders were drawn – as of that day not a single man knew! This destination was theirs to decide and to drive the world to, he said: together, Richard; you and I.

The Under Secretary's dauntless enthusiasm was like a torch to Richard's plastic soul: he was buckled and twisted in the heat of the flames. The long hours Richard consequently undertook to prove his conviction and loyalty (after all, once clasped, the hand of the hand that held the pen could not so easily be let go) meant it was therefore not until nearly three weeks after his visit to the Childs' house that he felt sufficiently assured of his position to request an afternoon to attend to a personal matter. It was a request, it should be said, made at a moment exactly contemporaneous to Sarah Childs casting her needlework aside, throwing her arms in the air, and crying in anguish of the treachery of men!

'Why of course, my dear fellow! Take all the time that you need!' the Under Secretary proclaimed with selfless effulgence. The construction of Europe would not be done on the whip like the pyramids at Giza, he said. He was not a Pharaoh!

Richard's devotion to the Under Secretary was not to say he had not thought about Hélène during this time. He most certainly had. His occupation had simply been the motor of his love.

Love? Already? Well, a little water every day makes the garden green.

Love, of course, was hitherto not a word which had touched either Richard's thoughts or lips. If it had been put to him as to why that should be before he entered Sarah Childs' front room, he would most likely have replied with imperishable solemnity that he neither knew the word's meaning, nor cared a fig for its source. Love, he would have said, was the lust of the flesh and the eyes; it was an obstacle to be crossed like a river in flood; it was a rock on the path to be kicked. As evidence he would have cited his time in Vienna. The pageantry played out by the emperor and his once fairy queen had deceived the people and rotted the woods through and through. It was a fantasy for fools, this love.

This, however, would be to look with his own eyes and not with those of others. For on the grand stage of continental seduction (and, wittingly or no, he had trod those very boards) Richard's performance was defiantly English. When he had sought to express interest, his looks were too fervent; when he tried to express fervour, he was thought to be drunk; when his gestures were subtle, they were roundly ignored; when his gestures were bold, he was thought to be rude. Worst of all, given his stage was Vienna, he abjured the idea of a dalliance being a byway to love, ignorant as he was that love is most often found by way of a dalliance. In short, he was like the crab of his birth: all pincers and shell.

If the unpleasant sight of his features in the hotel mirror had done anything it had been to highlight his own lack of youth. But his wondrous engagement with the Under Secretary had since confirmed his chosen path and equipped him with means. And whilst these means could in no wise be equated to a fortune, they nevertheless permitted him entry into the cadre to whom the acknowledged truth was applicable: that a single man in possession of one must be in want of a wife.

'*Viens*' – that was what she had said. '*Viens*' – that was how she bid him. '*Viens*' – the word blew like a zephyr through his soul. But it was her look that had infected his eye. It was as deep a brown as ever soil turned by the plough, as piercing as a sickle point. It was a beam of light that shone on his path. And in the instant it did, it was clear they already understood everything of the least importance about each other. By working at the orphanage she understood he too was an orphan; through exile from her native land she understood he too had suffered that pain. These were the shoots of productive love that sprouted from the earth. They were the solid foundation on which to build a home. All else, thereafter, would yield to the circumstances.

Some of these circumstances, naturally, had been beyond Richard's control. Not long after the encounter at the Childs' house the freezing air had warmed the necessary fractions of a degree to let fall a thick blanket of snow that covered the city to the four corners of its span – and far beyond. This had coincided with the long-threatened arrival of the strikes. The dockers struck first, were soon joined by the transport workers, then by the railway workers, and then – this being worst of all for those who hung their hat on service as life's true propellant – the waiters. And whether Mother Nature or the Bolsheviks was responsible for this outrage very much depended on how much time each individual was prepared to spend waiting for a bus, how much coffee one had to imbibe in a day, and how much confidence one placed in one's legs. Although Richard's confidence in his own could not have been greater, to have embarked on an expedition to the northern steppe of Crouch End at an earlier date would have clearly been impractical, had the Under Secretary's demands not made it impossible.

Come the day, there was still snow everywhere (though much had hardened to ice) and it remained savagely cold, not least on account of the wind. These elements he was exposed to without respite for the duration of the journey, the bus he caught being one only in name. An army lorry hastily converted to fill the public transportation need, a rickety staircase was tacked onto the back, there was no inside or cover, and there were only two narrow benches for seats. Forced to stand all the way, he alternated which hand was stuffed into his new Liberty's coat and which clung to the metal bar overhead. In spite of the temperature, though, the sweat still formed on the small of his back.

Three weeks was a considerable length of time to pass and then to arrive unannounced, he realised. But having made his request at the end of the day and been granted the next afternoon there had been scarce opportunity for him to signal intentions. Not that he would have done so: advance notice held out the prospect of early rejection. There were therefore multiple risks in his going in such fashion: she might not be there, she might be too busy, he might be unwanted. He might even have been forgotten! Thus did the butterflies fly in his stomach; thus did his legs become weaker; thus did the tension keep rising and pain the base of his spine; thus did he sweat.

Arriving at the orphanage, he had not been forgotten. Quite the opposite in fact. A broad, affectionate smile was accompanied by the thought expressed that *he* had forgotten *her*! Be that as it may, despite the warmth of her greeting and the welcome of his appearance, she retained sufficient reserve to tell that love was more than a look.

And never the twain shall meet.

Of course he had not forgotten, he said.

The orphanage was a large Victorian end-of-terrace house at the top of Crouch Hill. The house's pale brick façade found its colour and contrast in a series of narrow windows and bright red architraves, and a panorama of the heights of suburban north London had at its centre point the distant acropolis of Alexandra Palace.

He had arrived at just the right time (*au bon moment*), she said as they stood on the porch. The older girls had just begun their afternoon lessons and the younger ones were playing out in the yard. This meant she was free to give him a tour of the building... if he wanted? Of course he did, he said. But it was so small (*vraiment petit*), she said, that it would not take so long. Richard did not mind. There were only girls? he then asked as they passed beneath the lintel together. Yes, she said, only girls.

Hélène's dress was plain and earthen save a stretch of lace around the collar and some twilling at the hems. Her hair was held in a loose chignon, though its forest weight rebelled against the pins and clips; beneath the falling curls he glimpsed her neck: it was as smooth as the ribbed sea-sand.

And so the tour began.

The driving forces of conversation being commonly known, egotism, acquiescence, curiosity and confession are among the most popular. Time, however, remains the supreme force. For time marries all types and breeds all manner of talk. How long it is before this talk becomes barren depends not on what the individuals concerned wish to say to each other, but on what they do not.

It was very kind of him to come, she said. It was his pleasure, he replied. She must forgive him, he then said; he wished he could have come sooner, but because of the strikes and the snow... and he'd been so busy at work – he had a new job at the Ministry of X – he'd barely had a moment to step out of the office. That sounded very serious and important, she replied earnestly, if he never had time to leave work. It was, he said.

She had come to England (she said, when Richard asked) in 1915, and she had been working at the orphanage for almost two years. She was happy, she said, but she was often so tired; it was a long way to travel every day, and it was a lot of work with the girls. She needed so much sleep to recover: Mrs Childs did not understand this. But she did not want to leave the orphanage. She loved being there. The girls were like her little sisters (*mes petites frangines*), and the most important thing, for her, was that they were happy and safe. Did he have children? she asked, looking at him with the same intense, prying eyes as before. No, he replied; not yet.

He should learn to speak French properly, she said, flashing a coquettish smile; that way they could speak French to each other. It was so difficult for her to speak English all of the time. She could not express herself in the way that she could in French. Yes, said Richard;

it was the same for him when he had been in Vienna. People never understood how tiring it was to speak in a different language all day, trying to express what you felt. Yes, she said, like Mrs Childs.

Upon reaching the top of the house, they did no more than promptly turn and make their way back down the stairs again. In the courtyard at the back a small group of younger girls were gaggled up against the wall playing some rhythmical number game and clapping their hands. A pattering of footsteps behind Richard and Hélène announced one missing from the number. The girl's slim, bony frame was not allowed an instant egress; she was collared by Hélène and tightly embraced.

'How are you, *ma petite*? Is everything ok?' She stroked the girl's limp blonde hair and kissed her on the crown. The girl nodded. Hélène put her hand to the girl's forehead. 'Are you sure? *T'as pas chaud, non?*' The girl shook her head in restive befuddlement; Hélène was doubtful. 'Maybe we get the doctor to look at you later, *oui?*' The girl hid a scornful look, and for reply simply wriggled free of the noose to rejoin her comrades outside.

She would shortly have to get the girls into their class, she said. Yes, he said, and fell silent. After she would have a little break and would have to sit down. There was a tea room very close by, she said. He could take her there if he wanted? Of course, he said; he would very much like to.

Twenty minutes later they set off, with the school left in order. Hélène was dressed in the same navy overcoat she had worn on her debut in Sarah Childs' hallway. The tea room was on the high street at the foot of the hill, and as they descended, Richard's full concentration was deployed in making sure he didn't slip on the ice. Apart from a solitary observation of the distant palace the short walk was therefore conducted in silence.

The tea room had two large, bow-fronted windows of single glass panes, with a series of decorative panels along the top. They entered and took a table by the window.

Did she not want to go back to Belgium now that the war was over? Richard asked after they had ordered the tea. – No, she said, she would never go back to Belgium; everything had changed. Richard nodded and thought of his father. – Everything had changed for him too, he said. He had been in hospital in Vienna when the war started, and then he had been interned. He had known very little about the progress of the war. Occasionally he would read snippets from an Italian newspaper smuggled into the camp, and sometimes he would get news from a new internee, but mostly he had had no idea. It was strange to have been a prisoner of the war's violence, he said, and to have known almost nothing about it. – What was *interned*? she asked. Richard explained and she gave a sad nod. – But he was lucky, she said; she would have liked to have been in hospital and interned and to have known nothing about the violence of the war. – Yes, he said.

Her family had been forced to flee from their village (it was close to Louvain) when the Germans arrived, she said. Did he know Louvain? she asked. – No, he said. – She said nothing for a moment. It was better like that, she then said. She hated the Germans. She could still smell their filthy unwashed bodies, hear the clumping of their hobnailed boots, and see the rows of grey advancing through the dust. 'The good will pay with the bad,' she said; that's what they said: 'The good will pay with the bad'. – That was when they burned her house? he asked. She looked at him strangely. – Yes, she said, after a pause. And when the trenches were dug in the autumn, she said, they were fortunate to be on the side of the French; many families she knew had not been so lucky. Then they went to Arras. After her father refused to move any further, she said. The only thing he wanted to do was return to Belgium, even though it was impossible. But she had to get away, she said; she could not bear to be so close to the Germans. That was why she had come to England. – Her family was alive? he asked. She fell silent again, then fixed her eye boldly on him. – Yes, she said expressionlessly, but her father had died two years ago. There was only her mother and sister now. Why did he ask if her family was alive? she asked with a twitch of her lips – Mrs Childs had told him that she had no family, he said; she said she had no one. Hélène cursed the woman and her stupid inventions. – She was always making things up, she said; she was always lying, she said; she knew nothing, she said. Richard cursed her too. – She had always been like that, he said; that's what his father used to tell him. – But Mr

Childs is very nice, she said. He was always asking her if she wanted to go for a walk with him, or to go to church, or to do some other thing. – Did she go, he asked, to church? – No, she said. It was not the same church, and she was too angry with God. Richard nodded. He understood her.

Did she miss her mother and sister? he asked. – It was difficult with them, she said. Her mother was always favouring her sister and thinking she was the best. She did not get on with her sister; that was always how it was (*comme ça depuis toujours*), she said. Richard nodded and thought of his brother. He understood her. – That was always how it had been for him with his brother too, he said. – But she was sad she could not see her little sister, she said. She adored her and had wanted her to come to England with her, but her mother would not allow her. – She had *two* sisters? he asked. – Yes, she said.

Why was he in Austria before the war? she asked. – He said that he had been working for the *London Times*. He said he had wanted to try and show people how rotten the empire and the Habsburg monarchy were. He had wanted to mount a famous campaign so the whole world would see. But it was impossible, he said. The people did not want to see; they preferred to be blind. It was because of that that millions of innocent people had died, because of that that people like her had had to flee their homes and their country. She nodded. – It was always the innocent who paid, she said; it was always the innocent who had to flee. The good always paid with the bad, she said. – Yes, he said, but that would soon change.

'*Oui*,' she said.

Her deep eyes rested gently upon him, like two sun-kissed pebbles that had been placed on his chest. She flashed another thin-lipped smile, then she sipped her tea.

Yes, he thought, it was clear; she understood. She understood him.

Chapter 16

About a week later Richard was summoned into the Under Secretary's office. The Under Secretary was standing behind his desk, his head bowed, his face almost translucent from the reflection of the lamp off the polished walnut surface. He did not acknowledge Richard's entry, but continued instead to rhythmically tap the envelope on the desk before him with his middle finger, like a telegrapher entranced by the act of transmission. When at last he looked up he swiftly averted his eyes, as if the sight were too painful to behold. He scanned the room for a balm. A brisk movement of tergiversation drew him forth to stand in front of a painting hung between two large front windows – through which, despite the late afternoon gloaming, could be still discerned the foreshortened vista of iron railings, pavement, street, trees and square. The orange glow of the fire crept from the grate and enriched the blue hues of the carpet around him; but it did not extend to a height to illuminate the painting. Richard already knew the details though: it was the court and spectators of *The Championship Match*.

'I was there, you know,' the Under Secretary mused abstractly. 'That's me, hidden behind the post. Terrible match. Captain Dangleby, the chap serving –' the figure was indicated by a finger '– was a disgrace. The ball had to bounce five times before he ever believed his shots were not-up. He kept staring at the marker like a stuck pig. Ruined the game. You'd think an officer would have a bit of integrity and fair play about him, wouldn't you?' He fell silent before, with a solicitous glance back at Richard, he said in a strain touching appeal, 'One has a duty to behave with responsibility, no matter how much one is determined to win, don't you agree?'

'Of course.'

Richard's solid affirmation brought a reassured smile to the Under Secretary's lips. The change in countenance was fleeting. Turning to the fire, he took a poker from the rack, prodded the fluffy white edges of coal, and stared into the rousing flames with the glassy intensity of a pyromancer in search of his light. Then, with apparent decisiveness, he replaced the stoker, returned to the desk and picked up the envelope. With ebbing resolve he flapped it between his fingers, then placed it back on the desk and made a couple of indeterminate movements neither one way nor the other. He finally picked it up again and was shortly back in front of the fire.

Had Richard not been paddling in the deep pools of Hélène's eyes and charting the future course of their voyage together upon his summons to the office he would here have marked the disjuncture in the Under Secretary's usually serene motion. Had the polar lights of the lamp and fire not distracted him from the finer adumbrations of the scene he would have noted the discomfort which furrowed the Under Secretary's hitherto impeccable brow. And had the rough clamour of hooves and horns outside not been so loud, he would have detected the doubt in the Under Secretary's always assured tones. For these were the unmistakeable signs of his desperately conflicted emotions.

The Under Secretary held the envelope out to Richard.

'This is for you,' he said, his grasp remaining firm as Richard reached out to receive it. 'It contains a matter of some considerable urgency, and no little delicacy. That's why I'm entrusting it to your charge.'

'Yes, of course,' Richard averred with legatine fidelity.

'You are to cable the contents to the person and address on the envelope. Any future communication between you and the individual concerned – should it be required – is thereafter your responsibility. Is that clear?'

'Yes.' The envelope being hereupon released, a downward glance was insufficient for Richard to decipher either name or address. 'I'll keep you informed of everything,' he confirmed.

'No, no!' the Under Secretary shot out; a reflex made to snatch the envelope back. He mastered the instinct, but could not conceal the anxiousness in his tone. 'You don't need to inform me about anything – I don't need to know. The communication is only for you. Do you understand? *Only you.*'

There was a short silence as the Under Secretary fixed his celestial gaze on Richard, the fire's reflection rippling across the whites of his eyes.

'Yes,' said Richard.

The Under Secretary flashed another smile: a sign of relief, if not one of purgation. For, already knowing more than as much as he wished of the contents, it was this knowledge that lay at the heart of his tumultuous conflict. Its origins could be sourced to the previous day's breakfast.

*

However, before breakfast is partaken of it is necessary to expound upon an essential aspect of the Under Secretary's character. Private means and a public school meant that his entrance into the political sphere was one of conviction rather than profession. As a profession he esteemed it a low-born one practised by those who found the financial rewards of shopkeeping to be too marginal and the ethical demands of the law too taxing. Politics could therefore only be elevated to nobility if carried out with Periclean vision and Christian morality. For this reason did he loathe the Machiavellian arts of political intrigue: arts which infected the Continent and made the Channel an obligatory moat. All who knew him knew this. There was no deceit in his beliefs, no duplicity in his actions. It was, he believed, only by dickering in the details that mankind was dragged down from the mountainous peaks of great ideas to the sloughs of perfidy, vice and corruption. Nowhere was this credo epitomised better than during his morning game of real tennis with the professional at the Queen's Club. He did not debase himself with plotting galleries, chases and devising fiendishly spinning serves. All that mattered was the winning of sets. It was this grand-plan philosophy which he believed underpinned his ability to force every set to a deciding game, no matter how poorly he played. In the season his playing hours were a matter of regimen. It was consequently no surprise that when he walked off court the previous morning he should have been greeted by General Shawcross and invited to breakfast.

The general was well-known to the Under Secretary: he was a cousin of his sister-in-law and a regular guest on the 12th. He had retired from the army after the South African War, but been re-engaged by the War Office in late 1914 as an informal liaison between the Ministry and the king. 'The Buffer', he was known as. With a long, jowly face of chameleon complexion, a pair of hard, lugubrious eyes, and a mane of white hair valancing a narrow, bald head, he possessed an easy-going authoritarianism that suited the role. As such it was not long before he had become an essential reed-bank through which the rapid waters of information passed. The coming end of the war had threatened to uproot him though. And so, with that peculiar tenacity of weeds and old age, he had clung to his ground: he had inveigled himself onto any number of committees and subcommittees so as to ensure he remained a vital artery of information and could not be cut like a clot when the last shot was fired. In February 1919 such a person proved to be just the man the government and War Office were after.

Breakfast was gammon and eggs. General Shawcross was not a man for ostentation: he was perfectly at home with the rough and ready nature of the club's cafeteria facilities (the flooring was linoleum, the napery gingham, the food on the greasy). One did not come to a sports club to fuss with fine dining, he declared, before attacking his food with the same ferocity as he had once attacked the Dervish. Nor was he a man to beat about the bush: he had sought the Under Secretary specifically, he said. The Under Secretary replied with felicity (his morning's play having been superb – the professional had been fortunate as to only win on the last point of the match) that he would have been distraught to have breakfasted alone and not been sought by a soul. The general, always receptive to good humour when the subject was serious, laughed heartily – and considered that as sufficient preamble.

As the Under Secretary well knew, the general said, following the armistice the Austrian emperor had withdrawn to his hunting estate at Eckartsau, near the Czech border. Of course, unlike the Kaiser, he hadn't abdicated. It was a decision the general considered by far the most sensible, not least given his youth and initiatives to end the war early. But although he hadn't abdicated he was clearly no longer in power. This had created a problem. It wasn't a problem – the general interrupted himself – as far as *he* was concerned: the emperor was a damned sight better than the bunch of Reds and Jews the country had just elected. The Kaiser's impetuous act of abdication had been as foolish as his itching for war in the first place; now he'd created a political vacuum that threatened the return of good order. Anyway, said the general, whatever the rights and wrongs, the facts were still the facts.

'This is the present state of affairs,' he said. 'No disagreement with that?'

The Under Secretary signalled his generous accord and spooned some sugar into his coffee. The general, leaning back in his chair, took a bite of his toast, then resumed in his silky, stentorian timbre.

His Majesty had recently received a letter from Prince Sixtus, the emperor's brother-in-law: it was a request for support for the imperial family. However, this support, the general observed, was of the sort that was due from the Austrian government, and where it was not given, could naturally not come from elsewhere without their consent.

The Under Secretary, listening attentively, took the opportunity to interpose on a point of acuity. When had the request for support been made? he asked.

'Was it before or after the Austrian elections?'

'Oh before, before,' returned the general, offhand. 'Several weeks ago now, I should say.'

'Several *weeks*?'

'At least.'

'And what reply has been given?'

The general's mouth was full – hence the pause.

'What reply? Why, nothing's been said at all, of course,' he said amid a splutter of yolk. 'How could anything be said when we didn't know *how* to reply?'

'Surely some response must have been conveyed,' the Under Secretary pressed with a touch of pique – for he could not abide rudeness, 'if only to acknowledge receipt of the request?'

'Oh no,' the general replied, deeply guffawing. 'To have done that would have been tantamount to *acknowledging* that we didn't know how to reply.' The general buttered his toast and trimmed a slice of gammon to the dimensions required. 'So, anyway, the point is that as it stands now the War Office wants nothing whatsoever to do with the matter, the Foreign Office has told the foreign secretary they want nothing whatsoever to do with something the War Office wants nothing to do with, and the prime minister wants nothing to do with something that won't win him any votes. Of course, we've got no idea what the French position is, but then nor do the French,' he observed dryly, as his teeth cracked into the toast. After a few moments' loud mastication he swilled some coffee and continued, 'The problem for all of them is the king. The request was made to him personally, and he insists that something be done. He's horrified at the prospect of the same thing happening to the Habsburgs as to the tsar and his family. Eckartsau, Ekaterinburg – they even sound alike, don't they, eh?'

The Under Secretary eschewed his choice of comestibles and took a draught of his coffee instead. 'Yes, almost, I suppose,' he said.

'Well, not exactly alike – but we all understand His Majesty's fears, don't we, eh? Impossible not to, not when this damned Bolshie hullaballoo's running amok on our streets too now! Because it's not just a matter of what *might* happen to the family if they're left where they are: it's who it'd be done *by*. That's the predicament, you see. We can't let the Bolsheviks run riot and do as they please all over Europe, can we, eh?'

'Certainly not,' the Under Secretary said with measured disapproval, aware that the general had not specifically sought him merely to inform him of a predicament. His cup empty, he turned to the waiter and ordered more coffee.

'And some more toast!' the general cried out, disgruntled. 'They never give you enough bloody toast. They treat it like a damned delicacy. You can win the bloody Derby more easily than getting more bread in this country. Anyway, in short, the government has accepted it has a moral obligation to ensure the imperial family's safety. And so within the strict terms of this *moral obligation* it's agreed to the prince's request for support. We can't have a family butchered just for who they are now the war's over, can we? What'd it say about us if we win the war and let that sort of thing happen, eh? It's a question of what's morally right – that overrides any political concerns, don't you agree, Phillip? Eh?'

The Under Secretary's immediate reply was supplanted by the replenishments of coffee and toast. Thereafter he chose to remain pensive and silent: the general's step to Germanity was always a sign of intent. And whilst the general manifested a certain indifference to the Under Secretary's agreement or otherwise by helping himself to another mouthful of gammon, there was at the same time little escaping the expectant gleam that shone in his eyes while he did so. The Under Secretary could be in no doubt that upon his suitable response would depend the direction of their further discourse.

'Exactly,' he said, finally. 'The moral argument always supersedes the political. Given the circumstances it would be reprehensible to sit and do nothing.'

At this, The Buffer returned a look of deep satisfaction. 'Excellent. I knew you'd agree, Phillip. One must make decisions according to one's principles. Now, in terms of this support – this *moral* support, I stress – nothing military, you understand?'

'Quite so.'

'Well then, in these terms, the best person to effect this support has already been found: a colonel – a distant relation of the king, used to hunt with the Archduke Ferdinand in Austria before the war. Knows the country pretty well I gather. He's already in Italy doing some liaison work or other and the War Office has agreed to release him for the task. You see, it has to be absolutely clear that he's not acting in any official War Office capacity – as if they sent him. Because if it was understood that they'd sent him it'd be seen as support for the Habsburg throne, when it's nothing of the sort; it's only supporting the family. Of course we can't just send an officer and let him make up things on the hoof, hope things turn out for the best. Certainly not. So someone's got to be responsible for him, give him some direction when he needs it. Someone who's not going to be seen, should the question arise, as being linked to any *official* policy. You see?'

The Under Secretary did. Plainly. However, any circumspection was given no opportunity to express itself beyond the benign smile that remained settled on his face, for the general, having mounted the ramparts, keenly sat forward, brushed the crumbs from his tunic, and said in a pitch that was akin to a peroratory roar, 'I know you despise this confounded cloak-and-dagger stuff, Phillip. I do too. It's not what a military man sticks a feather in his cap for, that's for sure. Orders are orders in my book. There's none of this wash about official or unofficial. But that's what happens when you let these backsliding civilians have a hand in the country.' Whatever disapproval the general here attested to was promptly disavowed by the stiletto glint in his eyes, and he continued in the conspiratorial undertone of one for whom the rapid waters of information had produced a thirst as unquenchable as that of a bite from the serpent Dipsas. 'The prime minister has, however, asked me to you tell you personally that he has for some time looked with dispassion and equanimim... equanit... hang it, I can't even say the blasted word! That's that politician mumbo jumbo for you – equanimity – there we go, that's it, *equanimity* – on any proposal considering the future federation of the Danube states, so long as it was popularly endorsed by the people concerned. It's a subject he says he knows is very close to your heart.' Just how close the general was himself in ignorance of, though in the Under Secretary's fixed countenance not a hint of this truth could be gleaned. 'That such a federation might fall under the aegis of the present emperor, the prime minister considers a matter of eventuality – although one which should have no substantive bearing on the federation of the states themselves. To this end he is keen to impress his ardent wish that no precipitous attempt is made to promote such a federation as might have an injurious effect on the present negotiations in Paris. Idealism must have its time in the sun, he says, before pragmatism moves it back to the shade.' Concluding, the general collapsed into his seat and exhaled volubly, exhausted by the syllables. After a moment's respite he removed his cigarette case from his pocket. 'Good God, Phillip – I hope you understood all that, eh? You know, I'm just an old army codger, good for the saddle and a sabre – not that that's any worth any more, mind. But there you have it – that's what the prime minister wanted you to know. All perfectly clear to a smart fellow like yourself though, eh?'

In spite of an aspect of imperturbable serenity the Under Secretary felt a rush of excitement surge uncontrolled through his body. In the prime minister's open palm before him had been presented the dazzling jewel of all his ambition. To seize it – to possess it – would mean that the mark of his endeavours could not possibly fade. And it would be at the price of but the sleightest of hands. The general was not known as 'The Buffer' for nothing.

Shortly after the Under Secretary and General Shawcross had parted ways, the Under Secretary understood that the *someone* alluded to could of course not possibly be him. Certainly not. Direct communication between the colonel and the Under Secretary for the Ministry of X would be seen as just as official as anything sent from a great office of state. But if the responsible someone was, say, no more than an assistant secretary – why, that could never be understood as indicative of government *policy*. Moreover, a colonel of such pedigree would be highly unlikely to correspond on such a delicate mission – and, if he did, not with some junior clerk. All that was therefore needed for the prize to be grasped was but one simple telegram.

*

By the time the Under Secretary had drafted the telegram and called Richard into his office, knowledge and reflection had roused him to conflict. It was a conflict not just concerning the Machiavellian means, but whether he should share them with Richard. The fear of disillusionment had proved to be the sight that he could not behold. It threatened to expose him to the truth that he already knew: that, whatever the merits of the deed, deception lay at its core. And, with one deceit, so tempting would be the next. It would be the first thread in the unravelling of his very being! For this reason did he decide to veil the act, although he could hardly deny all *knowledge* of it.

'You should of course inform me if something urgent arises, Richard – of course,' he said in the firm, amenable tones with which he was accustomed to speaking. 'But it's highly unlikely there will be. You will likely send the telegram and never hear another word.'

And with that concord the act was concluded.

When Richard left the office and closed the door behind him he did two things: he firstly resolved on returning to the orphanage as soon as he could, and then he read the address on the telegram. It read:

Colonel Linton, Hotel San Danieli, Venice.

Part III

*Strange to no longer desire one's desires. Strange
to see meanings that clung together once, floating away
in every direction.*

Rainer Maria Rilke, *Duino Elegies*

Chapter 17

Colonel Linton's family line could be traced back with ne'er a hint of bastardy to before the Norman Conquest. His ancestors, it is said, descended with the dragons from the west. There was scarcely one not immortalised in some ancient lay as an allusive bird or wise old goat, and then, when ballads no longer sufficed as a record of lives, one whose portrait did not bear down from the panelled corridors and polished staircases of the great Linton estate. There were soldiers, courtiers, diplomats, explorers, financiers, two governors and one poet – among a host of others depicted in all their armoured, ruffed, bewigged and wing-collared majesty by the Van Eyck or Bellini of the day – those whose contribution to the grandeur of England lay not in such exploits as to require the penning of biographies or the erection of plinths, but in their simple devotion to the glory of the estate, through the landscaping of the rose gardens, the dotting of follies, or the adding of wings, wainscot and water features that provided a tapestry of the times quite as organic as the earth tilled by the farmers whose roots themselves could be aged to the days of yeomen.

And yet, despite this antiquity, there was not a one among them whose name was embellished by anything grander than a baronetcy. For to accede to the aristocratic peaks of dukedoms, marquisates, earldoms and Garters would have been nothing less than the certain sign of patronage and vulgarity, a diminishment well beneath the dignity of the ancient line of Linton.

The Lintons were English, most certainly, but Englishmen whose blood had for centuries been spilt on foreign soil. Among Colonel Linton's forebears, for example, one had gone on King Richard's crusade, one led the charge at Castillon, one been an envoy at Pavia, one conspired the death of Wallenstein, one defied the seraskier's guns atop the parapets of Vienna, and one thrashed like a flail by the batteries at Ismail.

And Colonel Linton himself? Well, he had hunted stag in the Styrian forests, shot grouse on the Hungarian steppe, steeplechased the Wallachian plains, hiked the Rodna valley, skied the Bohemians ridges, and washed his feet in the Danube in every land its waters passed through – each one of which he knew as intimately as the great oaks that ringed the 1,000 acres of Linton land in England.

So there could be no doubt: for a man such as he to communicate with some Tomnoddy secretary was out of the question. Nor was it required.

The telegram from London contained the usual soft-soap – of course it did – but Colonel Linton had not been decorated in two wars without being able to cut through that sort of humbug. His instruction to give the emperor and empress the *moral support of the British government* was as plain as the nose on his face: it finally recognised the need to stem the swelling tide of Bolshevism. A Colonel Carrington, he was informed, would provide an officer to assist in the mission upon his arrival in Vienna. And that was all he needed to know.

Thus apprised of the telegram's contents and scope Colonel Linton replaced it on the silver salver before him. His legs extravagantly crossed, he scratched an end of his neat brown moustache, took to his coffee, picked up his smouldering cigarette, inhaled on it deeply, and after a casual exhale, peered across the shimmering stage of the Venetian lagoon from the superior elevation of the hotel terrace.

The morning sun still slung low in the sky, the light kissed the water's surface like a million skimming pearls. The natural hood of Linton's heavy brow shielded his eyes from the worst of this glare, but through the dazzle and haze he could still make out the old Jutland destroyer idling in the distance; the sky's palette of bleached yellows and blues gave it an increasingly spectral appearance, like an iron *Fighting Temeraire* evanescing before him. It was supposed to be ferrying troops across the Adriatic to the British garrison at Fiume, but seemed to him to be doing far more idling than ferrying: it had not budged in a week. This being the case, Linton deemed it emblematic of naval decrepitude. An army man to his bootstraps, he was of a conviction inviolate that the Admiralty's capacity for self-aggrandisement was only outdone by a strategic fecklessness that never went a wit further than the procurement of more and bigger ships. Not that procurement meant they were used, certainly not: they were too expensive for that. For to use them risked losing them. And so, just as at Jutland, instead of winning the war in a day, they had merely tried not to lose it. When the ships weren't ferrying soldiers who actually fought, they therefore idled. The destroyer was his case in a nutshell.

Linton's choler at the sight once again rising, it was now given purpose by the demands of his mission. And so, with no direct train to Vienna for three days, he determined to put the damned thing to use. He promptly extinguished his cigarette, stood up with an attentive thump of his boots and returned briskly inside.

Upon reaching the bottom of the grand, marble-columned staircase that led to the hotel lobby (whither he was headed in order to cable the ship's captain) his path was crossed by a smart young naval officer hurrying past. Linton summoned the officer back. The questions he put to him were of nature acerbic and blunt: Was his ship going anywhere or just sightseeing through the winter? What was its schedule? When would it sail to Fiume?

Of beanpole physique, the young naval officer possessed a small, slim face and a puckering mouth. An expression of wide-eyed inscrutability was only broken by the occasional cursory twitch of his downy, long upper lip. His reply, when it came, was delivered in the equable tones of the slightly aloof and distracted. He said that, alas, the ship had nothing to do with him; but the colonel was in luck. He had dined with the captain – Captain Ellis (a charming fellow) – two days before and had understood it would be departing the next morning. The captain would be certain to accommodate the colonel if that was his wish. Would he like him to pass on the request?

Despite the offer manifesting good form, Linton found the young man's manner obnoxious; an air of affected courtesy he took as proof of either condescension or stupidity. And confound the man if his little grey eyes wouldn't stop darting all over the place like a couple of sprats! Linton retorted that it was not a request – he was not after a cabin on a paddle cruise. He said he would contact the captain himself and promptly dismissed the officer. Shortly after, a cable was despatched to the aforementioned captain stating (not requesting) that Linton would join the ship en route to Vienna.

At sunrise Linton sloshed through the foot-high water in St Mark's Square and took a launch to the ship. He was greeted by Captain Ellis on deck. One glance was enough to establish that there was nothing charming at all about the man: he was another po-faced, puffin-featured nautical cove, one who swore by the ensign, who could never stand straight, and believed that to be buried at sea was a choice. This was soon proven once they got under way when he joined Linton on the afterdeck for a smoke. With a broad, sloping, clean-shaven face, the captain's features had been wizened by the wind to such an extent it was as if he had been raised through the light of a threemaster's rigging. He smoked an old clay pipe, and his voice had been gravelled by years of licking salt from his lips. The captain said he had been at Jutland on one of the cruisers. As this was axiomatically the only 'action' the captain had witnessed in four years of war, he forthwith proceeded to recount the tedious, unabridged circumstances of that day's non-events in the dull lexicon of latitudes, longitudes, horizons, signals, reckonings and crossing t's. Linton recognised it as nothing more than the old tale told of one who had gone hunting once in his life, spotted a tiger, missed with his shot, and then dined for the rest of his days off the tale of having scared the animal off with the size of his gun.

When the German ships had slipped off the edge of the North Sea horizon for the umpteenth, and final, time, the captain, having run out of tobacco, remarked on the beautiful sunset and signalled his return to the bridge. As the declining sun nestled into the Alpine peaks aft, Linton watched on as he bobbed away in perfect time with the chop of the waves, then as he passed through the long, cylindrical shadows cast by the huge funnels and guns and climbed the steps up to the quarterdeck. Just as he was about to disappear from view when he reached the deck, however, he stopped.

Linton's angle of vision was acute: he could make out no more than the captain's head and shoulders, but by their sharp, twisting movements it was evident the captain had been assailed by a voice, the whereabouts of which Linton was not immediately certain. This was indeed the case, for a moment later the captain was engaged in a short conversation. It was inaudible to Linton above the roar of the engine and the sea. Upon the conversation's conclusion the captain resumed his passage back to the bridge. His interlocutor, whose approach from the far side of the deck had concealed his features to Linton below, then advanced sufficiently to disclose to Linton a high, pale forehead and brow. Whatever interest Linton possessed as to the man's identity could be described as parenthetical at best, and certainly no greater than that aroused by whether one pigeon beat another in a race to a discarded breadcrumb. But his curiosity, when piqued, was of the sort that demanded satisfaction. The figure above, however, stubbornly refused to advance any further and provide it. To gain a better perspective Linton therefore retreated to the taffrail. As he did the figure shied his head teasingly so only the tips of his eyebrows could be seen. Suppressing an oath of vexation, Linton pressed himself tight to the rail, assured a firm grip, and leaned as far as he could backwards. At the farthest extent of this manoeuvre the figure suddenly took a prominent step forward. Linton's shock at the sight was such that he might have plunged either way. As it was he lurched forward. Hidden by the deck, he was struck dumb: it was the very same young officer he had addressed in the hotel! The one who told him he *understood* the ship was leaving the next day! The one who had said he had nothing to do with it! Well – what the hell was the man playing at? Linton thought. Pretending to be a damned spy?

But Linton had neither the wit nor patience to seek answers to these questions. It was simply further proof of the bottle-brained nature of the nautical sort. Thus forbearing to see either captain or young officer again, he thereafter skulked in the shadows until darkness had fallen, before secluding himself in his cabin for the rest of the voyage. When the ship docked in Fiume in the early hours of the following day he was the very first to alight. On reaching the station in Fiume he caught the train to Zagreb; at Zagreb, the day after, another completed the journey to Vienna.

Arriving in this last, Linton was greeted by snow a foot deep and still falling. Outside the Südbahnhof the white drifts were furrowed with mazy lines ploughed by the many beetle-like forms that scurried out of the station around him with their full sacks of wood, oats, vegetable and rye plundered from the surrounding countryside. A solitary fiacre stood in the forecourt. Harnessed to an animal more nag than horse, with ribs spare like a beggar's outstretched fingers, Linton was briefly minded not to inflict further punishment on the beast and shoot it dead on the spot. But as sure as the meat would be inedible and he was exhausted after sixty hours of travel, he climbed into the carriage and directed the driver to his old haunt, the Bristol Hotel on the Ringstrasse.

Chapter 18

Le petit déjeuner: 1 × coffee (of barley: no milk, no sugar), 1 × small square of baked brown bread. Colonel Linton was not detained long in the breakfast room.

Where once he had dined with archdukes, ministers, counts and ambassadors, now the barely edible food took the biscuit – or would have, except that there were none, nor any electricity, nor heating, nor warm water, nor tea, nor bed sheets, nor blankets. Not that Linton was bothered by those sort of fripperies: he was not there for pleasure.

After breakfast he therefore immediately sent a cable to the emperor. In it he stated his arrival in Vienna, his present *logement*, and that he would set off for Eckartsau the moment he had secured transportation. Then, with the Military Mission only a short walk from the hotel, he left in determined pursuit of Colonel Carrington and his officer. That distance alone was sufficient for him to witness the pitiful state of the city. He spotted urchins scavenging bones and rubbish down a back alley, a few rusty shovels disinterring the carcasses of a tram and a horse from the snow, and a couple of broken ex-soldiers zittering along to the sound of their medals tingling beneath their threadbare greatcoats. Gone indeed was the glory of empire, he knew; it was ruin, ruin everywhere.

This shameful state, he was appalled to see, applied equally to the British Military Mission. Ascending to the third floor of an unprepossessing building he had to dodge dripping, rusted pipes, puddles in the stairwells, and lumps of broken plaster scattered everywhere. Linton disliked Colonel Carrington before he even laid eyes on him: any British officer prepared to tolerate that sort of dilapidation was an utter disgrace. And as soon he entered Carrington's poky little office with its shabby little desk and filthy little window he understood exactly the type of man he would be dealing with too: a desk-wallah for whom inaction was default, and action only sanctionable according to whether his grubby little paws could get a grip on the next rung on the ladder. It was an opinion further confirmed by Carrington's immaculately dressed paunch, his shifty eyes, and the fluff of white hair with which his ears were evidently stuffed, for the man was deaf as well as a fool.

'The *Bristol*,' Linton repeated impatiently.

'Ah yes, I thought as much,' Carrington returned with cog-clicking sagacity. He said he had received a message from the War Office alerting him to the colonel's coming two days before. The War Office's instruction to him was that after they had met – that being today, he noted trenchantly – he was to have no further involvement with the colonel's mission, whatever exactly that was.

'Good. Nor do I need it,' Linton said bluntly.

Carrington fell to a ruminative silence. Years of studied horticulture had taught him that to cut even a dead branch from a rose bush one had to take the utmost care in order to avoid being pricked by its thorns. After a moment he said he had conveyed the details of Linton's impending arrival to the medical officer – a Major Fendius – who had been at Eckartsau; the major had subsequently informed the emperor.

A medical officer was not what Linton had envisioned. But as a pig was better than a poke, and as he hadn't the slightest intention in wasting any more time in Carrington's plainly pointless presence, the major would have to do.

'Very good,' he said, turning to the door. 'I'll speak with him when I get there.'

The major had since returned to Berlin, Carrington put in hastily. Linton pivoted on his heels. Carrington, sitting, gestured for Linton to do likewise; the gesture was dismissed out of hand. This was a cause of some perturbation to Carrington, for it gave the impression of haste, and he hated to be rushed. Moreover, it manifested an attitude that appeared to confirm Herr Schulze's warning to him the previous day as the pair of them strolled the Prater in search of the last living swan – the one fed by the hand of Maria Theresa. The Herr Colonel was 'a very dangerous man to be having in Vienna,' the chief of police had asserted. 'He is a man who is making trouble for everyone. Yes, yes – *everyone*.'

In his deliberate, pragmatic tones Carrington therefore pointed out to Linton that whilst it was all well and good for the War Office in far distant Whitehall to say he was to have no further involvement, that was not the reality. He was the man on the spot, after all. Colonel Linton's mission, he said (whatever *exactly* it was) had placed him in a most invidious position.

With a scornful *de haut en bas* look Linton noted this position to be sedentary. The man was the worst kind of meddling buffoon! Linton's fine Grecian nose snorted with the intent of a steeplechaser charging a brook.

'Damn a horse, man – what position would you *like* to be in?'

Colonel Carrington was a man seldom ruffled by bluster. Even so, the force of Linton's charge saw him instinctively turn to defence. He glanced down at his desk drawer before, collecting himself, noting with equanimity that whatever secrecy might be attached to the colonel's mission, both Herr Bauer and Herr Schulze were already aware of his coming. They had asked *him* to clarify British intentions concerning Linton's presence in the country, he said.

Linton's contempt soared to new heights. Why, a colonel in the British Army being asked to clarify His Majesty's Government's intentions by a bunch a socialists and shirkers – the man should be *dégommé*! He ought to have reminded them who won the war and told them to go to the deuce!

'Our intention is to give the emperor the support he's asked for. Tell them *that*,' he said with distemper.

Carrington's drawer stuck as he opened it. In the process of wriggling it free he soberly reminded Linton that Austria had had its revolution. It had been the best type, he repeated, because no one had died. This being the case, the question that any person in his position was obliged to ask was what exactly the nature of the *moral support* was intended to be.

Linton could stand no more. The man on the spot? *Carrington* was certainly not. And as it had already been established he was to have nothing more to do with the mission, there was clearly no reason to stay.

'It's the support that will be given,' he fulminated, and spun again on his heels to leave. But he had almost forgotten. 'As it's not this Major chappie, I'll have my damned officer though.'

Carrington, having removed the letter he had been seeking from the drawer, stood up with it in hand. He asked in calm, solicitous terms what officer Linton was referring to.

Linton flushed his greatcoat behind him, unsheathed the telegram from his trouser pocket and plunged it like a dagger at Carrington. 'This one,' he said.

Carrington examined the telegram's contents scrupulously. On concluding, his response was functional. His orders came from the War Office; this one did not. He had received no order to provide Linton with an officer and knew nothing about it. Besides, he added (unnecessarily, but for the sake of good will), he had no such officer in Vienna to give. Linton had better ask – he glanced at the telegram and squinted at the bottom of the print – the fellow Wilson about it.

Linton's features were touched with apoplexy. No wonder the War Office didn't trust the rabbit-sucking fool with any information! 'Hell and scissors – why *are* you here, man?' he exclaimed. 'Is there anything you *do* know?'

Indeed there was. Carrington's decision not to give the letter presently in his hand to Herr Schulze in the Prater as he had originally intended had proven to be prudent: experience had taught him how to protect himself from the thorns. He offered Linton the letter by way of a parry.

After a moment of puzzled hesitation as to what on earth he was being given, Linton snatched the paper, unfolded it, and furiously read it.

'Where did you get this?' Linton barked as soon as he'd finished.

Carrington's response was matter-of-fact. He had received it shortly before the cable from the War Office. He was not inclined to believe there was a scrap of truth in it – most of the assassination plots he heard were nothing but rumours and will-o'-the-wisp.

'Then why the hell are you giving me this one?'

Carrington scratched his side whiskers in earnest. His calculation had been purely pragmatic. If Linton's mission were indeed for the extraction of the emperor – and, given events in Hungary, there was no doubt in his mind that it was – if Linton were to believe the emperor's life at imminent risk he would be forced to act precipitately to remove him from the sphere: specifically, Carrington's sphere. If there was any truth in the plot, Carrington would have handed it to just the right person at just the right time, and so done just the right thing. If there was no truth in it, the emperor would have still been removed, so he would have done just the right thing at just the right time in that case too. Either way, the swift removal of both Linton and emperor were prerequisites for the avoidance of trouble.

Carrington's straightforward reply was that he would normally have handed such a letter straight to Herr Schulze. But when the War Office telegram had arrived he had found the coincidence peculiar: the letter in his hand had come from Italy too. From Venice, even. In light of Colonel Linton's mission (*whatever exactly it was*) he thought it significant, and sensible, to pass the information directly to him. Carrington pointed out that it was not within his compass to verify the truth of such plots; the Military Mission, he stressed, was an entirely diplomatic position.

Linton pulled up his collar and put on his cap.

'I only hope, Colonel Carrington,' he said, angrily swinging open the door to depart, 'that your position does not change in the forthcoming days.' With that, and a slam of the door, he left.

As Linton thundered back down the stairwell beneath a black cloud of fury, he continued to rage at Carrington for having withheld the letter until this last moment. Why, what did he think – he would establish the truth of a plot *after* it happened? The man was beneath all contempt!

Linton's introversion meant it was only once the figure, which paused on the landing to let him pass and flashed a salute as he did, resumed its rapid ascent that Linton became alive to the fact this had happened. He stopped in time to look up and see the cut of a British officer's uniform enter the Military Mission above. And if combustible material had been placed anywhere near Linton he would have exploded.

Chapter 19

Whatever satisfaction Carrington felt at Linton's departure evaporated the instant Edward entered his office. He had forgotten about *him*. Now reminded, Edward's timing could not have been worse. Colonel Linton would have unquestionably passed him on the stairs, put two and three together, and concluded he had just been told a bare-faced lie about a British officer being spare in Vienna; he would have no regard for the facts. This disagreeable concatenation of the two men's appearance led to Carrington's features displaying the very antithesis of their usual calm.

'You – yes, now this lance corporal of yours,' he snapped, the colour in his cheeks the visible indicator of his annoyance if ever Edward happened to be deaf to the tone – and there was no point asking him to sit, he wouldn't be staying – 'what are you doing with him?'

Edward had no idea why the colonel had summoned him. He was not expecting the subject. He was not expecting the question.

'I'm not sure I follow. What do you mean, sir?'

'I mean precisely what I say – what are you doing with him? What's his punishment?'

There was a short, arithmetical silence before Edward's sums were concluded. And the moment they were, he replied in the smarting tones of an officer for whom such humdrum matters of discipline fell well within his compass and had nothing to do with the colonel. He was not some greenhorn subaltern.

'I've already dealt with the matter, sir,' he said.

'I didn't ask *if* you'd punished him, Wilson, I asked *what* punishment,' he barked. 'It's quite simple.' Carrington slapped his hand on the desk and threw himself back in his chair. His frustration was aired by a fathomless sigh. All he wanted was *quiet*!

The relief mission was not Carrington's responsibility – that was true. He had no authority over Edward's dispositions and deployments. Where he did have authority was over infractions of army discipline that came to the attention of the chief of police. As head of the Military Mission the army's reputation was his own, and whether that was threatened by a lance corporal or a colonel was one and the same: in such circumstances he had to take a hand. Moreover, having specifically warned Edward as to the perils of the black market, if the young man had been neither clear enough in his transmission of this warning to his men, or if they had chosen to ignore him, it could only be because he was but an *acting* captain and in need of a superior. The nettlesome business was thus:

Lance Corporal Bagley had secretly sought to procure some whisky on the black market to celebrate the news about the Labour Party's two-million election vote. He had approached one of the *Schiebers* and negotiated a mutually acceptable price. After some discussion he had paid a small deposit and was told he would receive the whisky in two days' time. Bagley had, however, naively agreed the price in the wildly fluctuating kroner. This meant that when he had gone to collect the whisky the *Schieber* had told him the rate of exchange had quadrupled (a claim quite probably true – give or take a percentage point here or there) and that the previously agreed price could only have stood if Bagley had paid the full amount in advance – which he had not. If the *Schieber*'s position was dubious, that was because it was the black market; he was a *shady dealer*, after all. After some dispute the *Schieber* had proposed that if Bagley paid in dollars then a far more advantageous deal could be struck. Bagley had no dollars. In their absence he was offered an amount of whisky considerably less than he had thought to receive. This exchange – conducted via assorted pidgin terms and finger gestures – had left Bagley thoroughly bewildered, and in the end convinced he was being robbed blind. Being of sporting nature, Bagley had sought to settle the matter with his fists.

Bagley had quickly confessed the incident to Edward. He had left the thieving bastard (pardon his French) with a couple of shiners, nothing more. Maybe the bottle-arsed pig (pardon his French) had a bruised rib or two, at worst. If the lying shit (pardon his French) had any broken bones, he had hardly touched him. He had used the putter (so to speak), not the driver.

Edward's mild reservations over the cause of the planned celebration were tempered by the cheerful hamster cheeks and guileless disposition with which it was admitted. And if he was not necessarily sympathetic to it, he tolerated it in the full knowledge that the men were in the country on sufferance. Likewise, being there for the ministration of the Viennese people, his moral equivalence reasoned they deserved better than to be gammoned over a bottle of hard-earned hooch. He therefore sufficed by punishing Bagley with a week's night shift and snow-shovelling duty to keep the depot entranceway clear, and giving him (and, later, the rest of the men) a stiff lecture about their responsibilities. As far as he was concerned that was the end of the matter.

Although Edward and Carrington both knew of the incident, it was not until their opening exchange in the office that Edward's maths resulted in him being aware that Carrington knew. What Edward did not know – and what Carrington did – was that the incident had been witnessed by a local Social Democratic Party official. This official had reported what he had seen (and, more pertinently, what he had *heard*) to his party superior, who had subsequently gone straight to Herr Schulze. Whilst black-market dealing and the beating-up of a civilian by a British soldier were certainly worthy of complaint to the Military Mission, of far greater concern was the language Bagley had used. During his pugilistic display he had repeatedly called the *Schieber* a '*Saujud*' – in rough parlance, a 'dirty Jew pig'. Bagley had mentioned nothing of this to Edward. This was either because he had no idea he had said it, or because he had thought it of no significance, being as it was but one foreign insult plucked from a dizzyingly thick lexicon acquired over the years – few of which he understood. Not that understanding would have made any eggs to him, but it did make eggs to the party superior. The party superior therefore told Herr Schulze that if something wasn't done he would go to the newspaper. The prospect of a report appearing that British soldiers (the plural always adding weight to a headline) had been beating up Viennese citizens (here the plural for dramatic effect) and been brazenly anti-Semitic was serious at such a volatile time. For this reason had Herr Schulze sought out Carrington (hence the meeting in the Prater) and requested the matter be dealt with in such a manner as to placate the party superior; he had made some suggestions to this end.

Carrington had no interest in running a fine comb through the tangled hairs of Bagley's misdemeanour. Nor did he have any actual interest in the punishment Edward had already applied. The only thing he wanted to do was to state the punishment that *would be* applied and move on. That said, with Edward's steely blue eyes deepening to solidity in front of him, he made deference to his position by detailing what he knew Edward to be ignorant of.

'You understand we can't have British soldiers brawling in the streets. It won't do. Calling the fellow a dirty little Jew for the whole world to hear – you know that's what your man called him, don't you? A *dirty Jewish pig*.' (Edward's negative was expected). 'No, I thought not. That's what one of these little party snitches who saw the whole thing said he did. So that's that. It doesn't matter what everyone else says and thinks. Good God, half the government's Jewish, Wilson – you should damned well know that. I thought you were in Vienna before the war.'

Edward said nothing. In a trice the object of his ire had swung from Carrington to Bagley. The sudden change was not just due to Bagley's stupidity and the crassness of the insult, but because he had said nothing to him about it. It had left him exposed before Carrington as an officer ignorant and incompetent.

Carrington, having anticipated the impact the unfortunate disclosure might have, hereby dropped his register to its customary one of pastoral solemnity. 'We have to show the locals that we don't stand for that sort of thing, dear boy. We have to abide by the behaviour expected of us and the conditions of peace.'

Edward's affirmation was muted, but sufficiently clear for Carrington to proceed.

'Good. Now,' he said, leaning forward like a judicial Solon, 'I'm sure whatever punishment you've given the lance corporal conforms perfectly with the King's Regulations, but you've not had the full recourse to the facts, have you? So I've decided to take that stripe from the lance corporal's shoulder. Consider it temporary if you like – he might get it back if he sticks around, I suppose. I was going to put him on the first train back to Italy just to get him out of the country, but I spoke to Major B the other day and he said he needs a man up in Berlin for a couple of weeks. So that's where he'll go. The major told me your mission here's about to end – said he'd spoken to you about that – so the chap would be going somewhere else either way.'

Edward returned a minimal nod to the edict.

'Very good,' said Carrington, satisfied. 'That's all. But I'll take it you'll remind your men to watch their language and steer clear of that black market – just as I told you before.'

Upon a final, silent confirmation, Edward was thereby dismissed. Just as he was about to leave, however, Carrington was recollected to the very beginning of their interview.

'Oh, and... Lieutenant – sorry, *Captain* – do be sure and keep yourself busy, won't you? There's nothing worse than bumping into someone who thinks you're at a loose end. That's when people end up getting into mischief. We don't want that happening, do we? Remember, calm seas, dear boy; calm seas.'

Edward had no idea what the colonel was talking about. Carrington, of course, knew exactly what he meant. And if he was to have any hope at all of being pensioned as a brigadier, the choppy waters had to be kept clear of his bay.

Chapter 20

Edward's natural character instinctively questioned authority. It also submitted to the thinnest veneer of logic as soon as the question was answered, before later reflection saw him scratch the veneer to reveal his instincts had been invariably sound all along.

Whilst he was standing in the office he was in complete agreement with Carrington: Bagley's behaviour warranted the maximum censure. He had brought disrepute to the army and deceived his commanding officer. When Edward left the building, however, the vane of his ire was blown back towards Carrington. Because there could be no doubt about it: Carrington had acted without the faintest regard for the consequences.

For Lance Corporal Bagley to be summarily despatched to Berlin was bad enough. But to be stripped of his rank? It was true that Bagley only had the stripe because no one had wanted it, but, now that he did have it, Edward was equally sure he would want to keep it, if for nothing else than the extra three shillings a week that it paid him. And all because of a loose tongue and a stray fist. Well, better a stray fist than a stray bullet.

Edward was satisfied that he had administered Bagley's punishment in thorough accordance with military law, to say nothing of plain common sense. Now Carrington expected him to impose a harsher one on the basis of what some lickspittle official claimed to have heard Bagley say when his dander was up. Why, if Edward did that, he knew he would lose every ounce of respect from the men: they would think him a flunkey and scab, and they would be right! And what then? He had heard of incidents in Italy after the armistice when, provoked by the pettiest disciplinary tyranny, men had struck work in solidarity. And what Edward could not overlook, and what Carrington did not know and he did, was the reason for Bagley's intended celebration in the first place. Edward's prior reservations on the matter had thus assumed portent. With the war over for four months, here the men still were, freezing in a foreign land, being swizzled by the locals, and stabbed in the back by the staff. Colonel

Carrington may have been indifferent to the men's fate, but Edward's responsibility to their care was as great now that the guns had stopped firing as it had been when they had never stopped firing. *He* would not forsake them.

Edward's febrile convolutions outside acted like a gyroscope to his legs: they took him in a whirlwind of motion through the heart of the city. When he finally came to a stop he had no idea where he was, beyond being in the middle of a narrow arcade of shops. A glance to his left startled him: the dark shop interior had emboldened his reflection to almost fantastic proportions. Sometimes, he then thought, as he began to look hard in the glass, it was true: he *did* look like an officer; when at others he knew he did not. Sometimes his tunic shaped as just the right cut, when at others it was ill-fitting and awkward. Sometimes his hair seemed waxed to perfection, when at others it felt lumpy and greasy. He stared at his sometimes reflection for a short time, half in expectation that at any moment the deeper, dirtier, other half lurking in the darkness would leap out and swallow him whole. But nothing leapt: he remained the same man that he saw. Whereat he turned his eyes away. At the very last degree of this reorientation, he turned back. There, he saw, tucked in a corner of the bric-a-brac window, was an old toy Vienna tram. It was exactly the same as the one Friedrich had mocked him for wanting to buy when he had first come to Vienna six years before. Edward glanced round the arcade; it was not the same shop though. A wry smile slowly lit up his face as he remembered that Friedrich had called him a tourist, that the shopkeeper had then raged and had thrown them both out of the shop, and then that Friedrich had laughed, said he had seen everything in Edward's eyes, and finally offered his hand of friendship. Friedrich was like a great prophet – that was what Oriana had once told him; he was always seeing things. Feeling, she had then said, was always better than thinking. And Edward had known she was right.

Supper at Kashia's had concluded with not a single mention of Oriana. After telling Edward about his brother, the tram, the hospital, and his recovery, Kashia had said she knew nothing more. Knowing nothing more either, Edward had had nothing to add. Thus had the conversation drifted banally to siblings, and little else that mattered besides. Once or twice, it was true, he had been on the cusp of muttering an incidental enquiry as to the whereabouts of Kashia's 'friend' and 'former (was she *former*?) roomer' – only to have it knocked from his lips by one of Millie's diversions. And then sensibility to Millie's feelings meant he had shied away from mentioning his former (was she *former*?) love, as if to do so risked putting a wall between them where presently only a window existed. Having wound himself to a pitch of nervous tension before his arrival, on his departure it was as if his cord had been snapped and left to dangle forlorn in the air.

This state had not seen out the night though. The cord had been quickly rewound and the nail had begun plucking once more. Because now, having come back – *having left!* – still he knew nothing. Kashia had said nothing; he had said nothing; the walls had said nothing – when all he wanted was to know what had happened: why had Oriana said nothing after he had left Vienna?

And so, three days later he had returned to the apartment. He had picked up the thread, retraced his steps hand in hand, and retrieved the pictures that had been lost in a dream. When he had arrived at the tenement the sight of an old lady hefting a bag of wood twice her size in the courtyard quickly returned Edward to the cold realities of the waking world. This world told him Kashia would not be there when he knocked; this world told the truth.

When he saw Millie next he asked her if she had seen Kashia. *Of course she had!* She had been to the soup kitchens and met some of her friends. *Of course she had!* She said Kashia and János had left their apartment and moved to another. She had been to visit them, but hadn't had time to tell Edward before. *Of course she had!* She was dreadfully sorry. *Of course she was!*

This conversation had taken place just before a huge train of thirty wagons of supplies had arrived, the unloading and distribution of which to the various depots had taken Edward and the men the best part of a week's round-the-clock work. By the time Edward had recovered from the exertion Millie was too busy to meet up, or too distracted, or too elusive – it didn't matter which (well, it *did*) – and it was a further two weeks before he saw her again. Then she said

Kashia and János had been kicked out of their new apartment and had moved to Budapest. The revelation had taken every breath of wind from his sails. It had left him feeling listless and numb, and with not the slightest interest in speaking to Kashia ever again, if ever he saw her. And it was then that the heavy snows came.

The only thing Colonel Carrington had been right about when he had spoken to Edward was that the relief mission was winding down. Of the company that had shepherded the first train from Italy some seven weeks earlier, only eight men remained under Edward's charge. Despite Carrington's parting exhortation there was, in fact, little for Edward to do beyond supervising the continued smooth running of the operation. With the numbing cold inducing apathy, and apathy worsening the effects of the cold, his principal task entailed staving off the men's disenchantment – as well, of course, as his own. But Carrington's reckless intervention had now changed matters.

After reflecting for several moments more in the window, a solution to the Bagley conundrum came to Edward: he knew precisely what he would do. Confident of both the acuity and moral rectitude of his plan, he stamped his seal on the wax with a fleeting smile of triumph. And then he had to move on: he had finally got hold of Millie and was to meet her at a café in the south of the city. And so, as soon as he got his bearings, that was where he went.

As he turned and strode briskly away it was clear he had not been the only person looking through the shop window. Someone else had been equally transfixed by the possibility that some deeper, dirtier, other half might leap out of the darkness with its claws at the heart. This person had been on the other side of the glass, looking out, not in. Then Edward had smiled. And the difference between a smile that is wry or triumphant and one that is malicious or scornful is no more than the fire in the eyes and the glint of a tooth. And Oriana had seen teeth.

Chapter 21

'Oh God, what's the matter with you?'

'You're late,' Edward said.

He had been too, but that was by the by; Millie was later. And lateness being entirely proportionate to the motive forces propelling each individual to an encounter, Edward's having been five minutes late – but needing to speak to Millie – made him feel like he was twenty. Millie, on the other hand, *being* twenty minutes late, but lacking the equivalent necessity of speaking to Edward, felt that as being five minutes late was neither here nor there, the fact that it was twenty was no more than a result of not being punctual. What mattered was that she was there, which she was.

'Am I?'

'Yes.'

'Sorry – I was busy.'

'Well I have to leave in twenty minutes.'

'That's fine, we've got plenty of time for a coffee.'

'It's not just coffee. I said I needed to speak to you about something.'

'Oh yeah – but you always say that.'

Millie plonked herself down on a thin wooden chair opposite Edward. The café was rudimentary: there was a bar, a few battered tables and chairs, a large mirror with rust spots on the glass, and some hand-printed election posters tacked to the walls. It was far removed from the ornate panelling and opulence of the famous Viennese cafés. It was the sort of place one entered, ordered a coffee or schnapps, moaned about something to the barman, had perhaps a hand or two at cards to forget about it, and then went home. Located opposite the tram depot, its principal custom was evident by the cluster of underemployed conductors and drivers propped at the counter. Edward's uniformed entry had aroused much curiosity among them, and the series of poke-and-prod-with-a-stick glances thrown in his direction whilst he was waiting for Millie was a supplementary irritation to her tardiness.

Millie's arrival changed everything though. The barman, having previously treated Edward with extreme suspicion and truculence, came speeding over to the table to greet her with sparkling, comradely eyes. His simpering enquiry as to what he might serve her touched on the feudal.

'Ooh, I don't know. What do I want?' she asked Edward.

'Wine?'

'Don't be a silly.' She glanced at the barman. 'I'll just have a – oh bugger, sorry!' She let out a coarse, gravelly laugh... and blamed Edward: 'That's your fault for making me speak English.' The barman's long sickle eyebrows arched with pleasure as he said he understood her English perfectly. But Millie would have none of that. '*Ich nehme eine Melange, bitte schön,*' she said. The barman was delighted at her German, praised her accent, admired her still-beautiful eyes, and as if attending to the wishes of Helen herself, with no more ado bustled back to the bar in pursuit of her choice.

'*Zweimal, bitte,*' Edward called out after, for another.

'Oops, sorry – I thought you didn't need anything.'

'I will do,' he said, draining the remainder of the bitter black brew from his cup. Millie unfastened the clip of her cape and took off her hat. She then pulled her chair up to the table and flopped her arms across it, whereat the table lurched to one side. This happening at the precise moment Edward set his cup down, the unpalatable dregs splashed over his overcoat.

'Whoops-a-daisy.'

'Millie!'

'Sorry.' She leaned forward to inspect the damage. 'Oh, that's nothing – a damp cloth and they'll be gone in a jiffy. You can hardly see anything anyway – not with all the other muck on it. God, that coat's disgusting.'

'It's not *disgusting*, Millie,' he returned, irked by the same breezy lack of concern with which she dismissed the coat's presentability as that with which she had just dismissed the time, as if her actions had no consequences and *he* were of no regard. He clunked the cup back on the table and made an ostentatious display of scrubbing the stains with his thumb. 'It's not been washed, that's all. It hasn't needed to be either – until now.'

His disagreeable tone soured Millie's expression. She was correspondingly brisk. 'Stop doing that with your fingers – you'll make it worse. Let's get a cloth.' Her rise to do so was belayed by a flap of the barman's arms: it was in hand for his *Fräulein*! She sat back down and said with the obstinate force of her present humour, 'Anyway, come on, it's funny.'

'What's funny?'

'Look – it's a hopper!'

'A *hopper*?'

She wobbled the table. 'That's a hopper,' she said, flashing a grin. 'It's what we call people who're missing part of their leg – they're hoppers.' She gave the table another demonstrable shake; Edward put a hand to his cup to prevent its tipping again. 'And he's a very hoppy hopper this one, isn't he? Hoppity hop hop hop. Let's have a look at him, shall we?' Upon which she promptly pushed back her chair, fell to her knees, and disappeared under the table like a rabbit down a hole.

'What are you doing, Millie?'

'Having a look to see if we can fix him.'

'Him?'

'Mr Table.'

The barman came over with the rag end of a cloth. Seeing it was not to be conferred directly to Millie he disposed of it on the table as if it were something unpleasant. He then proceeded to gaze with reverential longing down at a girl who would certainly be of use in *his* establishment. A moment later her head poked out from beneath. Her face flushing, she made a hammer gesture to the barman. Once more at her service, he hurried off in search of the requisite tool. Edward let out a huff that was half forbearance of the incorrigible, half impatience at the wilful.

'Leave it, Millie. I haven't got time.'

'Hang on. It'll only take a second. It's just a naughty nail that needs popping back in.' The barman returned with the sought-for mallet, and she promptly disappeared again. A hand reached up to clamp a corner of the table to its leg. One 'fiddlesticks' and a few solid thumps later it was all done. She got back up and gave the table a wobble test. It passed, to the inestimable satisfaction of her, the barman, and the admiring cluster at the bar. 'There we are. All better, aren't you, Mr Table?'

'Mr Table would've be fine in the first place if you hadn't thrown yourself over him.'

This remark, despite its drily humorous intent (for only in this way could Edward express his exasperated admiration at such a moment), was nonetheless taken as criticism.

'You're doing it again. Stop it,' she snapped peevishly.

'What?'

'That twitchy frowny thing with your eyebrows. It's really annoying.' His eyebrows twitched and frowned. 'See! You don't even know you're doing it! Well, come on then,' she said, settling back into her chair with a bend of the birch, 'what's your problem? What did you need to speak to me about?'

'It's not a *problem*, Millie. It's a *proposition*.'

Millie's eyes suddenly ballooned in alarm. 'What kind of proposition?' she said; then added warningly, 'Nothing silly I hope.'

Her suspicious, censorious tone roused Edward to indignity. Firstly, that she had even thought that was what he might have meant by a 'proposition'; and secondly, that even if it were (*which it wasn't*), that she should talk of it in such belittling fashion.

'The proposition – if that's what it's called – is whether you wanted to come to Germany.'

'To Germany? *Why?*'

To her tone of suspicion was added a hint of accusation. It caused Edward to trip over his words – and in so doing did nothing to quell her fears as to his lurking amorous intentions.

'Major B... asked me to... to ask you if you'd be interested in going there – to work.'

'Major B?'

'Yes. He's... he's asked me to go.'

'Hmm. To do what?'

'Search for missing POWs.'

'Why does he want me to come?'

'He needs a couple of nurses to help out.'

'Hmm.'

All of this was of course perfectly true: Major B had said as much on his brief visit to Vienna the previous week. He had asked Edward to head up a bureau in Breslau when the relief mission ended. He said there were stragglers all over the place: soldiers down mines, in hospitals, factories, prisons and asylums – he could scarcely believe the number of places where the Germans had squirrelled them away! On one side of the Hindenburg line prisoners had been sent to western France or England; on the other they had been dropped like ants into the vast expanse of Central and Eastern Europe. Of course, Major B had added in the same offhand, predetermined manner as Lieutenant Colonel Backhouse, Edward was welcome to refuse the post and wait for his papers – but what good would that do him? And although it was also true that Major B had spoken to him of Millie in regard to this posting, he had done so with a lascivious glint as he suggested that they'd be needing some poultry to give them a hand in the coop. Edward had flat-batted the suggestion, but had later applied common sense to it. She would of course be perfect. To have someone providing the necessary palliative care who was intrepid, forthright, practical and spoke (a little) German was a virtual prerequisite: it would not be bedpans on the ward.

'God, they'll think we're an old married couple if I start following you all over Europe,' said Millie, after a pause, the hint of accusation still on the tip of her tongue. 'I can't just drop everything like that. Anyway, why didn't Major B ask me himself?'

'What do you mean, himself?'

'Come and speak to *me* – not get you to do it for him.'

'Don't be ridiculous. He was only here for two days. He suggested you might be interested and to speak to you about it. That's all.'

'Thank *you*,' she replied sardonically.

'Well he was hardly going to go hunting all over Vienna for you just to ask that, was he? Honestly, you're acting as if it's a... plot, or something stupid like that.'

'I didn't say it was a *plot*. You just don't explain things very well.'

'I do, perfectly. But you're taking me asking you as if it's demeaning or... well, I've no idea what.'

'I don't. It's just it'd be nice if Major B didn't act as if I was a little girl holding your hand. I don't want to be treated as if I'm your...'

She was interrupted as the coffees were placed on the table. Millie's eyes brightened at the sight. 'Ooh, I forgot about the cake,' she said. She gave an excited clap of her hands at the prospect of confected distraction. 'Got to have cake. What do you reckon I should have?'

'I can't imagine you'll have much choice, Millie,' he said heavily, as if in the midst of a storm she had just proposed plumb-lining the ocean floor. 'If any.'

He was right. A minute later the Hobson's choice of a lump of dry, ersatz, sugarless *Kaiserschmarren* arrived – though even this was a provision of exception delivered to the beautiful *Fräulein* with the barman's fawning indulgence. Millie forked herself a mouthful of cake, then pushed the plate to Edward.

'Yum, yum. Have some.'

Edward checked his instinct to decline. Despite what he knew would in no wise be 'yum', he had come to understand that Millie treated food and drink as things almost sacramental. To refuse the offering would be tantamount to spitting in the pyx. He took up the fork. There was a short silence before Millie resumed in the placid tones of one for whom humours were no more constant than the shape of a cloud.

'So when you off then?'

'Where?' asked Edward, trying hard not to gag as he pushed the plate back.

'To Germany, silly.'

'I don't know exactly – I'm not even sure if I'll go yet. I might get my papers. And there's still a number of things to sort out here first, anyway.'

'Oh, I see. I thought it was all decided and you were going right away.'

'No. And it's not for another couple of weeks.'

'And it's to do with the POWs?'

'Yes.'

She trowelled the fork into the pastry crust thoughtfully. 'What would you be doing again if you did go?'

'Try and find them first of all, whoever they are – and wherever they are. Then work out how to get them back to England – or Australia, Canada… or who knows where. If we can, that is. If we can't, well, that's another thing. Major B reckons they're scattered all over the place, but I imagine they'll mostly be men trapped in tiny hospitals in the middle of nowhere: those who have amnesia, flu, typhus and things like that. They'll be pretty badly knocked about either way, I reckon. Anyway, that's why Major B needs a few nurses – when we find men like that.'

'Oh, I see,' Millie said, conceding legitimacy to the much-contended proposition. 'Sounds interesting. But I can't just leave the children in the hospital.'

'Like I said, it's not for a couple of weeks or so. Besides, I'm not sure you'll have much of a choice. When the relief mission ends you won't be staying. You'll have to go where the army sends you – further east, possibly, or back to Italy, or even England. You'd have to start working for one of the charities if you wanted to stay, I imagine – I'm just saying.' His swift adjunct was delivered in anticipation of a protest, but came there none. Millie's mood was reflective.

'Yes, yes, I know. I heard the other nurses talking about something like that the other day. I need to think about it.'

'It was an idea, Millie. Not an order. You can do as you please.'

'Yes, I know. Thank you. I don't want to go back to England, that's for sure.'

There was another short silence. Edward took a light step onto ground which he knew to be more suited to the present shift in her mood. 'How are the children, anyway? Are they getting better?'

'Oh yes – much!' she said. Her round face glowed with freckled cheeriness. 'As soon as you get some food and cod liver oil in them it doesn't take long for them to become springy again. It's getting hold of enough milk that's the biggest problem. We need some big cows out the back of the hospital. Then we'd be fine!'

'You need the depot back how it used to be.'

'What do you mean?'

'The depot centre – the one we're using for the supplies. It used to be the cattle market before the war.'

'Did it? Well, that's definitely what we need. A big shed full of cows. And then we could put one or two aside so we can sneak a little steak off every now and again. Just for us.'

An expressive appeal of her wide eyes and a gleeful clenching of teeth were the definitive signs of her ease. They were the signs that could do nothing other than bring a warm smile to Edward's face. As he basked in this gay, bright light the door to the café opened behind them. The blast of winter air immediately sucked Millie's attention away from Edward to the entrants.

'Hullo,' she said.

'Hello, Millie,' said Kashia. 'Hello, Edward.'

Kashia was dressed in a heavy brown overcoat with a tassled blue shawl wrapped tightly around her head, concealing her hair so completely that it gave a marbled, puritanical aspect to her little white face. She was not alone: a squat, muscular figure with hunched shoulders swaggered in behind her like a bulldog.

The intrusion pricked Edward. As the pair approached the table he felt a chill pierce his warmth. Kashia passed a familiar greeting with the barman as Edward and Millie rose from the table in welcome. When the four came together there was a short, awkward silence – before Kashia's companion, glancing first at Millie, threw out a leathery, gorilla hand at Edward and broke it with the gruff appellation.

'Zsolt.'

'Salt?'

'Oh God, yes, sorry,' Millie interjected. 'Not *salt*, silly, Zsolt. Zsolt – Edward. Edward, this is Zsolt.'

Edward was none the wiser as to what the name was as he took up the proffered hand. Zsolt's grip was powerful. It was supplemented by a pair of prominent green eyes which seemed to Edward to glow with the deep, prowling intensity of something that stalked the ancient forests at night. He wore a loose-fitting navy jacket, corduroy trousers, a flannel shirt and peaked cap; an old red kerchief was tied round his thick neck – evidently a flag to his labouring heart. On finally letting go of Edward's hand his wide, sloping nostrils flared and he removed his cap to reveal a bald head bristling with the same silver-black hairs as the rest of his coarse, jutting, unshaven face. He then turned to greet the cluster at the bar. Edward glanced meaningfully at Kashia: he thought him a wretched substitute for Friedrich.

'How are you, Edward?' said Kashia, undoing her shawl as the trio sat down.

'I'm fine, thank you,' he said in a clipped, sandpaper tone. 'Millie said you've moved to Hungary.' His eyes flicked to the bar to intimate the for why.

'Yes.'

'And... what was his name, János? He's gone too?'

'Yes. He is gone too, back to his home. It is better to be in Hungary – for all of us.' There was a pause before she added, 'But you're still here in Vienna. Is it different for you now?'

'Now?'

'Yes, now. You are spending much more time here. Is it still as full of all that wonderful *Gemütlichkeit* that you were finding before the war?'

Edward's eyes narrowed; his speech was curt.

'Of course it's different – how could it not be? There's been a war.'

'Not *our* war, but yes, that's true. I wanted to say only that when you are staying somewhere for just a little time you are remembering it – and the people – much more differently than when you are staying for longer. We are all different when it is snowing and cold. It makes a very big change to how we are feeling and behaving in the end of a summer, no?'

'I wasn't trying to feed and clothe the city last time,' he remarked acidly. 'That's different, isn't it?'

'Oh yes, you are nurse to the people of Vienna now, Edward,' she said with an ironic twitch of her colourless lips. 'That's true. Maybe you make even a better nurse than Millie.'

'I don't think so,' scoffed Millie aside.

'No, maybe not,' agreed Kashia.

'What are you doing back here in Vienna?' he asked.

'What am *I* doing here?' She let out a short, violent laugh as Zsolt rejoined the party and took up a chair between Millie and Kashia. Her pale eyes turned sheer. 'People always come back to Vienna, don't they? I come to visit some people. Zsolt comes for the same reason. He comes to meet you too.'

Despite the fact that Kashia was addressing Edward, this 'you' was not directed at him. It was directed at Millie. And it was only when Edward pursued the line of Kashia's look that he noticed Zsolt's attention was fixed not on she whom he had presumed his *amour* to be, but on Millie. His thick, hairy fingers, he saw, were twirling round the fingers of Millie's pliant, outstretched hand. Edward flashed a forced, rictus smile to all corners of the table.

'I see that,' he said. Crossing his legs, he threw his left arm over the back of the chair, pinned his shoulder to the wood, turned to Millie and said with dispassion, 'I didn't realise you knew each other.'

'Millie came to visit us in Budapest,' Kashia explained.

'Yes, Kashia invited me. I've never been there. It's beautiful. She and Zsolt gave me a tour of the city.'

As if the iteration of the name were some prearranged signal, Zsolt leaned forward and kissed her on the cheek. Edward pressed his arm tight to the wood.

'That's why I couldn't get hold of you,' he said.

'Probably. Why, were you trying to?'

'Yes. You were obviously busy.'

'You know me – I normally am.'

It was no good: he uncrossed his legs, crossed his arms, and beneath them drove his fingers fiercely into the muscles. But, like an iron to magnet, he could not help being drawn to the sight of Zsolt's fat, hairy fingers pawing at Millie. He thought it repulsive. Then, worse; he suddenly pictured them roaming the Budapest streets arm in arm – like some grotesque, Puckish parody of how he and Millie had gambolled carefree through the streets of Padova. He propped himself forward, as if compelled by a force far stronger than disgust.

'That's a bit OD, isn't it, Millie?' he said with playful malice, before turning instantly to Kashia to say, 'I wasn't expecting to see you. Millie didn't say anything.'

'We don't have to tell you everything. Sometimes it's a surprise.

This is a surprise for you, no? Millie told me she was meeting you and I wanted to see you. We haven't seen each other since you came to dinner.'

'I told Kashia you were looking for her,' explained Millie.

'Oh yes – yes, and I wanted to know why.'

In Kashia's cold, crystalline gaze Edward saw the unmistakeable gleam of the scalpel raised before him. His body wrestled in the chair as he tried to get loose.

'I don't remember now. It's not important.'

'Wasn't it about that girl you liked?' said Millie. 'Kashia told me all about it. Oleanna – that was her name, wasn't it?'

'Oriana,' corrected Kashia. She shook her head in disbelief. 'But it can't be that, Edward. You can't possibly be still thinking about *her*. It was just a bit of fun – *six years ago*. You must be finding someone more interesting than Oriana since then? But… maybe she has become like a picture to you. Maybe that is what you are seeing. Maybe she is like the girl who is looking out of a window, and it is winter, and all the ground is covered in snow and ice, and underneath the title says: "Forsaken". Maybe that's it.' Edward said nothing. Emotionlessly, theatrically, Kashia slowly reached forward, set the scalpel's edge to his skin, and gently pressed down: 'But you must think of the actions of a person. Yes, you must remember what they have done, not the feeling you have; the feeling is nothing when you remember someone. It is only what they have done that matters.'

'I think we need to find Edward a nice girl, don't you, Kashia?' said Millie lightly as she detached herself from Zsolt's tacky hands. 'Someone who he doesn't have to remember. Someone who's going to put up with him and his annoying habits.'

Edward turned on Millie at her treachery. '*Annoying habits?*' he sneered.

'Oh yes – you've no idea how many there are!' Millie laughed again.

'I think Millie knows you very well, Edward,' said Kashia. 'I think she is right, for sure.'

'A nice simple little thing that he can love. That's what he needs, isn't it, Kashia?'

'Yes. Something simple. But if he is still thinking of Oriana maybe he is not even knowing what love actually is. Maybe it's important to learn that first. It's not only slipping off petticoats and kissing in the rain. That is maybe romantic, yes – but it's not love, not in real life. Love is not just to make pretty pictures in the head.'

'He needs someone who can wash his overcoat too, and someone who can sew on a button for him – look, you can't even do it yourself.' Millie leaned over and tried to pull the button unthreading on his tunic lapel. 'It's not very good for a lieutenant – sorry, *captain* –' she gave him a teasing wink '– is it?'

'It's fine,' he said, recoiling from her touch.

'No it's not. Look – they're about to fall off. You get grumpy about a couple of coffee stains and you can't even take care of your buttons. I think that's more important if you're worried about looking like a proper officer.'

'That's the problem with the army,' said Kashia. 'There are too many men who don't know how to sew buttons, or mend shoes, or patch clothes, or do anything useful. All they can do is polish their guns so they shine when they fight; but that is not *useful*. And when they're not polishing and have nothing to do, they spend all of their time writing letters and making stupid pictures of love. It is for sure a woman would not do the same thing if *she* was in the army. We are not as interested in men as men are in us. That is the problem, you see, Edward. No – that is not a problem; it is a good thing. Because if only we were doing the things men are supposed to be doing, everything would be better; everything would be useful. *Then* there would be truth.'

Now, Edward said to himself, it had all become clear. At last he had discovered the truth: love to women was nothing but buttons. When a thread came loose it was pulled out and the button sewn back on. For it could not be lost. The tunic, once ripped in the field, the button trodden into the earth, crushed beneath bodies and boots, could not be worn gaping. The hole could not be unfilled, the skin not exposed to shiver or burn: a button would always have to be found to replace it. And – lo! that was the value of love. For did the tale of life take only six years to be told? Was it fiction when facts attained a certain age? Is the longer one loves without a love fit only to be howled out by the cries of foolishness? Of *uselessness*? There was a picture, yes, but there was a feeling too – of a body shaking on the stairs; or another, rolling from side to side in a shell hole to the sound of a bullet and sigh; or yet another, quivering, hungry, thirsting across invisible lines of mud and mountains for miles upon miles. Going back. It was always going back. That was what he was *doing*. That was the reason. And yet, what did all that mean to Millie and Kashia? It meant nothing but buttons.

Edward's rich blue eyes leapt wildly between Millie and Kashia. Yes, he told himself, he would leave them to it. He would strike out on his own. He would find his love again. And there, from the dark shadows of emptiness, he would return again with it cradled in his arms. And so, *then*:

Chapter 22

Ah yes, I have seen this *then* before. The white-winged sails billow boldly in the breeze, the church bells softly peal; the blue-green waters drift faceless to the shore, and the sun beams on the deck. Then first the clouds begin to rack, and the wind scants from the north. Soon the sea begins to lop and roll; the waves slap the thrashing prow: the froth sprays high, then falls like rain and washes the happy, sun-browned skin. This is how the attack begins: it is always the same; it is all laughter and deceit.

The clouds then mass; the ocean stills; the wind dies to a breathless lull: now comes the ice with winter. As the mighty frozen floes surround the ship, stuck to the hull as honey does to skin, the deadened waters slowly thick the blood with cold, and the sails turn deathly black. Lifeless, immovable, for a while the vessel rests – just like a painted ship upon a pure white sea; until the crushed beams splinter, the waters pour in, and all is sunk to the blackest of depths. And then – then there is no more then.

Oh yes, I have seen this. I have often heard the cry ring out – *Ah, love!*

So where, you might ask, is the proof? Oh yes, the question is always for *proof*. Where is the proof that she stood before the ice walls and shivered? Where is the proof that she was wrapped in blankets and scarves and cashmere and serge? Where is the proof that she *loved*? It is there – I say – in the crack in the stone, in the turn of the soil, beneath the rugged elms and the yew tree's shade. It is there in the liquid that seeps through the slits when the tunic is torn; it is there in the spots and stains on the cloth. So dig – I say – dig! Dig into the festering heap and scour it clean with brushes and nails. Feel the flow of the immemorial sap.

That God, I know, is insatiable: it is always wanting *more*. This I have learnt, and *I* do not lie. For if his blood had been clotted up like the mud, I too would have stamped my boots with this love through the shell holes, bullets and gas with my pail to catch that of another

– another whose *did* flow. Oh yes, as you would too! Stamping and catching and lapping, clicking your teeth as your tongue coloured red. That, after all, is where the life lies. That is what the salivating tongue hounds for as it follows the rippling artery, farther and deeper, down to its fountainhead source; it does not weep for the bodies washed up on the shore with the bottles and water wings.

So, I say, sail onward! Do not be packed by the ice and crushed. Do not drift in ever diminishing fragments in the sun's broiling glare until all is evaporation. Do not grow fainter like the perfume on the collar. Do not be swayed by jewels and shards of glass. Fill your ears with wax: do not listen to the bells – their peal has been forged from the guns. Reach down into the mud and clasp the button that has been torn from the breast! For that, I say, is *duration*. That is *permanence*.

*

Colonel Linton never ignored a letter. He cared nothing for the gossip of clubs or the prattle of the season: the idle tongue was full of lies and bile. But a letter – oh, a letter was different! In a letter there was always the truth! But if it can be said that to edit or amend a composition is to corrupt the genie of its source, then Colonel Linton was of exactly this view as to reading it twice. Repetition led to reflection; reflection bred doubt. He did not pore over syntax expecting a nuance. He read, understood, and acted.

Carrington's letter (wherever he had got it from) meant matters had become urgent. Linton knew perfectly well the emperor would not quit his estate unless assured of his position, or unless the risk to life was manifest. This was proven by the fact he was there and not with his feet up in a plush Swiss resort. And that, be it said, he considered just as it should be. For a king did not turn tail at every rustle he heard in the woods: he stood majestic and defiant, like the monarchical stag of the glen. It was only when the huntsman's rifle was slung from the shoulder that he silently disappeared in the mists. Any imminent threat to the emperor's life therefore depended on the estate's defensive dispositions. It was those Linton was in haste to discover. For a letter alone was not the muzzle of a gun.

On Linton's return to the hotel from the Military Mission there was a cable awaiting him. It was from the emperor; it lauded his safe arrival and told him to help himself to a car and driver from the royal garage. Linton wasted no time. At the garage, however, he found the only roadworthy vehicle to be the emperor's large Austro-Daimler, the Habsburg arms emblazoned on the doors. Linton may have sported many decorations, but none were for foolhardiness: the Red Guard would be taking potshots at every corner if he drove out in that! He promptly ordered the arms painted out. As soon as the paint had sufficiently dried, and the time being shortly before noon, he was driven out of Vienna.

The journey to Eckartsau took just over an hour. The final approach was made in the thickening light of the forest along a single track road. It was a morass of potholes, frozen mud, snow and ice, and the driver, wrestling the wheel like a boatswain his helm in the midst of a storm, was forced to skid and thresh all the way. A single Viennese policeman marked the crossing of the boundary into the imperial estate. Soon after, they reached the hunting lodge – its bright Maria Theresan yellow walls glowing like a buttercup of light in the wintry gloom – and came to a stop through the *porte cochère* at the rear. Linton's alarm was instant on arrival – although not for the driver: *he* collapsed at the wheel. Stepping out of the car he found himself waist to nose with a vicious Alsatian. The latter, by means of an occasional pause and twitch of the ears, seemed to evince an almost tragedian pleasure in the savagery the acoustics accredited its bark.

'Good afternoon, Herr Colonel. Welcome, welcome,' said an Austrian major of middle age, full figure, square jaw, smooth fleshy cheeks and a pair of wheedling, duplicitous eyes. 'I see you are meeting Gussl. He has no manners, I'm afraid – that is only his way to say hello. But he does not bite.'

That was not to say that Gussl didn't want to. And as Linton had learnt as a boy that volition was a poor restraint when it came to whether his father's jealous dog bit him or not (all that mattered was opportunity) he remained perfectly still; but he did not brush up flat with his address: he had seen only one policeman since arriving, he told the major sternly. He sincerely hoped there were more!

The major, momentarily stunned by what his sour expression

deemed Linton's uncourtly preamble, shortly replied that of course there were *more*. The majority of the guard had, however, been withdrawn the previous month on the orders of Herr Schulze – in spite of his own most fervent protests. The chief of police had given assurances that the imperial family and household were perfectly safe: those he left as the guard were his very best men. There were six.

'*Six!*'

'Of the best,' confirmed the major.

After a moment Linton grimly observed, 'And you, of course.'

'Of course, there is me too,' the major said in the spry, imperishable tones of his class, 'and Gussl, and some others of the household – although they have no bullets or guns. But my duty as an officer is to protect the emperor, not to stand on the fence, is it not, Herr Colonel?'

There was no time for Linton to retort to this last.

'*Mon cher Colonel Linton! Je suis ravi. Absolument ravi!*'

The emperor, entering the courtyard through a latticed door on the far side, strode up to Linton and shook his hand with notable feeling, upon which symbolic act Gussl resigned himself to a querulous growl. '*J'espère que vous n'avez pas trop souffert lors de ce si long voyage.*'

'*Point du tout, votre majesté,*' replied Linton formally.

The emperor was dressed in his field marshal's uniform with the full gamut of imperial medals displayed on his chest. Beneath a trimmed moustache his small mouth opened to an elliptical smile curtained by the upper row of his yellow-tipped teeth. Linton had encountered him but once before – and that when he was not even the heir. It had been on Archduke Franz Ferdinand's Konopiště estate in 1912 when the archduke's nephew had stayed for two days. Aside from his declining to hunt, and showing little interest when his uncle had brought out his fascinating compendium of hunting kills, Linton's impression of the young man (the little he had made) had been of one who conformed perfectly to the stolid precepts of the Habsburg monarchy: unprepossessing, largely unimaginative, a touch pious, prone to petulance, but nonetheless possessed of sufficient intelligence and sincerity as to make a palatable heir to his uncle should the need arise – which it had.

That said, whereas previously youth had allowed that the above characteristics might be susceptible to some deft Schwarzenbergian manipulation, in the person now present before him Linton found there to be something disconcertingly rigid. It was as if his uniform, medals and courtly French were the last stays of his frayed monarchical poise. In his thin face and sallow complexion were the strains of one diminished by hunger, illness (he at that very moment coughed weakly) and fatigue. And although his soft brown eyes expressed unmistakeable cordiality, Linton found a preponderant lifelessness to the declining arcs of his eyebrows, to his angular nose and to his flat, protruding chin, such as to suggest a face more becoming an effigy than a crown. The thought flashed through his mind that perhaps Switzerland *was* the best place for him. Few men, he had learnt, retained their stature in the absence of power: those who did merited exile; those who did not were happy to have it.

Gussl striking up with an attention-seeking bark, the emperor proceeded to irritably dismiss both dog and officer in a manner that barely distinguished the one from the other. He then proposed a walk in the grounds to Linton. He could not abide being cooped up in the house with so many people all day.

'This is a hunting lodge, *mon cher* Colonel Linton. Come, let us hunt!'

Linton thought the proposal excellent, be it as it may the emperor's absence of arms told it was merely purposive to the walk: it provided the perfect opportunity for him to assess the terrain. The emperor collected his walking stick and overcoat from the boot room and then conducted Linton back through the porte cochère and out into the forest wilds.

It was not long before the emperor spoke again of his heartfelt delight that the colonel was there, of his gratitude at King George's assistance, and of his humility at the kindness and generosity shown him by the British people. '*Voila ce que la vraie noblesse*,' he said. '*C'est surtout la courtoisie anglaise.*'

He had been to England once, he said; for the king's coronation: he had been sent in the place of his uncle. The images of that time were as vivid to him as if they had happened only yesterday! He remembered his arrival at Victoria station, where the red carpet covered every inch of the concrete and the air was suffused with the scent of – he was sure – at least a million carnations! He had later reviewed the navy at Spithead – he had never seen so many ships! He thought at the time it was impossible that a country would ever go to war against an empire as mighty as that! (Linton laconically remarked that that had been the Admiralty's view too.) But it was the coronation itself that had left the deepest impression. It had been the most magnificent thing, with its ancient rites dating back centuries, with its symbols of Christian kingship, with its solemn oaths sworn to God and all the peoples of the empire. That was what he had thought of when the Crown of St Stephen was placed on his head. He had remembered that the oaths were eternal and unbreakable, that that was the duty of kings.

'Et puis je suis revenu en Autriche, et je me suis marié. J'avoue que c'était le moment le plus heureux de ma vie, cher colonel.'

After this he fell to a reflective silence; Linton, preoccupied with the topography, had little interest in making idle conversation in order to break it. When the emperor eventually resumed it was in a peculiar strain of melancholy infused with indignant bewilderment. He had never imagined the provinces of his empire could be so vengeful towards Austria, he said. Never. Now he heard stories that the Czechs stole their coal, the Poles spoiled their potatoes, the Hungarians hoarded their wheat, and the Italians grabbed at every last morsel of land. He swung his stick in an arc and drove it into the earth like a stake into a foul poisoned heart. *'Je ne l'aurais jamais cru,'* he said. *'Jamais. Tout ça, après sept cents ans.'*

They came to a stop when they reached the broad, flat course of the Danube. On either side of the shallow, rocky banks sheets of ice spread across the water's edge like cold breath on a glass. Only the gentle purl of the river intruded on the stillness of the air. The emperor levelled his stick and pointed to the far distant bank. He said that patrols of the Red Guard had been occasionally spotted there, but that they had never tried to cross. They did not dare, he swore. It was the same for the patrols that prowled the edge of the estate. They were merely loyal men who had been turned just as a ravenous dog was when it was tossed a bone to gnaw on.

Linton was not so sanguine in outlook: he knew it only took *one*. Surveying their present exposed position any half-decent sniper might wipe the pair of them out in two simple shots, although even a half-decent sniper was hardly easy to find! It was also true that the freezing river with its vicious undercurrents formed at present a reliable moat. However, any notion the emperor had that the patrols of men were actually *loyal* he considered to be touching delusion. Whatever qualms such men possessed could be only attributed to cowardice: it would be cast off at the first holler and halloo of the mob, and then the first blackguardly shot of the gun. With the fierce, brazen cold starting to sting his fingers and cheeks, Linton thought it timely to articulate what had unsettled him since his arrival. And he did so in the bold terms befitting the ancient line of Linton.

'Your major – didn't tell me his name – said you've only six men. How can this be? How can the chief of police, this Herr Schulze fellow, have let this happen when – as you say – there are Red Guard patrols everywhere?'

The emperor shook his head with determination. It had nothing to do with Herr Schulze, he said in unequivocal tones. Herr Schulze had done everything possible to help them. It was the new government's fault. It was they who had ordered the men be removed. They were the ones who had stopped the supplies to the estate. They would not even allow Herr Schulze to send ammunition for the guns that they had. It was *them*! A glance up at the darkening sky was as if away from his bittermost thoughts; and the swift, low adjunct that followed told of a subject that he wished not pursued.

'*Venez, mon cher colonel. Nous devons rentrer avant qu'il ne soit trop tard.*'

Following the course of the river a little way, the emperor soon indicated a short cut back to the lodge; he turned off the track and led Linton into a dense thicket of trees and heavy undergrowth. An assortment of crooked, snow-covered boughs had to be awkwardly hurdled and ducked under before the pair exited into the wide expanse of a glade. As they walked in the open the crystalline silence was broken only by the soft crunch of their footfall and faint tinkling of the emperor's medals.

Then, all of a sudden, the break came: a boar broke cover ahead. The two men stopped dead, momentarily stunned as the beast thundered across the clearing. Linton was first to spring back to life: he whipped his pistol from its holster.

'No, no,' the emperor said, catching sight of the move. He threw his arm in front of Linton: 'Don't waste your bullets.'

Linton nearly swallowed his tongue. *Waste bullets?* He had never wasted a bullet in his life! He turned on the emperor, with scarlet complexion. 'Do you not hunt, Your Majesty?' he said hotly.

'Yes, yes… but, Colonel Linton… the bullets…'

'Bullets are for hunting.'

A sudden shake of the head signalled the emperor's self-admonition. 'Yes, yes – you're right. Forgive me.'

But it was too late to forgive: Linton turned back as the boar crossed the far line of the trees. His blood was up though: the slur on his marksmanship could not possibly stand. His eyes swelling, his boots made a restive dig at the ground.

'Then we should hunt,' he said plainly.

The imperial assent granted, the two set off at a canter.

Linton's pace was the faster by far: it peaked at a gallop. He soon crashed through the tree-line with a mighty leap, picked up the boar's tracks, and began battering his way through the pines trees in furious pursuit, as impervious to the nicks and flicks of the branches as if charging through a hail of oncoming bullets. Bounding a series of stumps, bushes and other whitened protrusions he then suddenly stopped; he threw himself behind a tree, his ruddied cheeks puffing like a bellows. Not twenty yards ahead he spotted the beast snuffling in the undergrowth. With a quick deep breath he levelled his pistol and took aim; his finger feathered the trigger. At the very instant of firing two shots rang out overhead. Linton turned to the sky. He could see only trees, but the brutal echo of gunshots still rang in his ear, and rang, and rang – like the devil's own bell. He quickly looked down – and saw the boar scuttle and vanish. He spun round and scanned the woods behind him: the emperor was nowhere to be seen. An icy panic momentarily addled his brain, before a heavy fist slamming the tree set his senses to rights. *Hell and scissors – where was the damned man?* With an air-scenting snort he launched himself from the tree and tracked impatiently back.

It took him no time to discover the bifurcation of prints. The emperor's had turned from his own at a right angle. *A right angle! Damn a horse – he had turned off on purpose!* Pursuing the mazy path of the footprints, he stalked the forest noiselessly, patiently, breathlessly. He stealthily worked his way down the side of a hollow. At the bottom he stopped. There, at last, he found the emperor: slumped on his haunches, his back to Linton, his grey overcoat fanned out in the snow around him. For all the world he seemed to Linton like one of the totemic, iced corpses that had dotted the mountain passes. But at Linton's approach the emperor stood; in doing so he revealed the frozen, eviscerated carcass of a stag at his feet. His head bowed, the emperor's muttered words were scarcely audible in spite of the silence.

'Quel malheur. Quel terrible malheur.'

He turned to Linton, an almost pathetic, uncomprehending sadness in the depths of his doe-brown eyes. In the same heavy, forlorn tone he explained that the poachers only ever took the liver and heart of the deer; everything else they left to rot. The *Jägers* told him they sold them to the Jews in Vienna. Not long ago there had been over 2,000 deer in the forest, he said; now there were barely 200. A deep sigh seemed to dredge the life from within to deposit without. All that killing, he said, to take only the heart.

Two more gunshots rang out in the echoing vault of the sky. The emperor looked to the very tips of the trees, and then at the world around him.

'*Dieu, que le son du cor est triste au fond des bois,*' he said. His eyes falling on Linton's unfired pistol, the merest hint of a smile formed at the corners of his lips; a smile ironic, bitter, and despairing. 'Someone is always shooting somewhere, *mon cher colonel*. Someone always has bullets. But not us. So we – *we* must be happy to eat only vegetables tonight, *n'est-ce pas?*'

Well, yes, Linton thought, masking a sneer of disdain – they would have to be *now*.

Chapter 23

'How do you find the cutlets, Colonel Linton?'

They were vegetable. That was the pretence of meat at dinner. Linton sucked the turnip from his teeth and turned to the empress. 'Excellent,' he said.

'My husband told me you spotted a wild boar this afternoon.'

'We did.'

'He said you very nearly managed to catch it.'

'Very nearly.'

'What a pity you didn't. Although I've understood they're surprisingly quick when they run.'

'They possess the speed of all good game,' he replied with restraint. 'It's no surprise once you've seen it, I assure you.'

'Well then I very much ought to see one at least once, don't you think, Colonel? An empress should not be surprised by anything served at her table, should she?'

'Indeed not,' he said, continuing in his manner of military thrift.

'Although perhaps if I did see it, I might not then care to see it shot. One thinks a good deal more of an animal when it is in flight than when it is nothing more than a head or cutlets presented on one's plate, doesn't one?'

'That's why a man should always eat what he hunts, Your Majesty. It teaches him respect for the animal.'

'And a lady?'

'A *lady?*'

'Should a lady always hunt what she eats too, Colonel Linton? Not just a man.'

Her dark brown eyes settled on Linton and flashed with a lively, *scherzando* air. Their tints of playfulness were not matched by her countenance. Beneath a chignoned mass of curling black hair overhanging a narrow, hemispherical forehead, the delicate lines of her square chin and straight lips showed not the least deviation to signal emotion.

'One's respect for one's fellow creatures should always be mutual,' he said.

'I doubt it could be mutual, Colonel Linton, surely? Unless, that is, you would on occasions contrive to have the quarry in pursuit of the hunter. If that were the case I might fear that such an animal would show as little pity for my plight as one of Mr Lenin's Bolsheviks.'

Linton drew his finger across his moustache to veil the twitch of pleasure at her spirit. 'I said *fellow* creatures, Your Majesty. I would not dishonour the noble boar by attributing to him the savagery of the Bolshevik.'

'Well, that is a thing, Colonel Linton. I confess I had never before thought of myself in fellowship with a—'

A flicker of lights interrupted her. The lights then went off, came back on for a moment, flickered briefly, before at last the current ran out. The room now plunged into darkness, the dim light from the fireplace at the far end shadowed the hurried movements of the footman across the ceiling and walls, and bestowed a penumbral mystery on the features at the table. The emperor, heretofore engaged with the Countess X and the officer, gave the table a furious thump.

'*Gott im Himmel!* I cannot even eat without this wretched machine breaking!' The violence of his outburst brought forth his cough, which punctuated his ensuing, spluttered words as he fixed on his wife. 'It is – so – infuriating. *Infuriating* – Zita!'

'There is not enough fuel, that is the problem, Herr Colonel,' the major explained to Linton. 'I have tried many times to—'

'There is not enough *anything*!' the emperor cried, thumping the table again. '*That* is the problem. There is nothing but – but – but trees and snow, and – dead animals.'

Linton instinctively glanced at the empress. But to look at her was to look at a countenance unmoved, a visage flawless and serene. After a duly respectful silence in which to allow the emperor's emotion to diffuse and abate, the countess turned to Linton, her large sapphire eyes like stars in the night.

'You *will* get us some fuel, won't you, colonel?' she said, her look appealing, her tone expectant. 'We're in darkness day and night here.

One is very nearly forced to guess which bed one is to find oneself sleeping in in the morning, you know.'

'I will be happy to ensure the countess finds the right one,' the major averred with the stolid rigour of his class.

The countess returned a lofty eye, and replied in an even loftier tone, 'I'm quite certain you would lead me to the wrong one.'

'Certainly not. My honour would not allow that to happen.'

'Your honour has allowed very little to happen.'

'Nothing at all. You have my word.'

'I'm sure your word is the very best that you've given.'

'Indeed,' the officer declared proudly.

The countess could be scarcely bothered to sigh.

'Now – enough, Claudia. Don't tease the major,' the emperor said with weary reproach as two precious candles were lit on the table by the footman's taper.

'Sometimes, Your Majesty,' the countess returned keenly, 'the only way a woman is permitted to tell the truth is to do so by teasing. The skin of a great many men is more easily breached by that than a bullet. Of course, I'm certain that does not apply to you, does it, Colonel Linton?' She redressed herself to the so-named forthwith; her eyes appealed now brighter than before. Set in a noble, aquiline face crowned with its head of still-lustrous blonde hair, theirs was a look of rich, haughty allure; a look of that particular superiority possessed by a woman who has bought a husband of ancient lineage out of penury, and done so on a whim. That, of course, was all her attraction: she had tried to seduce Linton before.

It had been at the Esterhazy ball in Vienna. Once introduced, she had not been coy in her advances, and so they had danced, laughed, and flirted with abandon. Had she not repeatedly talked of her husband Linton might have succumbed to much more. But in the way her tongue had licked the count's name from her lips and flung it about his ears with a sort of malicious ecstasy whenever her fingers had brushed his lapels, he had suspected her of thrilling more at her husband's cuckoldry than at his own being. That the count had since been killed in the war mattered little to Linton now: he had long since spied his reflection in his cuirass. But it was this flirtation that had set the seal on his amorous disenchantment.

He had returned to England in 1911 having served at both ends of the African continent and quickly fallen in love with the Lady Sarah. Her spry, caustic independence was like an island citadel whose only access was a path of sweetness as slender as the bridge of Al-Sirat. It was a lengthy pursuit over hard terrain, concluded at the last by a fall from his mount. And what, when he had picked himself up from the ground and wiped the muck from his face, after 12 months of letters, invitations, entreaties and sighs had he discovered that the exasperating Lady Sarah wanted? To receive letters, invitations, entreaties and sighs: that was what. 'What more could a lady wish for?' he had wondered while he chased; 'What was her motive?' he had puzzled long after he fell. Having thus found himself to be repeating these questions (however fleetingly) in the countess's company, he had resolved to ask them no more.

Linton looked at the countess coldly. 'It was a highly effective weapon in Flanders, certainly,' he said.

The countess laughed. Rebuffed thus, she dismissed him with a peacock turn of her cheek.

'I remember saying to Herr Köstler during the war – you know Herr Köstler, don't you?' she asked the emperor.

'Of course.'

'Well, I asked him if it had been the case that the Austrians had written such a short note to the Serbians in those sunny August days, was it not then the fault of the composer that I had been forced to sit through such a long and dreadful German opera? "My noble countess," he replied to me, quite out of temper, "it is no fault of the composer if the musician cannot play." There, Your Majesty, at least one person has got some truth out of that man by a little teasing: it was not the music that was to blame – it was how it was *played*.'

A crackle of electricity saw the lights return, and the major note to Linton with the worldly-wise sagacity of his class, 'Ah, you see, Herr Colonel, I tell the footman it is not always the fault of the fuel. Sometimes the machine becomes too cold, that is all.'

After a short hush, Linton emitted a low, sardonic laugh. 'Ha, ha.

To think, Your Majesty – before I arrived I read in the press stories of how the imperial family was living in all kinds of luxury, with lorries full of goods arriving daily!' He laughed again with a forked cutlet on display. 'The luxury of the rabbit and the bat – one of Aesop's tales, no doubt!'

A general descent into mirth was abruptly cut short.

'How can they write that, Colonel Linton? How can they say such lies? Is this *luxury*?'

Linton turned back to the empress. Her features appeared suddenly stark in the returned electrical glare. For a moment he thought it barely conceivable that the pale face and waif-like form, attired in a simple black dress with a collar of pearls no more ostentatious than had they been beads, belonged to the woman to whom he had shortly before been conversing, and not to some common Tuscan *signorina*.

'It is not,' he replied in stiff, respectful tones. 'It is the gleanings of the gutter press. They are the same the world over: they scrabble in the mud.'

'But they are lies, Colonel Linton. They are printing lies. How can they do such a thing? There is no luxury here,' she continued, her lips hardly moving despite the force of her words. 'And yet we are still here, Colonel Linton. Our telephone lines are tapped, we are watched day and night, we have only a handful of men and a handful of bullets – and yet we are still *here*. We have not abandoned our people. We have not run away like the Kaiser and Junkers: *they* have retired as if nothing had happened, as if the war had nothing to do with them. Now we hear the German people believe they have been lied to as well, that they have been cheated and deceived. Deceived? By whom? It is my husband who has been lied to, cheated and deceived – by *them*. He and my brother tried to finish the war – but *they* did not want to. They wanted to continue bombing ships with their submarines until we were destroyed. Until *we* were destroyed, Colonel Linton – *us* – because they cared nothing for Austria and the empire. They were happy to sacrifice *us* for Germany.

'Now the war is over there is no one in Austria who takes the blame either. It is a land full of musicians; there are no composers. They are happy to be all like Herr Adler. Do you know he told my husband last year that as *he* did not start the war, it was not *his* responsibility to end it? It was not my husband who started the war either – but Herr Adler, Herr Bauer and their friends want to make him the only person who is responsible for the millions that have been killed. They want to pretend that they did not volunteer to fight at the beginning too, that they have won the elections for Austria – and not for themselves. You see, Colonel Linton, they are the same as the Germans; they want to sacrifice us for them. But we will not let that happen. We will not abandon our people. My husband has not abdicated – he will never abdicate. Never, Colonel Linton.'

The empress's speech, delivered with the same vivacious gleam in her eyes, and the same rigid, inscrutable, almost divine poise as before, had a peculiarly invigorating effect on Linton. There was none of the countess coquetry, none of this Sarah skittishness. Instead there was a straightforward, homely, implacable resilience that could not but rouse him to his bottommost fibres. She was like a pillbox off which bombs and bullets would unceasingly bounce; at the end of which barrage, the emperor immediately charged out on the counter.

'*Austria shall be a federal state in which every race shall form its own political community in the district where it is settled.* That is what I proposed, and that is what I shall hold to: a free union of nations,' he said, a powerful, unafflicted force suddenly over-mastering his voice, as his eyes, repeatedly seeking his wife, lapped like tongues at a spring's nutrient source. 'I relinquished the government of the country for the sake of peace. I'd retired pending the restoration of order – to ensure the transition of power. But only for that. Everybody knows what I said. As the King of England would never abdicate and forsake his oaths, nor will I. Nor *can* I. It is only the throne that can provide the security for the new independent states, Colonel Linton. President Wilson must understand that. He must understand it is the only way to stop the provinces of the empire from becoming victims of the chaos of revolution – just as is happening now in Germany and Hungary. I did not understand how quickly these sentiments would spread when I acted in November. I thought by removing myself I would help to prevent them. But this is not the case. So we must restore the authority of the crown as soon as possible, Colonel Linton – to save them. Yes, yes, now you are here, Colonel Linton, you must help,' he said, the increasing excitement that animated his words reaching an almost fevered pitch, his accents flecked with wild caprice and decree. 'With maybe only five or ten thousand men – English, American… but not French, not Italians – we will very quickly bring back the order and stability of the throne. We will stop the Bolshevik conquest of Europe. That has always been the purpose of the Habsburgs and the Crown, after all – to defend the people from the barbarians. Yes, yes, that is why we are still here.'

Colonel Linton had long understood that the defence of Christendom was no longer a fight against Islam; it was a battle against godlessness. But the dinner had now proved to him one thing: for the Habsburgs to triumph and continue to rule, the emperor was nothing without the power of his wife.

Chapter 24

Of course, if the British government had any backbone the army would have been on the next train to Vienna. A few thousand men, a proper man on the spot and the deed would be done: the Bolsheviks would be crushed and order restored before the president had had time to put the jam on his toast. That would be true diplomacy. *Successful* diplomacy.

Alas, Linton knew, that sort of Palmerstonian brio had succumbed to the fad of the franchise. Politicians were too concerned with their seat to act for the good. Democracy was quite the worst thing when liberty was at stake.

Come the conclusion of dinner he had already determined his move though. He would make no mention of Carrington's letter: nothing could be presented which might induce the emperor to precipitately quit either Eckartsau or Austria. If the assassination attempt came it would have to be thwarted where they stood: the lodge would be their redoubt! And then, once thwarted, Linton's true mission would be to make certain that the news of such a base, cowardly attack on the imperial family (and an officer of the Guards from the victorious allies to boot) was known the world over. The powers could not be but stirred by fear and revulsion. Around the tables of Paris, accords would be reached to stop the barbarian Bolshevism from sweeping through Europe, as Kara Mustafa and the Tatar hordes had once done from the east. Led by the Habsburgs of a new Holy Empire, it would be for the defence of civilisation. The British government had asked Linton to provide the emperor with *moral support* – well, he would make certain it was moral to the hilt!

Damn it – he would do it for her!

The lack of arms and ammunition was Linton's most pressing concern. And for that he had no choice but to meet with Herr Schulze. To this end he would return to Vienna first thing the next morning.

The next morning dawned with a deep drifting blizzard. The car was snowed in and the road out impassable. There was not a hope of his leaving that day.

*

At the same time as Colonel Linton had been procuring the emperor's car from the royal garage the *previous* day, Edward, having stormed out of the café, had made straight for the telegraph office. He had cabled Major B accepting the post in Breslau: he said he would come *as soon as he could*. A postscript noted Nurse Fawley could not come. He had then returned to the depot to seek out Lance Corporal Bagley.

Edward's enquiry as to Bagley's whereabouts was met by Private Collins with a cold, glassy-eyed stare. He then informed Edward that Bagley and Yorston had left ten minutes before with an extra delivery of blankets for the distribution centres: 'Just like yer ordered 'em ter yesterday, sir.' Edward had no recollection that he had, but his turbulent mind was not about to argue the toss. Given the conditions of the roads Collins doubted they'd be back before dusk. The (new) punishment necessarily (and vexingly) postponed to the following day, Edward therefore proceeded to do what any man would when troubled by women and work: he went to a tavern and got drunk.

Rather more drunk than intended, in fact. The rare and welcome sight of an English soldier encouraged the innkeeper and an old sot at the bar to lubricate him out of taciturnity, not that much lubrication was needed. A couple of watery (though potent) beers quickly brought forth the revelation that Edward had had a previous flirtation (he used the word wisely) with a girl in Vienna, whereat the innkeeper's sensibilities were suitably touched. 'Ah, we have all loved the illusion once,' he said with a sigh, and poured him some type of schnapps. 'It is the illusion that makes us all dance,' he added, and poured him another.

'Such women were the playthings of the Viennese spirit,' mused the sot, who bought him some type of whisky.

'*Vienna, Vienna, only you*
Will be the town where my dreams come true,'

he sang, and stood him another. In spite of his alcoholic (he used the word advisedly) intake Edward remembered leaving the tavern as sober as a judge. It was only when he reached his hotel that he had found himself drunk as a lord. A splitting headache and ditchwater mouth were the morning consequence – the effects compounded by a packet of Woodbines and an empty stomach. The encounter with Bagley was consequently deferred to the afternoon.

On his eventual arrival at the depot he summoned Bagley to the small jerry-built office constructed at the back. The plan was elementary. There was no avoiding Bagley being sent to Berlin the next day; this would, however, be mitigated by Edward's light-hearted explanation that, with the relief mission about to end, it was the quickest route back home to Blighty. He would joke that Bagley's punishment was no longer shovelling snow, but putting up with Major B! The tricky part would follow. Bagley's original promotion had, technically, been nothing of the sort: it was merely an appointment, so he was still a lance jack. In writing to Major B detailing the incident Edward would consequently state that he had been about to recommend Bagley's official promotion to corporal due to his exceptional work during the mission and... well, he would come up with the rest of that bar later. Anyway, in light of the circumstances and the '*delicate question of morale*' he would propose Bagley's appointed rank be removed as punishment, and then reinstated as a meritorious *promotion*. Edward had every confidence Major B would see sense and back the judgement of his captain. Then *that* would be an end to the matter. Such was the plan.

Things did not go according to it. Even by the afternoon Edward's hangover was little improved. To Bagley he appeared like a man of the lash: his demeanour sullen, his tone gruff, his complexion wan, his patience limited. Nothing, in short, sounded to him like a joke. Bagley was thus led to understand not that *he* had done any wrong, but as a result of some slight from above, Captain Wilson was in turn kicking down. This was the usual vindictive recourse – exactly as Private Tate had always told him – of the petty bourgeois to the worker. And Tate had been right on another thing too: they'd send him anywhere so as he'd never come back.

As far as Edward was concerned, though, on being informed of the modified punishment Bagley had accepted his fate with the same hamster-cheeked cheerfulness as he had the appointment in the first place. He had paid up, looked pretty, thanked Edward, and saluted smartly as he left. And that, seemingly, *was* that.

At muster call next day Lance Corporal (strictly speaking – though Edward avoided any ranking address – *Private*) Bagley was absent. Edward's quip as to whether he had needed 'a driver' to get there was met by a parade of stonewall expressions. Further enquires as to where Bagley might be were met by a continued solidarity of silence. At this he felt an undeniable frisson, for it meant Bagley's absence was intentional. It meant, no less, that the men stood in defiance of his command. Edward's sudden urge to confess his benign stratagem was just as suddenly rejected: the men would see it as the wheedling device of a panic-struck officer to extricate himself from the consequences of his high-handed actions. Instead he decided to put his faith in one man alone. A man with whom he had shared trenches, shell holes, sunshine, bullets, whizz-bangs and blood; one man who had been by his side for two years, unflinching day after day; one man whose commitment to the army preceded the war, who knew the King's Regulations backwards, who knew his duty always forward. And so he dismissed the men and summoned Private Collins.

Private Collins had distrusted Edward from the moment he had volunteered to lead a raiding party on his first night in the line. Many a thrusting young subaltern had arrived and done exactly the same, of course – and many had met the same end – but Collins suspected Edward's motive had been due to some perverse moral compulsion, that he *had* to go forward. This he had glimpsed in a flash of moonlit blue in Edward's eyes, and he had watched out for this same ever since. Private Collins also had to go forward, but he did so for the same reasons a man went to work in the morning: routine, commitment, and a sense of general responsibility towards his colleagues and kin. He did not do it out of any sense of *morality*. Morality merely dragged one man down to share another's fate. This was he why he distrusted Edward. The only thing Edward had to his credit in Collins' book – and this, be it said, was worth far more than respect – was that he was lucky. Bullets missed him; shells soared over him; shrapnel barely grazed him; infections seemed uninterested in him. And if there was one thing twenty years of soldiering had taught Private Collins, it was to cling to luck far tighter than life. For this reason alone had he remained limpet-like by Edward's side for two years. Now, however, there was no longer cause to; so he dealt with Edward's questions for the most part monosyllabically.

'Have you seen Lance Corporal Bagley?'

'Yes, sir.'

'When?'

''Bout five o'clock, sir.'

'What, this morning?'

'No, sir.'

A short, expectant silence.

'Yesterday then?'

'Yes, sir.'

'Evening – after he came back with Yorston?'

'Yes, sir.'

'And you didn't see him again? You haven't seen him since?'

'No, sir.'

'And no one else has either?'

'Can't speak fer 'em. Can only say what I saw, sir.'

A puff of exasperation.

'But no one's said anything about having seen him, or not having seen him?'

'Men see each other and don't see each other all the time, sir.'

The only variation to Collins' stock, perfunctory responses came at the interview's close. After saluting he turned to the door, then looked Edward dead in the blue of his untrustworthy eye – as a cat should a king.

'When a man's not to be paid fer 'is labour,' he said, ''e 'as ter go where the labour's paid – sir.'

Edward's frustration briefly threatened to boil over to visible emotion. Because now, he understood, the war *had* ended. All the fraternity and shared blood of the past meant nothing to the future.

Faced with what he was sure was the real prospect of mutiny,

Edward's only hope was that duty won out once the point had been proven, and that Bagley's transgression (whatever it turned out to be) might not be too far gone to be brushed under the carpet. He gave the men a day to cool off and return to the fold. The next morning they had indeed done so: all except Bagley.

'So Lance Corporal Bagley's deserted?' he asked flatly.

Private Dawson was the first to reply, and he did so not with insubordination, but in a manner of plain, straightforward fact. 'Not a lance corporal, is 'e, sir?'

'War's over, sir,' said Addison.

'Exactly, sir. A man can't be a-desertin' when there's no one ter be a-fightin',' said Yorston.

Collins said nothing.

Here, at last, Edward gave full vent to his fury. Not to the men – no, certainly not! It was not *their* fault. The fault was all Carrington's! He was the one who had meddled. He was the one who had caused such a storm! It was *he* who had created the waves!

When Edward was once again on his own he tried to think clearly. There was still the possibility Bagley had simply been on the peg for two days, but that was unlikely given the serious consequences of now missing the train to Berlin. The probability seemed that he had thrown it all in and hoped somehow to make his own way back to England. The possibility, however, unpalatable as it was, was that he had jumped ship to join the Bolshevik cause. Edward had lately remarked socialist leanings in some of Bagley's actions and speech – but hadn't he in all of the men? Hadn't he done so in himself? It was only the incident with the *Schieber* that had brought them to note. But they had only been *leanings*, hadn't they? They were just the signs of a spot of trade unionism – not of communist militancy, surely? Then, Edward thought, even after all that fraternity and shared blood of the past, what did he actually know of the inner thoughts of the man? Of any of the men? Collins had proved that. Bagley, with his hamster cheeks, golf club and guileless smile – the character of a man was of more substance than that! The only thing Edward did know was he couldn't just let Bagley *go*: he couldn't just abandon him to the enemy without trying to find him. And so, having been done with Millie two days before, he found he needed her help, and Kashia's. Maybe they could give him an answer. As such he headed straight for the hospital.

As he walked briskly down the Ringstrasse an icy squeal of brakes brought him to a halt. He looked up and turned to the road.

'Captain—?'

'Colonel—'

'I know my damned rank, man. Your *name*, Captain – what is it?'

'Wilson. Captain Wilson, sir.'

A combination of one horse, main force, considerable throttle, much wood and several spades had succeeded in digging Linton's car out and dragging it up the drive that morning. An ever alert, eagle eye had then ascertained that the officer on the Ringstrasse was the very same as had passed him on Carrington's stairwell. Serendipity had provided his man at the critical moment! He ordered Edward to meet him at the Bristol Hotel at four o'clock sharp, then marched back to the car and continued on to the police commissariat.

Chapter 25

To arrive unannounced at the commissariat for the world and his dog to see was precisely the sort of troublemaking Herr Schulze had expected from Colonel Linton. Not that he had ever yet met him; as chief of police, and inspector before, it was his duty to know all *about* people, for people to know only *of* him. But experience told that any man connected to the late archduke was – like the archduke himself – bound to be a cause of political grief.

Following several moments of intense, glowering aggravation at the news, he dismissed his assistant with the curt response that the colonel should not be brought up to his office: *he* would come down. Schulze's next movements were those of consummate deliberation – not merely to allow him time to think, but to make Linton wait. He slowly stood up, moved out from behind his desk and carefully removed his thick blue overcoat from the stand by the door. With ceremonial precision did he do up the gleaming brass buttons to the top where they joined with the stiff, brocaded lapels. Returning to his desk he collected his cap and positioned it inch-perfect on his head. He next retrieved his calabash pipe from the console by the window, then first opened one desk drawer to remove a pair of black leather gloves, then another for his eyeglass and tobacco. Finally, accoutred with every formal beat necessity, he picked up his truncheon and left.

Marching in stately fashion down the stairs he espied Linton pacing the cavernous entrance hall, upon which his descent could be said to have even slowed just a touch.

'Ah, Herr Colonel – I have been most interested to make your acquaintance. Most interested indeed,' Schulze declared, wrestling his hands into his gloves as he made his final approach. 'I had understood you were in Eckartsau – with the emperor.'

'I was.'

A pinched-face man with sad, drooping cheeks, fine twirls rounding off a lavish moustache, and thick silver-black eyebrows foregrounding two keen, sunken eyes, Schulze flashed his squirrel front teeth in the guise of a smile.

'And now you are here.' A pause was for a forensic scan of Linton's problematical features, before he continued graciously, 'Yes, I am hearing a great many things about you. It is for sure we are most fortunate to be having someone like you here in Vienna in this time. Someone who is understanding the history and culture so well. Someone who is so loyal to the emperor.'

'The emperor has said the same of you,' Linton obliged in return.

At this, if Schulze had ever blushed once, he might here have blushed twice. 'I am only doing my duty, Herr Linton,' he said.

'No doubt.'

'Of course there is no doubt. Loyalty is the most important thing to people in our positions. It is why we are here, Herr Linton.'

'Indeed. Now—'

'*Now*, Herr Linton,' Schulze interrupted emphatically, his register lower, his assertion quite absolute, 'we shall take a little walk in the gardens. It is better to discuss some matters outside, don't you agree?'

Most certainly Linton agreed. At last there was someone who got straight to the point!

The gardens were in fact a small courtyard in the nexus of the drab commissariat blocks, the odd desultory shrub the only botanical shape protruding from the heavy dumping of snow. A circular pathway had been shovelled clear to access various nondescript doors, though the ice made the cobblestones treacherous. Schulze and Linton tramped the circuit like a couple of old lags.

'It is indeed a most unpleasant situation, that is for sure,' Schulze intoned after they had been talking some minutes. 'But already the people hear rumours that some countries want to make us into a federation with the old empire – with the very same countries that betray us at the end of the war! Not, of course, with the German people we belong to.'

'I'm not interested in rumours.'

'No, of course not, Herr Linton, you are not a policeman,' said Schulze, his contumely barely concealed in the twitch of his lips. 'Rumours and suspicion are the filling that makes our sandwich of facts. But, as I am saying before to you, you must understand that so long as the emperor is insisting to stay in so dangerous a place it is impossible for me to help him. Impossible. The government wants to force the emperor so he has no choice other than that he must leave.'

Linton fetched him a look of the narrowest breadth, then proceeded to be blunt, and to bluff; despite his earlier conviction Schulze would get straight to the point, he had now missed the thing altogether.

'To deprive the emperor of the means to defend his life is as much as to allow others to end it. Is that clear? So when His Majesty's Government reinstates the blockade of the country and no food trains are let in, we'll know where the blame lies. Then we'll see how popular you and your government friends are.'

'It is for sure they are not *my* friends, Herr Linton.'

'If you're theirs it's the same!'

Schulze's small mouth, with its inclination to gape like a door left ajar (the draught sparing the effort to open a window), displayed his teeth as a proof of their gnawing prowess. For the nut of human resistance could not always be cracked; sometimes the shell had to be ground down to reach the kernel of truth. He therefore stopped, removed his pipe from his pocket, and silently, meticulously, with almost exaggerated pretension, filled it with tobacco.

After observing this tedious process for nearly a minute, during which he progressively coloured the full spectrum of red, Linton eventually snapped, 'Well, what do you say?'

But Herr Schulze was not to be rushed; less so given the clearly successful result. At length he placed the pipe to his lips, struck a match, and with eyes steadfastly down puckered his lips to draw forth the smoke. Then, in the controlled tones of one lightly suppressing the merest hint of aggression, he said, 'The emperor is safe, Herr Linton. Perfectly safe. You have my word.'

'Safe? What do you mean *safe*?'

'Exactly that word.'

'You just said the place was too dangerous!'

'Safe – yes, yes,' explained Schulze between puffs, 'but only if he leaves.'

'*Leaves? Safe?* What the devil are you on about?'

'I am saying he is safe for now; that is certain: my spies are assuring me this. But this information cannot be true for always. With this situation we are in things can be changing very quickly. That is why he must leave.'

Linton let out a scornful blast and tossed his head in disgust. 'Your spies would be a damned sight more useful if they carried some ammunition and guns – not words. But that's what you get in a place like this, I suppose.'

Schulze nearly snapped the stem of his pipe. *In a place like this!* Who did the colonel think he was speaking to – an old sumpter at a *Beisl*? He glanced up at the cold, featureless walls. Why, the present location was ideal for the use of the truncheon. That would teach him some manners. His pipe fiercely clenched, he took a series of rapid, pacifying puffs to restrain his impulses.

How a bumptious little island like England had managed to conquer so much had always confounded Herr Schulze. The English possessed no culture to speak of, had produced no thinkers of note and given the world no rulers of wonder. Where was their Mozart or Bach; their Hegel or Kant; their Goethe, Grillparzer, Heine or Schiller; where was their Frederick the Great, their Luther, their Bismarck? They were nothing but a backwater blob off the mainland of Europe. His loathing of the country was only outdone by his jealousy of it. For, oh – how he envied their empire! How he craved their saltwater moat! How he pined for the unity of their isle without borders! And oh – oh! – how he longed to have to speak only one language! In place of giving vent to these wildly tortured emotions, he was instead surprised by a letter.

'Here,' said Linton impetuously, overwhelmed by a reckless presumption as he whipped Carrington's battered epistle from his pocket. 'I'm sure your little spies told you about this, eh?'

Schulze accepted the paper with the withering look he reserved for any eureka manifestation of evidence. At first he could not make out a thing that was written, so he removed his eyeglass and popped it in his left eye. A quick turn of the paper was for any mark of identification, but there was none. His eyebrows then proceeded to quiver with surprise on remarking the English script; his nose then sniffed as he read the contents; and, on concluding, a mocking turn of his lips would have been visible save for the greatest exertion of will.

He took a lengthy draw on his pipe before he asked in suitably grave tones, 'Where did you get this, Herr Linton?'

'What does *that* matter?' replied Linton, proud he had not only trumped both Carrington and Schulze, but the man's wretched spies too.

'It matters a great deal. It says an assassination is planned.'

'Exactly.'

'That is most serious.'

'Of course it damned well is!'

'But – don't you see what it says?'

'Of course I see. It's there in the letter!'

Schulze's marble eyes seemed to suddenly prism and tint, as if rolled in the brightest of lights. Despite Linton's assertion, it was clear he had seen nothing at all. A whole palette of colours was displayed that to Linton was one monochrome hue. Schulze resumed walking, the renewed vigour of his pace matched by the animated turn of his mind – of one whose supreme powers were fully charged with sifting the options unexpectedly placed in his hands. His response, by contrast, was one of negligent calculation. 'Yes, Herr Linton – but it is even more serious that it is the *Dósza* behind it.'

Linton knew his Hungarian history: the peasant revolt; the defeat of the Turk; the noble betrayal; Dósza set on his hot iron throne, with a hot iron crown on his head; then dismembered and fed to his men. But he'd paid no regard to the name when he'd read it.

'And? What difference does that make?'

'The difference is that they are the ones assassinating Count Tisza last year and leading the occupation in Budapest to start the revolution. They are trying to start a communist revolution here in December too by sending Herr Kun to Vienna – but I would not let them. I told Herr Adler I would resist the foreigners with all of my police. That is the only the reason it is not happening – because *I* am doing this. But now it is clear the *Dósza* want to try again; they want to start by killing the emperor – just like the tsar. Yes, it is for sure, there is no one more impatient for Austrian blood than the people of

Hungary.' He paused to scoop some snow from a shrub, fashioned it into a sphere, held it in his palm, and then, as if words alone were never sufficient to be testament to truth, demonstrably smashed it with his other gloved hand. 'But we will crush them – yes, just like we are doing seventy years ago too.'

Linton was lip-curlingly unimpressed by the show: he knew the Austrians had had the Russians do the crushing for them. And he responded with the appropriate sardonic disdain. 'They're Bolsheviks then.'

'The difference, Herr Linton,' said Schulze, his voice assuming the richness of portent, 'is that I know they are here in Vienna even now.'

'So those spies of yours haven't a clue after all.'

'Yes, yes, maybe,' Schulze agreed carelessly, 'but now we must act together very quickly. Very quickly indeed. We must make sure to protect the emperor. The *Dósza* do not play games. They come only to kill.'

'Protection is with *ammunition and arms* – as I said before. And with more than six damned men!'

'Yes, indeed.' Schulze fell to a silence of deep deliberation. After a moment his conclusion was masterful and direct. 'I can give you the ammunition, Herr Linton. Yes, of course. But it must be you who is taking it: it must only be going in the British lorries to Eckartsau. There cannot be any suspicion I am sending it. That is too dangerous. If the ammunition was discovered like that it is for sure the government would be making a terrible show against my Vienna police, saying the emperor is wanting to fight against the people to bring back the monarchy. Do you understand, Herr Linton – if this happens to someone so loyal as me there is safety for no one?'

Linton checked his response. After all, in any military operation a subordinate was given only the information pertaining to his objective. So there was no point talking of middles and ends to someone like Schulze when they were at the beginning. His accord granted in the form of a grunt, he pressed on forcefully.

'And the men – the arms?'

'Yes, of course, but we must be very careful, Herr Linton; these men cannot be either from my police or your soldiers,' said Schulze in a newly confidential tone befitting such an enterprise, a glimmer in the depths of eyes befitting its worth. 'The only people that can do this are the monarchists. Prince Strumboldt is the person to make sure this will happen. Yes, he is the only person to be trusted in this most dangerous time.'

'Good – then get on with it.'

'*Me?* No, no, Herr Linton – that is impossible. The chief of police contacts the leader of the monarchists? Quite impossible.'

'Well get someone else then.'

'It is not so simple as that, Herr Linton. We cannot contact by telegram or telephone: there are traitors everywhere listening. Someone must go to speak with him – in person. But it is too dangerous that I sent one of the Vienna police. No, that is impossible.'

'Damn a horse, man – what *is* possible?'

Schulze stopped dead. Fixing intently on Linton, his instruction was plain.

'The only thing possible is you go yourself,' he said. 'Such a man is trusting only the word of the British Army – *from a person so noble as you, Herr Linton* – to do this. Yes, yes, I am giving the ammunition and you are making certain the prince is sending the men and some arms. And you must go as soon as possible – otherwise there is too much time for things to be changing that we can do nothing about. Do you understand, Herr Linton? You must go immediately. *You.*'

Colonel Linton was certainly not about to let himself be packed off like a galopin – whatever the cause – by a glorified runner. Serendipitous it was that he had just got his hands on one who could be instead.

Chapter 26

'Sorry, sir – when?'

'*What?*'

'Catch the train when, sir?'

'Hell and scissors – *tonight*. Don't you listen, Wilson?'

Edward was trying to, but there was a lot to take in. What Edward *had* ascertained was that he was to head to the town of Dürnstein, an hour or more west of Vienna, to deliver a message to the prince. This, however, took no account of his own troubles and duties.

'But, sir, the relief mission orders—'

Linton nearly exploded. 'Damn a horse – officers don't "*but*", they *do*. Is that clear?'

The alacrity of Edward's confirmation mollified Linton. Every young officer was a disagreeable prig in his book – unless he was drunk; this one was clearly no different. Besides, the incipient caveat could not but rouse him to the irksome truth that he was ordering an officer away from his post (however briefly) on an assignment for which there was, strictly speaking, no *official* command. And if Colonel Linton regarded anything in life as sacrosanct it was military protocol. Moreover, as the embassy had to be confided orally, the information had to be shared. This, in moderated tones in the dingy corner of the basement Grille of the Bristol, he forthwith proceeded to do. He stated first that the order came straight from the Ministry of X.

When he had finished conveying the details of the message, he told Edward a telegram had already been sent to the prince notifying him that the Countess X would arrive on the late train (that was Edward, Linton clarified, though the prince would not know that; Edward would have to impersonate her coquetries as best he could – the Viennese loved their masques, after all!). Final confirmation was again sought that the above was clear.

Edward gave it – though the ruse about the countess was immediately lost in the convoluted twist of events. Only a couple of hours before, he was unpicking a Gordian knot on the Ringstrasse when the colonel had fallen upon him as if he were a column-dodging shifter. Nor had Millie been at the hospital when he had got there; so, unable to wait, he had had to leave her a message before hastening back to the hotel. Serendipity was therefore the very last word Edward would have used to describe their encounter!

The instruction concluded, Linton accompanied Edward back to the ground floor. A prearranged signal being made to the concierge, the concierge came promptly out from his desk and led them along a side corridor to a cloakroom. Inside Edward was presented with an overcoat: large, brown, and shabby, its aroma was notably fusty.

Linton explained with unvarnished contempt (and only modest deceit) that the ink-slinging official at the Ministry had insisted Edward not go in uniform. But – 'Hang it, I'll be damned if I'm going to let a British officer of mine meet the prince dressed up like some footy little spy! So this'll have to do.'

Edward's coffee-stained (but still *clean*) greatcoat was removed and replaced by the new (old) coat. The fit (if it could be said to have one) was loose, inclining to baggy. Once it was buttoned up, a thick scarf was added to hide his lapels, and a stiff woollen hat exchanged for his cap. Edward glanced down at his boots; so too did the colonel: their consternation was mutual and silent, until Linton said, 'Well, don't go crossing your damned legs on the train.'

Without further delay, Edward was hustled out of the cloakroom, then out into the snowy darkness; he was told to cable as soon as he was back.

Edward reached the Westbahnhof just after seven. When he did he was informed with Germanic brevity by the clerk at the ticket office that there was no station at Dürnstein: he would have to get off at Krems and take a – Edward didn't catch what he said above the noise of a train whistle; he asked the clerk to repeat it. The clerk's mechanical response was to point at the station clock: the train whistle was for *him*. Encumbered by the size and weight of his new attire, and unsure of which platform, Edward only just made it. Thereafter, the sudden whirlwind of confusion and intrigue swept aside his other concerns. After all, to act was to be happy: it was to be *anything*. In a state of permanent self-consciousness as to his garb and giveaway boots, he consequently spent the journey repeating the message to himself *ad infinitum* so as not to forget the least detail, while simultaneously fretting and plotting about how to reach Dürnstein from Krems. In the end a metropolitan mindset persuaded him there would be plentiful cabs at the station to carry him onwards when he got there.

At Krems the provincial reality was stark: there was not even so much as a husky for hire. Indeed, on exiting the station into the fathomless drift of impeccable snow, he might have been at an outpost on the winter tundra, such was the deserted level of nothingness. The handful of passengers who had got off the train with him quickly vanished into the depths of the night. All he could make out in the darkness were a few trees, apparently a road, a couple of unlit lamps, and a row of dwellings away to his left. Any evidence of greater habitation was concealed behind the adumbrated roll of the hills and the moonlit film that covered the valleys.

A sudden crunch of snow made him turn back. On the far side of the station there was just enough light emanating from the hall to give substance to a vague human form. The contusions of electric light and the moon shadowed a figure whose thick winter garments possessed a strange, unsexed lineament, as if a simple wire mesh had been sheathed in a Carmelite habit. Edward stared at the figure in the hope of catching an eye. But no eye could be caught; no face could be seen; not a word broke the silence. He looked left and right: there was still no one about. At length the predicament took charge of his tongue. He called out. He asked the way to Dürnstein, asked was it far, asked was there a cab anywhere… or could he make it on foot? – this last lest the question seem too much an attempt to solicit a lift from someone who was clearly awaiting just that. Still there was silence; still nothing moved. Then, all of a sudden, a monastic arm rose; it pointed behind him to the waning westerly moon. Edward turned and faced the orb. But if the direction were intended as a navigational aid a stick might have been thrown for all the good it did him: Edward had no idea where he was. He spun back with thankless intent, but the words stayed lodged in his throat: in the instant the figure had vanished. An oath on his lips, his ears pricked to the snort of a horse: it came from the moon – or somewhere beyond. He peered through the sheen of white light. At last, as if dangled at the end of a long silver thread, he discerned the shape of a carriage. He hurried towards it.

The driver was hunched over, the reins clasped in his hands, his eyes shut in apparent deep slumber. Edward rapped the side of the carriage. Was the carriage for hire? he asked; the driver barely stirred at the sound. Would he take him to Dürnstein? he pressed; the driver opened his eyes and looked dumbly around. Then Edward remembered: he asked in hushed, fevered tones if the driver was waiting for the Countess X? These words were like a coin dropped in the slot of an old pier attraction: the driver's mouth gaped and his eyes whirled with life; a cursory examination of Edward was then of one long-accustomed to ill-fitting coats cloaking all manner of life. He signalled for Edward to ascend.

The passage to Dürnstein was along a rocky strip of land through the Wachau valley, the winding road crumbling away to the icy black Danube on one side, a sheer escarpment rising Babel-like to the moon on the other. After what seemed to Edward like a journey of hours, the moonlit ruins of the medieval keep of Dürnstein castle loomed ahead on the hillside. As they entered the narrow streets of the town only the dim glow from an unshuttered window here and there broke the patchwork pattern of silver and shadow.

The carriage was drawn to a halt beside a high, plain wall. A footman received them, his face craggy and molten like the wax in the lantern that lit it. He led Edward through an iron gate postern and up a steep cobbled alley that hugged the shadows of the mighty Gothic buttress-work. At the top of the incline they entered a galleried courtyard, a sharp turn immediately taking them through a wooden door, where a narrow vaulted corridor was like the ingress to a crypt. The footman stopped. In the spare light of a single electric lamp he snuffed the candle and placed the lantern on a shallow recess. Turning to Edward, he reached out a long, skinny hand. Edward flinched, convinced the limb sought more than his clothes. An adjustment saw him lower his eyes and wriggle free of his misshapen apparel. The divestment complete, he straightened his back like a chrysalis released. He once more followed the footman.

At the far end of the passage they exited into the main castle corridor. The ornately panelled walls, sparsely appended by two rows of scallop-shaped lamps (though with even fewer bulbs working), seemed cast in the dusky, hard wood tones of a galleon's cabin at night. They crossed the entrance hall. There, three magnificent candelabra were positioned like giant flambeaux, their flaming incandescence illuminating the grand staircase and the heights far above. All around, vast tableaux of holy war were glimpsed and emboldened in the fiery light: the armour gleamed, the pennants flew, the valleys rolled with 20,000 men; then the walled towns fell, the fires raged, and somewhere in the smoke and fog a king was slain at Lützen. The corridor resumed; the darkness returned. As they passed along the hollow length Edward thought he heard a dissonant third pair of boots falling out with their rhythm. A final turn brought them to the threshold of a large room. They stopped. On one side was a series of tall latticed windows on top of a row of stone alcoves; on the other a great fireplace extruded a long, bare, brick wall, the light of a half-digested ration of logs radiating out across the flagstone floor. In front of the fire were two old armchairs with a small table beside each. On one, Edward noticed, was an empty wine glass. He looked up at the carved ceiling panels, the patterns of moonlight reflected from the waters of the Danube outside glittering and twinkling, as if being spun in a stroboscope. An instinct thought to put a hand out to stop it.

'An English...' began a firm, resonating voice, before pausing; a slight squint preceded the confirmation, '...*Ja, ja*, that's right – an English officer. *Ja*, I was thinking exactly that when I received the telegram this afternoon. I have known the Countess X for many years. She is a spirited and venturesome woman, but she is never taking a train, that is for certain.'

The prince was at the far end of the room. He stood, side-on to Edward, at the head of an impressive oak table on which was spread a mass of papers and leather-bound volumes. An oil lamp in the middle provided a broad canopy of investigative illumination, a single lamp so positioned in front of the prince to afford scrutiny of an item once chosen. The present selection was a large folio of coloured prints, above which his fingers hovered with apian impatience.

Of lean physique and average height, the prince possessed a small turtle-like face with wavy black hair, heavy eyes and a pair of fine, crescent-shaped eyebrows. His complexion was smooth and unblemished, and combined with skin tightly wrapped round his cheekbones and jaw, would have given the impression of a man considerably younger had he not, at that moment, returned his attention to the folios and the moonlight shone on his bald, Caesarian crown.

Although the prince's remark as to the countess's viatical habits did not seek confirmation, Edward thought courtesy obliged it. But if courtesy obliged, then he knew the correct form of princely address was also surely required – whatever it was.

'Yes, Your… Excellency,' he said.

The prince's lips wrinkled, as if he had just been fed a bitter lettuce leaf. He flashed a condescending smile.

'You do not need to flatter me, young man. Such terms are no use now. To the victor, the spoils.' At which, to emphasise his disdain for the subject, he turned one of the folios over. Leaning forward to inspect the new plate, an expression of entomological wonder came over him, as if he were a lepidopterist just presented with the wings of a most rare and exquisite butterfly. 'Who are you?' he suddenly asked, his eyes fixed on the plate.

'Lieutenant – Captain Wilson, Your… *sir*.'

'*Captain?*'

'No – I was just…'

An imperious flick of the wrist cut Edward short. '*Ja, ja* – there is no need to explain. The war is making everybody into officers. It is no longer a class; it is only a rank. It has no importance. Why are you coming here, that is all I have to know.'

'I've been sent by Colonel Linton…'

'That is who, not why.'

The opportunity for Edward to finish his sentence and expiate on the *why* was stymied as the prince then repeatedly muttered the colonel's name to himself. 'Linton, Linton, Linton – *ja, ja*, I am sure I am knowing this name.' Edward, despite being of a solicitous disposition, had no idea what to say. It did not matter. With the affected cordiality of a man who had just rowed with his wife and been left to deal with her guests, the prince remarked that as he had met so many men from all over the world, it was impossible to remember just one. 'They are all having exactly the same moustaches and beards!' That, he noted fastidiously, was why he shaved twice a day. The razor was what distinguished the noble from the savage. (Edward inadvertently fingered the brutish bristles on his lips). The prince beckoned him forth. 'Come here. I know how much the English love their history – everybody from an island is exactly the same. They think their history is more special, but they forget it is not only water that makes an island. Austria is an island too. It is the last island of the German race: it is surrounded by the blood and soil of barbarians.'

As Edward approached, the prince called to the footman still in the doorway for some cold meats and wine. The table was thereupon rapped like a blackboard to begin the instruction.

'This is the Golden Book of the Army,' said the prince. 'There are pictures of every great Austrian battle inside, and of every regiment of the Imperial Army. When I was a boy I was spending so many hours looking at the pictures in this book. I learnt everything about the army: the name of every battle and date, of every commander and foe; the colour of every tunic of the hussars; the shape of every hat of the dragoons; the number of stripes on every trouser of the lancers; the motto and crest of every regiment – everything, so that when I came to be in the army myself I would know from many kilometres away precisely which of my soldiers were fighting where in my battle.' A noble turn of his head displayed his wine-tinted cluster of teeth. 'Then the war comes and the Prussians make everybody to wear grey. But that can never destroy the beauty that is locked forever in the page. *Ja, ja*, I am sure you are never seeing anything so magnificent as this book, Captain-Lieutenant.'

If agreement were needed for the prince to continue, he continued without it; with both hands he carefully turned another folio.

Edward's eyes were drawn to the Tyrolean-peaked picture newly presented. It was titled beneath: '*The Defence of Bergisel*'.

'To serve God, the emperor, and the country has been the life-purpose – not just for me – but for every Austrian: they have been the highest ideals. It has been always impossible for me to imagine Austria without the emperor.' The prince stood up straight, his own wild blue eyes shadowed by the depth of his brow. He looked squarely at Edward. 'And yet, here we are – we have none. You have not experienced the downfall of your country, have you, Captain-Lieutenant?'

'No.'

'No – so it is impossible for you to understand the suffering that every patriotic Austrian has endured since the fall of the empire. Now,' he said with an abrupt shift of tone, holding his hand open to Edward, 'you are come here to give me a message, a message too secret for the Bolshevik telegraph. I will have it.'

Edward's prompt refutation of the anticipated form of despatch was met by the prince with ill humour. 'Too secret for even the pen,' he said peevishly. 'Then I am forced to listen to the captain-lieutenant speak, no? It is good I ask for the wine. Come then – speak.'

At the advocation the prince recovered his wine glass – concealed behind a pile of books on the table – strode over to the fire and sat down. A flick of his fingers commanded Edward to assume the seat opposite. Edward tractably did so, and then in deference to what was manifestly an inconvenient hour for the prince, he stiffened himself to relay the message as quickly, concisely and flawlessly as possible. The prince, however, for all his brusqueness theretofore, was in no haste to hear what had to be said, for as soon as Edward sat he was distracted.

'Colonel Linton – *ja, ja* – I remember him now!' he exclaimed, the contrast in his complexion and tone suggesting a greater delight at the feat of recollection than at the recollection itself. He had been introduced to the colonel by the Countess X at the Esterhazy ball in Vienna, he said. Later that evening, finding the countess alone, she had enquired of him as to whether he had seen the colonel. The prince could scarcely recall who he was! Promising to keep an eye out for the British officer, he had eventually discovered him in the gardens –

to his great chagrin, *in flagrante delicto* with a party of the archduke's circle. It was the last he had seen or wanted to see of the colonel: he loathed the archduke and his friends. If only, he wished, they had simply shot hares, shot hares, shot hares – like they ought to have done, then there would never have been any war. At least, not a war that would have been lost.

The footman soon returned with a carafe of wine and dish of cold meats. He set them on the table and picked up the empty wine glass beside Edward to replace it. It was only then Edward realised the glass he had earlier spotted belonged to someone else. He presumed the prince had therefore been passing a convivial evening with his wife or some guest and, forced to wait up for the late arrival, had only afterwards begun perusing the cherished volume. *That* would explain his humour.

'Pfff, leave it,' the Prince said in peremptory tones. 'There is only wine to go in again. The captain-lieutenant does not need another glass at this hour.'

With the glasses shortly filled, a further impatient flick of the prince's hand indicated Edward was to get on with his purpose. Edward first took a draught of the wine to alleviate the increasing dryness and soreness he felt at the back of his throat (a surreptitious turn of the glass could find no trace of lips) and then recounted the message. In the course of him doing so the prince did not once look at Edward, but kept his eyes fixed like steel in the very heart of the flames. It was an impassivity, a strange sterility that Edward was quickly alive to, and it stirred in him the necessity of uttering words that were not stilted or arid, but which flowed with an appropriate rhythm and cadence – in the cause of arousing the prince. So did he find himself likewise producing an emphasis here, inserting a pregnant pause there; decorating with a mild embellishment here, an adjectival flourish there – for the sake of inciting emotion. It was thus by a process entirely natural and instinctual – an almost soliloquising evocation – that Edward too began to truly comprehend the words that he spoke. Hitherto, through simple repetition on the train they had been nothing but a mimetic procedure. But now, suddenly, he was aware that he was no longer a cipher, that he was not just a courier: he was not the ink in the pen that flowed at the behest of another. The prince's actions would be forged according to the conviction and power of his very own speech.

And the instant he finished the prince rose decisively.

'Very good,' he said curtly, Edward mirroring his rise. 'You will have enough to eat and drink, I'm sure, Captain-Lieutenant. Gustav will make sure you reach the station in time to catch the morning train to Vienna. Goodnight.'

As Edward watched the prince stride to the door he stood, half in disbelief he might exit saying no more than that, half in submission to the truth that he would.

'Excuse me – Prince Strumboldt,' he suddenly burst out, his intemperance as startling to both as the intervention itself, and which for a moment bore no sequitur to the impulse of simply arresting the prince. 'What will I tell Colonel Linton?'

The prince stopped in the doorway. As he turned back, an entire transition of his countervailing thoughts could be read in the slow morphing of his features: once hard and implacable, they concluded by being supple and arch.

'Tell him I remember dancing with the Countess X. *Ja, ja* tell him that, Captain-Lieutenant.'

Had the prince's first thought not been supplanted by the second in the turn of his face, the pair's colloquy would surely have ended there and then. Edward's intemperance was not of the character to hammer at rock: one chip in the eye would have seen him retreat. As it was, the prince's sly, twinkle-eyed remark had the effect of electrifying his blood with bolts of lightning.

'I'll go back to him and say you'll do nothing – is that it? Is *that* it?' he shot out. Then he thought, but did not say, *For the slothful man saith, There is a lion without, I shall be slain the streets.*

The prince's cheeks coloured brightly; his proud, reptilian head shook with such violent, ineffable indignity that its only recourse seemed thereafter to burst. That it did not was because he was chilled by the wall of ice that confronted him in the profundity of Edward's blue eyes: there was something impenetrable, something almost familiar in them, he found. His expression of fury tempered, he glanced at the table and let out a sharp, ironic laugh.

'Ha ha! There is something in the wine glass! Ha ha!' In the split second that it took Edward to turn and return, the prince's Janus face had hardened again; his tone was once again brutal and caustic. '*Ja, ja*, the emperor's life is in danger. It is always in danger. I have that repeated to me like the cuckoo every hour. So I will tell you the same thing, Captain-Lieutenant. A year ago I told the emperor that the empire no longer exists; he would not listen. Six months ago I told him to give up the Crown of St Stephen; he did not do so. Three months ago I told him to leave the country; he is still here. That is the problem with the emperor – he is a Habsburg: he is too stupid and too stubborn. And when people are stupid and stubborn they should never wed an Italian. That makes them twice as stupid and twice as stubborn. When a monarchy becomes this stupid it does not deserve to exist.'

'So you'll do nothing?' Edward repeated, his ardour undimmed.

The prince stamped his boot. 'God, must I say the same thing all evening – *every day*? I have said what is to be done – it is for the emperor to *do*: he must get on a train and leave the country. It is simple. The fervour of these little revolutions never lasts – they all come to nothing on roast beef and apple pie. When it finishes, *then* he can come back. And when he does he will understand there is no empire to rule – there is only Austria. It is simple.'

It was simple for Edward too: the moral choice for action had become binary.

'So you won't help them – you'll let them be butchered. That's what I'll tell Colonel Linton. There'll be ammunition and no one to fire it.'

'There is always more ammunition than men to fire it. You should know that, Captain-Lieutenant,' the prince replied scornfully. 'If that were not true Herr Schulze would not ask me for what he does not want to give himself. You must understand, Captain-Lieutenant, that the best nationalists in Austria in this moment are German. They have no care for the emperor's life; what matters to them is that he does not exist – here, in Austria.'

'If he's killed then he won't, will he?'

The prince returned a careless shrug at the brazen rejoinder. 'That is one possibility, *ja, ja*. But it is what a man of honour accepts. When one is challenged to a duel it is one's duty to fight. Satisfaction has to be had. One cannot shed tears for a duellist who has fought for his honour and died.' A slight elevation of the chin presaged a final noble retreat. 'Or *did* not,' he said, sniffing. 'Like I said, that class does not exist any more. There is only the rank. So, *auf Wiedersehen*, Captain-Lieutenant.' With that, he spun on his heels and departed.

*

Edward was woken by Gustav at four thirty; he had not bothered to undress and had barely slept. He had been too hot, then too cold, continually tossed and then turned, and every time he had dropped off the sprites worked in his mouth with a brush and a chisel. The crisp, pre-dawn air during the ride back to Krems briefly chilled the infection away and invigorated him. But by the time the train arrived at the station, it was getting painful to swallow; by the time he was on it he was starting to shiver; by the time it got to Vienna his limbs felt like lead; by the time he reached the hotel he had to practically crawl up the stairs. The last thing he managed to do before curling up into a quivering, feverish ball of threadbare blanket and shabby overcoat was to have the porter send the obligatory telegram to the Bristol Hotel for Colonel Linton.

That the fog of fever led Edward to a cavalier choice of words in the above was certain. That had the fever not struck he would have been perceptive enough to remark the presence at the station in Krems of the same cowled figure that had pointed at the moon the night before was less so. As it was, this figure lingered on the platform, inspecting each one of the entraining passengers from beneath the lowered screen of their habit. It was not until the very last whistle that they had joined the train too. When they arrived in Vienna they then tracked Edward as he staggered through the snow, waited outside the hotel for some time after he had entered, then finally went in themselves. A brief exchange ensued with the porter. Upon its conclusion, the hood was lifted back over their head, and she left.

Chapter 27

The moment Colonel Linton had left the commissariat Herr Schulze got to work. He hastened back to his office and summoned his assistant. He told him two crates of ammunition were to be immediately despatched to the British relief depot, and that the crates were to be unmarked: they were to be accounted for under an 'international peacekeeping operation'.

Despite then being dismissed the assistant remained where he was. A young man with a high, shell-scarred forehead, there appeared at the corner of his mouth something akin to a smirk, as if the instruction had been some sort of a riddle. Schulze was unsettled: he was always unsettled by the lad. He couldn't work out if his permanent grin was the sign of common imbecility or of something more savage stitched under his scar. Normally, of course, such qualities he considered laudable in the constabulary, just not when they suggested violence against *him*. Schulze's next move was thus brisk – if not hasty: he opened the door, ushered the lad forcefully out, and called in his secretary with a shiver of relief. She was to send a cable, the content of which was a single word: *Tonight?*

Its reply was received in short order. It read: *Ariadne.*

In a former age, for the chief of police to have been seen at the Vienna Opera House in the box of a man who had seduced the whole of Viennese society (from the very top right down to the upper middle) would have been a mark of great social distinction. In the present it was one of suspicion. Schulze's entry into Ulrich Köstler's box was therefore one undertaken with the stealth of a panther. An engrossing lament, harlequinade or other *moment de crise* was the customary signal for the door to be silently opened, the screening curtain to stir, and the chair at the very back of the box to be imperceptibly filled. Köstler's own seat, so withdrawn from the balcony edge as to give the impression to any distracted, prying eye that the box itself was quite empty, discreetly shielded the occupant from even the slightest perforation of light.

Upon Schulze's spectral manifestation behind him, Köstler glanced at his fob watch, logged the precise position of the hands and returned the timepiece to its pocket. Then, as if transported by the sudden pathos of the music, his left arm swung up; it was held suspended with the tremulous note: Ariadne, waking from her slumber on the shores of Naxos, sighted the sails of Theseus' ship in the offing.

Schulze was not in the least interested by the goings-on on stage. He detested the opera. His nocturnal pleasures were staunchly buxom or beery. None of which were to be found in Ulrich Köstler's box, all of which were liberally dispensed at Frau Hentjen's tavern, whereto he was itching to head as soon as he had finished with Köstler.

Following a *tacet* interlude he leaned forward and growled impatiently, 'Is it over?'

'My dear friend,' returned Köstler in a whisper of lilting delight, 'it is only the beginning.' A half-turn embossed his avian profile on the theatrical background of lights. 'The thrill of the opera is not in the music or drama – it is in being surrounded by six hundred people in the darkness. Where else can one enjoy such intimacy without being observed? At the opera one may slip in and out of a box as undetected as the silk spun by the spider at night.' Returning his eyes to the stage, he left only the zephyr of his intonation behind. 'Just as you do, Herr Schulze.'

Schulze was in no mood for frivolity. He was too hungry, too thirsty, too...

'Herr Linton came to see me,' he said.

'Ah. And?'

'*And* – he came to see me. It's exactly as you said it would be.'

'Of course it is, my dear friend,' Köstler purred in reply. 'Why, before the war such a man would have added vigour and dynamism to the imperial cause. Sadly, the time passes. We age. The dance, we find, is no longer the same. The violinists are too clumsy with their bows, the pianists too thick with their fingers; our feet cannot follow the rhythm. We go to the ball and no longer find beauty, frissons, and love—' his large eyes reposed on Ariadne as she collapsed with bitter tears on her lips '– but infidelity, discord and drink. Ah yes, that was the time – before that happened. But when the day dawns anew we wake to discover that we have been thrown back on the very same shore as the one we have left. So soon another ship appears, and the play begins again.'

'Well the play will end now,' said Schulze, a low, malevolent drawl underscoring his vengeful intent.

There was a pause before Köstler coyly enquired, 'Which one?'

'Which do you think?'

'There are so many, my dear friend.'

Schulze was not there to twirl parasols. He had never needed to play the game of seduction to make his way in the world. He had become chief of police because he was the best man for the job: his abilities were supreme, his conviction unerring, his methods infallible. His was not a temperament to be ever subverted by a quibble or truth. *His* had not been the gilded path of a Linton entail or a Strumboldt bloodline. And so, in a relationship such as his with Ulrich Köstler – who had always lauded his pragmatism with such a smile as to suggest it was the only flaw that marked him out for distinction – he intended at last to prove its unvarnished effect.

'The prince's,' he said, then added in an undertone of ruthless exult, 'I've got him. I've got him! We'll get rid of them both now – we'll get rid of them *all*.'

Köstler said nothing, as if lost in the fathomless depths of the cave before him with nothing but the brutal echo of Schulze's voice for company. Then came the crescendo to bring light to his thoughts. For that, he knew, was the problem with the police: they always got carried away; they were always so *imprecise*; they possessed no *discretion*. One had to be so careful with the information placed in the hands of such men.

'Indeed?' he mused, at length.

'Indeed.'

'But – both?'

'Herr Linton knows,' Schulze muttered forcefully. 'He *knows*—'

'Quite so.'

'Yes – so I sent him to the prince. I gave him ammunition. Ha – you see!'

There was another profound, pensive interlude.

'And he's gone?' asked Köstler.

'Who?'

'The English colonel.'

'Yes.'

'*He* has?'

'I just said so, didn't I?' said Schulze, with the outrage of one for whom any doubt of his word had been customarily charged by the heel of his boot. 'Now the prince won't have a choice but to act. He can't sit and do nothing. And then – *then* –' an imaginary stripe was inflicted on Köstler's back by the word '– I've done it. *I* have, Herr Köstler. *Me*.'

'Perhaps, perhaps,' murmured Köstler, his subtle inflections hardening. 'But the Prince is nothing more than a name now, as I said. It is not the people with famous names and ancient lineage who will cause any trouble; it is those who no one has heard of. It is the people who are nothing – they are the ones we must fear.'

That the chief of Vienna police might fear anyone – let alone someone he had never heard of – was inconceivable to Herr Schulze. Ulrich Köstler might cower at every corner and shape with a cosh – but not him! He *was* the shadow! He *was* the cosh!

'*I'm* the one to be feared,' he said. 'Tell them. Tell them *that*.'

Then the person who no one had seen enter the box slipped noiselessly from the chair and out through the curtain.

The second he had left, Köstler flicked open the silver lid of his fob watch and checked the time. Precision, he knew (and Schulze did not), was the key to any exit or entrance. He withdrew a notebook from his jacket pocket and made an annotation on one of the pages. He then tore out the page, folded it, replaced the notebook in his pocket, and settled back in his chair to enjoy the performance.

A short time later he flipped the watch lid open again. A clash of cymbals and a drum roll presaged the coming storm; and as soon as they had, he had left.

Köstler passed quickly through the golden lights and red-papered walls of the opera house corridors. He made his way down to the foyer and, with a familiar nod to one of the ushers awaiting the intermission exodus, pushed through the double doors out onto the pavement. He stopped and glanced around, as if with no greater intent than a man observing the constellations and clouds while taking the night air. All life, it seemed, had been sucked into the opera house from the dark, snowy streets. A subtle gesture of his head was as if to indicate to a waiting fiacre driver that he had no need of their service. He removed his cigarette case from his jacket pocket and opened it. Selecting a cigarette, he patiently tapped an end against the engraved silver lid. At the anticipated explosion of applause redounding from within he put the cigarette to his lips and returned the case to his pocket. He listened closely for the sound of the interior doors opening; on hearing them, a match was struck and the cigarette lit. A moment later the outer doors began swinging. Köstler remained perfectly still, waiting, watching from out of the corner of his high, indifferent eye as the gentlemen thronged the freezing night for their cigarettes, cigars and society. He chose his moment with the utmost precision. Tipping his head to one side, he tucked his right hand (in the fingertips of which the folded paper could just be detected) across his waist beneath his left elbow, drew on his cigarette and wheeled round into the midst of the crowd.

'Ah, my dear friend,' he exclaimed as he weaved through the ranks of top hats and tails, 'I was hoping to find you here. A most excellent production, don't you think?'

As he reached out both hands towards the anointed friend, he did so with the cigarette smouldering in his left; in his right there was nothing: the note had already been taken.

Part IV

On n'aime point si l'on n'est aimé.

Rousseau, *La Nouvelle Heloise*

Chapter 28

Sarah Childs' conversion was practically Damascene. One moment she was hurling her needlework on the divan and muttering the foulest imprecations about the treachery of the male sex, the next she was dusting off the fine china, plumping the living room cushions, ordering the sugary appurtenances and inviting Richard (*such a delightful young man!*) to afternoon tea.

Her enthusiasm was in marked contrast to the despair (pursuant to the hurling of needlework) with which she had asked Hélène four days prior as to whether Richard had visited the orphanage yet. Because then, not only was she told he had visited, she was told he had done so *twice*. Vexing as it was that the girl had not already informed her of the *first* visit, Sarah Childs had eagerly seized on the news to ask when she would be seeing him next. Hélène's reply that she didn't know was delivered with a hint of a pout, a bit of a shrug, and half a sigh – gestures which Sarah Childs (untutored as she was in the fine arts of Gallic pouts, shrugs and sighs) immediately understood as the immemorial signs of a woman at the mercy of a man's whims; and the only thing she found more objectionable than a man's whims was a woman placing herself at their mercy. After all, no man bothered to visit a woman twice (*in Crouch End!*) unless to make the acquaintance of her lips. And so if two visits to such an out-of-the-way place did not a couple make, Sarah Childs was determined that two visits *and* afternoon tea certainly would!

Sarah Childs' machinations, it should be noted, were not entirely driven by her desire to expel the girl from the house. No – not *entirely*. While certainly nothing had changed in respect of Hélène having been imposed on her due to her husband's cavalier attitude to the marital oaths, there was more subtlety to her feminine designs than the attainment of domestic superiority.

It went without saying that Hélène's continental habits were a complicating factor in any man's courtship – her ready confession of helplessness being merely at one with her papist creed. Had Sarah

Childs been in Richard's position she wouldn't have touched her with a barge pole; still, that was his choice. Richard's demonstrable hopelessness was another matter altogether though. That he had taken so long to visit Hélène in the first place was bad enough, but a failure to fix a third encounter on conclusion of the second showed a shocking lack of understanding of a woman's expectations: there was a fine line between arousing them and being a disappointment to them; and although where exactly the line was was not for a man to know, suffice it to say that as soon as it was crossed no amount of arousal could make up for the disappointment. Even Sarah Childs knew that a hare had to be chased to the hole! Quite nearly thirty and without a wife of course told its own sorry tale. The result of this, however, was that Sarah Childs felt a burgeoning instinct towards Richard which could only be accurately summarised by the use of one word: maternal.

The necessity of this instinct was perforce the consequence of a lack of one. Adeline was no mother: she was all grace and herself. Sarah Childs had said exactly that (*and repeated it*) from the beginning. It was hardly surprising such a woman had been deceived by a charlatan so suddenly brought to the light as Jack Wilson, but even that only happened to one tacitly complicit in the temptations of a bold rolling eye. It was these flaws of nature that had led Adeline to give a kitten to be suckled by a hound. Richard's physical similarity to his mother (for all its unappealing qualities) at least meant Sarah Childs was able to clearly observe from her own elevated perspective (unsullied by motherhood as she was) the manifest failings of others. Thank heavens she was there to correct them!

The invitation was for Sunday. Joseph was informed by his wife of the event well in advance: that is to say, Saturday teatime. And as soon as he was (he had yet to remove the key from the front door, having entered) he was told not to bother taking his coat off as he had to collect the cake from the baker's.

Upon Joseph's second return to the house Sarah Childs wasted no time in unburdening herself of all she had gleaned from Richard's original visit, and which the tribulations of daily household management had led to her having neither the time nor the wits to divulge hitherto. These included such items as Richard being a prisoner in Germany during the war (Joseph had understood it was Austria. *No*, Germany, she said); that Richard was to sell the house in Ravenscourt Park (Joseph had understood he was now living there. *No*, Richard had told her himself that he would, she said); and that he was now working as a minister – though she had no clue at which Mission (Joseph believed it was rather a Ministry. *Yes*, that's exactly what she said, she said). The only thing she didn't know was why Richard had called in the first place. Still, she said peremptorily, Joseph would be able to ask him himself the next day, wouldn't he?

Joseph had already been apprised of Richard's circuitous path from Katzenau to the Ministry of X by Mr Campbell, the minister at the Ravenscourt Park Mission. Richard had been to see him shortly after his return, he said, though he had not returned to the Mission since. Notwithstanding Mr Campbell's usual placid, non-confrontational smile, Joseph Childs had detected a hint of reproach in his tone for this absence, tempered though it was by the observation that after six tumultuous years abroad some disorientation was only to be expected. As soon as Richard had re-established his bearings, Mr Campbell had piously attested, he was sure to be a credit to his great expectations. Further to this Joseph Childs knew no more. Death, disappearance and war had led to the Wilson family fading from being a topic of conversation among the congregation to being of parenthetical remark. His wife's disclosure that Richard had sought him out therefore came as a considerable surprise, if, in all honesty, no great shock. The surprise was in the time of the telling, not the happening. He considered it natural that a son should make enquiries of those who had borne witness to his father's last days. This, he was convinced, was why Richard had called.

Joseph's opening of the front door on Sunday afternoon was marked by a singular occurrence: Richard smiled. It was an awkward smile, true, but there was enough genuine warmth for Joseph to be distinctly taken aback. Six years before, all Richard had ever done was snipe and scowl at him. Joseph's recovery was swift though: no man possessed of the same earnest good faith as he could possibly harbour ill will towards a young man whom he had known since his birth, who had suffered the deprivations of four years' internment, and who had been orphaned by the second of his parents' sad, untimely deaths.

The positions in the sitting room were prearranged and soon assumed: Richard and Hélène together on the settee (a couple of extra cushions added to the wings to ensure the lovers sat as close together as possible); Joseph in his armchair; Sarah Childs and her needlework on the divan. The progression to tea-drinking, cake-eating and the usual formalities of informal conversation was as smooth as to be expected of an event four days in the planning.

It began, of course, with the weather, whence it moved to the orphanage, linked seamlessly to Richard's fortitude at making such a trek in such frightful weather (*twice!*), segued effortlessly to remark upon the excellent prospects of Richard's new employment (*a ministry!*), alighted with wonderment on how Hélène managed to put up with the discomfort of the London omnibuses – for Sarah Childs had caught the number 12 to Oxford Street the other day (*it was impossible to believe the lengths one had to go to just to find a pair of rabbit-skin gloves that fitted one properly!*) and had been jostled and jolted the whole way by the wretched contraption so she had ended up bruised like a peach; she couldn't imagine anyone having to go through such an ordeal every day (*and, my, with all those great hills in the north!*) – though of course it was no better on the Underground with the millions of people crammed into those tiny tunnels and passageways like ants in their molehills that made her feel so dreadfully claustrophobic (*why, if she had the choice, she would never set foot out of west London!*), before bifurcating artfully to hope that the cold wouldn't destroy the bulbs she'd planted before Christmas – for it had been a monumental effort to make sure the neighbours had kept their front gardens looking respectable during the war, which made it all the more important that the flowers should be in bloom for the first spring of peace... and so as soon as the snow cleared she would go to Kew Gardens (*had they neither of them been? Oh, really, they must visit!*) because the start of spring was always the best time to go (*why, was March only a week away now? Good heavens! Yes, yes, they simply had to go then!*) when there weren't all those terrible insects buzzing around that there were in the summer – once when she and Joseph had gone (*did Joseph remember?*) she had been attacked by a swarm of ghastly green, black and blue creatures with antennae and teeth, and they had sought refuge by sitting under a plane tree (*they had tried in the glasshouse but – dear Lord – it was even worse with the aphids and ticks!*) and Joseph had pointed at the men and women lying on the grass and wondered whether the two of them might be doing exactly the same in twenty years' time… and she had pretended not to understand him (*did Joseph remember that?*). The next day he had asked her to marry him. Oh yes, Joseph knew how to chase a hare to its hole!

Joseph smiled broadly. None of the above correlated with his recollection of events (not that he possessed a diary to check on the facts), but he knew the happiness of one's wife always excused the need for accuracy. And Sarah Childs was happy – to such an extent that the tea had run straight through her and she had to excuse herself. She waddled away up the stairs quite full – not just of tea, but of felicity and triumph: the lovers were positively beaming beside one other.

This was most certainly true. Not that there was occasion for them to do anything other than smile – that was not the purpose of tea. But with Sarah Childs' indisposition there came a short silence. Joseph then took the opportunity for more sober engagement: he asked Richard how he was finding the political demands of the post-war world at the Ministry.

Richard's engine required no more than this gentle turn of the crank: he fired instantly. He preached on the need to reorientate British policy towards the values it shared with their American cousins; then on federalisation as the means to secure the future peace of the world; then on how integral to the success of both was the abrogation of the Japanese alliance. He spoke with concision, confidence and fluency. Indeed, as Richard descried the alliance as a last pernicious prop of the imperial system of colonies and protection, for a moment Joseph believed he was listening to the father, not the son. There was the same evangelical spirit, certainly; there was the same righteous commitment; there was even a hint of the same adjectival vehemence – even if it did not possess quite the range. But there was also something lacking, Joseph thought. It was as if a core was missing, a root around which to bind, an axis upon which to spin. For all the rhetorical fluency he felt Richard was espousing nothing more than a basic political policy that was as changeable as any of Mr Chamberlain's old brightly coloured coats. Such a thing, he knew, could only be turned to permanence and conviction by faith. Without faith there was never anything to prevent what was morally wrong being seen as politically right.

Two things then happened: the first was that Sarah Childs returned and, catching the word 'protection' issued forth from Richard's lips, turned upon her husband with a look of the utmost violence and treachery; the second was that, to escape the daggered eyes of his wife, Joseph glanced up, down, left, right, nudged the rim of his spectacles up the slippery bridge of his nose, and finally sought succour in the face of Hélène. It was the first time he had looked at her since Richard had begun his descent, and it could be said that – whilst lacking the throat-slitting purport of his wife's look – an unmistakeable glint of treachery was detectable in his eyes too.

Hélène's streaming curls of deepest brown coiled from her brow, concealed her ears and ranged around the twisted, twining muscles of her neck. Her head, settled at an angle that inclined towards Richard, had yet not turned in the full. With a single eye – but, oh, a wild wide eye! – she gazed at Richard with a fascination and intensity that seemed to Joseph almost rapturous, almost devoted; and, as she did, their elbows brushed, her knee touched his, and her breast heaved like the rolling sea.

Could it possibly be she might love him true?

Joseph had pooh-poohed his wife's matchmaking ambitions the moment he had understood them. Her antipathy towards the girl's plight had been plain from the start. The afternoon tea, he had assured himself, was simply another of her kenspeckle schemes to oust her from the house: one doomed to failure like the others. Now, however, he was confronted with the prospect that there might not only actually exist a spark of amatory fire between Richard and Hélène, but that his wife might succeed in her crowning ambition. An arrow of anguish pierced him through at the thought. Hélène was too frail a creature to be cast into the world with a man whose words rang hollow as the drum. This Joseph knew, for he understood her.

The matter of refugees had been raised from the very earliest days of the war: it was the congregation's Christian duty, Mr Campbell had said, to succour and shelter the brutalised persons of Europe. Sarah Childs had been only too happy to succour; she was appalled at the notion of shelter: rumours of the Belgian reputation for poor hygiene, poor manners and other unpleasant foreign traits meant she considered duty to be a thing given out, not taken in. This had been the accepted position in the Childs' household until the advent of Joseph's financial troubles. It was then, upon enquiry, that Mr Campbell had told Joseph he knew of a young Belgian lady in need of lodgings; she was from Louvain, he had explained. Joseph had agreed to take her in there and then. He had heard the reports of the city, heard of executions and beatings, of innocents defiled, of bodies mutilated, of breasts burned, of fingers and ears hacked off and sold with their rings, and worse! He had no need to probe the details of Hélène's ordeal; they could be surmised by any man with a conscience – he too could hear the relentless pounding of the hobnailed boots and smell the putrid stench of the savage, unwashed men. And so when she had arrived at the house he had asked her no questions: sanctuary was all his words. She was his St Agatha to be saved.

After all she had suffered Joseph therefore had no intention of allowing his wife to now harry the girl into love because she was an *inconvenience*. No, he would not let her be driven away by guilt. He had a moral responsibility to protect her from the things that were detrimental. Why, if she were removed now it would be as if she had been removed from the world altogether! Of course, if in time affection might blossom into love between Richard and Hélène he would bless it. But love, he knew, was not simply gazing into each other's eyes; it was looking together in the same direction.

Joseph tapped the bridge of his spectacles, stumbled briefly over his words due to the haste with which he wished to speak them, and addressed the twain alternately.

Richard, he said, appeared to have so little time in his new employ it was a wonder he even had time to take tea! To which Richard smiled and agreed. Hélène, he said, was similarly so tired by her work at the orphanage that when she came home he barely knew if she was speaking English or French! To which Hélène, faintly smiling, said she sometimes didn't know that herself. Richard, he said (passing reference having been earlier made to an upcoming conference in America) was evidently engaged in an enterprise of signal import that would mean he'd be travelling the world for years to come! At which Richard hesitated, glanced to his right, and agreed. Hélène, he said, had often spoken of returning to Belgium at the end of the war. At which Hélène, looking him bold in the eye, said, *Oui, peut-être*.

If marriage had taught Sarah Childs anything it was that a knife was often a more faithful bedfellow than a husband. She offered the couple more tea and moved the subject on from Kew Gardens.

She and Joseph had been invited to a concert at Wigmore Hall by a friend from the congregation (*Had they?* asked Joseph; *they had*, she replied). She could not attend herself, and as Joseph didn't know a fiddle from a bow it would be pointless him going without her. It was somebody's very famous string concerto; it was on Wednesday. She had told her friend Richard and Hélène would go in their place.

'My dear, only if they can,' Joseph interrupted – a frantic rush of blood to his head. 'It's... it's very late notice and... and they do both have a lot of work to do.'

'Nonsense, Joseph. Nobody works in the evening. Helen certainly doesn't.'

'But *Hélène* is—'

'Well I've already told Mrs Clifford they'll be going,' Sarah Childs cut in sharply, her tone stiffened by the foreign affectation, 'and you know perfectly well how she is when people start fiddle-faddling over things once they're agreed.' She purveyed a smile of adamantine will at the object pair. 'Now, you two will go, *won't you*? I *do* hope so.'

A glance between Richard and Hélène could do nothing but accept the *fait accompli*. And the moment the contract was signed, Richard knew what he would do. So too did Joseph.

Chapter 29

The day of the concert soon came, and the Under Secretary's thoughts were anything but amatory. At five games all, and at the start of the decider, he spotted General Shawcross looming in the dedans behind him.

'Serve up,' the general said gamely – the first point was then lost. 'Stroke,' he called in the midst of the next – the general swore the ball clipped his lace. 'Change your serve,' he advised in a whisper – he did, and a double fault followed. 'Concentrate, Phillip, that's set point,' he reminded him bluffly – and hooked his nose to the netting. 'Chase a yard!' he roared in approval – though only the blind could agree with the call. The players changed ends and the Under Secretary prepared to receive. '*Au carreau!*' came the cry from the depths – and the ball was framed to the rafters.

The Under Secretary joined the general in the dedans after. They sat on the front row of the cold wooden benches in the semi-darkness.

'Bad luck, old boy. Looked like you hit the buffers in that last game there, eh?' the general said jovially.

The Under Secretary nearly did. Instead he smiled and muttered something about the size of the balls. The general apologised for the intrusion, but he had been asked to speak with the Under Secretary as a matter of urgency. He had been woken by the prime minister's secretary after he had gone to bed – or before he got up, he wasn't sure which. Either way it was an ungodly hour – the confounded telephone meant a man could be harassed day and night! And as privacy was paramount for what he now had to say, the location was perfect.

'Nowhere better in London to be sure of not being disturbed than the dedans at Queen's, is there, eh?' His eyebrows rose like the surf as his eyes swivelled and ranged, and he gave the bench a couple of slaps as he would to get his horse going. An alarming report had been received from Vienna, he said.

'Your man, Colonel Linton—'

'Not *mine*,' the Under Secretary corrected punctiliously.

'No, no, not *yours* – not literally. Yours only figuratively speaking, to distinguish the different individuals in the area.'

'I'm only aware of the one.'

'Come, come, Phillip – there's always more than *one*. You know that,' said the general, a touch crossly, for his wife had disapproved of the telephone caper, and he meant to share a pinch of her roughing. He leaned forward and bumped a ball from the netting with his fist. He then continued: the colonel had apparently procured (or intended to – the general was not there to split hairs) ammunition from the chief of the Vienna police to take to the emperor. The purpose of the colonel being in Austria, the general reminded the Under Secretary, was to get the imperial family *out* of the country, not to have some shoot-out like at the O.K. Corral. 'As you know, some of the prime minister's colleagues are itching for war with the Bolsheviks and they'll take any excuse to bounce the country into it.' Not that this prospect was entirely distasteful to the general, only it did play havoc with the grouse. But with his morning's objectives strictly defined, he was forthwith explicit. 'That'd put the kibosh on any idea of a federalism plan, you see. But the prime minister's quite sure you understand that, don't you, Phillip? Eh?'

The Under Secretary had forgotten his jumper: he sat in his white collared shirt and flannel trousers with a towel round his neck. Despite the chill he was still perspiring. He mopped his brow and, picking up the numerical strand shortly left off, enquired in a tone as unflappable as an ostrich's wings who it was again that the report had come from.

As long as General Shawcross still sported his rank there was no mistaking his caste; the same, however, could not be sworn of his loyalty. A man no longer able to cut and thrust was as useful to the modern army as a halberd or pike. The political bread and butter had become his trusty steed and his lance. This meant that, despite the disparity in age and good looks, he could joust with the Under Secretary on superior terms: some information was simply not to divulge.

'Good God, Phillip, you didn't think the prime minister would have a relative of the king strutting round Europe like one of those Kipling buccaneers, eh?'

'I thought he was recommended by the Foreign Office.'

'Precisely – that makes it even worse!' the general exclaimed, and almost guffawed. A couple of snorts and a loud blow into his handkerchief restored him to humour. 'The aim's to extricate the emperor from his predicament. That sort of thing can't be left to some fly-on-a-wheel, man on the spot like your colonel – not literally *your*, of course. The colonel's just there to speak a bit of Frog and give the emperor the old *Ak Dum*. But to be sure he can do this requires some proper intelligence and planning; that's what the prime minister understands. You can paint the Bolshie blighters in Austria whatever colour you like and it won't make a scrap of difference: nothing's changed there in a thousand years. But all those other countries – that's a different matter.' The door to the dedans was opened a crack, but upon a voice outside declaring there to be nothing of interest within, the opener promptly closed it again. The general resumed, his smooth baritone hushed. 'Hungary's the key to it. We've got to make sure that fool Károlyi keeps his Bolsheviks in check. And the only way to make sure that happens is for us to put a leash on the Czechs at Pozsony and remove the emperor for him. To keep the stupid count in power we have to stop the scent of royal blood from tickling the Bolshevik snouts, you see. Can't very well have them wiping our eyes on the emperor's estate, can we? Who knows where it'd end if that happened? No point saddling the right horse only to have the wrong rider holding the reins, is there, eh?'

The general concluding, the solution was elementary, and presented with a crack of the whip. 'Heavens Phillip, just hurry up and get your man – not *your*, literally, of course – to put the family on the first train to Switzerland. That's all the prime minister wants. Then we can all get a good night's sleep again and get on with the things which really matter, eh?'

The Under Secretary departed the club soon after with a gait of as perfect, languid serenity as ever a giraffe might be proud to possess. But in his countenance was painted the torment of his soul. That one sclerotic, backward people might subvert the divine cause of federalism was torture enough, but that his succumbing to the allure of deceit might be punished by the devastating consequences of failure was worse by far.

If this belief could be said to possess an element of self-flagellation, then the second victim of the Under Secretary's knotted whip was – quite naturally – *also* himself. How foolish he had been to follow the general's line and compose a telegram talking of the *moral support of the British government* to a soldier! He knew the only morality a soldier possessed was that delivered at the end of a gun barrel with the aid of – heaven help him! – *ammunition*! If self-consciousness was the true mark of genius then the Under Secretary clearly saw that the fault was all his.

Before the Under Secretary could think of composing another telegram to be sent to Colonel Linton, he had first to confirm whether any communication had yet passed between the colonel and Richard. His initial adjunct to Richard to inform him of anything *urgent* could well have been interpreted as nothing less than 1,000 men at the gates.

But nothing of importance had been received by Richard not to tell: the colonel had evidently considered there to be nothing of importance to send. In fact, it was clearly a matter of general unimportance all round: Richard had not given the colonel so much as a second thought since he sent the telegram.

The Under Secretary was not able to establish the above information until well into the afternoon though: illness to two of the minister's secretaries had seen Richard co-opted to a parliamentary subcommittee for the day. In the meantime he had busied himself with a preparatory draft for the colonel:

> *George most anxious to hear news of friend's safety over border. Anticipating imminent arrival in Switz. Stress train timetable fixed and no delays. No unexpected baggage or stops. Please confirm receipt asap.*

Having pored over it to ensure nothing was missing or – *worse* – open to interpretation, the Under Secretary was satisfied at the ambiguous compulsion of the name 'George'. The intimation of royal impatience would surely have the desired effect. All the telegram wanted was Richard's seal, for much as the Under Secretary earnestly wished to assume titular responsibility he feared any communication sent to the colonel at such a critical moment by anyone other than Richard might lead to confusion and – *even worse* – interpretation.

When the Under Secretary finally found Richard on his return to the Ministry, he did his utmost to conceal the pain of the blood on his back with his usual gentility. Richard was no less pained due to the ticking clock of the coming concert; he was less successful with its concealment.

Following a brief discussion where the Under Secretary ascertained the aforementioned absence of communication, he hurried back to his office and put the draft note into an envelope. He paused, removed the note and read it through a final time. He crossed out '*confirm receipt*' and put '*acknowledge understanding*' in its place. Into the envelope it went again and out the door he then flew.

Richard already had his hat and coat on.

'Ah Richard, you're leaving,' the Under Secretary said, his calmness of tone belying his perturbation at the sight.

'Yes. I asked yesterday. I'm going to a concert this evening.'

'So you did, indeed. Excellent, excellent. What is it?'

Richard had no idea. The Under Secretary wasn't interested in the answer, but good breeding was hard to repress. Richard's silence allowed the Under Secretary to briskly continue, 'Anyway, I'm sure you'll have a splendid time, whatever it is. I'm very jealous. It's just that, before you go, could I ask you to send this to our friend in Austria, Colonel Linton? It's rather –' he swapped the fallible word *urgent* for the more emphatic '– critical.'

The Under Secretary's sublime nature possessing a sensibility quite beyond that of the common man, upon this request he perceived a transformation in Richard's complexion that far surpassed its attribution to the customary end-of-day emotions of fatigue and dejection. Indeed, the Under Secretary very nearly winced at the sight, as if the flesh on his back had felt the scourge once again. Not that Richard could be excused from the task – but that hardly lessened the pain that was felt. The Under Secretary therefore sought to apply balm in accents that were, for all their inherent decree, palpably kind and compassionate.

'The whole issue of federalism can be said to hang upon this single thread, Richard,' he said. 'This *single* thread. If this is broken – well… well… it could be quite catastrophic. Not just for the cause, but for us too; both you and I, together, Richard.' He pressed the envelope into Richard's inflorescent fingers and laid a tender hand on his shoulder. 'It'll only take a minute. I'll make sure a taxi is waiting to take you to the concert as soon as you're done – that goes without saying. Of course it does. You won't miss a single scrape of the bow, I assure you.'

And how, when all was said and done, could Richard possibly reject such glorious, radiant offices? Love was an unpollinated flower when bereft of purpose; the stamen was worth nothing without the buzz above of the bee.

But it did not take a minute to transpose the message and send it. It did not take five, ten, fifteen, twenty or – but after twenty, who was honestly counting? The machine still wouldn't send the *fucking* thing! It was only after Richard's red mist dwindled to a whimper that the machine condescended to work and the message was despatched to the ether. There was no taxi waiting outside though, nor was there one in sight either. The Under Secretary's assurances had been nothing better than sawdust!

Thus did Richard arrive at the concert hall in a state of palpitating, public-transport-induced exhaustion – just as the final bell rang to summon the patrons to their seats. A few flush-faced apologies were all he could gabble to Hélène before the lights dimmed and the first scrape of the bow took place. It was not what he had planned, at all.

Chapter 30

None of this was to say the concert wasn't a godsend – it was: Richard could hardly have gone to the orphanage again, even if he had been invited. There were only so many times a man could profess an interest in the education of young girls without arousing suspicion. Towards the end of a second visit that had largely replicated the pattern of the first – his being bundled into the final minutes of a class as an article of professional curiosity (rather than aspiration, that is) upon arrival being the sole variation before the café adjournment – their intercourse had become suffocated by the surroundings to such an extent that Richard's desperation to conceive a more liberating future outing led to his mind's complete and utter congelation: he could only think of a trip to the zoo. Having no idea if she liked penguins or not he ended up proposing nothing. However, thanks to Sarah Childs and afternoon tea, any despair was short-lived. Indeed, the intervention had briefly led him to see her as something akin to his mothering angel.

The same warmth of feeling could in no wise be attributed to her husband. By the myopic way Joseph Childs' oleaginous features had squinted at him in the front room, Richard was reminded of the fact he was one of the people his father had despised most: he was a man happy to meddle in the affairs of others and never think it wrong. Yes, it was clear to Richard that *he* would never forget the debt. But what matter the opinions of Joseph Childs – when all the while Richard spoke the only thing that concerned him was the heat he felt from Hélène's gaze as it settled upon him? There were frissons too when their knees touched, and flutters when their elbows brushed; together they roused the fires of passion in his heart which nourished belief in his deeds. So he had never once needed to look at her to know how she felt!

Many fallacies have been lain down in the course of human history, but never has a greater one gained currency than of eyes being windows of the soul. They are not: they are the mirrors to the beholder.

Richard's plan had been to arrive at the concert hall early, propose supper, speak candidly, and lead Hélène strongly by the arm into the auditorium. That way, even if her immediate response might be tacit (words, after all, were superfluous to the expression of one's innermost feelings), her silence would be her consent, and the charms of music and propinquity would soon evince by gesture what coyness always made one reluctant to say.

His intentions thrown over by the Fates, Richard did not enjoy the music one bit. Better said, he did not listen to a note. He agitated throughout. Preoccupied by hands that refused to stop sweating he placed them flat on his lap, wiped them under his coat, clasped them tightly together, splayed them dryingly wide, and buried them under his arms, but nothing made any difference. The only thing that would stop them from sweating, he was sure, was if they were held by Hélène. And each time he thought of the solution the problem got worse. Further to the physical there was also the practical to resolve. For what was to happen when the music stopped? Their feet had to trip together in the night air somehow so that there was time enough for silence to work its magic without being swallowed in a tube tunnel or run over by a bus.

As he plotted these contingencies, once or twice in the darkness he glanced at Hélène just long enough to trace her proud profile down to the unruly mass of hair tumbling about her neck and shoulders. If truth were *not* to be told, these glances were for the vicarious thrill of espying her rapture at the music; if truth *were* to be told, then it was purely to know whether she glanced at him too. And she did, once or twice – after he glanced at her. But this was only detectable in the final fraction of a second that Richard himself turned away. He was therefore unable to catch the full portent of her enquiring eyes, which seemed to wonder whether there being something wrong was the explanation as to why he should keep turning to her when the musicians were playing in front. What she did ignore were the occasional grumblings of his stomach. That said, as soon as the bows were laid to rest, the lights had come up and the applause run dry, she no longer had cause to hold her tongue.

'Your stomach was not 'appy with the music?' she said playfully as they made their way out of the stalls.

Richard was too wound up to do anything but stick a mortified claw in the yarn. 'I'm terribly sorry – I haven't eaten. It didn't ruin the music, did it?'

'No, there is only the sound of one more instrument. But why are you not eating something before you are coming?'

'I thought... well – maybe it'd be better to...' The audience bottlenecking in the foyer, his answer was stifled by a couple of fur coats and boas braying beside him.

'...*seven years since we met*...'

'...*the last time in Venice*...'

'*And where are you living now*...?'

'*Is that in Surrey, or Sussex? – I can never remember*...'

They shuffled *en masse* along the narrow exit passage before being ejected onto the slushy pavement like the cultural effluvium they were. Richard quickly moved to one side and stood in front of the adjoining shop window to do up the overcoat he had intentionally left unbuttoned. He waited until, uncertain as Hélène had been as to what exactly he was doing, she wandered over and stood beside him, before resuming.

'I was just saying that I thought maybe it'd be better to have supper after.'

'After what?'

'The concert.'

'It is better to eat before, I think – to listen to your stomach. That is what I am doing.'

He glanced up from his buttons, a forced smile on his lips. 'Yes, you're right,' he said. The baldness of her statement leaving not even the tiniest chink of prandial light, he moved swiftly to contingency two. 'You're taking the Underground, I presume?'

A wrinkled brow treated the presumption as just that. 'No, I take the bus.'

'The Underground will be much quicker at this time of night,

I'm sure. I'm going to Ravenscourt Park, so we can get off at Hammersmith together.'

'But you are eating, *non?*'

'Oh – yes – I'll just have some biscuits when I get home. I'm quite tired actually. It's been a long day.'

'You are 'aving only biscuits for your dinner?'

'And some cheese too, no doubt,' he lied, before intoning in such a way as to recall the hardship she knew he had suffered, 'I survived on a lot less in Austria.'

She suppressed a laugh. 'Yes, but… you are not being in prison 'ere, are you?'

If there was in her question a hint of mockery, an immediate hardening of her aspect indicated it to be no more than a single current in an eddy of thought, followed as it was by a tone as cold as the north wind.

'*Je n'ai pas compris. Pourquoi tu viens avec moi?* Why are you going to Ravenscourt Park?'

'That's where I'm living.'

'But that is not where you tell me you are living last time.'

'Yes,' he said firmly, 'it is.'

She beheld him intently for a moment. The chill evening air had drawn what little colour the concert hall had given to his pale face, and there appeared the faintest glistening in the corner of one eye. Whether this was the effect of mirrors or windows could not with certainty be told, but its result was to force a concession.

'*Ok, je te fais confiance,*' she said prosaically, 'Shall we go?'

'Where to?'

'I go to Oxford Circus.'

Contingency three.

'Baker Street will be better. We can catch the Metropolitan Line to Hammersmith.'

'But it is much more distance to walk there, *non?*'

That was the point of contingency three.

'Only a little,' he said. 'But the train will be quicker and we won't have to change.'

She glanced at the crowd diminishing around them. She did not defer to his wisdom, only to the circumstances.

'As you like,' she said.

By this act, however, Richard knew she had displayed the strength of one whose submission was only consent in so far as it allotted time for him to prove the man that he was. So it was no longer a question of *if*; it was simply a matter of *when*. Yes, he understood her.

With no further words she followed his direction. A northward turn was soon taken and they began making their way up through Marylebone. The silence that signalled the start of their walk continued for a short while after, for if the matter of when had still to be settled, so had the where. It would have to be before they reached Hammersmith, that much was certain; it could not be risked to the end. And if it could not be risked to the end, nor could it be risked to the accompanying sound of rattling carriages. So if it was to be before they got to the bustle and tunnels of Baker Street, it also had to be before they reached the noise of horses and cars on the great Marylebone Road. And the infinitesimal fear that love, no matter how indisputable its existence, might vanish upon the crossing of a single unpropitious paving stone, car horn, or passerby's glance, prompting a response that was neither in her nature nor her will, caused his pace to fluctuate according to the dissonant rhythms of his heart. At last, as they passed by the pillars of the Hinde Street Methodist Mission, Richard – oblivious to the structure – anointed a place to himself a short way ahead. With that matter settled he was able to pick up with conversational poise.

'Did you enjoy the concert?'

'*Oui, merci* – but only for the music. I am not enjoying it for to say after that maybe one person is playing better than another, or that the second violin player is coming in late, or some things like that. I have no idea for the technique, only for the sound.'

'No, exactly.'

'But you – I am not so sure you are enjoying it, even for the sound. *Tu pensais à beaucoup de choses, je crois.*'

'I'm sorry... I—'

'*Exactement*,' she said. A mischievous smile flirted in the wide corners of her lips. 'I am saying you think of many things in the concert. You are not listening to the music.'

'That's what you do when you listen to music, isn't it – you think about things?'

'Maybe yes – maybe no. *Ça dépend de ce que tu penses.*'

'You surely can't decide what exactly to think about. It just happens.'

'But music is more the feeling when you are 'earing it. It is the emotion that you 'ave then.'

'The music makes you think of something first: a memory, or a – well... whatever it might be. The emotion comes from that – what you've thought of.'

The mildly dogmatic strain in which he voiced his opinion had a negating effect. She said nothing for a moment before, with a shrug, saying, 'Yes, maybe you are right.' Then, in a whimsical undertone, she repeated, 'Thinking or feeling; thinking or feeling', as if she had tossed a coin in the air and, watching it spin, would have to choose one side before it landed. 'Yes, thinking is better,' she concluded, but in a manner of such sudden, categorical certainty that it seemed to defy any vagary that the spun coin had had. 'Maybe it is possible only to think and not to feel – to be 'aving a memory or to be picturing something in the future, and to feel nothing about it? Yes, it is better not to feel, only to think. You can control that.'

'Maybe,' said Richard negligently, his mind having drifted elsewhere. The distance to the anointed spot being as yet too great for silence to cloak their passage, he assumed the mantle of guide.

'Do you know where we are?'

'*Oui* – London,' she said.

'No, the area.'

'It is the area between Oxford Circus and Baker Street.'

'Yes... but, just over there –' he pointed right, impermeable to her teasing jousts '– is Harley Street... where all the famous doctors are.'

She watched as his raised arm seemed to tremble as it pointed; it was swiftly lowered.

'*Ah oui, je sais* – but it's there?'

'Yes. So if you ever need a good doctor...'

'Ok, thank you.' She flashed a condescending smile. 'But I think those doctors are maybe too expensive for me. Maybe even for you too. Until one day when you are in charge of the Ministry and you can be 'aving any doctor you want, *non*?'

'Yes,' he replied. A violent throb of his heart saw it leap to his throat – for he knew: she understood him! 'Maybe not too expensive. I don't know. There are lots of other doctors though.'

'I hope so. It's very bad if they are all only on one street.'

'No, of course they aren't.'

Nearing the top of the street Richard could see the gates to the old parish church grounds were still open. A minimal gesture of his forearm indicated they should enter therein. In spite of there being no evident sign of a passageway cutting through to the station to explain the diversion, Hélène obeyed without a sound, as if resistance could be no more given by speech than an impulse could be vanquished by an act. Amid a cluster of ancient Wych elms, two lamps stood at a diagonal either side of a cobbled elliptical pathway, providing a ghostly, mist-speckled sheen to the numerous headstones scattered around.

Richard suddenly stopped. On the far side of the path he spotted the unmistakeable leporine spring of Mr Bellman silhouetted against the colossal wall of the nave. But before he even thought to call out the shape had disappeared down an alley running between the church walls. Richard was sure it was him; either that or some phantom doppelgänger was roaming the London streets.

'You are wanting to ask me something,' said Hélène.

'Pardon?'

'You are stopping so you can ask me something, *non*?'

They stood directly beneath the first lamp. Richard was caught full in the twin beams of her proud, searchlight eyes. In the instant he felt a wave of denial overwhelm him, for in denial was triumph. Yes, he would prove he was not afraid, and by doing that her presumption would be scorned. He would declare loftily that he had no idea what she was talking about, refute the contention, proceed to the station in dudgeon, and abandon her to reflect on traducing his motives. But before he could say any of this – if, indeed, he *could* have said any of this – she continued in a voice piercing and hard, far closer to admonishment than enquiry.

'*Mais pourquoi?* Why are you wanting to ask me this?'

His eyes slunk away, flitting to one side. But it was the shining light of truth, he then realised, that now shone full upon him. And in that lucid brilliance he immediately understood that the key was in his breast. Oh, foolish Galatian that he was! He looked up at her, his eyes unabashed.

'Because I love you,' he said.

There was a short silence.

'Maybe yes, maybe no,' she replied at length, in subdued tones.

'What do you mean?' Without waiting for a reply, he said quickly, 'You're angry.'

'Why should I be angry?'

'You should not be.'

'I am not,' she said. In negation her complexion was suddenly transformed. No longer did the bold contours of her face seem to strike out as a wave rises before it beats the shore; rather did they appear rounded by an aspect of patience – even forbearance – that masked an urge which, being of an influence of far greater potency, was yet the more vague for its being so. 'But to tell me you love me is not a question. What is the question you are wanting to ask me?'

There could be no denial now: love had only one consequence. And as a matter of this consequence he felt permeated by the serenity of true faith, and the words flowed from his lips.

'It's the only natural question to ask when you love someone: will you be my wife?'

The ensuing silence was only notable for the inscrutability with which she attended the question, and the dispassion with which she replied.

'And is that natural?'

'It is.'

'To ask a woman to marry you before even that you tell her you love her?'

'Did I need to tell you with words?'

'*Oui,*' she said, then almost instantly countered, '*Mais non.*'

'The two are inseparable, aren't they? You don't tell someone you love them if you don't want to marry them, do you? You don't say that if you're going to abandon them.'

'*Non – pas si tu dis la verité.*'

'*L'amour est toujours la verité,*' he said.

'But I – I...' she started, her voice ringing with determination, before she stopped, not due to a want of strength to continue, but to a doubt as to what exactly it was she *could* say. She pushed her thin white thumb and forefinger between the open lapels of her jacket and under her muffler. It was a movement as like to locate and tackle an itch. After several moments her hand no longer moved, but seemed to rest peaceably upon the object she had sought. Her hand then jerked forward. The small metal object twirled in her fingers at the end of a chain caught a sliver of light: Richard blinked. By the time his eyes had recovered from the flash the cruciform shape had been concealed again. Her large eyes stared at him brazenly, powerfully, almost in defiance of herself as she stuttered, 'But I – I... can I – *non* – I *can* only be what you think that I am. Nothing more. *Tu comprends?*'

Of course he understood – and in the slight movement of his head was told all she needed to know. The utterance of but one false word then seeming as liable to tip her final word one way as another, Richard waited in silence. And he waited, and waited, and waited. Until, at length, he determined that he would submit to the feminine urges he knew to be striving within her, and ask the question to which no answer was needed.

'Do you lo—'

'Yes,' she said. A strand of coiling hair that had swung down across her cheek was looped behind her ear. Finally, driven not by an accession of will, but by a force outside of her, and more worthy, she plunged. 'Yes,' she repeated, 'I will be your wife.'

Richard smiled. He was happy. From the very moment she had infected his eye in Sarah Childs' front room he had always known the truth. Yes, he understood her.

Chapter 31

Colonel Linton passed a restless night after Edward's departure to Dürnstein. Whilst the prince had taken only a few minutes to remember him, it had taken Linton a good deal longer to remember the prince. This was to be expected; after all, he had met so many princes, archdukes, counts and barons over the years that to distinguish one minor noble with some backwater *puszta* from another was like naming a shrimp in a fisherman's net. It was only once he had retired that the prince's turtle features and immaculately shaven visage had come back to him.

He had been looking for the Countess X for his next promised waltz at the ball and had asked the prince if he had seen her. The prince's '*nein*' had been objectionably curt. Shortly after he had caught the pair dancing to his waltz, and as they twirled together both of their eyes had seemed to sparkle with delight at the man deprived of her arm. This disagreeable recollection had quickly incited one after another, and Linton's sleepless hours had thus got smaller and smaller. In the very smallest he had finally dismissed the need for any help from the prince. There was only one force, he realised, that could be relied on to give proper support to the empress at such a perilous juncture: the British Army. An attack on *them* would end equivocation: the British government would be forced to act. The men of Captain Wilson's relief mission, he concluded, would have to become his.

He roused himself in the morning with full military vigour. A flannel wash was followed by a shave, a trim of his moustache and the combing and re-waxing of his hair. Some items of personal correspondence were attended to before he proceeded to the breakfast room, where he took coffee, ignored the inedible offerings, and then set out for the relief mission's depot.

When he arrived at the depot he discovered the men inspecting Herr Schulze's two crates of ammunition as if they were the eighth wonder of the world. Addison imparted one a desultory kick.

'What the fuck's them fer?' he said.

'Not fired a bullet ter know what it does yet, eh?' said Collins.

'Yeah, an' the fuckin' rest,' came the acid reply.

'Gettin' ready for the next war, aren't we,' said Dawson. He flashed a gummy grin at Yorston. 'Yors!'

Yorston's marionette limb shot in the air. 'Mine!'

'Still in for the seven, aren't yer?' Dawson prodded him archly.

'Erm... sorry... that's *duration* fer me.'

'Oh – so sorry.'

'*So* sorry.'

'Bet it's one o' Captain—'

Collins' grizzled accusation was interrupted by the colonel's approach; it brought the men to sudden attention. Besides being unexpected, his presence, unknown as it was, was also the cause of suspicion: no colonel ever appeared in the line to ask the men how they were.

'Nothin' ter do wiv more fightin', is it, sir?' said Addison humourlessly.

Linton knew instantly the men had gone soft: that was exactly the sort of question they asked when they hadn't been busy. Of the two foes in war, time was always the most deadly. So what they needed was action. His response was straightforward.

'That's what you're here for,' he said. His instructions as to their new mission were then delivered with all the *Ak Dum* required: they would be taking two lorries of relief supplies to Eckartsau the next morning; all the preparations were to be completed by dusk.

'What's Ickysaw, sir?'

'Bloomin' dinosaur, innit, Yors,' Addison muttered aside.

Linton ignored them both and stated plainly it was for the imperial household.

'An' the ammo's for their relief, sir?' asked Collins. His delivery was as flat as a fish, imparted with a look as dumb as a mule, but it brought a colour to Linton's cheeks that was a virtual mirror of its perceived bolshiness. Linton retorted that they'd be damned well relieved to have it if they were shot at!

Dawson glanced down at the crates. 'Lucky it's just the four of us then, eh, sir?' he said.

Despite this remark's similar savour of bolshiness to Collins', Linton condoned it. For if the chief of police's loyalty were to be measured in bullets, then two crates were the revolver to the Maxim gun. There were barely enough to load the guns already at the lodge, let alone any more. But in the restless permutations of the previous night Linton had half anticipated as much. He was fully aware that the first thing a policeman did when he heard a shot in the dark was to find out which way the cat jumped. After all, no man who professed *that much* loyalty could truly be trusted. He therefore tartly replied that they'd have plenty of bullets between them!

'But what 'appens if we're stopped on the way, sir?'

Linton's temper here became even shorter. He barked that if someone tried to do so then they should run the fools over!

'Save on the ammo, eh?'

Linton had had enough of their backchat. He forthwith demanded a tour of the depot. Inside he delineated which supplies were to be loaded, ordered extra mechanical checks made on the lorries and, when satisfied the instructions had been understood, said he would return in the afternoon to inspect their progress. He then left, and headed back to the Bristol in the expectation of receiving Edward's telegrammed reply.

His expectation was more than fulfilled; he read the contents with unalloyed relish! Not the bit at the beginning about the prince's refusal to help, or the bit at the end about Edward having a fever, but the bit in the middle which called the prince a '*sliverly blackguard and coward*'. In those four words Linton's estimation of Edward soared from priggish incompetence to the heights of mild competence. For that was just what the prince was! As such he graced his young captain with a few hours' sleep to get over his sniffles. But it was a grace not entirely selfless in motive: Edward's absence allowed him to complete the preparations without some junior raising quibbles all day.

On Linton's return to the depot, instead of finding four men outside inspecting two crates, he found four men inspecting an engine. The first of the two lorries having earlier been driven out for Collins to check the differential, the radiator had suddenly exploded. The bonnet had since been folded open, much head-scratching discussion had, and a bolt here and there tightened. The conclusion of this was the point at which Linton reappeared.

Colonel Linton knew all about horses, not a stick about engines. He consequently assumed a superintendent detachment, watching on as Addison fetched a can and refilled the radiator. Once this was done Dawson returned to the cab, with Yorston and Addison positioned as spotters for any cracks or leaks, and Collins taking an overview. A single thumb up saw the engine cranked into life. After a period of pleasingly smooth running Linton was sufficiently satisfied to stride forward to the vehicle. But the moment he reached it the radiator exploded again. His tunic and overcoat receiving the full force of the water, a number of oaths coloured the air before he stormed inside to dry himself off by the brazier.

Some twenty minutes later he re-emerged (minus his soaked overcoat) to check on the men. The light of a dull day had already turned fast to the gloom of midwinter, but, gloom or no gloom, Linton did not need the full beam of the equatorial sun to know what he saw – and his horror was such he could barely spit out the words:

'What the – Get that... that... that *object* out of there – now!'

For the little Linton did know about engines was that no woman should ever be let near one.

'She were just...'

'I don't give a damn what she's *just*, private – I'm not having some flag-about box up my engine. You – out – now!'

You being Millie, her attention turned from engine to colonel. Beneath her nurse's hat was a smear of grease the width of her forehead. She purveyed the jolly, pig-headed expression of one well accustomed to censure – and equally accustomed to ignoring it.

'I was explaining that we had the same problem with one of the tractors on—'

'I'm not interested in your wretched tractors – that's a *lorry*.'

'Yes, but—'

'Is someone sick?'

'Sorry, sir, I—'

'Is someone sick? Is one of the men here *sick*?'

Miffed and perplexed, Millie scanned the men's faces. 'I don't think so – not yet,' she concluded bullishly.

'Excellent,' returned Linton, 'so you can trot off back to the bandage-and-balloon shop until one of them is. I'm sure there're plenty of things for you to do there.'

Millie's cheeks flushed to their freckled roots.

'I was actually looking for Edw— Captain Wilson,' she said, a fine vibrato in her voice betraying the heavy slight to her pride.

'Well he's not going to be under the bonnet of a lorry, is he, my jam?'

Linton marched forward to shoo her away. That the men displayed a collective displeasure at this act was obvious, but he was just as displeased with them. He nonetheless stopped, and by a deft change of tone deferred to her whimsical sex.

'He's got a fever, or something like that. There you are – a chap who needs a pretty nurse to buck him with a smile and some cocoa. So, off you go. And when you see him tell him he needs to be at the depot at six thirty sharp in the morning.'

Millie returned a smile as hard as teak, and promptly spun on her heels. She was summoned instantly back by a click of Linton's fingers. She bit her lip hard as she turned to face him again, a *bum-de-dum-dum-dum* refrain ringing loud in her head.

Linton had already taken his notebook out of his pocket to scribble something down. He tore out the page and gave it to her. The note read: *Mr Ciotti, Bristol Hotel.*

'Might as well make yourself useful,' he explained. 'Can't have an officer with a cold without his overcoat, can we? So you can pop by the hotel first. This chap'll know where it is. You can give it to the captain when you see him.'

In issuing this instruction, it should be said, Linton fully believed he was doing the captain a favour worthy of his new estimation: the girl was clearly all spoons on him. So now he'd given her an official reason to see him. Done with the girl, he pivoted back to the men.

'Well is the damned thing fixed yet?'

Chapter 32

Fortunately Millie was at a loose end. A day off had coincided with both Kashia and Zsolt being busy, so she had gone to find Edward. Not that she wouldn't have done this if the others hadn't been busy (the message he left her had said the matter was urgent), it was just – *well* – something *always* seemed to be urgent with him. As a result, and as he evidently needed more watering than the other flowers in her garden, sometimes she was busy, and sometimes she couldn't be bothered, but that was her choice.

However, the news of Edward's fever had an unsettling effect on her: it aroused the curious contradictions of her heart to which she was most defiantly resistant. Although the city had been largely spared the flu epidemic and he most likely had nothing more than a chill (that would explain his behaviour in the café at least), she couldn't be sure this was the case. But an impulse to take care of him (of which affection might be considered a disagreeably unquantifiable part) was counterbalanced by an equally strong impulse that he not for one moment believe that she had ever felt such an impulse. Furthermore, whereas the day had begun with it being her choice to visit Edward, it had since turned into an obligation, and Millie hated nothing more than that she should be *obliged* to do something, regardless of whether she wanted to or not. All of which led to her departing the depot in an obstreperous humour – at Linton, at herself, and at Edward for making her feel like she did.

The biggest nuisance about having to collect the overcoat was that Millie now had to go back into the centre of the city before heading north again to reach Edward's hotel. It meant most of the day would be lost. This was confirmed by her arriving at the Bristol to find the concierge, the said Mr Ciotti, had popped out shortly before and that the receptionist had no idea where such a coat had been put; but he said Mr Ciotti was bound not to be long if she could wait. In the light of Millie's business the receptionist took the opportunity to say that if she saw Colonel Linton could she let him know that a telegram from

London had arrived. Millie's 'yes' was dutiful – though she flippantly remarked that she hoped to do her best to avoid him! The receptionist beamed at her candour – and was discreet in lamenting that he wished he could too! After a short, impatient wait, Millie declared the whole situation a pretty kettle of fish, and huffed that instead of hanging around in the lobby she would have a goosey gander at the opera house opposite. Following a translation the receptionist laughed. He thought it a splendid idea. It was such a pity he could not take her himself!

Millie exited the hotel and crossed the street in front of the opera house. The dark, lumbering clouds carried a greater portent of more snow than they did snow itself, but with the bone-chilling wind she paused only briefly to check the announces for *Ariadne auf Naxos* before going inside. It being still some time before the first of the evening's audience was due to arrive, the foyer was empty apart from a single gentlemen making enquiries at the ticket booth; she saw only his back as she passed him. Marvelling at the plush red interior, at the ornate gold-leafing, at the intricate plasterwork, and at the exquisite details of the cornices around and above her, she slowly gravitated up the grand staircase towards the auditorium doors. Halfway up her attention was drawn back below: the ere fluent German of the gentleman enquirer was being punctuated by idiomatic English exasperation. She went down to have a look. The face of the speaker at the ticket booth now visible, she recognised it instantly; she immediately strode over to him. She stopped just far enough away so as not to intrude on his conversation, but close enough so that she would be the first thing his eyes fell on when it had finished. And this is precisely what happened.

The gentleman was somewhat startled: he did not recognise her at all! And although, once he had recovered his equilibrium, he confessed himself delighted to be approached in such game fashion by such a charming young lady, he was sure her identification was mistaken. Millie was equally sure that it wasn't. He had been at the railway station in Budapest two weeks ago, she said; she had said goodbye to her friend Kashia on the platform, and when she had looked out of the carriage window she had seen the two talking together. She had seen him – though, of course, he had not seen her; she had no idea he was even English until now! The gentleman's little grey eyes darted about the foyer like a couple of sprats trapped in a bag. His smile, hitherto rigid and tense, then relaxed with a cursory twitch of his long upper lip. Why, *yes*, that was right, he said with simpering felicity – he had indeed been at the station. He shuffled away from the booth to explain: he had just arrived in the city and, not speaking a word of Hungarian, had overheard them speaking in English, and so had leapt on the chance for directions. Kashia – yes, that was her name; he had quite forgotten – had been most wonderfully helpful. She must thank her again for him.

'Well, well, fancy that for a coincidence,' he said.

There was a short pause. Millie, smiling appealingly, did not move. What she might have added – had she remembered or even deemed it important – was that, when she had looked out of the carriage window, she had only been drawn to the gentleman's face because she was sure she recognised it then too – from the hospital, in Italy.

To fill the indeterminate, half-expectant silence, the gentleman said he was expecting to meet someone at the opera house but he had mistaken the time: he was too early. He had been hoping to leave a message at the ticket booth but they refused to accept it. Millie replied that that was (more or less) what she was doing too: she was waiting for someone.

'Well, well, fancy that for a coincidence too,' the gentleman again mewed in his mannered, superior tones.

After a further silence the gentleman was induced to propose that such a coincidence merited a drink, did it not? Could he offer the young lady a coffee while they waited? Perhaps something warmer, even, as a toast to attendance?

'Something warmer's always better,' beamed Millie.

Thus of a mind the pair left the opera house and, turning right, proceeded to an establishment the gentleman knew on the far side of the Ringstrasse.

The gentleman was considerably taller than Millie. His face was slim, his skin was white, and between an effeminate nose and a puckering mouth was the downy blonde hair of a hard-won moustache. But even with this latter disguise – and even shorn of their uniform – they were still the unmistakeable biscuit-and-weevil features that Colonel Linton would have instantly recognised as belonging to a certain bottle-brained nautical sort.

Millie and the young gentleman (or naval officer, if clothing should be the definition of a man) took a table in the corner and were soon served with two glasses of wine. Their conversation took in a couple of war anecdotes, some social commentary on the state of the country, and a few basics concerning their present occupations. Millie's being self-evident, the young gentlemen explained that he had been seconded from the navy to help with the reconstruction of the railways in Europe: it was the family business in England.

As soon as the young gentleman finished his wine (Millie's glass was already empty) he suggested another – if Millie had time? Millie did: it was her day off. She could do as she pleased. Besides, she told herself, with the Bristol only over the road, and given Edward was not expecting her at all, it hardly mattered whether she reached his at twenty minutes past the hour, or twenty minutes to whatever hour. What mattered was that she would be there, which she would be. With the ordering of the second glass the young gentleman excused himself: he had to check to see if his friend had arrived; he would return to Millie post-haste.

Millie's solitary state was fleeting: the instant the young gentleman departed he was replaced by another. The replacement was more distinguished, in both age and appearance. He possessed a gleaming bald head, a furzy white beard and a generous moustache lightly curled at the points, and his little dark eyes were set deep beneath a heavy, sloping brow that joined his nose like the tip of an arrow. Standing at the end of the table he displayed a girth of such substance as to suggest the hardships of war had only been surfeit.

The *Fräulein* must forgive his intrusion, he said. He had been listening to them talking and would consider it a grave discourtesy if he did not express his admiration and gratitude for all the work that the fine English nurses were doing in his city. He had travelled much in his life, including to England (where he still had some friends), and would never understand what had brought their countries to war. He shook his head with unmeasured sadness – and helped himself to a seat. So now their countries were friends again it surely demanded a toast. The *Fräulein* must allow him to buy her a drink. Her glass being yet full, Millie could hardly refuse. But the drink would not be wine, the gentleman said. No, no – a proper toast could be only had with a schnapps. The schnapps served, the toast had, the gentleman thereupon proceeded to some earnest enquiries as to Millie's life and work as a nurse, and before. In the midst of these investigations the gentleman's younger counterpart returned.

Millie asked the latter if he had found his friend, which he had. His friend had been most jealous to hear he had such a charming companion to engage him while he waited.

'Yes, yes, charming indeed,' the bewhiskered gentleman put in, adding with an extravagant, self-effacing twinkle, 'Of course, I am too old to be having a nurse alone with me all of the evening; but too young to be having her all of the day either, that is for sure!' So now that the *Fräulein*'s companion had found his friend – the opera was always the best place to do that, he averred – he would no longer impose on the pair; he would continue reading his newspaper alone. His movement to then do so was deliberate, if at all.

Millie would not hear of his parting. They would not be staying long, she said – she had to visit a friend who was sick – but they must first have a drink all together. The gentleman considered it an honour, and promptly ordered a round. After all, he said, spreading his arms and gazing around the splendour of the establishment, with its fittings of natural wood, marble, mirrors and art deco ceiling, when one was attired correctly it was a pleasure to profit from the equivalent company! The round of schnapps soon drunk the younger gentleman, feeling obliged (if only mildly rivalrous), ordered another in turn – the arrival of which prompted Millie to declare that she would have to leave after that.

'Yes, yes, that is always the fate of the poor nurse,' intoned the elder gentleman, raising his glass to good health. 'She is always having to sacrifice her amusement in order to be tending to the sick.'

The jest brought an obstinate flush to Millie's freckles. It was impossible, she resolved, that they could part with her not having paid for a drink, which she insisted on doing. The final round (after the present one) would be hers to buy.

The elder gentleman roared with delight; then scowled at a joyless thought. 'Ha! Yes – it is for sure the *Fräulein* is reminding me of my son. Yes, yes, it was impossible for me to be telling him what to do either. It is for sure he was never listening to his father.' Looking at Millie, he let out an ironic laugh. 'I was always thinking it is better to be having a daughter – but now I am not sure.'

'No, nor me!' Millie laughed too.

The final round was not long in coming. The younger gentleman who, since his return to the table, had retained an air of good-natured – though unquestionably aloof and distracted – taciturnity, was by an unsuspecting increment of alcohol drawn forth to loquacity. It was a loquacity the elder gentleman greeted with great satisfaction. What was the gentleman's name again, the younger asked; he hadn't quite caught it.

'Herr Braunthal.'

Ah, yes. And what did he do?

Herr Braunthal slapped his thigh and guffawed. 'No, no, I do not *do*, young man – not at my age. I am only advising. Just a little. But you are doing what, young man?' Herr Braunthal being told – though he already knew (he had been listening *very* closely) – he returned a nod of sagacious investment. 'Most interesting,' he said. 'Yes, yes, most interesting – and most important for my country.'

Millie, for whom the increment of alcohol, equivalent to the young gentleman's, was discernible only by the depth of her laugh and a rash appearing on her neck, glanced up at the clock by the bar – at exactly the moment the young gentleman did too. Now, she told herself stiffly, she really had to be going. Upon which vow three more drinks arrived at the table.

Herr Braunthal apologised, but it was out of the question that the beautiful *Fräulein* from England could buy the last drink. A toast was consequently raised to the prosperity and wonder of the railways.

After that round then, Millie swore to herself, she would definitely leave to collect the overcoat from the hotel and be a nurse to Edward; after the last drink.

Chapter 33

Edward woke with a start. A thin band of coppery light opposite was the only mark in the solid black space. For several seconds he had no idea where he was; then the door was pounded again. A chill of panic shot through him: Colonel Carrington had discovered his plan; furious, he had come to punish and disgrace him. Springing from his bed, he lunged at the door, but the key was not in the lock; he spun round and fumbled on the bedside table. A muffled clunk telling the key was knocked to the floor, he dropped to his knees and frantically clawed at the carpet. At last in hand, he scrambled up and shoved they key in the lock. A mere half-turn was needed before the bolt disengaged – and the door was barged open. Edward was thrown back on the bed, as if struck by a wave. The door was then shut. A couple of fevered strides took the entrant across the room to the window; a furtive glimpse was snatched at the alley below. The entrant turned round. In the impenetrable void nothing could be seen beyond a vague silhouette.

Edward flailed an arm at the table, but the act was symbolic: he had no clue where his gun was. Prostrate, unarmed, a towering spectre before him, he redressed himself fiercely to assume an advantage.

'Who the...?'

'I need petrol.'

'What? *Petrol?*' Edward was thrown by the word. 'I – I – I haven't got any damned petrol. Who the—?'

'Of course you do. At the depot – with all the other supplies. *I know.*'

The figure's limbs suddenly convulsed with the power of speech: its colossal form swayed forward, as if an electrical current had been charged to its body. In the lurid strip of red-orange light a set of teeth flashed, the hollows and shafts of its cadaverous face presenting an ungodly, nightmarish aspect. But this time the vision was real: flesh and blood stood before Edward; it was no Alpine illusion.

A sneering grin tore up Friedrich's cheeks, unbridled scorn on his lips as he said, 'You are wanting to say it is not for me, no? That it is British petrol and not for the Austrians – even though it is here – in Vienna – in *my* city? Ha! Yes – it's always the same: the foreigners are always pretending to help, but when we have to defend ourselves you do nothing. No, it is not in your interest to *do*. It is better for you we are slaughtered. Ha! Yes – I knew it would be pointless to come to here.' Three imperious steps returned him to the door. His hand gripping the doorknob, he stopped. The angle of his neck and salient profile alone informed his look rested on Edward, and not on some mote to be flicked on the floor. He remained in this pose of panther-like stillness, a statue crafted not for the aesthete, but as incitement to Edward's purest emotion.

From the stunned vacuum of silence a response was at last sucked.

'Well – well, what for?' asked Edward.

'Burning the Reichstag – Pff – *a motor car*.'

'What *for*?' Edward snapped at the sarcastic retort.

'You know already,' Friedrich snapped back. 'You know what they're going to do. You know I must get to the emperor before the bullets.' He let go the door knob and jerked his head to the window, a glimmer catching in the white of his eye. It was a light that penetrated the deepest depths of the ocean; it fell on all the rivets and bones and crushed wooden beams that had sunk to the bottom and littered the floor. And in that fractional instant Edward saw all that was shown him: it was what he had seen too when he had confronted the prince. So of course he *knew*. He knew a man and his kin were either killed, or were not. *He* therefore either did, or did not. The moral choice had not changed with the resurrection of Friedrich: it was still binary.

Compulsion coursed through his body as he asked, '*Now?* – *Tonight?*'

'Tonight – today – what does it matter the time?'

Edward spun round, disorientated; then found his watch on the table. 'What *is* the time?' he said.

'It is tonight – today. What does it matter the time? It is only the petrol that matters.'

Edward tilted the watch to the light; the hands were at four. A glance at the window confirmed it was night, though not of what day. However, Friedrich was right – what did that matter? He sprang to his feet, found his gun on the sideboard and grabbed his coat from the bed. He stuck his arms in the sleeves.

'That is your cloak for the night?'

Edward had already halted his vestment before Friedrich spoke, confused by the size and smell of the garment. He then recalled the exchange.

'No, it's not,' he said sharply. He stripped himself of the article and tossed it back on the bed. He stood, ready as he was. With a smirk suppressed by the darkness, Friedrich promptly swung the door open. As the pair hastened out, a note pushed under the door was trampled and torn beneath the heels of two sets of boots.

The bitter night was swirling with tiny pellets of snow. Turning down a side road, Friedrich immediately opened the door to a little two-door Steyr. Edward stopped, suspicious.

'I thought you didn't have any petrol?' he said.

'No – not *enough*.'

Any thoughts Edward had of Friedrich's deception were swept aside by the wind. His fever may have been purged by a deep, sweaty sleep, but in the freezing outside, and deprived of his coat, his clammy underclothes had turned in a mere second to ice. He therefore opened the door and got in the car. The engine turned at first asking.

*

As they drove off into the snow-speckled night, opposite the hotel, sheltered from the elements and concealed by the shadows beneath a tenement archway, the very same slight mantled figure that had tracked Edward's fevered arrival the morning before, here marked his befriended departure. It was a sight that brought the fierce, fleeting glint of the tiger to her once patient eyes; that he should have dared to come back – *after all that*. With steps at once restless and precise, for a moment she seemed chained behind the bars of an invisible black cage, her fingers clawing at the walls all about her. Then, suddenly, she leapt out of the darkness; in the freedom of ice she proceeded with such a swiftness of foot that scarce a trace could be seen in the snow.

*

'Who? You must get there before *whose* bullets?'

The question broke a lengthy silence. Or perhaps it wasn't lengthy at all – the wild, delirious shifts from sleeping to waking, and from inside to out, had stripped the hour of its temporal truth. Only the shuddering chassis and the pervasive smell of leather and petrol attested that Friedrich was truly there at the wheel. It was this sentient reality that brought a cool, military rationale to Edward's enquiry. In response a half-smile flicked Friedrich's lips.

'You are still asking the best questions, that is for sure,' he said; then added succinctly, 'Everyone's.'

'So what is it you think you're going to do when you get there?'

'Me?'

'Yes – you.'

'I will make certain the emperor does not leave. That is what I will do.'

'What?'

'Exactly – that is *what* I will do.'

Edward started; a heady frisson of rage surged at this knife plunged in his back. So he *had* been deceived! Friedrich was using him to abet in the emperor's murder! He was being duped and exploited by someone whose earthly existence had but minutes before secretly thrilled with its stark revelation. Now – well, Friedrich likely didn't even need petrol! Edward's hand flew out to the door handle—

'Ha! But you are not knowing so much I am thinking. Ha!' Friedrich exclaimed triumphantly. An icy camber in the road briefly took his attention; Edward's grip on the handle turned with it from flight into safety. The bend negotiated, Friedrich resumed, in expositional tones, as if he had never left off. 'So I explain it to you. It is, as some people always say, *simple*. If the emperor leaves the country now he will never come back. Never. So he must stay in Austria until the Paris treaty is signed. That is the only way he will be recognised as the King of Austria – as our symbol of independence. If he is leaving people will be thinking that he belongs to an empire that does not exist any more. If he is leaving one thing only is happening: Austria is dead.'

There was a pause. Edward, swallowing Friedrich's indigestible words, then asked in the disputative tones of one for whom something bilious had stuck in his throat, 'Austria is dead?'

'Yes, Austria.'

'And what on earth makes you think the emperor will listen to *you*?' Edward scoffed.

Friedrich's reply was of proud, elementary assurance. 'Because we are the only ones who want him to stay,' he said. 'We – the true monarchists – know that it is the only hope for Austria to survive. The emperor knows that too. That is why he listens to me – and not to the stupid prince.'

The image of the table by the fire came to Edward first, then the echoing footsteps, then the wine glass, then the hooded form at the station, then the prince. So that was how Friedrich had found him! He had followed him every step of the way! Admitting entry to Edward's shaft of enlightenment, Friedrich pressed on serenely.

'I am learning these surprises happen always very often in life. Then they are becoming quite normal. Very quickly nothing is a surprise. That is when you are truly learning about people, when you are truly understanding them and seeing into their eyes. You too must be learning this, no?'

Frantically unjumbling his chaotic thoughts Edward suddenly recognised the corners of the depot's approach. So he gave neither answer, direction, nor utterance, but merely waited for the car to quietly draw up alongside the depot's high corrugated wall.

*

Private Yorston had been dozing in the midst of his fire-spaniel shift; the sound of the car therefore woke him with exactly the same panicked bewilderment as Edward had shortly before felt: he had no clue of the time either. That it was Captain Wilson he found at the door and not the colonel consequently came as a relief. Indeed, understanding the captain would be there in the morning, Yorston was hardly surprised that he was.

'Morning, sir. Feelin' better?'

Edward was similarly relieved to find Private Yorston there and not

Private Collins, the former's pasty skin reddened by the brazier and his eyes glazed with just-woken candour.

'Yes. Thank you, Private—'

'Be chilly tonight without yer coat, eh, sir?'

Edward needed no such reminding. 'Yes – but Yorston – I need petrol.'

'Now, sir?'

'Yes. Now.'

"Course, sir. Ah be a-thinkin' just that an 'our ago, yer know – that the colonel might be a-needin' some.'

'Yes, yes, exactly.'

'Be a going with 'im, will 'ee be, sir?' Yorston's eyes were distracted by the figure behind Edward. Edward shot a look back.

'No,' he said firmly.

Yorston was not referring to Friedrich, but was content either way.

'Good, sir. The more we be the better, ah be thinking. Just in case, eh, sir?'

'Yes.'

Edward had no idea what Yorston was on about; he could only guess that the colonel was Linton. But if that was the case it meant the colonel had apparently given the men orders of which he knew nothing. At this thought Edward's indignant choler returned to the fore. After all, they were *his* men: they were *his* to shepherd and command; they were not for any Colonel Linton or Carrington to dispose of like toy soldiers on the nursery floor. He would not be treated like an insignificant nothing to be flicked to one side! So as Yorston slipped inside and shortly returned with the sought-after petrol, it was clear the first thing he needed to do was to get to the Bristol Hotel and find out what was going on. Taking the petrol from Yorston, he returned bristling to the car and relayed it to the waiting Friedrich, standing by the door. Friedrich removed it to the boot and hid it under some matting. They both got back in and a moment later were gone.

*

Colonel Linton was already up: he had risen at precisely the same time as Edward, but this was due to no pounding of his door. Rather had he returned to the hotel the previous evening to have his blood boiled by not one, but *two* messages. The first was from Mr Ciotti: he said a nurse had come to collect the captain's overcoat while he was out but had not come back as she'd said she would. *Hell and scissors – why could these damned women never do what they said they would? He'd not sent her just to go and catch fleas!* Suddenly doubting that she even had the wits to remember Edward's order, Linton immediately despatched a message to his hotel; expressly demanding confirmation of receipt, he had got none before retiring. *Damn it – she'd taken him out on the razzle!* Thus had Linton risen at the hour he had to check there was still no reply (there wasn't), and then to go and drag his wretched officer out of bed by his ear, for whilst the lorries would travel in daylight to confute any suspicions of a clandestine mission, he himself intended to part in advance in the car, under cover of dark. An impetuous character might be prone to leap at the odd fence blind, but fool was he who did it on another's mount.

All this, however, paled into insignificance beside his fury at the second message: the cable from London. *Wilson – why it was a damned dog of a name!* That an ink-slinging cur should possess the gall to 'stress' things to him and talk of the king as if he knew him himself was farcical – were it not such an outrage. If Linton's resolve beforehand had been stiff, the cable had now made it hidebound. He was the man on the spot; the footlicker Wilson was not. This was the only thing Linton was prepared to *acknowledge* as he thundered out of the Bristol Hotel and onto the Ringstrasse in the snowy black morning.

*

'The war is making liars of us all, no?'

'What do you mean?'

'You were lying perfectly to your soldier there,' said Friedrich, a twinkle in his wide, lacertian eye, 'the same as you are lying in your clothes too.'

Friedrich had spoken just as Edward was to instruct him of their parting. For whilst his refutation to Yorston of accompanying Friedrich had been a reflex response, Edward's moral obligation had not exceeded the basic provision of petrol. Refusing to take Friedrich's bait he therefore maintained a stubborn, incorruptible silence as they headed south into the city centre, awaiting his moment of descent.

'It is making liars of those who are still living, that is,' Friedrich persisted, matter-of-factly. A further pause was met by further silence. 'Those who are not liars are already dead.'

'And those who were?' said Edward, finally biting.

It was all that was needed: Friedrich was once more triumphant.

'Ha! Exactly! I know you are thinking like this! I can see it in your eyes – just like I always did! Ha! Yes, you are thinking I am fighting for the Habsburgs and the empire. You are thinking exactly like *her*.'

There could be no doubt who *her* was: the last word was uttered with such seething contempt that it could only pertain to a woman once loved. And even though it was clear to Edward that he had indeed only known Friedrich *a little* (Kashia had certainly been right about that), the effect on him was still as if he had been crushed between their violent collision of rocks.

'I am. You *did*,' he said between lips stiff, barely parted.

'And you fought too. Like you had to—'

'I had to because I… I… well, what should I have done – *nothing?*'

'Maybe nothing is better.'

'Maybe it is,' said Edward, offhand.

Friedrich's counter was splenetic and instant. 'No, it isn't! Because it is the same – you are not fighting for your Methodist God, and I am not fighting for the empire. We are fighting only because we must – to save ourselves from destruction.'

'The destruction was caused by you and the Germans.'

'No – I fought to stop it! For the same reason I fight now. I am fighting against those who are diseased with the fear of aggression – against those who are already too big! Bolsheviks, Jews, Germans – they are all exactly the same. Now it is only the monarchy that can save Austria from being destroyed. So we are the ones who must resist. *We*, who are the better Germans.'

Friedrich's changeling convictions cut no ice with Edward. He knew he had fought in the war because he had had to, and he had done so knowing that if any man said and did not – that if belief were found only in words – then he was no better than dead. *But Friedrich?* When he had first come to Vienna all Friedrich had done was denounce the Habsburgs and the empire. Now, here he was, admitting that he *had* run headlong into the war and kissed the feet of the Habsburg boot, the same boot of the same tyrant that had once crushed the Austrian skull and had its blood on its heel. His re-emergence into light was therefore not just as a man reformed in thought, but one transfigured beyond all recognition by it. It was an apostasy that far exceeded any simple negation of belief: it was treachery right through the heart. And in recognising this Edward was overwhelmed by a feeling of moral revulsion, that the good that had been provoked in him by the turning of the prince's back might be subverted by one whose motives were craven.

'Stop the car,' he said.

'What for?'

Edward's hesitation was both cause and logistics; his conclusion was curt.

'I have to see the colonel.'

'And that is making what purpose?'

'The purpose is my orders.'

'Orders! Ha!' Friedrich gave an equine snort of derision. 'Orders are given by people who do not know what to do to those who have to be told what to do.'

'Then I'll make sure he knows.'

'Pff – and he is doing what? Sending a letter? No, he will do nothing – just like that stupid prince. Do you understand? They do not want the emperor to live; they care only that he is gone. But – ok, ok, I stop the car and you leave. You leave – and I will *do* on my own.'

A peevish foot to the brake brought the car to a juddering halt. Edward opened his door to get out; his arm was snatched as he did.

'Is that it?' Friedrich's whole face was contorted, then, in a pitch of wild, incredulous disdain he repeated, '*Is that it?* You are leaving to see a colonel who will care nothing for the things that you tell him, not even that it is *you* that is telling him. You are leaving for *that*?'

Edward wrenched his arm free and swung a leg to get out. 'Maybe,' he said, but he made no further move. After a short silence of inaction Friedrich threw himself back in his seat. He let out a savage, mocking laugh.

'Ha! Yes, yes – that is what you are always liking the most! You are liking the little games! Ha! Yes, the colonel is playing with you just like this, and after you are seeing him and telling him everything, then he is tossing you aside – just like Oriana. Ha! You see, even at this very moment I know that is who you are thinking about. Ha!'

'Don't be stupid,' Edward snapped.

Nor was there any doubt of this truth: he was not, nor had he been once. Now that Friedrich had said it, however, he did. And in that twinkling, comet-like thought, the tail wagged once again; it wagged with a furious, unstoppable beat. Friedrich leapt upon it as it careered through the sky.

'Yes, yes – *her*. Ha! Yes, always the little secretary girl, no?' One hand was set to the steering wheel, another to the gear stick. 'Good. Now you close the door and I am telling you what is happening. Yes, yes – that is giving you a much better reason for coming than the life of an emperor, for sure.' A cursory signal was made at the door. 'Yes, close it, quickly. *Now* I will take you to see the chandeliers that light the snow.'

Edward's eyes darted left and right. They had stopped on the Ringstrasse. The wide boulevard was being covered by a fresh screen of snow; it was deserted save for the bristling, military gait of a man in the distance whose direction was clear, even if his features were not. And then, that simply, drawn like the iron to the magnet, the door was closed.

*

The young gentleman of ere maritime attire might have wished to continue drinking with Millie if, upon delivery of his final message to Ulrich Köstler in a secluded passage behind the opera house foyer, he had not been bequeathed one in return. His own confirmed the guarantees made by the minister in London to ensure the prevention of bloodshed and the maintenance of order, and that a haemorrhage could only be stopped by the appropriate cut: this was the concluding rite of his secret assignation, or it should have been. Such, however, had been Köstler's powers of seductive persuasion that he had found it impossible to refuse his last passionate entreaty.

There was no time for a cable to London, Köstler said breathlessly: he feared the chief of police had quite lost his head – he threatened to spread bullets all over the country. If this happened then the English colonel might well find the means to fire them. Such a thing would shatter the whole glass equilibrium. It would lead to blood on the walls and blood on their hands. So their mutual friend had to know this – at once – before it was too late. Köstler himself was in a race to forestall a catastrophic Rubicon act. The young gentleman was consequently the only person he could trust to deliver his note. Swiftly providing the when and the where, he caressed the young gentleman's anxious, lip-twitching pucker by stressing it would be at an hour most suited to the thrill of the night; it was a place to be slipped in and out of completely unseen. Then, releasing the note, Ulrich Köstler promptly vanished with the stealth of one who had almost never been seen.

The young gentleman's pleasure at Millie's company had not been matched by that for Herr Braunthal: he abhorred his nosy pomposity. He had suffered him purely for Millie – and in the hope he might leave; and then, when all hope was abandoned, as an end in itself until his nocturnal encounter. When the time had arrived he brought their association to a close; his departure roused Millie and Herr Braunthal to likewise adjourn from the table. Herr Braunthal declaring his fortune to be heading in the same direction as the *Fräulein*, the young gentleman had lamented that his was in the opposite. Upon their parting of ways outside the young gentleman had briefly watched on as the Herr Braunthal and Millie disappeared into the dark evening snow towards the Ringstrasse; *they were almost arm in arm!*

The young gentleman's *opposite* direction had only been so in order to extract himself from company; rather was it circuitous. After a westerly beginning he therefore looped back and took a parallel south-easterly route passing through the Karlsplatz as he made his way to the Stadtpark. Entering the park he found the lamplights extinguished, just as Köstler had advised, and so was able to glide across it like a shadow traversing the deep desert dunes. He soon descended the icy steps to the canal. A single set of footprints were the sole disturbance to the pristine white surface of the narrow towpath, dimly lit by reflections skimming the frozen waters beside. He followed the line of the prints, carefully placing his own feet in their mark. At a short distance they arced to a stop; in the shadows a man stood with his back to the high wall. A cap pulled low over his brow, his face was wrapped in a scarf with only a slit for his eyes. The young gentleman did not stop, but continued along the path; he was immediately followed. A moment later, in muffled, barely intelligible tones, the man behind spoke. The gentleman turned round to face him; as he did a sliver of light caught the hollow of a crushed, sunken eye opposite like a glittering pearl. The young gentleman replied fluently – *Nem tudom*: he didn't speak Hungarian. In return two words were spluttered in English – *For Kashia*. Upon this signal the gentleman removed Köstler's note from his pocket and handed it to the man with the pearl in his eye. He then turned round again and continued along down the towpath.

*

'That is the problem with the English,' reproached Friedrich. 'They are always wanting to see the pretty painting – they care nothing about the creation.' He leaned forward and smeared the mist from the windscreen with his sleeve. A glance at Edward was to confirm he was listening. 'You know, when Oriana was sending you letters after you are leaving Vienna, I was laughing at her: the same person who is saying you will never come back is writing letters to you. What is the point, Oriana, I was telling her, but she was always saying nothing. Then, one day, Kashia tells me Oriana is receiving a letter from you where you say that maybe you *do* come back. Ha!' He thumped the steering wheel in elation. 'It takes six years – but it's true: you *do*! But she tells me that when Oriana is reading the letter she is so angry that her whole body is shaking. It is like the reality that you come back is too terrifying for her, that she is wanting only to think of you being so far away, while she sits on the shore and looks out to the sea, so sad you have left her. So she stops writing. She says nothing, only stops.

And like this everything ends. Poof!' In a puff of his lips she was gone. 'So that is Oriana. Now you discover the truth, you see how banal it is: it is maybe not even worth to come in the car with me, no?'

Friedrich mistimed a gear in his excitement; the grind of the clutch was like the horn of some massive, invisible liner sounded in the ocean of night. With the Danube behind them they slowly began traversing the exposed plains east of Vienna. There the wind whipped, hurling the snow at the car in violent gusts like fistfuls of sand; it rattled the windows; the chassis shook; the winter air whistled in through every crack. And all the while it did Edward's eyes remained frozen, imbedded deep in the tunnelled darkness ahead.

After a silence Friedrich's next glance was artful, his tone comradely. 'But that is not the end. It is never the end. I know – because you are like me: you are always thinking of the creation. So there is only one thing that is making any of it interesting, and that is the one impossible question that you are always asking to yourself: *Why?* It is such a stupid word, no? So ugly too. But this is the word that creates the only true beauty of the world.'

As if an obligation had at last to be met, Edward asked in a desultory undertone, 'And now? What is she—?'

'*Pff.* She is dead – she is alive. What does that matter? What matters is that you have come back.'

The question's peremptory, haughty dismissal made no impression on Edward's stolid, lifeless aspect: he continued to stare through the windscreen as if at a sheer, solid, insurmountable wall of ice. Suddenly a spark flashed in his eye. But *then*? he thought. Now that he had come back – what *then*?

Then there was light: a star appeared up ahead. That, he told himself, would be his guide of redemption; that would lead him onwards. And so he watched, mesmerised as the light slowly expanded, getting ever brighter and brighter. Finally blurring, it split into two. Then it dazzled and glared.

Friedrich threw the car right; the axle lurching left, a wrenched counter-turn was put to the wheel. The car seemed to leap with the contrary force – then ploughed into a drift at the side of the road. Behind them a lorry barrelled on like a boulder. Friedrich sat up straight; his door was blocked by the snow. He turned to Edward. A sharp pain in his neck made him wince and put his hand to protect it. His features were flecked with dashes of red on his cheeks and temple; they were marks almost tribal.

'Get out. Look at it!'

Edward bridled at Friedrich's imperious command. 'At what?' he said.

'The lorry. See if it stops.'

Edward got out in dudgeon and studied the diminishing glare.

'Is it stopping?' asked Friedrich impatiently.

'No.'

There was silence.

'*And now?*'

'I don't think so.'

'Is it still there? Can you *see* it?'

Edward could – just about – but it had reached a distance at which detection of motion was impossible; only the final extinguishing of the light would prove that. And the light, though it remained an infinitesimal speck on the black horizon, resisted erasure like a stubborn spot on a coat.

'Well?'

'I don't know,' said Edward, squinting. 'It might have stopped. Why?'

Friedrich gave no reply; instead he straddled the passenger seat and clambered out. His hand pressed to his neck, he squinted at the speck too. He then ran round to the front of the car and set his back to the radiator.

'Come on. We must get it out of the snow.'

Edward did not demur. He took up a position by the open passenger door, his hands pressed to the frame. Upon a count of two they pushed the car back into the road. They paused to look at the light.

'It's definitely stopped,' Edward concluded.

'Yes. And if they are stopped it is only to come back.' Where Friedrich's voice had previously resonated with indignation and anger, there now seemed to toll something closer to portent and terror, as if he had suddenly genuflected before the gleam of a sovereign blade that had risen above him. Edward looked at Friedrich, but to do so was to catch only a bold flash of eyes and a rapier grin. 'You see, that is also why I am wanting to keep a British officer with me. They are not attacking us then, that is for sure.'

'Who's *they*?'

'The people who want us dead.'

Edward had no chance to renounce the pheasant alliance: Friedrich swung round the bonnet and leapt into the car. Edward glanced again at the light. Without doubt it shone brighter; he got back in the car. But the portent and terror that had moments before tolled in Friedrich's voice had not disappeared with the rapier and flash: it was there in the tormented pallor of his face as his fingers hung, suspended, over the ignition button, as if everything had been ossified in the midst of the act. In the strange, no-man's-land stasis, Edward seized command of the operation.

'It's too late. We'll get barely two hundred yards before they catch us up – whoever they are – or whoever you think they are. Anyway, as you said, no one's going to attack a British officer, are they? I'll make sure nothing happens to you.'

An instinctive glance back triggered a like movement in Friedrich.

'You're right, it is too late,' Friedrich agreed heavily. He let his finger drop from the button like a stone from a height. 'It is always too late.' Falling silent he bowed his head in an attitude of fateful solemnity. An instant later his head rose, as if pulled back to life by the jerk of a puppeteer's strings. His teeth were set in a grimace and his eyes sparkled with bitter defiance. 'But I will not wait for them here. No, not *them*. Not for people like that – who talk of equality but know nothing about liberty.' He suddenly flung open the door and launched himself into the snow. 'Come on!' he cried.

'Where are you going? *Friedrich!*'

In a split second there was nothing to see; in the dim headlamp penumbra there were only deep gouges in the snow where his body had been.

'Come on!' exhorted a fathomless cry.

Edward twisted in his seat. No one would attack *him*, he knew. But then, he reasoned – who would honestly care who he was? *Ting-a-ling-a-ling, ting-a-ling-a-ling*, rang the bell in his head. He clamped his hands to his ears – then thumped the door in his anger; that fear belonged to Friedrich, not him! Why should he be tainted with that? And, even if he got out of the car, where the hell would he go? Follow Friedrich? A man who was a traitor, a man who was dead? He looked anxiously back: the windscreen was a dazzling mirror of light; any moment, he knew, the light would split into two and be upon him. Thinking no more, he jumped out of the car, rounded the front, and fell into Friedrich's staggering snowprints. Ahead, up an incline, he discerned a struggling shape.

'Friedrich—'

'Come on!'

'*Where?* Where the hell are we going?'

No answer was given. No sound broke the night other than the approaching rumble of wheels and the breathy crunching of snow. Edward slipped and fell in the drift. Impetuously, furiously, he scrabbled to his feet and drove himself on, blindly up the steepening bank: on and on, always forward, through the snow, through the ice, through the mud, through the darkness, never once looking back – until his flailing arms met a wall. The huge, rough, mossy blocks seemed to crumble at his touch, as if about to give way and see him tumble into a great black abyss. He looked to the road: the lorry had stopped; its yellow-tinged headlamps fanned light across the snowy expanse like a crepuscular glaze.

'Friedrich? Friedrich?' he hissed. He dropped to the base of the wall in pursuit of his prints.

'Here!' came an invisible growl to his right. '*Come on!*'

Edward hurried forward, his fingers running along the wall as he went. A massive, predatory force suddenly grabbed his lapels; it jerked him left, dragging him into a narrow fissure between two high, outbuilding walls. He was pinned to the stone. In front of him Friedrich's face caught a trace of elemental light; it shimmered in his wild, distended eyes, as if some fierce, lacerating attraction had been drawn from a celestial source to alight on its spot. A downward thrust of Friedrich's arm was then like a piston, and was followed by an upward: his fist flying at Edward, it splayed at the last on his chest. Edward looked down. A scrap of paper had been affixed to his heart.

'You see – this is what happens when someone cannot create – they can only destroy. They hunt, and they hunt, until they have blood, until they feel nothing.' His twisted inflexions of triumph and rage were interjected by a short, violent laugh. 'But the devils also believe, don't they? Ha! You see – I too have learnt.' He turned his head, disappearing his face, to scan the length of the fissure. Stuffing the paper into Edward's fingers, he re-gripped Edward's lapels and pulled him forward. 'Come on – this way. I know where to go.'

As they ran, tumbling together, at the end of the fissure a spot of nebular light struck the top of the wall. Edward glanced up at it – just as a force tugged him harder. But Friedrich did not hesitate as he stormed into the open.

Nor did Kashia.

She stood regal, emotionless, her outstretched arm rigid as a lance as Friedrich fell dead in the snow. Malignant was the infection; excision the cure. She turned to Edward: head, eyes, arm, pistol – all in one smooth, clinical motion. In a transcendent visage her eyes appeared pure and white, as if the full glare of the moon had pierced the clouds and was reflected in them by the crystalline snow. Trapped in her relentless, implacable gaze, Edward felt utterly powerless.

'Read it,' she said.

A barely perceptible movement of gun was made to his hand. Edward remained frozen; then he realised; he submitted: he unfolded the note in his fingers. The crumpled German script was hard to decipher. At length he read as commanded:

'*In loyalty my vow I have fulfilled. They hunt for our king.*'

He looked at Kashia forlornly, ignorantly, his blue eyes empty as the ocean. Facing her cold, marbled features an icy chill permeated his core; he shivered intensely.

'Leave no footprints when you walk in the snow – that is what he wrote too,' she finally said – her voice, unwavering, one of brutal dispassion. 'Fear is only for the known: that is what he wrote to *me*. You see – that is what men do: they lie.'

In the pale and ghastly glow of her orb-like eyes Edward's head was slowly drawn down to the body that lay at his feet. Friedrich had fallen on his back; an expression of near ecstasy was writhen in the gruesome twists of his face. Only the broad lapels of his unbuttoned overcoat flaring out in the snow gave the impression of a shadow that was no longer there. Edward shivered again. But then, he thought, Friedrich's coat would surely now serve him. Yes, that would keep him warm in the snow – in the place of his own. And so, he decided, he would kneel before Kashia, and he would take it.

*

No more – I say. *No more!* The view is clear: there are no longer spires or shards littering the path and blocking the sight of the world. So do not be turned by the old vanishing lie – it is not solid; it melts in the air with every faint gasp of invisible breath – for there is only the truth. That, I say, is permanence. That is God. That is the ever-ascending being which stands eternal, transfigured on the heights. I know! For that, I say, is *then*.

Acknowledgements

In the lengthy gestation of a novel numerous thank yous are inevitably due. Firstly, to the resources, without which there would be neither research nor book: the fantastic King's College library, and all the gems in the stacks; Quaker House library; the Royal Collection at Windsor; and, of course, the Imperial War Museum. Two wonderful location guides came in the form of Enrico Ladisa and James Bromiley Davis, and *devo ringraziare* Enrico again for the sandwich (and beer!) negotiated at a deserted Alpine outpost en route to the 'mouth of hell'. Thanks also go to Ken Casler for his patient and precise comments on the initial drafts, to my mother for her (sometimes less patient) comments, and for providing a place to get the thing from head onto paper – twice! And thank you K for tolerating a year (just the one!) of me being disconnected. Finally, thanks to all those who have somehow infiltrated my mind and found some part of themselves spewed out into this book; you have given some good lines.

Last of all – to all those supporters listed below and at the front of this book who have so generously helped finance the creation of the printed word, my unending gratitude… and a warning: there is more red to come.

Patrons

Martin Allmey
Paul Brown
Lucy Caulfield
Lee Childs
Dec Cousins
Lesley Craig
Graham Defries
Freddie Dixon
Bill Fisher
Simon Harris
Rachel Heslop
William 'Bill' Holmberg
Johari Ismail
Benjamin Jacquin
Alex Jones
Martin Kiefer
Christopher Kurkjian
Enrico Ladisa
Christopher Lindsey
Matt Mowat
Carlo Navato
Robert Nicholson
George Nodder
Tom O'Nolan
Tim Poolman
Fred Satow
Mark Smith
Jolyon Symonds
Christopher Vigrass
Wendalynn Wordsmith
Audrey Yeung

Patrons

Marin Alsop
Paul Brown
Lucy Caulfield
Lee Child
Dee Cousins
Lesley Crisp
Graham Davies
Freddie Dixon
Bill Fisher
Simon Harris
Rachel Healey
William Bill Holmberg
Johan Israel
Benjamin Jacques
Alex Jones
Martin Kiefer
Christopher Kirkman
Enrico Lelke
Christopher Lindsay
Matt Mowen
Cadu Navarro
Robert Nicholson
George Nudder
Tom O'Brien
Jim Roulston
Fred Sams
Mark Smith
JoAnn Symonds
Christopher Vignes
Wendelyn Wordsmith
Audrey Young